LEARNING

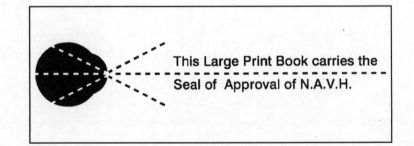
This Large Print Book carries the
Seal of Approval of N.A.V.H.

BAILEY FLANIGAN SERIES, BOOK 2

LEARNING

KAREN KINGSBURY

THORNDIKE PRESS
A part of Gale, Cengage Learning

GALE
CENGAGE Learning

Detroit • New York • San Francisco • New Haven, Conn • Waterville, Maine • London

GALE
CENGAGE Learning™

LIBRARY OF CONGRESS CATALOGING-IN-PUBLICATION DATA

Kingsbury, Karen.
  Learning / by Karen Kingsbury.
    p. cm. — (Thorndike Press large print Christian fiction)
  (Bailey Flanagan series ; bk. 2)
  ISBN-13: 978-1-4104-3900-0 (hardcover)
  ISBN-10: 1-4104-3900-3 (hardcover)
  1. Large type books. I. Title.
PS3561.I4873L4 2011b
                    813'.54—dc22 2011019931

Published in 2011 by arrangement with The Zondervan Corporation LLC.

Printed in the United States of America
1 2 3 4 5 6 7 15 14 13 12 11

DEDICATION

To Donald, my Prince Charming . . .

Can you believe that our Tyler has graduated from high school? How did the journey go so fast, the years fly so quickly that already we are here? I think about the day I found out I was having a boy — our first son. I remember you standing in the entryway of our little rental house, your eyes wide. "Well? What is it?" I'd gone to the doctor appointment by myself because you had school that morning, leading the kids in the classroom. I waited a minute, enjoying the suspense, and then I grinned at you. "We're having a boy!" I remember that before you could think about the politically correct response, you pumped your fist and shouted, "Yes!" I love that you were so excited to have a son, and between us I've loved everything about raising that little boy. I remember him standing in your cowboy boots, his four-year-old chest puffed out as

5

he stood next to you. A mirror image of his daddy. I know God has great plans ahead for Ty . . . and for all our kids. But it's bittersweet beyond words that already he has graduated. Thank you, Donald, for being the sort of daddy our boys have always wanted to imitate. They see you, and they know for sure that's who they want to be. You, the man of God, the one helping our family at every turn, praying for us. Stable, funny, loving, and always, always there for us. I pray that God will help us hold onto the lasts in the years to come as our other four boys hurry their way toward the front door. Along the way, I will cherish being at your side, watching you fill our home with laughter and love. God walked us through the baby stage and the walking stage, He walked us through the off-to-school stage and now, somehow, He'll walk us through the years of letting go. Quiet days lie ahead, but for now, my love, hold my hand and let's run the journey together. You and our boys, making memories. I look at you and still see the blond, blue-eyed guy who would ride his bike to my house and read the Bible with me before a movie date. You stuck with me back then and you stand by me now — when I need you more than ever. I love you, my husband, my best friend, my Prince

Charming. Stay with me, by my side, and let's watch our children take wing. Always and always . . . The ride is breathtakingly beautiful. I pray it lasts far into our twilight years. Until then, I'll enjoy not always knowing where I end and you begin. I love you always and forever.

To Kelsey, my precious daughter . . .

Only one year left of college, and I am amazed at how far you've come, Kelsey . . . how much you've grown. Your time in California — though some of the most painful days in your life and mine, for reasons we both understand — was a time God used to raise you into the strikingly beautiful young woman you are today, inside and out. I have watched you learn to love serving and listening and helping others, more than you care for yourself. I remember one day not long ago when you were still in California — alone and heartbroken — and you called. "Listen to this," you cried out, hope filling your voice. "These are some great Bible verses I found today. They're perfect for where God has me." You didn't know this, but your dad and I were in our room, and you were on speakerphone. The two of us exchanged a look — the sort of look that could only be shared between two parents who have prayed a lifetime for a child only to see God's answer in a single moment. I know you've had a hard year, sweetheart. But the truth is God cleared away the old and wrong to make way for the new and right. Wherever he is, honey, God is preparing him for that time when the two of you will meet and fall in love. Until then, you keep being the light of our family, the laughter of our hearts . . . and that one-in-a-million girl who inspired an entire series. My precious "Bailey Flanigan," I pray that God will bless you mightily in the years to come, and that you will always know how He used this time in your life to draw you close to Him, and to prepare you for what's ahead. In the meantime, you'll be in my heart every moment. And wherever you sing and dance for Him, we'll be in the front row! I love you, sweetheart.

To Tyler, my lasting song . . .

For eighteen years, I wasn't sure I could survive the goodbye, Ty. But the ride was so wonderful, so enjoyable that I could do nothing but celebrate as you grew from a baby to a toddler . . . and from those toddler days to your preschool years when you first began singing. I could do nothing but smile as you started school and proposed to

8

that darling girl in your kindergarten class. "I had a ring, Mommy . . . so I asked her to marry me." Never mind that I was letting my baby go; I was helpless to do anything but rejoice as you began performing in earnest, gracing the stage of Christian Youth Theater and making your Papa happier than he'd ever been. One day I turned around and you were in high school . . . the home-schooling years behind us and taking on every challenge you could find at our wonderful Christian high school. National Honor Society, choir leader, your first hit single in stores everywhere, basketball and soccer and cross-country — you made your high school years one adventure after another for all of us, and I found myself pushing thoughts of tomorrow out of my mind. The moments were simply too bright, your love for Jesus, your life far too compelling to do anything but enjoy the ride. But deep inside I always knew it would lead to this: your high school graduation. This month as you walked the stage with your classmates, I could hardly see for my tears. Precious son, I know that God has amazing plans ahead for you. He is your reason, your passion, your commitment to succeed . . . through Him, for Him, and by Him. But still I can hardly believe you're all grown up. Just know this, Ty. Wherever your journey of faith and music takes you, we'll always be there — cheering you on. I sometimes think about your Papa, and how proud he would be to watch the young man you've become. I still see him there in his favorite chair, the one by the fireplace, closest to the piano. He couldn't listen to you play and sing without getting tears in his eyes, and I can't either. This is the time of your life you've been waiting for. Life is your stage, Ty! Go change the world for Jesus, and let your very bright light touch the lives of everyone who needs it. Thank you for the hours of joy you bring our family, and I promise to stop and listen a little longer when I hear you singing. Your dad and I are proud of you. We're proud of your talent and your compassion for people and your place in our family. However your dreams unfold, we'll be in the front row to watch them happen. Hold on to Jesus, son. I love you.

To Sean, my happy sunshine . . .

I'm so glad you're on this side of your knee surgery. What a hard time for you, Sean . . . and what a time of growth in so many ways. Some years don't turn out like we planned, and this year that was all too true for you, sweet Sean. A blown out knee the third game of the football season, which led to surgery and a time of healing and rehab. You never let me see you down, never complained. But my heart broke at the pain you went through . . . and how you had to miss out on basketball season because your injury was that bad. But here's what God has taught me through this: Sometimes His greatest gift happens in the healing. When we are quiet enough to hear Him, quiet enough to listen to His leading. I have watched you spend hours shooting free throws, hours dribbling the basketball and playing the drums so that when the school gathered for worship every Monday of the past school year — you were there keeping the beat. Who would have thought so much good could've come from something so painful? But then . . . isn't that the lesson of the cross? Jesus loves you, Sean. Even more than we do. He promises that with Him, all things work to the good. And somewhere down the road I believe you'll look back at this time and see it as a turning point. A time when God was very close to you, indeed. You still need to remind yourself of the truth. You can do everything through Christ who gives you strength. And you can, Sean. You proved that this year by suffering

11

adversity, and in His strength, rising to the challenge. You remain a bright sunbeam, bringing warmth to everyone around you. And now you are an example of an all-star faith as well. I'm proud of you, Sean. I love you so much. I pray God will use your dependence on Him to always make a difference in the lives around you. You're a precious gift, son. Keep smiling and keep seeking God's best for your life.

To Josh, my tenderhearted perfectionist . . .

I'm so glad that this past winter you got back into premier soccer, and playing a game God has truly gifted you to play. Of course, you continue to amaze the opposition whatever sport, and for that I will always be proud of you, Josh. You train and play and lead with your whole heart. I don't know which records will fall or how many people will one day know of your feats on the field, but I do know this: It's so much more important that you have grown just as much in your faith. When God gives us talents, we must always remember where they come from. Who they come from. You have done this, dear son, and now you are ready to take on the world. Well, maybe not quite yet. But you're ready to take on the off-season, and give God the glory along the way. I remember when we first got word that your birthmother in Haiti had survived the terrible earthquake, after all. You only smiled and nodded. "I know," you said. "You do?" I was confused. None of us had known how she had fared for months after the quake. "I know she's okay — either way. In heaven or here. Because I prayed for her." Yes, Josh, you may laugh and tease a lot, but we know your heart. We have no doubt that someday we'll see your name in headlines and that — if God allows it — you'll play sports for a college team. You're that good, and everyone around you says so. Now flashback to that single moment in a broken-down Haitian orphanage. There I was meeting Sean and EJ for the first time when you walked up. You reached up with your small fingers, brushed back my bangs, and said, "Hi, Mommy. I love you." It might've taken six months of paperwork, but I knew as I heard those words that you belonged with us. The picture becomes clearer all the time. Keep being a leader on the field and off. One day people will say, "Hmmm. Karen Kingsbury? Isn't she Josh's mom?" I can't wait. You have an unlimited future, son, and I'll forever be cheering on the sidelines. Keep God first in your life. I love you always.

To EJ, my chosen one . . .

EJ, my jokester, you are finishing your first year in high school and what a year it has been! Varsity football . . . varsity basketball . . . and varsity soccer. And everywhere you go people say, "That EJ . . . God sure has gifted him with a ton of talent!" But the thing is, now that you've gotten through a year of high school I can say that maybe . . . finally . . . you're starting to believe it too. God has brought you so far, EJ, and now you stand on the brink of becoming everything He has planned for you to become. At our Christian school you have found friends and a deeper faith and a fire for pursuing the talents God has given you. All the things we have prayed for you! As you start high school, you are one of our top students, and we couldn't be happier for you. But even beyond your grades and your natural way of leading your peers in the right path, we are blessed to have you in our family for so many reasons. You are wonderful with our pets — always the first to feed them and pet them and look out for them — and you are a willing worker when it comes to chores. Besides all that, you make us laugh — oftentimes right out loud. I've always believed

14

that getting through life's little difficulties and challenges requires a lot of laughter — and I thank you for bringing that to our home. You're a wonderful boy with such potential. I'm amazed because you're so talented. I'm praying you'll have a strong passion to use your gifts for God as you return to high school in the fall. Because, EJ, God has great plans for you, and we want to be the first to congratulate you as you work to discover those. Thanks for your giving heart, EJ. I love you so.

To Austin, my miracle boy . . .

I think we'll look back on your seventh grade year as the time when you became obsessed with basketball. It was something you loved as a very little boy, back when people would ask you your name and you'd respond by saying, "Michael Jordan." Yes, you're finding out just how talented you are on a basketball court, and we can only dream about where God will take you. But even more than basketball, one highlight from your past school year will always stand out in my mind. The time when you found out there was an eighth grade boy who always sat alone at lunchtime. You made a determination to be that boy's friend — but even then the first I knew about it was when your teacher told me, "That Austin is probably my favorite student in the whole school. I don't think anyone has a kinder heart." Then again after you tried out for the select basketball team in our area, and made the A team, your coach came up to me and said, "It took about a minute to know I wanted Austin on my team. He can play great . . . but it was his attitude, and the way he was with the other kids. Such a leader. I knew I had to have him." Wow, buddy . . . do you know how proud of you I am? The fact that you're almost as tall as your daddy now just reminds me that this wonderful amazing time together won't last forever. Austin, I look at you and I see a young man with an ocean of determination and leadership ability, a young man who is first to thank his coach, first to shake the hand of the ref, and last to leave the classroom because you're so busy cleaning up and expressing your gratitude to your teacher. Sure you still struggle in a few areas, and sometimes your competitive drive can get you in trouble with your brothers. But truly, Austin, you can do anything as long as you keep God first. I believe you have the chance to go all the way with your dreams of playing sports, and I'm grateful to have a front-row seat. Play hard and don't ever give up, and always remember to be grateful and humble — two traits that will take you further than speed and strength any day. Not every infant who goes in for emergency heart surgery comes back out again. But even then, through our tears, we were certain we'd see you somewhere — here or there. The fact that God has blessed you with the here and now is proof that He has amazing plans for you. How great that you are seizing them with everything inside you, with every breath. Keep on, precious son. We are here for you, praying for you, cheering for you. No one believes more than we do. I've said it before, and it's true. Heaven has windows, and I'm convinced Papa's still cheering for you, son. Especially this year. Please don't forget that or him. You're my youngest, my last, Austin. I'm holding on to every moment, for sure. Thanks for giving me so many wonderful reasons to treasure today. I thank God for you, for the miracle of your life. I love you, Austin.

And to God Almighty, the Author of Life, who has — for now — blessed me with these.

ACKNOWLEDGMENTS

No book comes together without a great and talented team of people making it happen. For that reason, a special thanks to my friends at Zondervan who combined efforts with a number of people who were passionate about Life-Changing Fiction™ to make *Learning* all it could be. A special thanks to Moe Girkins — whose commitment to excellence at Zondervan was unparalleled, and to Steve Sammons, who may be one of the only execs in publishing who actually gets the big picture of what we're doing for the kingdom. Also, of course, a special thanks to my dedicated editor, Sue Brower, and to Don Gates and Alicia Mey, my marketing team. Thanks also to the creative staff and to the sales force at Zondervan who work tirelessly to put this book in your hands.

Also, thanks to my amazing agent, Rick Christian, president of Alive Communica-

19

tions. Rick, you've always believed only the best for me. When we talk about the highest possible goals, you see them as doable, reachable. You are a brilliant manager of my career, and I thank God for you. But even with all you do for my ministry of writing, I am doubly grateful for your encouragement and prayers. Every time I finish a book, you send me a letter that deserves to be framed, and when something big happens, yours is the first call I receive. Thank you for that. But even more, the fact that you and Debbie are praying for me and my family keeps me confident every morning that God will continue to breathe life into the stories in my heart. Thank you for being so much more than a brilliant agent.

A special thank you to my husband, who puts up with me on deadline and doesn't mind driving through Taco Bell after a football game if I've been editing all day. This wild ride wouldn't be possible without you, Donald. Your love keeps me writing; your prayers keep me believing that God has a plan in this ministry of Life-Changing Fiction™. And thanks for the hours you put in working with the guestbook entries on my website. It's a full-time job, and I am grateful for your concern for my reader friends. I look forward to that time every day when you read through them, sharing them with me and releasing them to the public, lifting up the prayer requests. Thank you, honey, and thanks to all my kids, who pull together, bringing me iced green tea, and understanding my sometimes crazy schedule. I love that you know you're still first, before any deadline.

Thank you also to my mom, Anne Kingsbury, and to my sisters, Tricia and Sue. Mom, you are amazing as my assistant — working day and night sorting through the mail from my readers. I appreciate you more than you'll ever know. Traveling with you these past years for Extraordinary Women and Women of Joy events has given us times together we will always treasure.

Tricia, you are the best executive assistant I could ever hope to have. I appreciate your loyalty and honesty, the way you include me in every decision, and the daily exciting website changes. My site has been a different place since you stepped in, and the hits have grown a hundredfold. Along the way, the readers have so much more to help them in their faith, so much more than a story. Please know that I pray for God's blessings on you always, for your dedication to helping me in this season of writing, and for your wonderful son, Andrew. And aren't we having such a good time too? God works all things to the good!

Sue, I believe you should've been a counselor! From your home far from mine, you get batches of reader letters every day, and you diligently answer them using God's wisdom and His Word. When readers get a response from "Karen's sister Susan," I hope they know how carefully you've prayed for them and for the responses you give. Thank you for truly loving what you do, Sue. You're gifted with people, and I'm blessed to have you aboard.

And to Randy Graves, a very special thank you. Randy, you and your family have been friends to our family for more than a decade, and now as my business manager and the executive director of my One Chance Foundation, you are an integral part of all we do. What a blessing to call you my friend and coworker. I pray that God always allows us to continue working together this way.

Thanks also to Olga Kalachik, my office assistant, who helps organize my supplies and storage areas, and who prepares our home for the marketing events and research gatherings that take place here on a regular basis. I appreciate all you're doing to make sure I have time to write. You're wonderful,

Olga, and I pray God continues to bless you and your precious family.

I also want to thank my friends at Premier — Roy Morgan and your team, along with my friends at Extraordinary Women and Women of Joy. How wonderful to be a part of what God is doing through all of you. Thank you for including me in your family on the road.

Thanks also to my forever friends and family, the ones who have been there and continue to be there. Your love has been a tangible source of comfort, pulling us through the tough times and making us know how very blessed we are to have you in our lives.

And the greatest thanks to God. You put a story in my heart, with a million other hearts in mind — something I could never do. I'm grateful to be a small part of what you're doing! The gift is yours. I pray I might use it for years to come in a way that will bring you honor and glory.

FOREVER IN FICTION®

For a number of years now, I've had the privilege of offering Forever in Fiction®* as an auction item at fundraisers across the country. Most of my more recent books have had Forever in Fiction characters, and I love that you, my reader friends, look forward to reading this section to see which characters in the coming pages are actually inspired by real-life people.

In *Learning,* I bring you three very special Forever in Fiction characters — all of whom are friends with my character Betty Keller. Betty offers her home as a place for Bailey Flanigan to live while she's in New York City, and Betty's three friends are part of her weekly summer Bible study. Each brings their own unique personality, likes, and strengths to the study — creating a rich

*Forever in Fiction is a registered trademark owned by Karen Kingsbury.

context from which Bailey is able to learn much. And learning is the whole point of this chapter in Bailey's life.

The first of Betty Keller's three friends is my auction winner — Barbara Owens. Barbara won the Forever in Fiction package at the Owasso Community Resources Benefit Auction in April, 2009. A beautiful woman known by her friends and family as being friendly and orderly, passionate and giving, Barbara is also the CEO of her own company. No one ever forgets Barbara's smile, or the way she helps those in need. She is married with three children and seven grandchildren, and she likes to decorate, sew, cross-stitch, and spend time with her family. Barbara, I hope that you enjoy seeing your name here in *Learning,* and that in years to come you and your family will be touched when they read about your character here, Forever in Fiction.

The second of my Forever in Fiction winners won the Crossings Christian School Auction in March, 2009. She chose to name her mother Maria "Irma" Rangel as a character in my Forever in Fiction program. Irma has been married more than fifty years to Al, and together they have four daughters and five grandchildren. The family loves to gather around Irma at any get-together, where she's often the silliest one in the mix. She loves telling jokes and laughing, and she is loving and loyal to all people — especially her family.

Irma retired from working on an assembly line and she lives a simple, quiet life. People easily recognize the petite Irma for her high cheekbones, olive-toned skin, and full smile — features that make her extremely beautiful, especially in her younger days. Irma, I am certain you and your daughter will smile when you read about yourself here in *Learning,* where you will be Forever in Fiction.

Finally, the third winner is Laura Rogers, who won the Simmons Cooper Cancer Institute Auction in October, 2009. Laura chose to honor her mother Sara Quillian, who died at the age of seventy-three. Sara was married for more than fifty years, and together she and her husband raised five children and enjoyed seven grandchildren. Sara was a trailblazer for her time, and worked as the first female editor of her university newspaper. She went to law school for a year, just to prove she could. She was an intelligent woman, always in the middle of all things social.

Sara constantly opened her house to the friends of her kids, or Campus Crusades workers. She also frequently hosted missionaries in her home and her pastor and his wife, for dinner. Sara was opinionated in her love for God, church, family, and a good conversation. She liked iced coffee and she loved a new pair of red shoes. Laura, I hope that you smile when you see your mother as a character here in *Learning,* and that you will forever be touched by the way she has been honored here, Forever in Fiction.

A special thanks to all three of my auction winners and your belief in the power of story. I pray that the donations you made to your respective charities will go on to change lives, the way I pray lives will be changed by the impact of the message in *Learning.* May God bless you for your love and generosity.

For those of you who are not familiar with Forever in Fiction, it is my way of involving you, the readers, in my stories, while raising money for charities. The winning bidder of a Forever in Fiction package has the right to have his or her name or the name of a loved one written into one of my novels, forever in fiction.

To date, Forever in Fiction has raised more than $200,000 at charity auctions. Obviously, I am only able to donate a limited number of these each year. For that reason, I have set a fairly high minimum bid on this package so that the maximum funds are raised for charities. All money goes to the charity events. If you are interested in receiving a Forever in Fiction package for your auction, write to *office@Karen Kingsbury.com* and in the subject line write: "Forever in Fiction."

ONE

Cody Coleman anchored himself near the hospital room window and wondered for the hundredth time what he was doing here. Why he was holding vigil for a young woman in a coma while Bailey Flanigan was leaving Indiana — maybe for good? He stared at the rainy parking lot twelve stories down and a realization hit him. It had been just twenty-four hours since Bailey stopped by the hospital to tell him goodbye. A full day of wondering and remembering and missing Bailey more than he could put into words. But none of that changed the reality of his situation: He was sitting bedside with Cheyenne Williams, pleading with God to save her life.

The machines around her whirred and beeped and reminded him that Cheyenne was alive. But everything else was tenuous . . . her condition, her prognosis. Her future.

Cody moved to the chair beside her bed and looked around the room. A sofa sleeper clung to one wall, the place where Cody had stayed most nights since the accident. Someone had to be here if Cheyenne woke up. When she woke up.

Cody's eyes fell on his guitar. He brought it hoping music might help bring Cheyenne around. He wasn't very good at it, and he could play only a couple songs. But they were songs that spoke of God's faithfulness, His mercy, and grace. If Cheyenne could hear . . . if any part of her was still connected to the world around them, then these songs would help. Cody believed that. Besides, he had told her that he was playing the guitar a little. They'd texted about it the day before her accident. Cody still had the conversation on his phone. He pulled it out of his pocket and thumbed through his text messages until he found the conversation with her.

So you'll play for me . . . one of these days?

At the time, he laughed at the text, and his response hadn't promised anything: *I better practice first.*

Don't practice . . . just play . . . all music is beautiful, Cody.

It was Cheyenne's last line . . . *all music is beautiful* . . . that convinced him to bring his guitar to the hospital. Other than a few times when he'd gone home to change clothes and shower, or when he was teaching or coaching, he was here. Last night — after Bailey's goodbye — he'd even slept here.

Because if he went home with the box of things Bailey had given him, if he looked through the box and remembered every good and wonderful thing about being with her, he might never come back. Why be here when Cheyenne woke up if he didn't have feelings for her, if he wasn't going to be here through her recovery and maybe afterwards?

Instead he stayed and kept reminding himself of what Tara had told him. Tara, who once long ago dreamed about having Cheyenne as a daughter-in-law. He could still see the earnest look in her eyes when she pulled him aside that evening after dinner. *Maybe God saved you from Iraq for Cheyenne . . .*

Cody stared at the beautiful girl in the bed, at her peaceful expression and the way her body lay so perfectly still. Maybe Tara was right. It was all he could think about, and so he hadn't gone home last night. He'd stayed right here beside Cheyenne, sleeping when he needed to and praying, of course. Always praying.

Cody stood and stretched. Tara would be here soon. She had called and told him she'd be by for a few hours after church. This ordeal had to be so hard on her. She'd lost her son to the war in Iraq, and now the young woman who would've married him was fighting for her life.

The room was quiet other than the sound of the machines. Cody walked to his guitar and picked it up. If she wanted to hear him play, he would play. And never mind that he wasn't all that good.

He sat back down at her bedside and found the right chords. The song was an old one, something he'd heard in chapel every now and then while he was serving overseas. The music filled the room, and Cody was surprised. It didn't sound half bad. "Great is thy faithfulness . . . Oh, God my Father . . . there is no shadow of turning with thee . . ."

The doctor had explained that Cheyenne might not remember him. She could have amnesia or any number of traumatic brain injury symptoms. Her list of damaged body parts was long and frightening. The impact of the truck hitting her broadside as it ran the red light had slammed her head against the inside doorframe. The swelling in her skull had stopped, but there was no way to tell just how damaged her brain might be.

In addition, she'd suffered a lacerated liver and internal bleeding. Emergency surgery her first day in the hospital had stabilized her, but there was no telling exactly how extensive the damage to her organs was. In addition, she had a broken lower right leg, broken ankle, and fractured wrist. She would likely need surgery to repair the broken leg, and possibly surgery on her back, as well.

Despite all this, Cody kept singing. There was something stripped down and raw about the hymn and its painfully honest message. No matter what a person might go through, God was faithful. He was merciful and loving . . . and His abundance was new again every morning. Like he'd once heard Bailey's father, Jim Flanigan, say. "We can have as much of God as we want."

Cody needed a lot of Him right now. He closed his eyes and kept singing. "All I have needed, thy hand hath provided . . . great is thy faithfulness, Lord unto me."

He finished that last line and was just about to head into the chorus when Cheyenne moved. Not a lot or with any sound, but her fingers flexed, and then her arm shifted a few inches on the blanket. Cody breathed sharply and set his guitar down at his side.

"Cheyenne . . . It's Cody. Can you hear me?"

Again she moved, and this time she winced.

Cody sat up straighter, his heart thudding hard inside him. If she could feel pain . . . if she could respond like that, then she had to be better off than they thought, right? "Cheyenne . . . it's Cody. I'm here."

She breathed in deeper than before, deeper than she'd breathed since the accident. And that meant she was responding to his voice. She had to be. Slowly, like someone coming out of a winterlong sleep, Cheyenne tried to blink, tried three times before her eyes opened just the slightest crack.

Cody looked over his shoulder at the door to her hospital room. Should he call for the nurse . . . tell someone what was happening? He looked back at Cheyenne and decided to wait. Better to put his full attention on her right now and not worry about what the doctors would say, what tests they might want to run now that she was showing signs of consciousness. At least for the first few minutes.

More blinking, more movement — and again she made an expression that showed how much pain she was in. "Cheyenne . . . I'm here." He stood and leaned over the bed, touching her healthy hand with the lightest sensation. "It's Cody . . . can you hear me?"

Cheyenne turned her head so slowly it was hard to tell she was moving at all. But she did move, and this time she blinked a little faster than before and her eyes remained open. As they did, they found his and they held. She was looking right at him — staring at him. Cody hadn't known her for very long, but he knew her well enough to be absolutely sure about this: Cheyenne remembered him. Her eyes searched his, and she seemed to have a thousand things to say.

"Can you talk?" He didn't want to push her, but he was desperate to know exactly how much of her might come back . . . her mind, her intelligence, her kindness . . . her love for God and people.

She moved her mouth a few times and then closed her eyes, clearly exhausted.

"Don't work too hard. It's okay. You don't have to say anything. As long as you can understand me."

Again, she opened her eyes and looked straight at him, and — in a way that was unmistakable — she nodded. Yes . . . she

37

could hear him. She could understand. She blinked again and the slightest sound came from her throat.

"Are you trying to talk?"

She nodded again.

"It's okay . . . you can talk later . . . you're very tired, Chey . . . don't overdo it." Once more he wondered if he should call for the nurse. But she looked a little less uncomfortable than before, so he let her have this moment. He moved his hand gently over her dark hair. "Does it hurt . . . are you in pain?" His voice was soft, his tone quiet so she wouldn't feel startled in any way.

A sigh came from her and she nodded again. But then the corners of her mouth lifted just a little and a hint of the familiar sparkle danced in her eyes. Almost as if to say, *Of course it hurts.* But none of that mattered as long as she was alive.

Still again she opened her mouth, and this time in a scratchy whisper she began to speak. "Cody . . ."

She knew his name! A fierce sense of protection and caring came over him. This precious girl had been through so much, so many seasons of heartache. How could she face the days ahead without someone who looked out for her, who understood and appreciated her? He ran his thumb over her brow. "I'm here for you . . . I'll stay no matter what."

Peace filled in the pained lines on her forehead and she nodded, more slowly this time. Her eyes looked deep into his soul, to the places that might've doubted the wisdom of being here. "Please . . . stay."

"I will." Cody felt the commitment to the outer edges of his heart. He put his hand alongside her face, speaking close to her, directly to her lonely soul. "You have my word, Chey . . . I'm not going anywhere."

She was still looking at him when her eyes gradually closed again. With a soft exhale, she seemed to fall back asleep. This time Cody acted quickly, pushing the call button and summoning the nurse. Over the next hour, the doctors did tests, assessing her in every possible way. They woke her up and managed to hold a conversation with her while Cody watched from the other side of the room.

"You were in an accident, Cheyenne . . . do you know that?" The doctor was a tall thin woman with compassionate eyes. "Do you remember the accident?"

Cheyenne looked across the room at Cody, and then back at the doctor. "I . . . remember the truck."

Again Cody's heart rejoiced. If Cheyenne

could remember the truck, then she could remember just about anything, right? Which meant maybe her brain had survived without any damage at all! He stood, watching the scene play out, realizing how much of Cheyenne's future rode on the assessment.

When it was over, when she was asleep once more, Tara arrived. She seemed to take in the commotion in Cheyenne's room as she rushed in, breathless, right up to Cody's side. "My baby girl . . . did she wake up?"

"Yes." Cody led her outside Cheyenne's room where they could talk. He smiled bigger than he had in a long time. "She remembered me."

"Cody." Tara raised one eyebrow at him. "What are you . . . a crazy man?" She gave a single chuckle. "Of *course* she remembered you. Do you own a mirror, Cody Coleman?"

He laughed quietly. "No, but that's not all. She remembered the accident, the truck . . . she seems exactly the same."

Tara grew very still and she closed her eyes. This was what they'd worried about, that Cheyenne would wake up somehow damaged, different. Less than she'd been before the accident. But by all signs, Cheyenne's personality — at least that much — was intact and Tara looked beyond relieved.

Tara brought her hands to her face. "Thank You, Jesus . . . You brought her back to us." When she opened her eyes she hugged Cody's neck. "God's going to work out the details, Cody . . . see? It's just like I told you."

The doctor called them out into the hall then, and explained her initial thoughts on Cheyenne's condition. Chey was cognitively whole — a tremendous relief and a resounding miracle. The doctor smiled, and her eyes seemed to give a glimpse to her own personal faith. "I've seen God work in hospital rooms, and this was a tremendous example." The woman's smile dropped off some. "However, the physical tests didn't go as well. She couldn't respond to simple commands — touching her finger to her nose, lifting her good leg . . . that sort of thing."

"What does that mean?" Tara's eyes were wide again and her hands began to shake.

"This was another possibility." The doctor hesitated. "Her brain damage may be in the area of her brain responsible for motor skills."

"So . . . she might never walk again?" Cody wasn't afraid of the possibility. After his own injuries in Iraq, he didn't view physical trauma as anything more than another mountain to conquer. But still, he wanted to know.

"I believe she can learn to walk in time." The doctor looked over her notes. "But I don't think she'll walk out of this hospital room."

Tara asked how Cheyenne was doing right now. "Can we see her again?"

"I gave her something for pain. She'll sleep for the next several hours." The doctor smiled again, empathetic to their concerns. "You're always welcome to stay."

A sense of exhaustion came over Cody and he leaned against the wall. He hadn't slept well last night, so if this was a time when Cheyenne would sleep for a few hours, he figured maybe it was time to go home. He could shower and grab a change of clothes. And he could take the box Bailey had given him home to his apartment. He shared his plan with Tara and she agreed. "I'll stay here . . . in case she needs anything."

Cody thanked her, and after taking one more look in at Cheyenne, he found the box from Bailey behind the hospital chair and set off. The hospital was outside Indianapolis, ten minutes from his apartment near the city campus of Indiana University. His roommate wasn't home when he walked inside, and Cody was grateful. He needed

42

an hour or so alone. Just him and God and whatever Bailey had given him in the box.

He took it to his room, shut the door behind him, and opened the blinds. It was the last day of April, and a thunderstorm was headed their way. He could see out the window the dark clouds gathering in the distance. The way they were gathering in his heart.

For a long time he held the box in his hands and looked at it . . . just looked at it and remembered his conversation with her the day before.

She was leaving . . . he understood that much. Bailey had gotten a role in the Broadway musical *Hairspray,* and tonight she would already be in New York City. Ready to start rehearsals.

He ran his hand along the box lid and tried to imagine her cleaning her room, going through a lifetime of memories and keepsakes, treasures from her childhood and high school days. Along the way she'd come across whatever was in this box, and she'd set the items aside. As she cleaned, she must've known she would take the box to him the day before she left.

But what she hadn't known about was his involvement with Cheyenne.

She had no right to be mad at him, of

43

course. Not about Cheyenne. Not when she was seeing Brandon Paul. Cody could still picture the way Brandon and Bailey looked together at her house that day, moving boxes across her front porch. He had come to her house that afternoon to find common ground with her. But after seeing Brandon, Cody had turned around and driven away. He hadn't seen Bailey again until yesterday. So she couldn't be upset that there was someone new in his life.

But maybe she did have a right to be upset about the fact that he hadn't called her once since January.

That's what she told him as they stood facing each other in that brightly lit hospital waiting room a few doors down from Cheyenne yesterday. He closed his eyes and he could still hear the pain in her voice.

"You promised to be my friend." Her eyes held a hurt so raw, Cody had to look away. Even so, she continued. "But you know what, Cody? You never meant it."

She was right, but he didn't say so. Instead he let her stand there in the waiting room, hoping for an answer that never came. Cody breathed in long and slow and ran his hand over the top of the box again. If he were painfully honest with himself, deep inside he had never meant to keep the promise of being Bailey's friend.

Not when he was still in love with her.

Cody ran his hand over his head and felt the blow of that reality, felt it like a physical pain. He never would've done anything to hurt her, and yet he had. The rest of his life he would regret that.

Finally, in an effort that felt beyond his own strength, he lifted the lid off the box. He'd lived with the Flanigans through the last half of high school until he'd joined the Army, until he left for Iraq. After that he'd shared two years with Bailey at Indiana University in Bloomington — Thursday Campus Crusade meetings and long walks around Lake Monroe. They had reached a point last summer when it looked like they'd never be apart again.

Then the Fourth of July picnic . . . where they finally admitted their feelings for each other. For all the crazy things Cody had been through in life, the last thing he saw coming was that his mother might get arrested for drugs again, or that her dealer boyfriend might make death threats against not only his mom, but also Cody and whomever Cody might be with.

And that meant Bailey.

He had moved to Indianapolis after that, without telling her goodbye. She was busy

45

making the movie *Unlocked* with Brandon Paul, and Cody began putting as much distance between them as possible. He wouldn't put her in danger. Period. And if that's what his mother's life — his life — had come to . . . a dangerous situation for Bailey . . . then his time with Bailey was over.

And now there was Cheyenne to complicate matters.

Cody breathed in deep and lifted a stack of pages off the top. He unfolded the first one and immediately understood what it was. Copies of diary pages from Bailey's journal. He felt a catch in his heart, and he folded the papers again. Later . . . he would read them later. When he wasn't on his way back to the hospital . . . when his heart could take missing her.

Next in the box were a few paperback books he'd been missing, and three issues of *Sports Illustrated* he'd set aside back when he lived with the Flanigans. He laid them on the bed and pulled a stuffed Tigger from the box. A smile tugged at his lips. It seemed like yesterday, he and Bailey at the county fair . . . competing against each other in the squirt gun contest, seeing who could pop the balloon first. When they tied, he gave her a Winnie the Pooh, and she gave him a

Tigger. He'd always wondered what had happened to the little guy.

Next in the box was a broken pair of sunglasses — just the left half. The ache in his chest deepened. He had broken them on the Fourth of July . . . hours before their private walk around the lake and the conversation that had led to what felt like a dating relationship. On one of the happiest days of his life he had stepped on his sunglasses and broken them in half. For the next half hour, he and Bailey each wore one half, laughing all the while. "So that we'll always see eye to eye," he'd told her.

The thing that stuck out to him now wasn't that she had included this half pair of sunglasses in the box of his things. But that she'd kept the other half. She still kept it.

He closed his eyes and longed for one more conversation with her, one more chance to tell her how much she'd meant to him over the years, and to assure her that he would never love anyone the way he had loved her. But that wouldn't have been fair — not now, in light of how life had changed for both of them.

Finally he reached the bottom of the box and there . . . there after so many years of missing it . . . was the one item he'd spent hours looking for. The friendship ring Bailey had given him when she was still in high school. The verse engraved across the front read, *Philippians 4:13 — I can do all things through Christ who gives me strength.* Bailey had dismissed the importance of the ring when she'd given it to him. Maybe because she was young, and he was already out of high school — as if she didn't want him to think she meant anything romantic by the gesture.

But even so he could hear her, feel her hand on his arm as she gave him the ring. "I've never had a friend like you, Cody." She assured him that he didn't have to wear it, but he wouldn't consider such a possibility. The ring meant more to him than Bailey ever could've known, and he had worn it until one summer day when he took it off to do yard work with Bailey's father and brothers. Somehow, it had gotten moved and he hadn't seen it again.

Until now.

He turned the ring over in his fingers and wished once more that the girl who had given it to him might still be here, assuring him one more time that she had never had a friend like him. Cody looked at the ring for a long while, and then he did the only thing he could do. He slipped it on the forefinger of his right hand. He might not have a friendship with Bailey or the chance to see her again. But he could keep the ring. He needed the message now more than ever. He could do all things through Christ . . . even letting go of Bailey Flanigan . . . and being there for Cheyenne.

The thought of Cheyenne reminded him that he needed to get back. He hadn't been the right sort of friend to Bailey, and he'd broken promises he never should've made. But now he'd made a promise to Cheyenne . . . that he wasn't going to leave her . . . that she could count on him. For however long . . . whatever that meant.

Cody twisted the ring, savoring the familiar way it felt against his finger. Yes, Cheyenne could count on him . . . as long as God provided the strength for him to be there for her. Cody had promised he'd stay.

And this time, he wasn't going to break his promise.

TWO

The lights of New York City glowed in the night sky as Bailey Flanigan and her mom arrived in busy, bustling Times Square. They shared a quick dinner at Sbarro on Broadway across from the DoubleTree, and headed to their room at the Marriott Marquis. Since her mom had slept the entire flight in, and because of the noise of the city and even the restaurant, Bailey still hadn't found a time to tell her mom about her meeting yesterday with Cody. Finally, alone in their hotel room, Bailey sat on the edge of the bed near the pillow and tried to remember every detail.

"I feel terrible for the girl . . . her name's Cheyenne." Bailey sat cross-legged, her long hair in a side ponytail. "But still . . . I had no idea he'd moved on."

Her mom took the chair a few feet away, and a sad, knowing sort of look filled her face. "I figured you had more in that heart

50

of yours than the goodbyes you said to your dad and your brothers."

Bailey nodded. "It was a lot. Too much to talk about." She exhaled, feeling the weariness from earlier that day. "I wasn't sure I could take all those goodbyes." She tilted her head, thoughtful. "Isn't it so weird, Mom? I mean, like, I've said goodbye to not only my childhood, but to my family. Now . . ." she didn't want to cry again, and her eyes were dry. But that didn't make the situation easier to accept. "Now they'll grow up without me. Like, when I see them again they'll be taller and older looking."

Her mom's eyes looked a little damp. "We'll visit. We're coming the first weekend after you join the show."

"I'm glad." Bailey wasn't distraught, not really. Her moving just made life so different, their family so unlike what it had ever been before. "So, yes, Cody was on my mind. We . . . we didn't talk much at the hospital."

"Maybe he's feeling hurt too. Have you thought about that?" Always her mom had been a great listener, even when she didn't agree with Bailey. This was one of those times. "I mean, sweetheart, he has to know about Brandon Paul. He came to our house and saw the two of you. And then he drove away."

"Right, and he should've talked to me." Bailey leaned against the headboard. "Cody's always running, Mom . . . I'm tired of that." She set her heart's resolve, unwilling to spend the evening feeling sad about Cody. "Besides, he has Cheyenne. And he clearly has her. He was sitting by her side like . . . like they were married or something."

"Honey, . . ." again caution rang quietly in her mom's voice. "He's doing what anyone would do in the situation. Cheyenne is fighting for her life." She paused, her eyes still on Bailey. "Did you see anyone else there?"

"An older woman. But that's all."

"So Cheyenne probably needs him."

Bailey hadn't thought about that. Despite the girl's injuries all Bailey had seen was Cody sitting by her bedside. As if he cared for her more than anyone in the world. Like he maybe even loved her. She felt suddenly terrible for her assumptions. "You're right. I can't tell anything from what I saw." She looked out the window at the dazzling lights, and she remembered again where she was and why she was here — and that she wasn't going back home at the end of the

52

week. "Anyway, it doesn't matter. We said our goodbyes."

Bailey spent the next hour talking about how Cody had begged her to stay longer, and how he'd asked her to sit by him while he went through the things in the box. But how she had hurried away, anxious to be done with the visit. "I think I learned something." Resignation sounded in her voice. It was the saddest part of saying goodbye to Cody, this realization that had stayed with her since then. "I can't be Cody's friend. I care too much about him."

"Hmm." Her mom's face was open and kind . . . not the least bit judgmental. "I understand." She wasn't in a hurry, clearly wanting Bailey to feel her support. "How are things with Brandon?"

Bailey felt a smile start in her heart and work its way to her face. "He's great. I mean . . . every time we talk I feel the possibility a little more." She explained how Brandon had plans to visit often and for whatever reasons he could think of.

"I'm sure." Her mom laughed. "Especially if he would fly to Indiana to help you clean your room."

The conversation lasted well into the night, until finally they were both too tired to keep their eyes open. As Bailey fell asleep she recounted the time with her mom, how close the two of them were. Tonight's talk was the sort of one she couldn't have on a regular basis once her mom returned to Bloomington on Wednesday.

She reminded herself to appreciate this time with her mom, and she thanked God for the opportunity — both that night and the next day as they took a car into the city and saw *Mary Poppins.* By then, the sadness from the night before had faded, and after the play Bailey and her mom set out down Seventh Avenue toward Forty-second Street — and past the J. Markham Theater where Bailey would perform. The *Hairspray* marquis looked twenty feet high and the lights around it shone even now in the brightest sunlight.

"I can't believe it." Her mom slid closer to Bailey in the backseat of the cab and gave her a quick side hug. "This is where you'll be working!"

They asked the driver to stop, and they jumped out of the car and took pictures in front of the theater. The building was locked and empty now, since it was only ten in the morning. Rehearsals took place a few blocks away. But still Bailey wanted to capture this moment, and she took a final photo using her phone. Then with a few taps of her fingers she texted it to Connor with this caption: *Working on Broadway . . . God is great!*

They were back in the car when Bailey felt her phone vibrate and saw Connor's response. *He's got big plans for you, Bailey . . . glad to see you smiling today!*

A warmth spread through her, and she felt the certainty of being exactly where God wanted her to be.

She gave the driver directions to the rehearsal location: Big City Studios on Fifty-fourth Street. Traffic was bad — but then that was always the case. "We could've walked faster," her mom whispered to her, grinning.

"I know . . . I think that's what I love about New York. You're never alone."

"That's for sure." They both laughed, and fifteen minutes later the driver reached the studio. They asked him to be back in an hour, and they hurried inside. A guard at the front door looked over Bailey's paperwork, checked their IDs, and let them inside. As soon as they walked into the lobby of the rehearsal space, they heard the music. On the other side of the door the cast was practicing the song "Without Love," and suddenly Bailey's heart soared with what lay ahead. It was really happening! She belonged here . . . performing on Broadway.

Quietly they crept in the back door of the studio and looked for a seat along the rear wall. Francesca Tilly, the show's director, had asked them to come. But that didn't mean she would want her rehearsal interrupted. The space was large enough for the entire cast to be spread out, and from what Bailey could tell, everyone knew the dance. But this was how they stayed strong. They practiced until the movements were like breathing.

The moment the song ended, Francesca clapped her hands and pointed toward the back of the room. "Alright, family, turn around." Twenty-some dancers did as she asked, curious looks on their faces. "This is your newest sister. She'll begin rehearsals Wednesday." Francesca smiled big toward Bailey and her mom. "Welcome, Bailey Flanigan. And Bailey's mother, I assume. We're glad you're here."

Bailey had the sense this was how Francesca always introduced the newest cast members, because the guys and girls smiled and waved, and there were a few who called out, "Hi, Bailey . . . glad you're here." Or some other such thing.

She returned the waves, and so did her mom.

As soon as the cast turned back to Francesca, the director dropped the friendly persona and scowled at each of them, her eyes moving over them the way they had over the hundred girls who had tried out with Bailey. "Now . . . I was at the show over the weekend . . . I know, I know . . . I didn't tell you I'd be there. But when you sang "Welcome to the Sixties," I felt like you wanted me to leave!" her voice boomed through the rehearsal space. "I absolutely did not feel welcome, because none of you — that's right none of you — looked like you were enjoying yourself."

Bailey smothered a smile behind her hand. Her friend Tim Reed was dating a girl who used to be in the *Hairspray* cast, and a few months ago when Bailey had auditioned, the girl had warned her. Francesca was very, very difficult to work for. But Bailey liked that she demanded perfection. How many directors would tell a cast of professional singers and dancers that they hadn't looked like they were enjoying themselves? Not many, Bailey figured. That's what set Francesca apart from the others. And it was why she was grateful she'd be starting her Broadway career here under the critical but careful hand of Ms. Tilly.

The director was explaining that the number should be so fun, people will have to hold back from jumping into the aisles and dancing along. "That's the sort of welcome we want people to feel when they watch this number. Like they've just been reintroduced into the era of the sixties, and they wish with every heartbeat they could get on stage and join you."

They watched for nearly an hour, and Bailey soaked in every correction, every bit of direction Francesca gave them. Being here was good. She would come to her first rehearsal that much more prepared. Finally, Bailey's mom gave her a gentle nudge, and Bailey stood. The driver would be waiting. Besides, it was time to meet her new landlords, Bob and Betty Keller. Bailey followed her mother to the car, which was already waiting out front.

"That was amazing." Her mom's look was part exhaustion, part nervousness. "I can't imagine performing in front of her."

"It'll be fun." Bailey slid into the backseat and made room for her mom to join her. "She only wants everyone to be better."

"But the way she does it . . . I'd be crying in ten minutes."

Bailey laughed, imagining Francesca's reaction if one of her dancers broke into tears. "I don't think you'd work long on Broadway."

"You got that right." Her mom pulled a folder from her purse and gave the driver the address for the Kellers'. "We're running a little early . . . but they're expecting us."

This time they tipped the driver as he helped unload their suitcases from the back of the car. The hotel was only eight blocks from the Kellers' house. They really hadn't needed a driver that morning, if it weren't for their heavy bags. Bailey was glad the *Hairspray* producers had provided one, for that reason alone. Once the car pulled away, Bailey spotted a man selling roses not far down the street. "Let's buy some. For Betty."

"Good idea." Her mom pulled two suitcases, while Bailey pulled the other two, and they walked shoulder-to-shoulder down the crowded street until they reached the florist. They bought yellow roses and then headed to the apartment building where the Kellers lived. A doorman stood at the entrance, and when they explained who they were, he buzzed the Kellers and welcomed them into the lobby. Bailey's mom whispered to her, "I like that they have security."

Bailey smiled to herself, grateful to God.

She had worried about how safe she would be in New York, and prayed to leave the matter in the Lord's hands. And now here He had answered her prayers abundantly. Not only was she safe, but completely taken care of. They wheeled the suitcases into the elevator, rode it to the eleventh floor, and as they stepped off, a pretty white-haired woman was waiting for them.

"You must be Bailey and Jenny." Her smile filled her face and she held out her hands. First she hugged Jenny, then Bailey. "Aren't you the prettiest thing?" She stepped back, her hands still on Bailey's shoulders. "You'll be marvelous on that *Hairspray* stage." She looked back at Jenny. "Come on . . . I have lunch ready, and Bob's setting the table."

Bailey handed the roses to the woman. "These are for you. Thank you so much for having me . . . you have no idea how much this means."

"Oh, dear . . . it's our pleasure. We haven't had a Broadway actress living with us for far too long. Having girls like you . . . it keeps us young. We're going to have a wonderful time together."

"Yes, ma'am."

"Oh, dear . . . please," the woman grinned at her and gave her another quick hug. "Call

60

me Betty."

"Okay." Bailey laughed at herself for thinking this situation might be even the slightest bit awkward. "Thank you, Betty."

Bailey could tell immediately that she was going to love Betty Keller. The woman reminded her of Elizabeth Baxter — the matriarch of Bloomington's Baxter family and the first wife of John Baxter. Elizabeth had died of cancer several years back, but her genuine kindness and warmth for everyone she met lived on in the memories of all who knew her. Bailey was no exception.

They went into the Kellers' apartment, and the view caught Bailey by surprise. She stopped, and a quiet gasp sounded on her lips. The entire far two walls of the living room were made of glass, and they offered a view of not only the city streets below, but also of Central Park. "Your view . . . it's breathtaking."

"Thank you." Bob walked up and introduced himself. He was completely bald with a tanned face and dimples when he smiled that made him look half his age. He gave a silly shrug. "Of course, I can't take credit for the view, actually. Not really. That's God's doing."

"But it is always surprising to people how close the park is when you're this high up.

61

It's just a few blocks away, really."

Bailey imagined sitting on the Kellers' sofa looking out that window. She would journal here and read her Bible here and even on the craziest day, after crazy difficult rehearsals with Francesca, she would have this respite to come home to. "It's perfect. Really."

Her mom agreed, and for a few minutes they talked about the flight in, and the stop at rehearsals earlier today, and all that lay ahead for Bailey once she began working with the rest of the cast.

"Francesca is a friend of ours," Betty winked. "Most people don't know that. We're . . . well, we're very different." She slipped her arm around Bob's waist. "We love Jesus in our house," she smiled at Bailey, "as you know. Francesca . . . well, she's not a believer. She has made that clear a vast number of times, isn't that right, Bob?"

"It is. She doesn't believe a word of it." He winked again. "Not yet, at least."

Bailey felt a ripple of anxiety. She knew about Francesca's lack of faith. Tim's girlfriend had told her that. But this confirmation was just a little chilling. "Does she . . . does she hold it against you if you believe?" If so, then fine. Bailey was ready for the challenge. But she wanted to know now, rather than find out later.

"Not really." Betty led them through the living room, around a corner, and down a hallway. She looked back at Bailey. "The thing to remember is, you must show your love as a Christian on Broadway. No one wants to hear about your faith. They must see it."

Wise words, Bailey told herself. She nodded. "I'll remember that."

Bob had stayed back in the kitchen, putting the finishing touches on the lunch. Now Betty opened the first door on the right and stood back while Bailey and her mom entered first. "This is your room." She put her hand on Bailey's shoulder. "I hope it'll work for you."

Again Bailey wanted to stop and catch her breath. The room had plush white carpeting and an elevated queen bed, with pale yellow and white bedding. The walls were a deep taupe, and the trim was painted the whitest possible white. All that and she had a window — one that overlooked a part of the street below and more of Central Park. "Mrs. Kel —" Bailey caught herself. "Betty . . . it's beautiful. Beyond anything I ever imagined."

"Well, good." She stood back, happy with

the situation. "That's how God works."

"Sound familiar?" Bailey's mom moved Bailey's suitcases into the far corner of the room. "Not that we'll always have a view of Central Park," she laughed quietly. "But He'll always exceed what we can imagine Him to do, the ways He comforts us and leads us."

"Amen." Betty turned smiling eyes at Bailey's mother. "You remind me of my oldest daughter. I'm sure the two of you would've been friends."

Bailey looked forward to learning more about Betty and Bob, about their family and their lives together, and about their adventures on Broadway. After she'd looked around her new room and noted the large empty closet space and the small attached bathroom and shower, they moved back to the living room. Along the way, Betty explained that she and Francesca had performed in the same cast of *Forty-Second Street* back in the day. "Not a person on Broadway would've figured Francesca would be a director one day," Betty said. "She was the least serious person in the cast. But something happened to her back then. It's a long story." Betty looked back at Bailey. "I'm sure we'll have lots of time to talk later, when you get in your routine."

They all agreed, and for the next hour they shared lunch and talked about how Bob was the cook between the two of them. "I got tired of eating crunchy pasta and microwave dinners." He chuckled, a fond look on his face. "Bless my Betty's heart. She's a much better singer than she is a cook."

Bailey flashed a nervous grin at her mother. The same could be said for her, she was sure. She might have to spend a little time with Bob . . . learn a little about cooking. Now, before she was really on her own. The meal ended, and Betty and Bob encouraged them to have a look at the city, take a walk to the park. Like old friends, Betty and Bob seemed to understand how important the time between Bailey and her mother was. Bailey appreciated their consideration, and she told her mom so when they were back outside on the street. "I'm going to like Bob and Betty." She walked with a spring in her step. The sun warmed her shoulders and the air was a perfect temperature. "They already seem like family."

"Exactly." She looked at Bailey, her expression curious. "Didn't you think Betty was a little like —"

"Elizabeth Baxter?" Bailey laughed.

"Really? Did you see it too?" Her mom

stopped, taken by the fact.

"Mom, seriously . . . she was just like her. I thought it the moment we walked off the elevator." Bailey loved this, the way she and her mom saw so much of life the same way, how they had similar viewpoints and revelations throughout the day. It was one of the many things she was going to miss when they were living a thousand miles away from each other.

The rest of the day went quickly, and after a fun night at the Kellers', Bailey and her mom spent the next afternoon shopping.

"Have you thought about how much money you'll make?" Her mom looked through a rack of sweaters and stopped to meet Bailey's eyes. They were at H&M, a discount clothing store on Fifth Avenue. "We haven't really talked about it."

Bailey knew the answer. She would make as much in a month as some people made in a year. It was an amount that didn't make sense to her, since she would've gladly performed on Broadway for free. And the Kellers had already made it clear they wouldn't take rent. She had a year-long contract, so truly she would be able to give and save a significant amount — depending on how long the producers kept her on the show.

"I know. I guess it hasn't really sunk in." Bailey looked through a rack of exercise pants — perfect for rehearsals.

That night Bailey and her mom took the Kellers out to dinner, to one of their favorite restaurants — the R Lounge at Two Times Square on the second floor of the Renaissance Hotel on West Forty-eighth Street and Seventh Avenue. The place was quiet, and the views of Times Square were the best in the city. There they learned a little more about Betty and Bob. They had three children — two who lived in upstate New York with their families, and a third who was making his way. That's how the Kellers described him. *He was making his way.* Bailey wasn't sure what that meant, but she guessed she would find out in time.

Bailey and her mom turned in early that night, since she had rehearsal at nine the next morning. Originally Bailey had been told she'd start rehearsing a few weeks after her arrival, but Francesca changed that. The director wanted her to join the production as soon as possible. As for tomorrow's rehearsal, her mom had been invited to watch. As they arrived at the studio and Bailey took her place with the other dancers, she was grateful again that her mom was there. This way when they talked about

67

Bailey's experience with Francesca and the practices, and even the various people in the cast — her mom would know what she was talking about. Because she'd taken the time to be here now.

Francesca gave the cast a brief description of Bailey's character. "I'll have you know that this young dancer won her spot with a resounding audition." Francesca gave a pointed look to Bailey. "Respect her, family. She is your sister, your peer, and your equal. She will play ensemble, and she will understudy for Penny." She looked them over the way a teacher might look over her slightly disheveled first grade class. "Alright then, let's begin. We'll work first on the song that's most appropriate for the occasion." She smiled to herself, and in that moment Bailey could see how much the director enjoyed her job. She pointed at her assistant, poised over an iPod and speakers. "Cue 'The New Girl in Town.' "

Bailey smiled and then immediately forced herself to be serious. No matter the irony, it was time to learn. The others were here to help her catch on, and she would slow them down until she did. "Alright, Bailey, . . . line up behind the last line of dancers and watch feet. Only feet. We'll go through it once, and then I'll break it down."

Two hours passed in a blur of music and dancing and memorized movement. When they were done, Bailey was confident of the steps in "New Girl," and she had a vague idea of how to get through "Run and Tell That." But she had a mountain of work ahead — enough that she felt dazed and dizzy as Francesca dismissed them.

"Don't let her get to you." A thin blonde came up to her as they were leaving. "I'm Chrissy Stonelake. I understudy for Amber."

Bailey shook her hand, and both girls apologized for being sweaty. Bailey laughed, grateful to have a friend in the cast. But even as she did, she noticed how thin Chrissy was. Too thin. And there were dark circles under her eyes. Bailey wondered if one day she'd be close enough to Chrissy to find out about the dark circles. "I figured she'd work us this hard, but being here . . . going through it . . . nothing could've really prepared me for this."

"I know." The girl seemed like she was trying to look confident, or like maybe the rehearsal had caused her to feel alive and complete. "But you'll learn more from Francesca than anyone in the business." She grinned as she grabbed her bag. "Our rule in the family — she always calls us her family — is just do what she says and bring a

lot of water." She waved. "See you tomorrow."

Bailey said the same, and found her bag
along the wall. Her mom waited nearby, and
as they walked out they shared a smile.
"That was incredible." Bailey wondered if
her legs had the strength to carry her down
the steps to the waiting car. Again, the
producers had provided a ride. This time so
they could take Bailey's mom to the airport.
Her flight was set to leave in three hours.

"You did great." Her mom took Bailey's
bag from her, found a small towel inside,
and handed it to her. "She really worked
you."

"I loved it . . ." Bailey's laugh gave away
how tired she really was. "I mean, I'm not
sure I can take ten steps after that, but
still . . . I loved it."

"You'll catch on quickly." Her mom had a
single small bag herself, and they slipped it
in the car. Already Bailey could hear a difference in her voice, the awareness of how
little time they had together.

On the way to the airport they talked
about their morning conversation with the
Kellers. Bob and Betty had already decided
they would walk with Bailey to the theater
every time she had a show, and they'd wait
for her at the end of the night to walk her

home again. As for rehearsals, Bailey would have access to a car any time she wanted. Part of the package of being a tenant in the Kellers' apartment building. "We'll make sure the car picks her up and gets her to rehearsals and then brings her back when they're finished," Bob told them. "It's part of our role . . . the way we handle hosting a young star like Bailey."

Now her mom smiled at the term. "I heard him say that, how he called you a young star, and I looked across the breakfast table at you." There was a tenderness in her mother's voice. "I wanted to say, no . . . you weren't a young star. You were my little girl. My Bailey . . . and that, I don't know, somehow I guess I expected you to come back home with me when you were done playing pretend on Broadway." She reached over and put her fingers over Bailey's. "But then I only had to remember how I've seen you perform . . . what you're capable of doing. And I realized they were right. You're a young star on Broadway, Bailey."

"Not really." She understood what her mom meant, but she didn't like the term. "I never think about people being stars or . . . I don't know, having fans. Like some people are above others . . . better somehow."

Her mom angled her head, thoughtful. "I

love that about you. I mean . . . they were only saying it in the kindest way. But you're right . . . people are people."

Bailey smiled. "It's what you and Dad always taught us."

"And now . . . sweet girl . . . you get the chance to live that out here in New York City." She leaned in close and hugged Bailey. "You'll be brilliant, honey. And everyone will see something different about you, how you're not like anyone else. And along the way, I'm absolutely sure people will be changed." She pulled back, her eyes still on Bailey's. "Maybe even —"

"Francesca Tilly?" They hesitated for a moment and laughed. Because once more, one last time before her mother would return to life in Bloomington and Bailey would start her own here in New York, they had finished each other's thoughts.

The ride to the airport was too fast, and as the driver pulled up to the American Airlines drop-off area, Bailey felt her throat tighten. It was one thing to walk around the city with her mom, marveling at the sights and being grateful about her new place and her incredible opportunity. One thing to go through an intense rehearsal with Francesca barking orders at her one on top of the other while her mom was watching. Her mother was her best friend, after all.

But now . . .

Her mom set her bag down and they stood facing each other on the curb. "When you were born . . . I would stare at you for hours and somehow believe that this day would never come." Tears gathered in her eyes, and she spoke just loud enough to be heard above the occasional passing car. "I couldn't imagine it . . . you all grown up and leaving."

"I know . . . me either." Bailey took her mother's hands. "You're my best friend, Mom. We'll talk every day. No matter how long I stay here."

Her mom didn't say that even if they talked every few hours it would never be the same . . . she didn't mention that there was no way around the fact this was a very real and dramatic ending to a special time in their lives. Instead she smiled through her tears. "You'll stay a long time . . . I know that." She kissed Bailey's cheek. "Because you're that good, honey."

Bailey only looked at her mom for a while, memorizing the support and confidence her mom had for her. "Do you think . . . do you think I can do this?" Her voice had fallen to a choked whisper.

"Yes." There wasn't the slightest hesitation in her mom's response. "You can do this . . . and you will be brilliant, Bailey. You will." She smiled, gathering her composure. "I've loved every minute of raising you . . . my only girl. But you're ready, sweetheart. Go shine brightly for Jesus."

"I will." It was all she could say before the tears broke for her too. She flung herself into her mother's arms and they stayed that way, clinging to each other for a long time. Finally, Bailey eased back first. "You need to go."

"Yes." Her mom sniffed, and took the handle of her bag. "I love you, Bailey."

"I love you too. Thanks for everything, Mom. You and Dad . . . we wouldn't be who we are without you."

There were no more words, nothing else either of them could say. They simply let their eyes speak the volumes between them, recapping a lifetime they couldn't fit into this final moment. Her mom waved as she walked to the revolving glass door, and Bailey did the same. And after a few seconds, her mom walked out of sight.

A shiver came over Bailey as the realization hit with a finality she'd never felt in all her life. This was it. She was on her own in New York City, ready to tackle her greatest dream and her biggest fears. As she climbed into the car, she reminded herself that everything would be okay, because God had brought her here, and He had provided the perfect place for her to live, the perfect way for her to get safely around the city, and the toughest director in New York City. Bailey smiled through her tears as she climbed back in the car.

She could hardly wait for tomorrow.

THREE

The painting was almost finished, and Ashley Baxter Blake wondered if it might be her best of all. In it there was her husband, Landon, and Cole, her son — the two of them on the Little League field. Cole in his uniform up to bat, and Landon behind him in his manager's uniform, adjusting his son's swing, giving him a final pep talk before his turn at bat.

It was a moment Ashley had watched in person a number of times, but here . . . captured on canvas, there seemed almost no difference between the image in her mind and the one before her. She set her paintbrush down and listened to the noise from downstairs. She could hear the sound of a movie — *Prince of Egypt* maybe — but there were none of the usual happy voices.

A chill ran down her arms. Ever since he'd come home from his time in the hospital, Landon hadn't been the same. She worried about him when he left for a walk or when he was out by himself. What if he had another asthma attack? And what if this time no one saw him and the inhaler didn't work? Her worry was hard on Landon, but Ashley wasn't sure how to change it. A part of her didn't think Landon should be out alone, not as long as his lungs were so unstable.

The dynamic was strange, because since they'd first fallen in love, Landon had been the strong one, the stable one. He never let anything faze him, never gave in to the possibility that something might set him off course. From the time they'd first become friends, she was the one with the mood swings, the one who had run off to Paris to paint, and who had come home pregnant and alone. Landon? He was dependable, the one she could count on. Always there, always steady.

But all that had changed in a week.

"Look at it as a vacation," Ashley had told him. "You haven't had this much time off in way too long." But no matter how she tried to convince him, the truth was, he'd been put on medical leave. Until doctors could determine if he really had polymyositis he couldn't be cleared to return to work.

Polymyositis . . .

Ashley let the word rumble around in her mind, where it regularly wreaked havoc on her peace and sanity. She had googled the disease for hours but she hadn't found a single positive anecdote or discussion. The progression was often quick . . . lung transplants were usually needed once it affected breathing. And after a lung transplant, less than thirty percent of the patients were alive ten years later.

Ashley still didn't hear anything but the cartoon from downstairs. Her mind began to race, rushing down the stairs ahead of her. What if he collapsed in the bathroom or outdoors with the dog? He paid no attention to the fact that if an attack hit when he was alone, he might not make it out of the attack alive.

She exhaled in a burst, stood, and removed her paint apron. Moving fast enough that she probably looked a little frantic, she hurried to the stairs. "Landon, . . . are you there?"

No answer. Ashley quickened her pace. *Dear God . . . I can't keep doing this; he has to find the right medication. Please, Father . . . wherever he is, help him.* He was probably outside by the fishpond. He'd said something about working on it today. But if he'd been outside and passed out he might've fallen into the water and then — "Landon!"

"Mommy." Devin ran from the family room to the bottom of the stairs and met her. "Are you okay? You sound scared."

She pulled up, her breathing faster than it should've been. "Honey, do you know where Daddy is?"

"I'm out here." His voice came from the kitchen.

Ashley could've collapsed there on the floor. He was okay . . . he wasn't passed out near the fishpond or drowning in the water or suffocating in the bathroom or —

"Mommy." Devin scrunched up his face, curious. "You still look scared."

She forced a quick laugh and stooped down to his level. "No, buddy . . . I'm fine. I just want to talk to Daddy."

"Really?" Devin looked doubtful. "About something scary?"

Her son had always been perceptive, but at times like this Ashley wished he might not grasp her emotions so completely. "No, sweetie. Nothing scary." In light of his concerns, Devin looked afraid now too. She put her hands on either side of his face and kissed the tip of his nose. "Everything's fine, Devin. Really. Go back and watch the movie with your sister."

After a few seconds he smiled at her, but

79

his eyes still held a slight doubt. Then he ran off to the family room to do as she asked. Ashley felt foolish for overreacting, but this was the pattern lately. She would go about the house finding him every half hour or so, just to make sure he was breathing. Usually she tried to be discreet, but today . . . with her imagination getting so far ahead of her . . . she had let her fear practically consume her.

"Ashley?" Landon sounded slightly frustrated. "What did you want?"

She walked to the kitchen and found him sitting at the kitchen table, staring out the window to the backyard, a cup of hot coffee in his hands. He glanced at her but only for a moment. "I agree with Devin . . . you sounded terrified." He took a slow sip of his coffee. "We've gone over this, Ash."

Irritation rose within her, more at herself than at him. "I'm sorry." She took the seat beside him and touched his shoulder. "Can you look at me, Landon? Please."

He sighed and turned his chair so he could see her. "What . . . you were upstairs painting and you had the sudden thought that I was . . . I don't know . . . pruning the rosebushes and an asthma attack came over me and dropped me to the ground?"

She managed a sheepish shrug. "I was

thinking the fishpond."

His almost-angry look softened. For a long time he looked at her, searching her eyes as if he was trying to understand what made her worry the way she did. But then he chuckled in defeat and looked down at his coffee. "I'm fine." His eyes found hers again. "The doctor said I can resume normal activity."

"But . . . you're still coughing." Her voice was soft. She didn't want to push the matter or make him angry. They'd never had to worry about tension between them, not in all their lives until now. "Doesn't that mean the inhaler isn't working . . . or the steroids need to be stronger?"

"No. It means my lungs are still healing." He sounded tired, weary. "We can't do this, Ash." He shook his head. "Talk about my breathing . . . my lungs . . . my asthma. Every hour of the day . . . every day of the week." His shoulders sank some. "I can't do it."

"I'm sorry." She ran her fingers along his shoulder, his back. "I'm trying to learn how to live with all this and . . . I guess it's just hard."

"It's hard for me, you mean." He waved his hand toward the family room. "Your life is just as it always was. Working with the kids, teaching them how to read and color and taking them on play dates with your sisters." He took another drink of his coffee. "You're still painting and running our home and doing everything you ever did." He wasn't angry with her — she knew him that well. But his voice was louder than before. "Have you thought about me? I'm supposed to be out there fighting fires, protecting the city, and rescuing people." He set his coffee cup down a little too hard and rocked his chair back onto its back legs. Then he stood and paced to the sink and back to the table. "Look at me, Ashley . . . I'm going stir-crazy and I've only been home two weeks. I feel like I'm . . . like I'm useless."

She wasn't sure what to say, but she had to try. "What about the vacation idea?"

"That's ridiculous." This time his response was more of a yell. "Ashley, they're telling me I might never go back to work. How can I think of that as a vacation?"

"Landon, please." Her tone pleaded with him to lower his voice, to get control of himself. "This isn't my fault."

He seemed to hold his breath for a minute, and for half a second she wondered if his anger was causing him to go into an attack. But then he exhaled slowly, like he was searching for control again. He sat back down and took her hands gently in his. "I know it's not your fault. This isn't about fault. And yes, I love the kids and you. Being home for a few days has been great."

Understanding filled her with a warmth she hadn't felt until now. "You miss it . . . being at the station. Is that it?"

"Of course I miss it." An exasperated laugh sounded quietly on his lips. "It's what I do, Ash, . . . I'm a firefighter. I can't sit home and wait for the next round of tests."

A different sort of panic pushed its way into Ashley's heart. She hadn't thought about this aspect of his lung disease. She'd been too worried about his survival to think about what might happen if he did live. "You could work investigations . . . or teach. You could get involved in coaching or you could —"

"Ash . . . don't you see?" The pain in his voice, the hurt in his eyes was more than she had seen since their early days, back when he wasn't sure if she loved him. "I fight fires. That's what I love. It's like," he pointed his thumb toward the stairs, "if you couldn't paint."

Ashley sat back. There had been times in her life when she relied on the canvas, times when she wasn't sure she could live if she didn't paint. She had always believed that creating a piece of art was proof of God in her life. His gift to her . . . and her gift to use for Him. She covered Landon's hand with her own. "I . . . I didn't see it that way."

They heard the sound of quick feet and suddenly Devin stood in the doorway. "Are you guys fighting?"

Ashley and Landon shared a hurried look, one that expressed their mutual regret that their conversation had caused Devin to worry yet again. Landon walked to him and put a hand on their son's shoulder. "We're just talking, buddy."

"Talking loud." His brow lowered, and he looked wounded. "You didn't have a nice tone." His anger lifted a little, and he looked at Ashley. "I have to have a nice tone with Nessa, remember?" He put his hands on his hips. "So you have to have a nice tone too, right?"

"Yes." Landon ran his hand along Devin's blond hair. "I'm sorry, Dev . . . I'll watch my tone, okay?"

"Okay." His lips curved into a relieved smile. "You too, Mommy?"

Ashley's heart ached. "Better tones all around."

"We haffa be friends . . . all the time." His smile filled his face this time. "Right?"

"Right." Ashley joined Landon as they answered him at the same time. She stood and joined the guys, putting her arm around Devin and looking long and hard into his eyes. "I'm sorry . . . Daddy and I love each other very much. And you're right. We're best friends."

Devin gave a satisfied nod and returned to the other room with his sister. Ashley peaked in on them and saw that Nessa had her pink blanket. She looked lost in the movie — right at the scene where God parts the Red Sea. "This is the part where God works a miracle, right Mommy?" Devin called back to her as he settled in next to Janessa.

"Yes." She slipped her arm around Landon's waist. "This is the best part."

"And God is working a miracle for Daddy too, right?"

"Exactly." She hesitated, but not long enough to alarm him. "That's exactly what God is going to do."

She and Landon wandered back into the kitchen, and Landon sat down at the table again. He put his head in his hands. For a long time she only looked at him, wondering what God might have next for them. He had saved Landon from the house fire, breathed life into him, and helped him recover enough to be here — home where he belonged. But what about the future? Devin was right — they all needed to be best friends, especially Ashley and Landon. But if he couldn't fight fires, then they would need a different sort of miracle — something Ashley hadn't prayed for once since Landon had come home. Not so much that he'd live.

But that he'd have a purpose in doing so.

FOUR

By mid-May Bailey's life was a blur of rehearsals and workouts and conversations with Francesca Tilly. She was learning her part, but Francesca still wanted more from her, sharper movements, better expressions. There were days she wasn't sure she was ready for opening night. At the end of each day, when she finally had a single spare moment, she would skype alone in her room with her family, and once in a while with Brandon Paul. Some nights she even had time for Facebook. It was a fun outlet, a way to keep in touch with the high school girls who had befriended her because of her role in the movie *Unlocked.*

They wanted to know how she had lived out her faith on the set and whether she'd played a part in Brandon Paul's decision to become a Christian. They asked for advice about guys and their friends, parents, and siblings. Bailey felt herself drawn to respond to them every night before she turned in. She'd give them Bible verses and ideas about standing strong for God and for purity. "And always tell your mom everything." She'd written that to more girls than she could remember.

Most of them knew Bailey had been cast in *Hairspray.* So on the Monday before her opening night, she signed onto Facebook and updated her status to read: *Tomorrow night my dream of performing on Broadway will become a reality. I miss my family like crazy, but I love everything about my time in New York so far. I'm not sure I'm ready . . . but I can't believe God would let me get to this point! Thanks for praying for me! Here's a verse I read earlier today: "Commit your plans to the Lord, and they will succeed." Proverbs 16:3. XOXO.*

She hit the *share* button, and the update went live. Already she had a couple thousand friends . . . and that had to be mostly word of mouth, because she'd stayed out of the newspapers and magazines. Before she signed off, she did the one thing she knew she shouldn't do. In the search line she typed the name Cody Coleman. He'd started a Facebook page a few weeks ago — something Connor had told her about. Bailey hadn't asked him to be her friend, and he hadn't asked her. But neither of them really needed to be official Facebook friends. Their pages were open to public viewing.

A quick scan of Cody's page told her nothing had changed. No new updates since two days ago when he wrote only, "Don't underestimate the Lyle Buckaroos. This team has more heart than any group of football players in the state of Indiana."

From what Bailey could tell, Cody had started the page to update his players about Lyle football. The only girls he was friends with — yes, Bailey had looked — was Tara, who'd been with him in the hospital after Cheyenne's accident, and Andi Ellison, who was also Bailey's friend.

And, of course, Cheyenne.

Every week Cody updated his Facebook with information about her progress. She had survived the accident with no brain damage, and now she was healing from her broken bones, and learning to walk again. So far Cody had posted no photos of her, and his info page still showed his relationship status as single. Bailey thought that was strange. Clearly they were dating. No, they were more than dating. They were becoming the sort of close that could only happen through tragedy. Cody was everything to

Cheyenne . . . though Bailey couldn't see her page. Her information was private. But if she could, it wasn't hard to imagine the pictures. Cody and Cheyenne in the rehab clinic, him helping her stretch her leg muscles, Cody walking beside her down the hallway, the two of them sharing dinner together.

Bailey signed off and, as she did, she heard the sound of someone getting onto Skype. In a hurry she opened the Skype program and saw that it was Brandon Paul. Brandon was her friend on Facebook and on Skype . . . but he went by the name His Only . . . a tribute to the way he felt about Jesus, and the only possibility he might have of flying under the radar when it came to social media.

She hit the small green telephone icon at the top of the Skype box, and then just as quickly, she clicked the *video* button. Instantly she could see herself in a small box on her screen. He answered on the first ring, and just like that, they were looking at each other. Brandon, his face life-size in the full screen, and in the far left corner a tiny box that showed how she looked to him on the other end.

"Hi . . ."

"Hi." His voice was soft, his eyes dancing.

"How many nights in a row is this?"

She giggled. "I haven't counted."

"I have." He was sitting in his office chair and he leaned back, a grin spread across his face. "This is our sixteenth night."

"I love it." Bailey let herself get lost in his eyes. Skype was crazy that way . . . it was a computer screen, yes. But because the image was life-size and because they could talk in real time to each other, skyping was more like talking to someone through a window. Only maybe better. Because their faces were so close, their eyes so connected. "How was your day?"

"Better now." He angled his head. "I miss you. Really bad."

"I miss you too." It was true. These past few weeks skyping together had brought them closer. "I look forward to this." She felt her smile drop off. "Especially lately."

"You better." He chuckled and then seemed to realize the change in her mood. "Why especially lately?"

Bailey hesitated, not sure how much she should say. She didn't want his pity . . . but she could definitely use his prayers. "I don't know . . . I might not be ready. A couple of the ensemble girls sort of hinted that maybe the part was given to me." She hesitated. "You know, because of my part in *Un-*

91

locked."

"That's ridiculous." Brandon's eyes flashed. "You trained hard for that part." He raked his fingers through his hair and jerked back in his seat. "Remember the director? She said you were the strongest dancer that day."

"Yeah . . . but since then she's been hard on me. And I deserve it." She hadn't admitted this to anyone except her mom. "The dancers here are so good."

"They've been on the show for months. Of course they're good. After the first show, you'll be fine." Brandon's expression eased and he smiled. "Now . . . about the way I miss you . . ."

Her worries left and a lighthearted laugh came easily across her lips. "You have a one-track mind."

"True." He leaned close. For a second he brought his face so close that only his eyeball filled the screen. Then he leaned back and laughed once more. "I sit here all day . . . waiting and watching . . . wondering when you'll finally find the time to go home and get on your computer."

"Oh, right." Her laughter filled her room, and her heart felt light at the sound. "That's you, Brandon. So bored . . . nothing to do but sit around waiting for me to get on Skype."

"Well . . . that and my movie."

"How's it going?" He was doing an emotional film about a father and a son, set in the world of NASCAR. The movie was called *Chasing Sunsets,* and it was based on a bestselling novel that was still one of the hottest books on the *New York Times* list.

"Let's put it this way . . . at some point earlier this afternoon, I was flying around a race track at nearly two-hundred miles an hour."

"What?" She leaned forward, as surprised as she was concerned. "Are you serious? That's too fast . . . I mean, you were a passenger, right?"

"Yes . . . But next week I'll drive."

"At two-hundred miles an hour?"

"Maybe." He laughed again. "Okay, maybe half that."

"Hmmm." She wasn't sure how she felt about him racing as part of his moviemaking. "Shouldn't you have a stunt double?"

"And miss all the fun?" His eyes sparkled with the challenge. "Come on, Bailey . . . You should know me better than that."

"So . . ." she relaxed a little. He would be fine . . . no one would let him get hurt. "What was it like . . . in a car that fast?"

"It's the weirdest thing . . ." A sense of adventure shone in his eyes. "At first it's like you can't believe you're going that fast. But at a certain speed — I don't know, maybe a hundred and eighty or so — everything starts to feel like it's in slow motion. The edges are blurred, and the only thing you can really make out is the track ahead of you."

Bailey imagined herself in a car moving that fast. "Sounds crazy."

"It is." The familiar flirting returned to his expression. "But you know what?"

"What?"

"Even though the director told me to think about how the car might handle, which groove to be in, and whether I'd sling-shot the car ahead of me . . ." He nodded a few times, his eyes sparkling. "And even though I did that for the first two laps . . . by the third time around the track, you know what I was thinking?"

"How soon you could get out of there?"

"No." He moved closer to the screen, his expression locked on hers. His eyes had never looked more sincere. "I was thinking about you."

"Brandon, . . ." She laughed a little, but she didn't look away. He had this effect on her more often lately, making her dizzy, fill-

94

ing her senses with his presence even when he was three-thousand miles away. The teasing in her tone kept the conversation fun. "Come on . . . be serious."

"I am." He tossed his hands in the air and gave her his best helpless expression. "I can only imagine if I were behind the wheel. They'd radio me to pit and I'd just keep driving . . . around and around and around. Thinking about Bailey Flanigan."

For the slightest instant she felt a whisper of fear. From the time she met Brandon, she hadn't expected anything to come of their friendship. He was so different from her, his visibility and the life he lived. If she let herself fall for him, at some point she'd have to deal with the big questions: *Where would they live? How would she tolerate the public eye? What parts of his past would she need to know about?* Questions she wasn't ready to consider. But she would have to deal with them at some point. Because at the rate they were going, she wasn't sure she could stop herself from falling for him.

"What are you thinking?" This was another difference with having a video conversation on Skype. In a phone call, a person could hide in the little silences between conversation points. But here . . . face to face . . . emotional depth was harder to miss.

She smiled. "You know me too well."

"I try." He settled back in his chair again, studying her. "Have I told you how much I miss you?"

"Once or twice." She picked up a pen and paper and doodled a picture of the *Hairspray* marquee. "Well, . . . I better get some sleep."

"Me too." He gave her a look of mock seriousness. "I've never been so tired."

She laughed out loud. "You always do that . . . you make me laugh whenever you want."

"Not whenever I want." His voice softened. "Otherwise I'd make you laugh in the morning and at lunchtime and at night . . . and we'd never have to rely on Skype again."

The thought sounded wonderful. The last time she and Brandon were together — at her house when she was packing her things for New York — she'd enjoyed every minute. "With your life, we'd probably spend more time on Skype than together."

He opened his mouth, mock indignation flashing in his expression. "Hardly."

"Oh, yeah," she giggled at him, at the way he was always such an actor. "Your movie shoots take you all over the world."

"Yes, but . . ." His look was still overly dramatic. "You're forgetting something."

"What's that?" She was closer to the

screen now, her eyes melting into his.

"Every movie I make . . . from this point on . . . is going to star you and me together." He shrugged, as if the matter had already been decided. "We're too good a team. I've already decided. Of course . . . when you open tomorrow you'll take Broadway by storm, and then I may have to figure a way to sweeten the deal. You know, to convince you."

"You're crazy, Brandon." Again she laughed. "Okay . . . seriously. I really have to go."

"Okay. I'll be thinking about you tomorrow night." He gave her a sweetly stern look. "Don't be down on yourself. You'll do great. And I'll be praying for you."

"Thanks."

He held his arms out in a circle. "This is me hugging you."

She laughed and tried to keep a straight face as she did the same thing. "This is awkward . . . but here's me doing the same thing."

His fingers came close to the screen until they took up most of it. "And this is me touching your heart." This time he wasn't kidding.

His eyes made her feel breathless, not sure what she was supposed to say or where they were taking this. But she did the only thing she could do. She brought her fingers to the top of the screen where the camera was located and she saw in the small box at the bottom of her screen that the effect was the same for him as when he'd done it for her. "There. That's me touching yours."

"You didn't need to do that, Bailey." His smile mesmerized her . . . and again she had to work to keep from being swept away.

"Why?"

"Because . . . you already touch my heart. Every hour . . . every day. Without Skype or texting or even saying a single word."

She tilted her head, her smile reaching all the way through her. "Goodnight, Brandon."

"Goodnight."

She hated ending a Skype conversation with Brandon, hated watching his image disappear from the screen. But she had no choice. She needed her sleep. Tomorrow she had a run-through early in the day, and then a quick lunch break, and after dinner she would perform her part in *Hairspray* for the first time.

As the computer screen went black, Bailey slid her chair over and looked through her Bible on her desktop. She had been reading Philippians lately, and tonight she was on chapter four. But as she found her place, something else caught her attention. She looked up and her eyes fell on the photo of her and Cody, the only one of the two of them that she had put up in her new room. The one they had taken after a long walk last summer.

Everything about her face, her look, shouted that she was in love. Her eyes danced and his spoke volumes about how much he cared for her. How he would always care. Next to the photo was the Winnie the Pooh, and the other half of the sunglasses — the pair Cody had broken at the Lake Monroe beach last Fourth of July. Maybe it was time to take the picture down. She hadn't heard from him at all, which meant that no matter how difficult that meeting at the hospital had been for him, he had moved on. If he thought about her, he would text or call. Something.

She reached toward the picture to take it down or turn it around . . . anything but seeing Cody's face stare at her while she tried to read her Bible. Anger stiffened the edges of her soul and she bit the inside of her lip. How could he care so little about her? Even tonight . . . when he had to know she was having her first performance some-time soon. He wasn't a nice guy . . . that was all she could figure. She'd been wrong about him all along.

But just as she was about to grab the photo and fling it across the room or at least toss it under her bed, she hesitated. He was part of her past. The picture was no different than the ones of her family and her kitty, Gus . . . no different than the one of Andi Ellison and her, or the photo of Tim Reed from their time in *Scrooge* a few winters back. Just an old friend who made up a piece of her past.

Nothing more.

Fine. She would leave the picture up. But still as she turned her attention to the Scriptures she felt the bitterness of his rejection, the hurt of his betrayal. He had promised he'd be her friend always, but now . . . now he didn't act like she was alive.

A long sigh rattled up from her chest, and she focused on the words before her. They were both familiar and comforting: *Rejoice in the Lord always. I will say it again: Rejoice! Let your gentleness be evident to all, the Lord is near.*

Bailey stopped. Always when she had read this section of Philippians, she had felt reassured by that last line. Be gentle because God was close by. It made her realize that as a believer, she would never be alone —

no matter how difficult life became. But here . . . for the first time, the words screamed an entirely different message.

What are you trying to tell me, Lord . . . that I need to be more gentle?

There was no response, but Bailey tried to imagine how her heart and soul must've looked a minute ago when she was thinking the most angry thoughts at Cody Coleman. God didn't want her to be angry . . . He wanted her to be gentle. In this moment, that was the message of Philippians 4:5, Bailey was absolutely certain. And the only way to be gentle was to forgive him.

She closed her Bible and stared at the picture of Cody again. Tears stung at her eyes, but she blinked them away. Suddenly her anger and inability to forgive him felt like a mountain resting on her chest . . . making it hard to feel gentle about anything. Amazing that after a fun Skype date with Brandon she could still feel so upset by Cody.

Dear Lord, I don't want to hold anything against him . . . but I can feel it in my heart . . . I'm still so mad. So hurt.

Then some of her anger melted away.

Let your gentleness be evident to all, daughter . . . I am with you always.

God was speaking to her, she had no

doubt. He was using the Bible — the way He often did when she prayed — making His will known to her by bringing a verse to mind. The realization was sobering. She couldn't hold a grudge against Cody and be gentle at the same time.

Bailey drew a slow breath and relaxed a little as she exhaled. If she was going to deal with her anger toward Cody she would have to start somewhere. Maybe if he were out of sight, she wouldn't think about him. The way he clearly didn't think about her. This time, without second-guessing herself, she did the only thing she could do.

She took Cody's photo and dropped to her knees. Then she gently sent it sliding beneath her pretty bed, all the way up against the opposite floorboard. That way she wouldn't have to look at his face again.

Even if she wanted to.

Cody had started his Facebook page for two reasons: to update the kids at Lyle High about the football program . . . and to keep them posted on Cheyenne's progress. Cody sat in his bed, his legs stretched out, his laptop open. Facebook also gave him a chance to keep up on his players, all of whom were his friends on the social media site now.

He clicked to Arnie Hurley's page. Arnie was a senior, the starting quarterback. But his profile picture looked like something from a honeymoon album. He and his girlfriend, arms around each other, the two of them locked in a significant kiss — the sort of kiss that could lead any guy to places he didn't really want to go. "Nice," Cody muttered, frustrated. He'd have to have a talk with Arnie. Rumor was the kid was sneaking into his girlfriend's room every other night. Cody hadn't believed that until now.

Cody clicked out of Arnie's profile and opened the one belonging to Marcos Brown. His most recent status update said only: "Working on the farm. Again." Marcos lived with his cousin's family on a farm at the outskirts of town. Three years ago, his mother died of the flu, and his father was a lifer at the state penitentiary, convicted of killing his boss in an argument over a pay raise, according to the school principal, Ms. Baker.

As it turned out, the boy's uncle demanded hard work and lots of it — and he didn't believe much in sports. The man also thought doing homework was a sign of weakness, which meant Marcos was pulling an *F* in two classes and a *D* in another. If he didn't pick up his grades, he wouldn't be able to play next year — and he was easily their biggest lineman. Cody made a mental note to talk to Marcos tomorrow.

He checked a few other players' pages and caught what looked like beer in the background of a couple photos. The more Cody looked through the profiles of his players, the more he became convinced he needed a meeting. He wasn't taking a group of non-committed kids into football summer camp this year. Not when so much was riding on the coming season. The whole town expected them to fail. If Coach Oliver couldn't do anything with the Lyle Buckaroos — then Cody couldn't possibly be better. He was too young. That was the mind-set.

"You've heard of a rebuilding year," one of the old men told him after practice last week. "Well, we're looking for this to be a five-year rebuilding project." He gave Cody a sharp but friendly slap in the shoulder. "It'll take that long for you to look a day older than them boys out there on the field."

Cody was aware of the doubts around Lyle. He could live with that. What he couldn't live with — absolutely not — was standing by and watching his players throw away their chances. Whether for a girl or for grades or because they'd gotten sucked into the same partying that had nearly destroyed Cody. He wasn't there just to teach them how to win football games. It was his job to teach them about life. The way his coach, Jim Flanigan, had taught him.

He was about to turn in when he saw that Cheyenne had posted something a few minutes ago. She was doing so much better than any of them had expected. Her situation was very serious for a few weeks after the accident. But once she began talking, it became evident that her personality was intact, her ability to reason and remember and feel — exactly as it had been before her injuries. But her physical body had been a mess of broken bones and nerve damage.

After two weeks in the hospital, she'd been moved to an inpatient rehab facility in Indianapolis, where Cody stopped in to see her at least once a day. She was making tremendous strides — and once already he'd visited with a group of his players. They all knew about the accident, since it had happened during practice. Cody felt it important to keep them up on her recovery. Especially since he and the team had been praying for her every day.

He clicked her name and went to her Facebook page. Her status read: *Thank You, God, for Cody . . . he's been there for me every step along the way. Literally . . . I couldn't have done this without him.*

A smile tugged on his lips and he looked for a long time at her picture. It was a snapshot of Cheyenne and Kassie — the little girl Chey had visited so often, who had died of leukemia. The girl's loss was still hard for Cheyenne, and the photo was a way of keeping her memory alive. But tonight Cody couldn't take his eyes off Cheyenne, the love in her eyes, the peace on her face. She was a very special person, and no matter what happened between them in the months to come, Cody definitely had feelings for her.

Cody clicked the *like* button on Chey's status and then went to his own: *Football meeting tomorrow after school . . . Oh, and Cheyenne is walking twice as fast now as she did when she arrived at the rehab center. Keep praying!*

He was about to sign off, when he went to Bailey's page. His eyes scanned her update, and he felt himself grow utterly still. Tomorrow night she would begin her role in *Hairspray* . . . her first night on Broadway. Bailey was working for her dreams, realizing them. A hundred people had commented beneath her update, congratulating her and promising to pray. But what about him? Had he let

106

her know he was proud of her or that he cared about this milestone in her life? No . . . he'd done nothing at all. Nothing kind, no brief conversation where he might tell her how happy he really was for her. He was right about his decision to let Bailey go. He couldn't be her friend, couldn't stand by while she moved onto a life without him, while she dated Brandon Paul. But alone in his room he realized again how his actions must've looked to her. Almost like that of an enemy. And there was nothing he could do about it.

Because his silence would always say more than his words ever could.

FIVE

Bailey couldn't stop shaking. She was ready to walk to the theater, and what little dinner she could force herself to eat she had already eaten. Her dance bag held her shoes and a change of clothes, water bottles, and her makeup. She stepped outside her room and walked down the hall.

Bob and Betty were finishing tea at the kitchen table. So far Bailey loved everything about them. They shared a love Bailey wanted to learn more about, and once the madness of her daily rehearsals settled down, she planned to do just that.

"You look like a vision." Betty was on her feet. She walked to Bailey and touched the side of her face, her arm. "You shine with the love of God, Bailey Flanigan. Something tells me you won't be in the ensemble for long."

"Thanks . . . that means so much." She gave an exaggerated exhale. "Especially right now."

"You'll be fine." She gave Bailey's hand a quick squeeze. "Well, Bob," she turned to her husband. "Let's pray for her."

"Definitely." He came to them and put an arm around each of their shoulders. "Father, we lift up Bailey Flanigan to You. She is nervous, as well she should be. For it is only in our nervousness and inability that we find strength to succeed in You."

Bailey smiled and the feeling eased her nerves. She loved the Kellers, the way they took care of her and treated her like their own daughter.

Bob continued, asking God to stand guard over Bailey throughout the night, as she performed her part and as she made an impression on the producers and director. "She is prepared, Lord . . . now go with her and help her shine. In Jesus' name, amen."

The couple exchanged a look, and Betty gave Bailey a hurried grin. "Bob used to pray for us that way, back when we first met. We were in the same show on Broadway, and Bob figured we needed all the prayer we could get." She smiled at her husband. "So we prayed together every night before we went on."

Another piece of this couple's story, a reason why they shared such a happy marriage. Bailey wasn't surprised that they prayed together. "Thanks, Bob . . . I need to pray every night too. For sure, that much."

Bob and Betty walked her to the theater, and along the way they bought her three long-stemmed white roses. "Because I just know you're going to be a triple threat." Betty gave her a quick hug. When they reached the front of the theater, the couple bought tickets and walked her to the stage door. Francesca Tilly was very aware of the empty seats. She told them at every rehearsal that if they didn't keep it fun, if people didn't feel welcomed to the sixties, then she couldn't guarantee how long the show would stay open.

"Should I be worried? That there are still open seats?" Bailey paused near the stage door and searched the eyes of her new friends.

"No, dear." Betty smiled and shook her head. "They won't close *Hairspray* for a very long time. Maybe not ever."

"I hope not. I hadn't really thought about it until now." Bailey stood a little straighter and took a deep breath. "Well, . . . I guess this is it."

"You'll be perfect." Betty leaned close and kissed her cheek. "Go get 'em."

"Thank you." Bailey searched the older woman's eyes. "You're a gift from God, Betty." She turned to Betty's husband. "You too, Bob. I don't know if I would've survived those rehearsals if it weren't for you."

"Nah," Betty waved off the compliment. "Just doing our job. You'd do the same thing if you were in our place."

Bailey bid the two of them goodbye and walked across the backstage toward the girls' dressing room. The couple planned to go home after the performance, since Bailey was going out for pizza with the cast. She'd catch a cab back home — something they all agreed was a safe choice. The costume room was empty as Bailey stepped inside and she realized she was a little early. But that was perfect. She needed this time to focus, to go over the songs and dance moves one more time in her head.

On a long clothes rack, she found a costume bag with her name pinned to it. A thrill ran through her veins as she unzipped it and looked at the two dresses inside. They were both adorable. For most scenes she would wear the white dress trimmed in pink with a big pink sash and matching pink socks. Bailey was to wear her hair in a single ponytail, with a pink ribbon that hung the length of it. She found a place in front of

111

the mirror and plugged in her curling iron. When she was finished turning her long hair into ringlets, she tied her ribbon and was about to spray the style in place when Chrissy walked into the dressing room.

"Hi." Bailey could barely contain her excitement. She was the only member of the cast whose first show was tonight. To everyone else it might have been just another night on Broadway, but certainly not to Bailey.

"Hey." Chrissy looked surprised to see her. "That's right . . ." She looked Bailey over and grinned. "It's your first night."

"It is." Bailey clutched her hands together, her eyes wide. "I'm praying I won't mess up."

"Come on, Bailey." Chrissy had bleached blond hair and too-thin long legs and she played an ensemble role, same as Bailey. And like Bailey, she understudied for one of the lead roles — the role of Amber. "You give your all at every rehearsal. And you have connections like crazy. A movie credit with Brandon Paul. I mean . . . you'll be a lead in no time." Something about Chrissy's tone sounded defeated.

"Thanks . . . I guess." Bailey wasn't sure she liked Chrissy's comments. "I sort of like to think I earned my spot."

"Well, yeah . . ." Chrissy uttered a light laugh. "I didn't mean it like that."

Bailey hoped not. Especially after the rumblings from other cast members that she'd taken the easy road to Broadway, or that her connections were the only reason she was here. Bailey watched Chrissy take a spot in front of the long mirror. "I've watched you rehearse the Amber role." Bailey had wanted to tell her this for a while. "Chrissy, you're perfect." The girl who played Amber now was rude and arrogant. She wanted nothing to do with Bailey, and she'd made that clear from the beginning — Francesca's thoughts on the cast being family or not.

Bailey gave her hair a few light spritzes with the finishing spray. As she did, Chrissy peeled off her sweatshirt and prepared to slip into her dress — a pale blue number with as many pretty bows and matching hair ties as the one Bailey wore. But in a rush Bailey could no longer focus on Chrissy's dress, or her own costume, or anything but what was suddenly and certainly painfully obvious.

Bailey had noticed this before, but not as dramatically as right now: Chrissy was bone thin. Her shoulders jutted out like balls at the end of a couple of sticks. The ribs across her back all jutted out, and her spine was bruised — probably the result of all the sit-ups Francesca ordered from them each day.

Moving as quickly as she possibly could, Chrissy slipped her dress over her head. "What?" She must've caught Bailey looking at her. For the first time since they'd known each other, Chrissy's tone wasn't as kind as usual. "Is something wrong?"

"Chrissy . . ." There was a knowing in Bailey's tone and in her expression . . . she could see it in the mirror. She didn't want to have to spell out the obvious. "Are . . . are you okay?" Bailey had wondered a time or two whether her new friend might struggle with anorexia. Her dance clothes made it clear that she was too thin. But now there was no denying the obvious. Chrissy had a problem, for sure.

"I'm fine." She laughed, but it sounded pinched, unnatural. "I've had a cold . . . I get a little underweight."

Was she kidding? Bailey wanted to scream at her, tell her that she desperately needed help. But instead all she could do was look at Chrissy for a long moment. The girl hid her problem well. Her arms weren't as thin as her legs, and since the dress she wore on stage had a longer skirt, she had so far danced her way under the radar. Francesca had told them a few times just since Bailey had arrived that eating disorders would destroy a girl's career as fast as drugs or drinking. "All things in moderation," Francesca had told them. It was a mantra of sorts when she talked to them about their personal lives. So had she pulled Chrissy aside and urged her to get help? Or were her comments more of a suggestion for the cast, her way of addressing Chrissy's troubles in a passive manner?

Because Chrissy's problem was both obvious and dramatic, and Bailey had no idea what to do. If Chrissy wouldn't admit she needed help, Bailey wasn't sure she could do anything. She would make a point to talk to her later — maybe after the show. For now she only smiled nervously at her. "I'm here for you . . . if you want to talk."

"Thanks." Chrissy applied her makeup in silence after that.

Bailey finished up first and reported to the green room. There were so many hurting people on the *Hairspray* cast. Two of the guys were gay, and Bailey had overheard them talking in rehearsals about their partners — both of whom were dying of AIDS. Bailey had a feeling several of the other guys were gay too, but she didn't ask.

Already one of them had pulled her aside

during a rehearsal last week. "Look . . . everyone's talking about you. How you're a Bible fanatic." His angry tone softened a little. "I'd just like to ask you not to judge us . . . you know, those of us who are gay. God loves us too."

The comment left Bailey speechless. Of course God loved them. He loved all people. But that didn't change the Bible's viewpoint on homosexuality or taking care of the body, and so far she had no idea how she was supposed to respond. She didn't want to come across as self-righteous or judgmental. She wasn't perfect, after all. She struggled with anger at Cody and doubts about her abilities and place in the *Hairspray* cast. But at the same time she was anxious to offer them the hope of God. The conflict remained, and she still had no idea how to treat the situation. Christians had taken so much heat for being judgmental that Bailey wasn't sure she could say anything.

For now, Bailey put all those thoughts from her mind. This was her opening night, and she could hardly wait to get on stage. Out there they didn't have to worry about eating disorders or AIDS or any other struggle except her own — to keep up with the rest of the cast. Tonight they would be just a group of kids dancing their way through the sixties, looking for racial equality.

Francesca found her in the green room ten minutes before show time. She walked up quickly and put her hands on Bailey's shoulders. "Are you ready for this, Ms. Flanigan?"

Bailey gulped. "Yes, ma'am. I hope so . . . I mean, yes. Yes, I am."

Francesca studied her. "You bring a good name to this show." She sized her up and down, as if she were still forming an opinion of Bailey. "Keep working hard and you'll do well. I believe that."

Bailey thanked her, but she felt defeated. A good name? Was that really why she was here? Because her name and her connection to the movie *Unlocked* brought buzz to a show that hadn't been selling out lately? She felt the blood leave her face, and her fingers tingled the way they had once when she'd fainted after a blood test. She couldn't be about to step on stage for her first night on Broadway not sure if she belonged. The doubt would paralyze her. No wonder the cast was whispering about her, calling her out about her faith and her connections. For a long moment she thought about putting in her time tonight and then resigning. If she wasn't good enough, then she didn't want anyone's charity.

Breathe, she told herself. *Dear God . . . help me lean on You. Help me be good enough . . . please.*

The response was straight out of a devotion Bailey had read earlier that morning:

Daughter, remember in this life you will have trouble . . .

In this life she would have trouble. But the rest of the verse was where she focused her attention. Because God had already overcome the world, and He'd already overcome her anxiety about tonight.

She took a deep breath and remembered something her mother had told her earlier that week. "Not all things will be easy for you, Bailey. It's the hard things that grow us. If you need to get stronger as a performer, then you'll get stronger."

Bailey headed out to her place in the wings. She and the others in the ensemble didn't make their appearance until a couple scenes into the show. The whole time she let Francesca's words stay with her. She needed to be ready. No way around it.

The house was filling up, but not like it needed to be. "We need to get those seats filled," Chrissy whispered to her in the shadows. "Otherwise they'll pull the show. They'll only be patient for so long."

More pressure to perform. Bailey willed her breathing to slow down, prayed that her heartbeat wouldn't get too far ahead of her. She would get better, and together they would make the show so great people would flock to see it. Bailey just got here. If she could be strong enough to stay, she couldn't bear to think about the show closing.

"We need to pray," Bailey spoke in a whisper too — more to herself than to Chrissy. "For the show to do something good. So it'll stay open."

"No . . ." Chrissy's face held a sadness that she probably hadn't intended to reveal. "We don't need prayer. We need an audience."

Again Bailey saw the opportunity to talk, the chance to share exactly what her faith meant with a girl who seemed at least a little curious. But Bailey still had no idea how to take the conversation from talk about rehearsals and shows and the intensity of their director to a place where the faith she so desperately clung to would be evident.

And maybe even something one of her castmates might claim as their own.

SIX

The show went by more quickly than Bailey expected.

One minute she was taking the stage for "Nicest Kids in Town," and the next they were through with the intermission and headed into "You Can't Stop the Beat." Bailey felt like she was running through syrup. The singing, the dancing . . . the expressions she was required to give for every part of every number when she was on stage — all of it made her feel half a step behind. Even so, she was doing this, she really was — singing and dancing on Broadway!

Far too soon, she was singing "Mama, I'm a Big Girl Now" with the rest of the cast, giving every move, every note everything she had. And like that . . . the show was over. Bailey and the other ensemble dancers were first to take their bows, and as they did Bailey felt tears fill her eyes.

Whatever had happened on stage, whatever terrible way Bailey felt about her performance, the audience must've felt differently. Because they were on their feet — from the beginning of the curtain call to the end. Bailey hurried off stage right as another set of dancers took a bow, the leads were next, and finally the sweet-natured girl who played Tracy, the show's star. The actress wasn't at every rehearsal, so Bailey hadn't connected with her. But she seemed kind, and she was brilliantly talented.

Breathless and laughing from the exhilaration of the night, Bailey waited with the others until the curtain hit the stage. Then she exited down the stairs toward the green room. As she did, one of the stage hands approached her. He held a bouquet of at least a dozen long-stemmed red roses. A few of the dancers hesitated and stared at the roses, then at her. Two of them whispered something to each other and then looked at her as they walked off. Bailey had no idea what they were thinking. It was her first night, after all.

"What in the world . . . ?" Bailey laughed once, still trying to catch her breath. Had her parents sent these? She took the flowers and thanked the guy, but almost immediately she realized there was no card on the flowers. "I'm sorry." She touched the man's elbow. "Do you know . . . who these are from?"

A grin appeared on the man's face. "Some guy." He pointed to the opposite side of the stage. "He's waiting for you over there. By the back door."

For half a heartbeat Bailey wondered if it might be Cody, if maybe he'd been silent these past weeks because he was planning a surprise for her opening night. But as she walked behind the backstage, in the aisle between the heavy velvet curtains, she caught a glimpse of someone on the other side, someone working his way into her heart a little more every day.

"Brandon!" She had the flowers in one hand, but she hugged him anyway, holding onto his neck and breathing in the smell of him, the thrill of him. "I can't believe this." She was laughing, half breathless, half stunned. "Why didn't you tell me?"

"And miss out on this moment?" He drew back enough to see her face. "You were absolutely amazing tonight. Every minute you were on stage you shone brighter than anyone in the cast."

"I felt like I was dancing in quicksand," Bailey frowned.

"Are you kidding?" He held her shoulders

and stared at her. "Did you hear that applause? They loved you. They loved the whole show."

It was true, and her frown didn't last. It couldn't. Not when her heart couldn't stop smiling. "Brandon . . . you're really here."

He laughed out loud. "Like I could stay away."

Her head was spinning, but she put her finger to her lips, laughing in more of a whisper now. "We have to be quiet. The rest of the cast . . ."

"Sorry." He chuckled and dropped his voice. He slid his arms down around her waist, and she eased hers around his neck. "You're so beautiful, Bailey . . . from the inside out." He took a step back, and his expression became almost bewildered. "Seriously, I had no idea you could sing and dance like that." He leaned his shoulder into the nearest wall, his eyes never leaving hers. "No wonder you don't want Hollywood. For a ride like that every night, I'd switch to Broadway too." He shook his head, his awe as genuine as his laugh. "And none of this dancing in quicksand. Be serious. It makes what I do look pretty boring."

She took his hand with her free one. Her surprise was wearing off, and now she wanted him to know how much it meant to her that he was here, that he cared this much. "Not when I was with you . . . never boring, Brandon." She breathed in his presence, the smell of his jacket and his cologne and the look in his eyes. "I loved being on the set with you. Every minute."

He had no easy comeback. Rather his expression shifted to that of a teenager, smitten beyond words, and speechless in the presence of the girl he was falling for. He shrugged one shoulder and flashed her a crooked grin. "What can I say? It was fun."

"Yes." She swung his hand lightly, enjoying the playfulness they shared. "And someday," she made a face, "if I last on Broadway . . . I'll have to take a break so we can do that love story."

He took a step closer, looking so deeply into her she could feel his heart. "Oh, we'll do the love story, Bailey . . . I have no doubt."

This was something else she loved about Brandon. He was confident. He didn't take no for an answer, even after all this time. Every other girl Brandon Paul had ever fallen for would've been his by the end of the night. Not her . . . not hardly. If Bailey knew him as well as she thought she did, she was more of a challenge than anything he had ever gone after. But not once did he show his discouragement.

"You look happy, Bailey, do you know that?" He brushed his knuckles lightly against her cheek. "It was worth every mile to see you this happy."

"Thanks. I thought I was going to collapse out there." She was dizzy again, her stomach nervous and excited and thrilled all at once. Brandon had come! For her opening night! She held the flowers to her face and captured the smell of them. "They're beautiful."

"Not as much as you." He looked like he might kiss her, here in the dark shadows behind the stage. But then he took a step back and slipped his hands in his pockets. He wore dark jeans and a light brown long-sleeved thermal. He also wore a dark hoodie, which would help keep him from being recognized.

"You look great." She tilted her head. Suddenly the night stretched out in front of them with endless possibilities of where they could go . . . what they could see in the city together.

"Especially this." Brandon adjusted his baseball cap and made a funny face. "Gotta love the hat. Can't go anywhere without it. That and the sweatshirt. Thought about bringing the dark glasses, but at night they

125

might only make things worse."

She laughed out loud at the picture of him walking New York City streets with dark sunglasses at night. The hoodie was a better idea. Between the cap and the sweatshirt, people wouldn't recognize him. He flipped the hat backwards and nodded toward the commotion on the other side of the stage. "Let's put the flowers in the dressing room."

"Okay." She hesitated. "Do you . . . want me to introduce you to the cast?"

"Sure." Brandon had an easy way about him. He clearly wasn't worried that one of the cast would alert the paparazzi. They were entertainers too, after all. "Do you have plans with them? Tonight, I mean."

"I did." She smiled. The whole night felt better now that he was here. "But they can wait." She gave him another quick hug. "I have plans with you now." Once more she took his hand in hers, and she led him down the aisle and to the green room. On the way, she almost changed her mind. Already the cast thought she was here because of her association with Brandon and *Unlocked.* Seeing him here would only fuel their doubts about her talent. But she didn't care. A few of the cast had already left, but most of the dancers were still there. They looked her direction as she entered the room. "Hey, everyone . . . I'd like you to meet Brandon Paul."

There was a hesitation, the sort that was to be expected. The cast might be in the same business as Brandon, but still he was a household name, easily the most familiar face in Hollywood. The guys nodded in his direction, and a few uttered their greetings. Two of the girls began to giggle, and one of them grabbed a piece of paper and a pen from her purse. "Sorry . . . I hate to do this, but can I have your autograph for my sister?"

Brandon's laugh came easily. He was comfortable in this environment — in any environment, for that matter. He understood that his celebrity came with certain requirements, responsibilities — and he bore them without arrogance or grumbling. He signed the paper and posed for a quick phone picture with the girl and her friend.

Chrissy came up then. "Hi, Brandon . . . I love your work." She looked at Bailey. "I've wanted to tell you . . . I loved you in *Unlocked*."

"Thanks." Bailey had been so busy learning her part, she hadn't realized that by now most of the cast had probably seen her movie. Was that the reason they had seemed colder toward her lately? Because they were bugged that an on-screen actress would win a part on Broadway? Or was her mediocrity on stage the cause? She wasn't sure, but she could hardly ask about it here. She made a mental note to talk to Chrissy about her perceptions another time.

Chrissy was going on, telling Brandon how amazing he had been in the movie, and how she'd been a fan forever. While she talked, her hands shook, and again it was obvious that she was far too thin. The bones in her arms and wrists made her look almost skeletal. She pulled her phone from her purse and asked one of the other cast to take a picture of her with Bailey and Brandon. After the photo was snapped, Chrissy turned to Bailey. "You did good tonight, Bailey, . . . really." She hugged Bailey. "I know you were worried, but you did just fine."

Just fine. Bailey wondered if her new friend would've chosen different words if she'd been amazing tonight, or if she'd wowed them beyond what they had expected. The compliment came off feeling like a consolation somehow.

As she and Chrissy and Brandon talked, several of the other dancers gathered their things and left — most of them with a friendly wave or a "Nice to meet you." But

a group of dancers — several guys and a couple girls — whispered among themselves, and one of them covered a ripple of laughter. She wasn't sure, but she thought she'd heard one of them say something about her thinking she was better than everyone else. Whatever they were talking about, Bailey doubted it was kind.

Oh, well. Not everyone was going to like her. That was okay. Maybe she'd find out later what their deal was.

Brandon must have picked up on what they were thinking and saying, because he looked at the time on his phone. "We better go."

"Definitely." She crossed the room to a sink, added water to the vase the flowers had come in, and set them on her makeup table. They said a quick goodbye to the others still in the room.

Chrissy slung her bag over her shoulder. She smiled, but in a wistful sort of way. "Go have a blast, Bailey. You deserve it."

She deserved it? Bailey wasn't sure what Chrissy meant. The two of them didn't know each other well enough for the comment to be based on anything Chrissy might know about Bailey. She would talk to her about it later. For now Bailey hugged her friend goodbye, and again she felt how frail

the girl was. She couldn't have weighed a hundred pounds. Suddenly Bailey knew she had to bring up the subject, had to urge Chrissy to get help. She was so thin she could be in danger.

When Chrissy was gone, after Bailey had changed into her street clothes and she and Brandon were alone again, Bailey turned to him. "Okay . . . I'm ready."

"Good . . . the horse should be there by now."

"What?" Bailey stopped just short of the stage door and turned to him. "What horse?"

"You know me, Bailey." He held his hands out, his eyes dancing. "Always full of surprises." He took her bag and led her outside. As they walked, he flipped his hat around, tugged the bill low, and slipped his hood over his head, so that his eyes couldn't be seen as long as he kept his head down. The night air was cool enough that Brandon's disguise looked very natural. "Come on," he whispered. "Let's go fast."

Members of the audience still waited outside, holding out their playbills and getting autographs from the cast as they walked out the door. But Bailey was new, and she was ensemble. No one would be looking for her — unless maybe they read the program

130

and saw that she was in the current hit film *Unlocked.* She chuckled to herself. With Brandon leading the way, they'd never guess she was anything more than a friend of one of the cast members maybe. He moved quickly, and where the rest of the cast turned left out the door and walked along the line of fans, signing autographs, Brandon led her to the right. They pressed past a few people milling about and darted to the curb.

Like he'd promised, waiting there was a striking black carriage with a pretty roof — fringe and all. The driver was dressed in a tuxedo, and his two horses were stately and proud, decorative tassels on their headdresses. Brandon helped her inside, and then he slipped in beside her. They were pulling away when one of the women waiting for an autograph turned and pointed. "Hey . . . that's Brandon Paul and Bailey Flanigan!"

A flurry of gasps and camera phones shot up from the crowd, but by the time they might capture a picture, Bailey and Brandon were gone.

"Not bad, huh?"

Bailey sat back in the carriage, laughing at what it was like to be him. "Actually . . . better than I thought. You were ready."

"I'm always ready." He winked at her. "See, Bailey, . . . my life isn't that crazy." He gave an exaggerated look over his shoulder and behind the carriage. He tossed his hands. "No paparazzi." He turned so he could see her better, the teasing that she loved about him written in his expression. "Just like being with any other guy."

This time she laughed out loud. "Okay . . . I'll tell myself that."

Clearly Brandon had planned this out, because the driver knew where to go. As they rode, Brandon studied her, searched her heart. "I've been looking forward to this for a month. Ever since I was at your house helping you pack." He grinned. "Your mom knew about it, by the way. I told her . . . just in case they were going to be here tonight."

"They're coming this weekend. The whole family — they'll watch it Saturday night."

"I know." He puffed out his chest and crossed his fingers. "Your mom and I are like this."

"Okay." She felt the joy of his presence through to her soul. Again she laughed, because that's the effect he had on her. She couldn't stop smiling. "I'll have to talk to her about that later."

"Yes. You do that." He sank a little deeper

into the back of the carriage and looked at her, just looked right into her eyes for a long moment. "You can never stop singing and dancing, Bailey. You're way too good."

"Hmmm . . . I wasn't sure tonight." Her voice was quieter now, and despite the honking yellow cabs and roar of traffic and noise from the jam-packed sidewalks, the moment became more intimate. Like they were the only ones in the city.

"You were scared, that's all." He took her hands in his, and gently he ran his thumb over her fingers. "You were perfect. Like I knew you'd be. I mean, you're so pretty and you're one of the best actors I've worked with." He wasn't teasing, and in his serious-ness Brandon showed a vulnerability that was almost more attractive than his usual easy confidence. "But watching you to-night . . . you were amazing."

"Thanks." Bailey allowed her eyes to stay locked on his. They were comfortable to-gether — no matter how much time had passed or how few nights like this they'd ever shared. "I can tell you mean it."

"Definitely." His teasing eyes were back. "I mean, if you would've bombed I'd just tell you straight out." He took on a heavy New York accent. "Bailey, are you *kiddin'* me? That was *terrible!*"

She giggled at him, at the way he could become any character he wanted in as much time as it took him to breathe in. They were headed toward Fifth Avenue — at least she thought so. A quick glance outside the carriage and she saw Radio City Music Hall. "Where are we going?"

"To London . . . or the Bahamas . . . or France." He laughed. "If we had more time, anyway. But since we're both actors, I suppose we can pretend."

"Meaning . . . you're not going to answer me." She turned to him again, and found that he'd slid a little closer. "I mean . . . do you have a plan?"

"Bailey, . . ." He still had her hands in his, and again his eyes worked their way straight through her. "I told you. I always have a plan."

She grinned, and at the depths of her being she knew he was telling the truth. This trip to New York, his time with her, none of it was an accident or by chance. He might want to seem spontaneous, but he had a plan.

Bailey believed that with all her heart.

SEVEN

He was asking her about the rest of the cast when the driver pulled the carriage to the curb. The man looked like he might've been from another country. If he knew who Brandon was, he didn't let it show.

Only then did Bailey realize where they were. "The Empire State Building!" she gasped. "What a great idea!" They climbed out of the carriage, and Bailey looked straight up. "I've never been here."

"Me either." Brandon said a few words to the driver about being back in an hour. Then he took Bailey's hand and led her to the door. His baseball cap was still pulled low over his eyes, the hood still in place. "I decided I'm way too old to have never been to the top of the Empire State Building."

She loved this, the way he could turn any activity into an event, a memory she would treasure always. "Oh, yes, . . . way too old." He walked in and went to the right, where a guard was standing. Immediately the man acknowledged Brandon, as if the two of them had talked before. At the same time, the guy snapped into motion. "Right this way," he said. He nodded at Brandon and smiled at Bailey.

What had Brandon done? She felt a chill of excitement run down her arms and back. They would have their own escort to the top, was that it? The guard took them to an elevator marked *Express.* They waited less than a minute, not long enough for the other tourists and passersby to understand what was happening, to catch a glimpse of Brandon beneath the hood or to figure out whether Bailey looked familiar.

Then the elevator shot them to the top of the building in less than a minute. Halfway up Bailey felt a popping in her eardrum. She looked at the numbers whizzing by on the lighted panel. "A hundred floors? We're going up a hundred floors?"

"No, . . ." Brandon looked at the guard, and the man winked at him. "Tell her, Joey."

"We're going to the 103rd floor, miss." The man's accent was as thick as the one Brandon had pretended to have just minutes ago. He waved his thumb at Brandon. "Your boyfriend here called weeks ago. Worked it out with the bigs upstairs. No one gets onto the 103rd floor . . ." Joey grinned at Brandon. "Except him." The man lifted his hands and let them fall to his sides. "They just lifted the security ban a few years ago. Even still, only high-ranking officials and government types usually get up here." He shrugged. "Pays to be famous, that's what I always say."

"Brandon!" She squeezed his hand. "That's so high!"

"It's a clear night." Joey smiled. "Should be perfect."

Bailey wanted to tell him that it already was, that she couldn't have imagined a more perfect night than the one Brandon had already given her. But the elevator was opening, and as they stepped out, Bailey stopped. Her hand flew to her mouth and she stared at the expanse of city below her. "Brandon . . ." His name was barely a whisper on her lips. "It's like we're flying, like a dream."

He leaned close and spoke softly near her ear. "Being with you . . . is a dream."

Brandon nodded to Joey, who stepped out and to the side, where he took a discreet position to the right of the elevator. He kept his eyes straight ahead, the perfect guard. Brandon had obviously arranged for all of this, the special guard, the ride to the 103rd floor . . . and now the added safety of knowing that Joey was going to watch over them while they were up here. Bailey felt like a princess, and everything below her looked like some magical kingdom. "I've seen pictures . . ." Bailey walked beside him as they went to the railing and looked out. Her heart raced within her, the feeling of being so high above the city so exhilarating she could hardly draw a breath. "But they were nothing to being up here . . . to seeing it for myself."

He removed his hood and turned his baseball cap around so she could see his eyes better. Then he slipped his arm around her shoulders and held her close. "Joey tells me . . . every few steps the view changes . . . it's another entirely different look at the city."

"Mmm." Bailey snuggled in close to him. The wind was chilly up here, and she could feel the building sway ever so slightly. "It's absolutely beautiful."

"On a clear day, I guess you can see almost eighty miles in any direction."

"Which means . . ." She looked up at him, and she could feel her eyes shining.

He understood what she meant, and he smiled. "Which means we'll have to come back up here again . . . in the daytime."

"Exactly." She leaned her head against his shoulder, and for a long while they stayed like that, quiet, caught up in the view of the city and what it was like being together this way — all alone, with the rest of the world far below them.

Finally he took her hand again and they walked partway around the observatory. The floor was open air, but with a roof and a safety railing system that would've prevented anyone from falling or jumping off. They stopped far enough away from the elevator that they were no longer in eye contact with Joey. Which was just as well . . . because Bailey liked the feeling — she and Brandon up here, no one else but the two of them.

"See that dark area?" He pointed toward a place in the distance where there were no lights. "I think that's Central Park."

"Oh, right . . . it must be." Again she felt a shiver of cold. The wind was even stronger on this side of the building, and even though it was mid-May, it couldn't have been much over forty degrees tonight.

"You're cold." He turned to her and again he eased his arms around her waist. "Here . . . let me keep you warm."

His sweatshirt and thermal didn't seem like much, but his body was much warmer than hers, and the nearness of him cut the chill immediately. She wore jeans almost the same color as his, a long-sleeved flowing sort of shirt, and a lightweight jacket with a high collar. It was one of her favorite outfits, and she was grateful she'd worn it. She looked into his eyes, and she was certain beyond a doubt that this was the better view. Even here on the 103rd floor. "Your eyes are so pretty . . . do you know that?"

"Eyes are a window to the soul." His look warmed her even more than his body. "Right?"

"Very nice."

"And the eyes are the lamp of the body."

"Hmm. You've been reading your Bible."

"I have." His eyes grew more serious, but his smile remained. "I love reading the Bible. It makes sense of the whole world — even Hollywood."

"Especially Hollywood."

"Yes." He chuckled and gave a single shake of his head as if to say he knew it well. "Especially there." He paused, never once looking away. "So if the eyes are the window to the soul . . . then it's no wonder you like my eyes." He framed her face with his hands, the two of them lost in each other. "Because . . . Bailey, you've captured my soul." He came closer, and for a few seconds

140

she wondered if he might kiss her. But instead he brushed the side of his face against hers. He looked at her again. "When you see into my eyes, you're seeing the reflection of yourself . . . the way you live inside me — whether you're with me or not."

His words couldn't have been more beautiful if they were scripted. She wasn't sure what to say, and for a long time she said nothing. Was this really happening? She and Brandon Paul at the very top of the Empire State Building? And was he really telling her that he'd moved past the crush he had on her, and that now . . . now he was in love with her? Her body trembled, and not because of the cold. She took a long breath and stepped back — even though she didn't want to. Brandon was passionate about everything he did, everything he said. If he really felt this way for her, then they would both need to be careful. Even now she felt herself almost drugged by his presence.

"Come on." She heard the desire in her voice, and she was embarrassed by it. She had to be so careful . . . so on her guard. Brandon had much more experience at this sort of thing, but now they both wanted to honor God with whatever this was between them. "We need to see the rest of the view."

If he knew how caught up in the moment she was, he didn't show it. He respected her decision to walk a little, and he allowed the conversation to lighten. They took turns pointing out landmarks — the Brooklyn Bridge and the financial district, the place where the Twin Towers had stood.

As they walked they talked about his current movie and his co-stars. "They're hard to work with . . ." This was the first time Brandon had admitted anything other than joy and happiness about his life or his work or his feelings about the people around him. She was glad he trusted her enough to talk about it. "I've caught a few of them laughing about me . . . you know, my new faith." He grinned in a way that said he wasn't going to lose sleep over the fact. "There's nothing I can do about it."

"I get that feeling from a few of my castmates too. Like they think I'm judging them because of what I believe."

"Do they know? That you're a Christian?" Brandon stopped and leaned on the railing.

"Yes, they know." Bailey had thought about it a little since the show had ended. She'd told Chrissy about how she'd prayed for the show to go well . . . and a few of the other girls had probably heard her. She talked about her faith like she breathed. It wasn't something she thought about first. Bailey guessed the girls might've shared her comment with the guys who seemed to be whispering about her. "They already think I'm young . . . and that I only won my spot because of *Unlocked.* They know I don't drink or pop pills. I'm pretty different, I guess."

Brandon sighed. "You'd think that would be a good thing." He shook his head. A slight bit of frustration worked its way into his tone. "I mean, I used to be out of control. Drinking . . . drugs," a shadow of shame fell over his face, "doing things with girls . . . stuff I never should've done." He worked the muscles in his jaw and looked out at the city for a long minute. "When I think about how I used to be it . . . it makes me sick."

"But your peers had no problem with it." Bailey's voice was soft. She understood. "Funny how the world is, huh?"

"Yeah. Because they were doing the same things." He shrugged again, and his expression relaxed. "The Bible talks about that too. 'In this world you will have trouble . . .' "

" 'But be of good cheer, for He has overcome the world.' Exactly what I was thinking earlier tonight. Before the show."

143

"The whole thing . . . the world . . ." He took her hands and drew her close once more. "That's why I had to see you this weekend. I could take only so much on the set without feeling you in my arms, looking into your eyes. Not through a computer, but here. Like this . . . in person."

Again Bailey wondered if he might kiss her. A part of her wanted him to, wanted it as badly as she wanted her next heartbeat. But she wasn't ready to agree to a relationship with him, so that meant she had no right kissing him. However magical such a moment — here high above the city — might feel.

"What are you thinking?" Again he put his hand alongside her face, his touch feather light against her skin.

"About you . . ." She couldn't break eye contact, couldn't look away. Her heart beat so loudly within her she wondered if he could hear it.

"Mmm." He came closer still, his face inches from hers. "That's the most wonderful thing I've heard all night."

She smiled, holding onto the moment. "Thank you . . . for bringing me here."

"It's the best night I've had since . . ." He looked like he might be racking his brain, going over every possible other night in his life. "Best night since I stood on the balcony of my house with this crazy beautiful girl and the stars dancing overhead . . . to the sound of the pounding surf."

"You know . . ." Her voice was soft against his cheek. "You could be a poet . . . if the acting thing doesn't work out."

"Thanks. I'll keep that in mind." He leaned back, his breathing just the slightest bit faster than before. "I have an idea." He ran his fingers along her hair, down her arm.

"Hmm." For a few seconds she could hardly remember where they were, or that they didn't have forever to be like this. "Whatever it is . . . I should probably say no."

"Bailey, . . ." He didn't laugh, didn't look away. "I wouldn't ask you to do something you wouldn't want to do . . . something that would hurt both of us or . . . disappoint God."

This was the boldest Brandon had been. He had a storied past, everyone knew that. But now that he was a Christian, he had changed in every possible way. Still, Bailey wasn't sure if he had adopted God's view on sex. Now, though, he'd made himself extremely clear. He understood that there was a line of purity, and he would neither cross it nor ask her to cross it. She put her arms loosely around his waist, curious. "What's your idea?"

"Well . . ." The teasing was back. "About that love story . . . the one we both still want to shoot someday."

"Yes." She could only imagine how much fun they'd have on a movie like that. But with her working here on Broadway the odds of it ever happening were slim. At least for now. "I read the script. Or maybe I wrote it." She giggled at the ultra-serious face he was making. "I love it."

"Right. Me too." He stroked his chin, his expression a mix of teasing and lighthearted flirting. "So . . . if we're going to take our craft seriously, then we should rehearse a little — maybe right now. Because otherwise — since we hardly have any time together — we won't wow the producers when it comes time to make the movie."

She looked at him for a long while, but then a bout of laughter caught her off guard, and she took a step back, laughing hard for a few seconds. "Brandon, . . . it's impossible to take you seriously."

"Good." He caught her by the waist and swung her in his arms. "Because guess what?" His voice was back to normal. "This night . . . was all the rehearsal we'll need."

They hugged again, for a long time. She

still wished he'd kiss her, but she was grateful beyond words that he didn't. Before they walked back to the elevator, he held her in his arms again, their faces so close that he needed only a whisper to be heard. "Bailey, . . . I won't forget this night."

"Me either." She felt herself falling . . . and from this high over New York City the feeling was headier than anything she could remember. "Everything about it . . . every minute was perfect."

"Good." He eased his face alongside hers and stayed that way for a few seconds, their cheeks touching, clearly fighting the temptation they both had to be feeling. When he drew back, his eyes held a resolve she hadn't seen there before. "I'm going to convince you, Bailey. One of these days . . . I will."

"Convince me?" She knew what he meant, but she wanted to drag out the moment.

"That I love you . . . that I've fallen for you and nothing . . . nothing will make me give up."

"Not distance?" She giggled, swaying gently with him.

"Not distance."

"Not time?"

"No." He laughed quietly. "Not time."

"Or anything else?"

"No. Especially not something so small as

147

our jobs." He brought his face close to hers again and slowly, like breath against her skin, he kissed her cheek. "Are you ready, Bailey? Are you ready to try?"

As quickly as he had made her laugh a minute ago, panic welled within her. She blinked twice, searching his eyes, willing the right words to come. She didn't want to make him wait. But she had to be honest — he deserved that most of all. "More ready . . . than I was yesterday."

He thought about that for a long moment, and a smile gradually lifted the corners of his mouth. "Okay . . . I can live with that." He stepped back then. "Come on, pretty girl. I need to get you home."

They made their way back to Joey and down the elevator. Along the way Joey made small talk, telling them trivial facts about the building and the famous people who had made it up to the 103rd floor. "But you . . . you might be the most famous in a long time." He nodded at Brandon, and then looked at her. "You too, miss." His cheeks reddened. "I saw your movie. It was fantastic."

Bailey thanked him, and Brandon slipped the guy a hundred-dollar bill. "You were great, Joey. I'll ask for you next time."

"Sounds great." He raised an eyebrow, his

accent thick. "I'm here to serve."

"Next time?" Bailey still felt like she was in a dream.

"Absolutely." Brandon looked at her, to the questioning places of her heart. "We'll be back."

He fixed his baseball cap and slipped his hood up one more time. Bailey wasn't sure what to expect when they reached the street level. With Brandon they could step out of an elevator and find a throng of people waiting. But whatever he'd done to prepare for this night, he'd done it well. There were only a few tourists milling about in the lobby, and a handful more waiting for the public elevator. Brandon was good at avoiding eye contact, expert at blending in. No one gave them a second look as they exited the express elevator and walked outside to where the carriage was waiting.

When they were seated, Brandon covered their laps with a blanket from the back shelf. She leaned her head on his shoulder and he took her fingers in his. "Aren't I supposed to lose a slipper or something?" She smiled up at him.

"No . . . this isn't that story." Brandon didn't break eye contact, wouldn't look away. His smile made her feel like the most cherished girl ever, his voice soft against her

149

skin. "Remember, Bailey? Cinderella lost her slipper because the prince let her go." He ran his free hand alongside her face, and again his touch was as gentle as the night breeze. "I won't do that. Not ever."

Dizziness swept over her one more time, and she rested her head on his shoulder for the rest of the ride. If she wasn't careful, she'd tell him yes, she was ready for a relationship, ready for a commitment. Because right now she would've said just about anything to keep him from leaving. *Be smart,* she told herself.

Jesus, please . . . help me know what to do . . . whether this is right or not.

Bailey waited, but there was no answer. Just the peacefulness of being here in the carriage beside him.

When they reached the Kellers' apartment, Brandon paid the driver and jogged to a waiting black Suburban. He said something to that driver as well and then hurried back to her side. The situation was just dawning on her. "You had a driver waiting here? Which means that . . ."

"I have a plane to catch." He smiled. "Well, actually it can leave whenever I want."

She laughed at his reality. Of course he'd flown on a private jet. He would create too much madness if he flew commercially. "So you really came just for this? My opening night and . . ."

"And the best few hours of my life." He wasn't teasing. "Hey . . . think about coming out to LA . . . when you have a break. Okay?"

"I will." She felt all lit up inside, like it might be days before the glow from this night would wear off. If it ever did. She thanked him again and they hugged once more. Not the long hugs they'd shared on the 103rd floor, but a respectful hug that told her he wouldn't put her reputation on the line, not now or ever. He stepped back and gave her a lighthearted wink. "Think about my question."

He didn't need to clarify which question. She waved goodbye and, after a lingering look, she turned and walked into the building. Long after she'd gone up to the eleventh floor and crept quietly into the darkened apartment, Bailey let the question play in her mind. She took it to God and remembered again and again how he had asked her. Was she ready? Was she ready for the friendship they shared to be something more? Bailey wasn't sure if she had an answer now, but she knew one thing for sure.

After tonight, she was close.

EIGHT

School was out — both at Indiana University and at Lyle High, which meant Cody had a great deal more time on his hands. The break was perfect, because Cheyenne was out of rehab, living with Tara. Though Cody still had daily practice with the football team, this first week of June he had become Cheyenne's full-time helper.

He jogged up the steps of Tara's house. She was so sweet, Cheyenne. So happy with whatever help she received from him. Not once had he heard her complain or show her frustration over her predicament. And because of her good attitude, she was relearning much of her lost physical skills at a record pace. Cody couldn't have been more proud of her. He knocked once. "Cheyenne, . . . it's me."

"Come in." Her voice held a smile, the way it always did.

Cody carried a bag of groceries and other

items, and as he let himself in he took it to the coffee table in the middle of the front room. He had another surprise for her today, one he could hardly wait to tell her. He smiled over his shoulder as he set the bag down. "I brought you a few things. Ice cream . . . licorice . . . all the healthy snacks." She'd lost weight since the accident. Her doctor wanted her to increase her calories until she regained her strength. He hurried the ice cream to Tara's freezer and returned, wiping his hands on his jeans. "It's hot out there. The ice cream almost didn't make it."

Cheyenne watched him, her eyes soft. "Cody . . . you didn't have to do that." She propped herself up on Tara's sofa, a stack of books and magazines at her side. She could use her walker to get to the bathroom. But her doctor preferred she wait until someone was there to walk with her. Just in case. She swung her legs tentatively over the edge of the sofa. "I'm sorry . . . that you have to do this." Her eyes were honest, marked by a gratitude that knew no limits. "There are better ways you could spend your summer. I know that."

"Chey . . . we've been over this." He offered her his arm. The truth was, she had helped him as much as he had helped her.

His flashbacks of the war in Iraq didn't come nearly as often now. His counselor thought she knew the reason. He had purpose again . . . and that purpose lived in the person of Cheyenne Williams. "Let's walk to the bathroom."

They'd moved past the point of embarrassment or awkwardness. He'd been there for her during rehab when the strain of simply getting out of the hospital bed had been enough to make her throw up on the linoleum floor. With all he'd seen her go through, they had become very close. He helped her to her feet, then positioned her walker in front of her. She needed to do most of the work herself — it was part of the process. "Okay . . . you ready?"

"Yes." Cheyenne's mom was white, her father black, a combination that made her beautiful skin look constantly tanned. Combined with her shoulder-length straight dark hair, Cheyenne was beautiful in a way that hadn't been marred by the accident. Even here, struggling to walk down the hallway, she was stunning. She stopped and worked to catch her breath.

"Here . . . lean on me for a minute." Cody eased her arm around his shoulders. "You don't want to overdo it."

"I'm not." She breathed in sharp and

tightened her grip on the walker. Her smile was marked by the effort, but she nodded despite the difficulty. "I'm okay. Let's go."

"A few seconds." He was adamant. She tended to push herself too hard, and this was one of those times.

For a long beat she hesitated, looking at him, clearly appreciating his kindness. But the mood shifted, and her expression told him she could feel the change too. "I . . . I couldn't do this without you." Her voice was tender, like everything about her.

Cody was caught in the moment, aware of the change between them. This wasn't the first time he'd felt his feelings shift. He had started out as Cheyenne's friend, but now . . . now he wondered whether God wasn't making it still clearer that she was in his life for an even greater reason. He waited several seconds, allowing himself to get lost in her warmth — even for this brief moment. "I told you, Chey." He touched her cheek, caring for her with everything he was. "I'm not going anywhere."

They made it to the bathroom, and from that point she managed by herself. Once she was inside, she flipped on the fan and closed the door. He waited outside in the hall, and his mind turned to Art Collins. What must it have been like to be Art, to be away from this marvelous girl for such a long time and to know that when he came back, the two of them would get married? Cody leaned against the wall and pictured his friend, his buddy Art. Had he known when the bullet hit him? Did he realize in that instant that he'd never see Cheyenne again?

For the first time in a long time, the images flashed in his mind. Horrific images of bloody limbs and utter destruction . . . dust and gunfire flying through the air in a whirl of terrible noise and death. Always death. He blinked hard and the images disappeared. If Art had known . . . would he want Cody to be here now? Standing in his place . . . helping Cheyenne through her injuries, through her season of healing? Maybe even falling for her?

He let the thought stand in the doorway of his soul for a long time, two minutes maybe. The answer was yes, right? Like Tara said, God had spared Cody and since things hadn't worked out with Bailey . . . this must be the reason. So he could be here for Cheyenne.

For a single instant, he looked down at the ring on his right index finger, the friendship ring from Bailey. Wherever she was, she'd moved on. He had seen her Facebook page, the pictures from her opening night. And there was another photo: one of her and a guy. He wasn't tagged in the picture and the guy's face wasn't clear, but Cody knew who it was. He would've recognized Brandon Paul's build, his profile anywhere.

Her profile still said she was single, but by the expression on her face she wouldn't be for long. Cody pictured the two of them, the way they'd looked in the photo. Brandon had clearly made his way to New York to see her show, and somehow he'd kept the event from the paparazzi. Cody gritted his teeth and tried to put her out of his mind. He wanted to feel happy for her, glad she'd found what he couldn't give her: a happy life, safe and whole.

But he wasn't there yet.

"Okay, I'm ready." Cheyenne turned off the fan, opened the door, and with painstaking attention to detail, she moved her walker back into the hall. They took minutes moving down the hall and through the kitchen, and once when she tripped he stopped her from falling. Frustration made her furrow her brow. "I'm sorry . . . I . . . I have to work harder."

"It's okay." Cody made sure she was steady. "You're doing great."

Again she smiled at him, but only briefly.

It took all her concentration to make it the rest of the way to the sofa. When she finally sat down, he expected her to look exhausted. But instead her eyes were bright, like the walk had breathed new life into her day, her disposition. "That was wonderful. Just moving again."

Cody understood. He'd gone through a similar rehabilitation after his injuries in Iraq. It was one more reason why he empathized with her. They shared a common bond of overcoming. "Okay . . . since you don't look too tired, I have a surprise for you."

"Really?" Her eyes danced, and again the bond between them felt like more than friendship. "You spoil me, Cody."

"Someone should." His voice was softer than before, and he couldn't have meant the words more. Cheyenne had been abandoned by her mother when she was young. She met Art in high school, and by then she had already determined to live an entirely different life than the one she'd had as a child. Their first date was at a Sunday morning church service.

Cody sat on the opposite arm of the sofa and studied her, the beautiful survivor seated across from him. "The football team can't wait to see you." He gave her a more

159

serious smile. "They've been praying for you, Chey. They made you something and . . . well, I told them I'd see if you were up for a trip to Lyle this afternoon."

Football practice was set for an hour later. Normally he would stop in and see her, help her however he could, and then head out to Lyle. After his team's workout, he'd come back and hang out with her until Tara got home. Even then he usually stayed well into the evening. "So . . . you up for a drive?"

Cheyenne's expression shifted from a childlike excitement to a teary-eyed look. "I feel . . . I guess I'm overwhelmed." She dabbed at a single tear before it could make its way down her cheek. "They didn't think I'd live . . . and the doctor worried about whether I'd ever walk. And now . . . something I used to love doing . . . I can finally go to your practice." She didn't come out and say it — the fact that she'd been on the way to see him coaching when she'd been broadsided by the truck. But the fact remained. In some ways this trip would be symbolic — finishing what she'd set out to do that afternoon. She sniffed softly. "Yes, Cody . . . yes, I'd love to."

"Good." He felt the sting of tears in his own eyes, aware of how important this trip was to her. "You think you'll be okay?"

"Yes." She uttered a sound that was more laugh than cry. "A million times yes."

He helped her to the door, and then had her wait at the top step. "I've thought this through." She wasn't ready for stairs yet, so he took her walker and ran it lightly down the steps to the sidewalk. Then he came back and swept her into his arms. She held onto his neck, and he cradled her close to his middle, careful with every step as he made his way down to where her walker waited.

"You don't weigh anything." He set her down gently, making sure she had perfect control of the walker before he took his place beside her. "You're going to get the biggest bowl of ice cream tonight. Just wait."

They both laughed at the idea as they inched their way toward Cody's pickup. "Tara will probably make me eat two bowls."

"She loves you." Cody admired the woman more every passing week. She worked hard all day, and then came home and played nurse to Cheyenne in ways Cody couldn't. It was a beautiful thing that Tara maintained her relationship with Cheyenne despite the fact that Art was no longer in their lives.

The trip to Lyle was marked by easy

161

conversation, and Cheyenne seemed happy and relaxed. Cody had wondered how she'd feel, taking this ride so soon after the accident that had nearly killed her. Halfway there she turned to him. "God has taken away my fear . . . isn't that amazing?"

"About driving?"

"Yes, that." She nodded, her face marked by a peace that could never have been from the world. "But about everything else too." She smiled at him, a smile rich with the sort of depth that couldn't be faked. "When Art went to war, I was terrified. Every day I worried that he might get hurt or captured . . . he might get killed." Her storytelling was slower than before. Not because she had brain damage, but because she simply was still recovering. "Even after I heard the news that Art wasn't coming home, I was still afraid." She leaned back against the seat, quiet for a moment. "I was afraid of the heartache . . . afraid I couldn't survive his funeral service." She turned slightly, wincing from the pain that was clearly still a part of her. "I was afraid of being alone."

"That makes sense." Cody tightened his grip on the steering wheel and kept his eyes on the road. "I've felt all those feelings." He didn't say that he'd felt them about Bailey.

162

This wasn't the time.

"Anyway." She looked straight ahead again. "I'm not afraid of anything anymore. I have God Almighty . . . I have my salvation." She smiled bigger than before. "I'll get to see Art again, and we'll have forever to hang around in heaven. And in the middle of my most difficult days, I have Tara." She looked at him again. "And I have you." She lifted her thin shoulder briefly. "What could I possibly be afraid of?"

Cody wanted to pull over and hug her. The way she viewed life, the trials she'd come through, her attitude was enough to give him new confidence in God . . . in his future. In the plans the Lord had for him. Maybe even the plans He had for the two of them.

He spent the last half hour telling her about his counseling, how his flashbacks had been less frequent and how he'd felt more at peace lately.

"God is doing something . . . in both our lives." She wasn't flirting with him. Just a matter-of-fact knowing. God was at work.

"The truth is . . ." Cody glanced at her, wanting her to know how much he cared. "He's using you to change me, Chey. He is."

"I know." She reached over and put her

hand on his shoulder, but only for a few seconds. Her endurance wouldn't allow anything longer. "God told me that."

Chey's faith was as attractive as her beautiful heart. The way she believed was different than Bailey, because Cheyenne hadn't known God all her life. Unlike Bailey, Cheyenne believed out of desperation, because she'd found God in the midst of a childhood marked by abandonment and tragedy. Because of that, her faith held the sort of depth that could only come after a person had passed through the fire.

Cody felt stronger just being with her.

He made another two turns, and then he pointed to the distance. "There it is. The stadium." He had purposefully taken a different path to the school, avoiding the intersection where she'd been hit. "The guys should be there."

She adjusted herself, sitting up straighter than before. "Can . . . I sit in the car? Or did you have another plan?"

"No." He chuckled. "You'll definitely sit in the car. This is enough adventure for one day without trying to make it into the bleachers."

"True."

They pulled into the parking lot, and Cody drove to the back of the school where the field was. Sure enough, his guys were gathered in the end zone and, as they came closer, all of them turned and as a group they began to clap. Not just a polite applause, but by the time Cody pulled up in the spot closest to them, they were cheering full force. Shouting and hollering their joy over the fact that she was there. Alive and healing and *there.*

Then, as Cody turned off his engine, the guys picked something up off a nearby bench and unfolded a paper banner that had to be at least twenty feet long. Written in black paint and decorated with dozens of colorful flowers was a sign that read: "Welcome back, Cheyenne! We love you!"

Again tears filled Cody's eyes as he took in the moment. Cheyenne put her hand to her mouth and shook her head. This time she didn't stop the tears that slid onto her cheeks. "Cody . . . for me?"

"What can I say?" He gave the guys a thumbs up. "The guys love you."

After that, the team set the sign down and came to the car. As they did, a few of the guys snapped pictures of Cody and Chey in his truck. Then each of them took a turn at the window, holding Cheyenne's hand or telling her they were praying for her. The last guy was Marcos Brown. He handed her a large card sealed in an envelope. Written across the front was Cheyenne's name. "This is for you . . . everyone signed it."

"Thank you." Cheyenne held out her hand. The action must've taken most of her concentration and strength, but she did it anyway. "I don't believe we've formally met. I'm Cheyenne Williams."

His smile was shy and a little flustered. "I'm Marcos Brown. Nice to meet you, ma'am."

She took the card and thanked him. And with one more smile, Cody patted her knee and joined his team on the field. The guys worked harder than ever — and though some of them had issues off the field that Cody needed to address, for now he was impressed with the way they gave their all, the effort they applied to every drill, every play. Every time he prayed about the football players at Lyle High, Cody felt the Lord answer him the same way.

Big things were about to happen.

Just a few months ago, these high school boys hadn't believed they were worthwhile people, let alone football players. Now, though, Cody could sense a change in them. They had purpose and vision and together they were capable of not only winning football games, but of doing well as a team.

166

The way they had done well today.

When practice was over, he took Cheyenne back to Tara's house and laughed while Tara encouraged her to eat not one, but two bowls of ice cream. When Tara took a phone call in the other room, Cody turned to Cheyenne.

"We haven't prayed together in a few days."

A shyness filled her face. "I . . . I didn't want to ask. I know you pray for me all the time."

"Still . . . we need to pray together." Cody clenched his teeth for a second or two. He shouldn't have waited so long. Gently he took her hand in his. "Let's not wait another minute." He bowed his head and closed his eyes, picturing all the ways Cheyenne still needed a miracle. "Father, we lift Cheyenne to You, and we thank You for the way You've healed her so far. We pray now for continued healing, for a miracle that her physical strength will return soon."

Cheyenne responded with quiet murmurs, agreeing with everything Cody prayed.

When he finished, with their eyes still closed and their hands still joined, Cheyenne took over. "Father, I pray that Cody might know how grateful I am . . . and that You would continue to grow this bond . . .

whatever this is we share together."

Cody understood her honesty. They both felt their friendship pushing into new territories. Like she'd told him earlier, she wasn't afraid of anything. Not even dating, if that's where this was headed.

"I love when you pray." He searched her heart . . . looking for what could've possibly caused a girl as damaged as Cheyenne to love God so fully. "Your faith makes me stronger, Chey. It does."

He helped her to her feet. When they were facing each other, she smiled at him. "Today was perfect."

"It was." He put his hands on her shoulders, remembering again how his team had surprised her. "Thanks for being adventurous."

"Are you kidding?" Her eyes sparkled, her expression more familiar to him — the way it had been before her accident. "Best day since the accident."

"Good." He pulled her into a careful hug. Again he felt something change in his heart, in the way he felt toward her. Like if this were a different place, if she were well and this were the end of another sort of night together, he might consider kissing her. The thought took him by surprise and caused him to step back sooner than he might've otherwise. "Goodnight, Chey . . . Heal up."

The drive home didn't take long — ten minutes maybe. Along the way Cody wondered about Chey's prayer, the part where she asked God to continue growing the bond between them — whatever it might be. Cody looked at his computer as he walked into his room, and for a moment he thought about going on Facebook. Checking up on his players . . . seeing if Bailey had posted any new photos.

But instead he brushed his teeth, changed into a pair of shorts, and climbed into bed. His prayer that night was not the usual one for inner peace, or the prayer that God might take away the nightmares and flashbacks. The Lord was already answering that prayer — more so every day. Rather, he prayed that God would make it clear what he was supposed to do with his feelings for Cheyenne, and whether she was the girl he was supposed to love, the girl he should maybe even marry someday. But no matter how long he prayed, a part of his heart still ached for Bailey. So instead he changed up his prayer again, asking God this time for an undivided heart. And as he fell asleep, he added one more request. That the Lord would make him a whole lot more like

169

Cheyenne. Not afraid of anything.
Even falling in love again.

NINE

The show was dark on Monday — no performances. So Bailey had time to spend with Betty and Bob Keller, something she had come to look forward to. It was the first Monday in June, and this morning Betty was resuming her summer group Bible study. Every Monday morning throughout the summer, three of her friends would stop in for an hour-long Bible discussion — at least according to Betty. "We see each other here and there during the other seasons." Betty had smiled, talking about her friends. "But we know how busy we can get. That's why we keep our weekly meetings to just the summertime."

The study would start in five minutes, and Bailey was still fixing her hair in her room. But already she could hear the voices of the other women. She hurried herself, aware that she'd be ready by now if she hadn't gone on Facebook this morning. Her intent, as always, was to update her page with something encouraging for the girls who had befriended her. Bailey liked to think of the couple thousand people who followed her on Facebook as genuine friends . . . and her page the place where they met in something of a virtual living room. A place to hang out.

She'd found a verse from Ezra 10:4 that seemed especially fitting. "Rise up; this matter is in your hands. We will support you, so take courage and do it!" The verse was powerful for Bailey . . . just reading it made her feel stronger. It reminded her of how she had moved on after Cody, how she had been forced to rely on God's strength and rise up to the matter. Also how she had relied on the support from her family — and even from Brandon — to have the courage to move on. Maybe a few of her Facebook friends were going through similar situations, and the Ezra verse might speak to them.

Bailey ran the brush through her hair. The trouble with the verse was that it brought Cody's name to mind — the way so many moments in a day still did. And that caused her to check his Facebook page. She'd told herself a hundred times that looking in on Cody wasn't healthy. She didn't need to know what he was doing or how his football team was coming along. It wasn't smart for her to analyze his page, reading his wall or checking out his information to see if he was still single. Every time she looked in on him, she only walked away feeling worse, rejected all over again. And every time she asked herself the same question: How could he go on like nothing was wrong? Like they hadn't just walked away from the greatest love either of them might ever know?

But today was worse than ever. All along she'd known that at some point she would look at his Facebook and find a picture of Cheyenne and him. It was inevitable, since he was spending his time with her. Bailey had read every one of Cody's updates on Cheyenne, how she was healing and coming along after the accident. Of course he was with her. But still, she'd never seen a picture of them together.

Until this morning.

Bailey listened for the women's voices in the front room. They would talk for a few minutes first — Betty had told her that much. If she wanted to join the Bible study, she still had a little time. She dropped to her desk chair once more and in a few clicks she was back on Cody's page. His profile picture was the same — a group shot of him and a few of the players. He looked as handsome as ever, his face more chiseled maybe. Stronger — if that were possible.

The photo was something Cody was tagged in, and it was taken by one of the players, Arnie Hurley. It was posted last night — Sunday — and it showed Cody and Cheyenne sitting in his pickup truck while half the football team held a sign welcoming her back. Since she was sitting in the truck, Bailey couldn't make out exactly what she looked like. But what she could see shook her confidence completely.

Cheyenne was gorgeous — striking cheekbones and big brown eyes. Straight dark hair to her shoulders. Bailey had never felt more plain in all her life. She leaned close to the screen and tried to get a better look. When Cheyenne was fighting for her life in a hospital bed, she'd looked nothing like she did now. But that made sense — what with her head bandaged and the swelling in her face after the accident. Now she looked like a supermodel.

Bailey breathed out, fighting the defeat that welled in her heart. No wonder Cody hadn't called her. He was clearly in love with Cheyenne. He could tell her he didn't feel worthy of her love or try to convince her that their lives were too different for a relationship between them to work. But the truth was here — in the Facebook photo. Cody's face was lit up, his smile as genuine as the look in his eyes. He was happy and committed to her. There was no other way to read the picture.

Bailey checked his information page once more and saw that he was still listed as single. Which made no sense. He should be truthful and just tell the world how it was. He was in a relationship with Cheyenne Williams.

Bailey clicked the X at the top left corner of the page and Facebook immediately disappeared. *Great . . . you did it again.* Her time on Facebook had made her late, and still she had to go back one more time, take one more look. Bailey didn't know what was wrong with her, why she couldn't let him go. She had no reason to think about Cody now. Especially when things with Brandon were better than ever.

She stood, took her Bible from the nightstand next to her bed, and headed out to join the others. As she approached, they were so lost in conversation it took a few moments for them to notice her. Each of them had a Starbucks drink, and their Bibles weren't opened yet. *Perfect timing,* Bailey told herself.

Betty noticed her first. "Bailey, . . . come in. Take a chair." She motioned to the seat beside her, one she had obviously left open on purpose so that Bailey would have a place to sit. "We were just catching up."

The other women raised their cups and the tallest of the four grinned at Betty. "Here, here. We need our catch-up time."

"Alright . . . this is Bailey Flanigan. She's a new Broadway dancer, starring in *Hairspray*." Betty smiled at her and patted her knee. "Bailey is brilliantly talented and she has a strong love for God. He has amazing plans for her, right?"

Bailey felt nothing of the sort, not after the way she was struggling in her stage role, and especially not after looking at Cody's Facebook page. She tried to shake her discouragement. "Yes." She remembered to smile. "That's my prayer, anyway."

"It's a promise!" The tall woman held her index finger upward, as if to heaven. "God's already decided that His plans for you are good, right?" She looked at her friends.

"Right." A woman across the room nodded sweetly. She wore bright red shoes and a smile that lit the room. "You can pray that God will help you understand those plans. But you don't have to worry. He definitely has good plans for you."

176

Already a sense of peace pressed in around Bailey. She was going to love this Bible study . . . these women and the knowledge they possessed. Bailey had missed meeting for a regular Bible study — something she had always done on campus at Indiana University. This time would be good for her. "Thanks." She looked at both the women who had added to the conversation. "I needed to hear that."

"Alright." Betty was clearly the leader, the one who kept them on track. "Let's have everyone introduce themselves. Tell a little about your life and why you're part of this group."

She looked at her tall friend, the one on her other side. "Barbara, you go first."

"Very well." Barbara sat straight and spoke in a way that was eloquent and clear. "I'm Barbara Owens, the baby of the group . . . though we won't say exactly what that means," she laughed, and the others joined in. She took a sip of her drink and waited for the room to settle again. "I'm married to the love of my life." A soft look filled her eyes. "We have three kids and seven grandchildren." She paused, but only because she wasn't in a rush. Everything about Barbara emanated confidence. She was very pretty, and something told Bailey she had been

177

successful in her life.

Barbara still had the floor. "Let's see . . . I love to decorate and sew . . . and I make a new cross-stitch wall hanging for my house every year."

"And you're the CEO of your own company." Betty gave her a friendly elbow in the ribs. "Don't be modest."

"Oh, that," again Betty laughed. "Yes, I grew up on a ranch in Texas, and today I'm the CEO of my own New York company." She paused. "I met Betty at a Pilates class downtown and by the end of the afternoon we were swapping Bible verses and promising we'd get together that weekend with our husbands." She smiled and put her hand briefly on Betty's shoulder. "We've been like sisters ever since. I wouldn't miss our summer Bible study."

Betty's expression showed how much Barbara meant to her. She moved to the next woman in the circle, the one with the red shoes. The woman didn't need to be asked twice. "Hi, Bailey . . . my name is Sara Quillian, and I live in the apartment building here. I met Betty and Bob at one of the building's rooftop barbecues. Betty was talking about Jesus in no time, and we began making a point of finding time to be together. We've been friends for a decade."

"At least." Betty crossed her legs at the ankles and shot a kind smile across the room. "You and I are in charge of telling the people in this building about Jesus, right?"

"Exactly." Sara took a quick breath and explained how she had been a child in World War II when she first realized how important it was to live for God. "We don't have time to hold a grudge against someone. They could be gone before sundown."

Bailey let the words hit deep inside her heart. Was there a message here from God? She thought about Sara's words . . . how a person could be gone by sundown. The way Cody might've been killed in Iraq or Cheyenne in her terrible wreck. She wasn't sure if she carried a grudge against Cody, but it was something she needed to think about. Sooner rather than later.

Sara went on explaining that she had been married more than fifty years, and that she hoped for another fifty more. Bailey smiled at the thought. Was that how she would feel fifty years from now . . . like her only wish might be for another half a century with the man she loved? Was Brandon a guy she could love like that? The image from Cody's Facebook page shot through her mind . . . Cody and his new girl. Bailey let the thought go and focused on what Sara was saying.

"I was the first female editor of my university's school paper." She paused. "Believers need to be visible," she nodded, her eyes sparkling despite the wrinkles around them. "That's why I love that you're performing on Broadway, Bailey. We're no light at all if we're not a light in a visible place."

Bailey nodded, as Sara's wisdom sank in. "My parents say that."

"Your parents are right." Sara eased her feet in front of her, and for a few seconds she gazed at her shoes. "I love a pair of new red shoes . . . have I mentioned that?"

"Not in the past hour." The fourth woman was more petite and quieter than the others. She had a pretty face and a sparkly smile. It was easy to see how stunning the woman must've been when she was younger. She grinned at Bailey. "I'm Irma . . . It's not my turn yet, but I had to say that."

Again they all laughed, and Bailey was struck by the closeness among them. These friends had learned the secret of accepting one another exactly as they were. The thought reminded Bailey that she should call Andi Ellison soon. Her friend from Indiana University was living in Los Angeles now, but with a little effort they could still stay in touch.

Betty looked at Bailey. "Sara's full of godly wisdom. Something she won't tell you." She glanced back at her friend. "Her home is the regular stop for several local pastors and Campus Crusade workers. She loves her family and she thinks it's important for women to be strong in our society."

Bailey listened, curious. Strength wasn't usually something she aspired to. "How do you mean . . . we should be strong?" She turned to Sara.

"Strong in society, vocal about our beliefs." Her eyes were kind, but they held a no-nonsense look. "For you, that might mean speaking up for your faith, being the voice of truth for your cast."

"She's right." Irma was the silliest in the group, Bailey could tell. But in this moment she was very serious. "It might not be enough to shine on stage. God might be asking more of you."

Bailey thought about Chrissy and her obvious anorexia . . . and the members of the cast who seemed to sneer at her faith or her connection with Brandon. Bailey had no idea how she might be more vocal with them, but she believed this: If she asked God for help . . . He would show her. "Thanks . . . I'll think about that."

It was Irma's turn. She rustled herself as

tall as she could. "I'm Irma, and I'm vertically challenged, but like I always tell my kids — I'm more fun per inch than anyone I know."

Again the ladies raised their coffee drinks and a couple of them clapped in agreement. "No argument here." Betty tilted her head, her eyes on Irma. "Why don't you start with your name and save the jokes for later, honey."

"Right." Irma pointed at Betty. "You did say that." She turned to Bailey. "I'm Maria Rangel, but most people call me Irma."

"All people," Betty pointed out.

"Okay," Irma shrugged. "All people. Anyway, let's see. I began this Bible study when I met Betty at church twenty-two years ago. My family and my faith are everything to me. Oh . . ." she pointed her finger in the air as if she wasn't quite finished, "and I've been married fifty years to the man of my dreams — Al Rangel." She stopped long enough to gaze upward, as if she were lost in romantic thoughts about Al.

Bailey giggled. She enjoyed these women, their wisdom and faith, their combined years of happy, successful marriages. She had much to learn from them — and already she looked forward to the summer Monday mornings they would share. Irma explained that she liked to travel and how she'd been to the Holy Land and to Greece and several times back to her hometown in Mexico.

"But you should know this," she leaned over her legs and brought her voice to a whisper. "I had heart surgery in 2009." She shook her head and waved her hand, like she was dismissing an irritating fly at a summer picnic. "We don't talk about that much . . . except to let it serve as a reminder." She sat up again and looked around the room. "What's the reminder, girls?"

A chorus of their voices responded almost in unison. "Love well . . . laugh often . . . and live for Christ."

"Exactly." She laughed at her own story. "You have one chance to get it right, Bailey. When it comes to your God . . . your family . . . your time on Broadway." She allowed the dreamy look to return to her eyes. "And the man you fall in love with."

"Good point." Barbara looked thoughtfully at Bailey. "Are you in love yet, Miss Bailey?"

"Ummm . . ." She laughed, not ready for the question.

"Take your time, dear; it's your turn." Betty clearly didn't want Bailey to feel flustered by the straightforward question.

Betty didn't need to worry. Bailey liked this, being forced to think about her life . . . why she was here . . . and whether she was in love or not. This was a safe setting, a place where she could be honest and learn something along the way. "I'm Bailey, obviously." She smiled so they could see she was relaxed. "I moved here a little more than a month ago — around the first of May. I'm the oldest of six kids, and the rest are all boys."

Irma gasped. "Your poor mother . . . she must be a saint." She smoothed the wrinkles in her wool skirt. "I had all girls. Four of them."

"Sisters would've been great." Bailey laughed. "But boys are a lot of fun, actually. I love having brothers." The group weighed in on how much food boys ate and the blessing of having sons.

Irma raised her eyebrows as if she were offended. "Okay . . . so I missed that blessing." She burst into a series of giggles. "Let's just say I was blessed by missing the blessing of boys. Raising girls was heaven on earth."

Bailey loved Irma's spunk. But gradually the room turned its attention to her again and Bailey picked up where she left off. "My dad's one of the football coaches for the Indianapolis Colts, and my brothers all play football." She told them a little about each of the boys, including the fact that three of her brothers were adopted from Haiti.

"Well, I'll be . . ." Irma sat back in her chair, not teasing for once. "Your mother really is a saint."

Like she'd done before, Bailey explained that adopting the boys ten years earlier had been good for all of them. "It was crazy at first, but it was a family decision . . . and God has blessed us all through it." She told them about her part in *Hairspray,* and the role she'd played opposite Brandon Paul in *Unlocked.*

"Brandon Paul!" Barbara slid to the edge of her seat, her eyes wide. "*The* Brandon Paul?"

"Yes." Bailey giggled again. "I guess I was pretty vocal about my faith when we filmed the movie." She paused, glad for the chance to remind herself. "Brandon became a Christian the last week on the set. My dad even baptized him."

Another gasp from Irma. "I read about that! So that's what happened!"

"See . . ." Sara nodded, her approving smile aimed at Bailey. "That's what it means to be strong. Good girl, Bailey."

She smiled and felt the heat in her cheeks. "It wasn't me."

"It never is." Betty turned a kind look her way. "It's always God in us, anytime we do any good at all."

"So . . . that takes us back to the original question?" Barbara must've made a very good CEO. She had no trouble directing the conversation, and she did so with a clarity and gentleness that would've made her an easy leader to follow.

Bailey stifled another laugh and looked at her lap for a long moment. She wasn't sure how much to say, but she could be honest with these women. Nothing she might say would ever make it beyond the four walls of the Kellers' apartment. Bailey took a quick breath. "Well . . . Brandon and I talk a lot."

"Brandon Paul?" Irma's eyes were wide again. "So then . . . is he your Al?"

Bailey pictured Brandon, the way he'd looked holding her in his arms on the 103rd floor of the Empire State Building . . . or how it had felt riding in the carriage beside him through the streets of New York City. She smiled at the memory, but even as she did she felt herself shrug. "I'm not sure . . . I'm really not sure." She looked at the faces around her, all of them so grounded in their faith, so solid in their love for the men they'd married.

"I've been wanting to ask you, Bailey . . ." Betty's voice was quieter than before, her question pointed and careful. "You don't have to answer if you don't want to, but what about the photograph that used to sit on your desk? The one of you and that handsome young man."

Bailey felt her heart sink. "That's Cody. I loved him for a very long time, but . . . he's out of my life now. Someone from my past." She smiled, more to convince herself than any of the ladies in the room. "I'm over him."

"Is that why you took the picture down?" Again Betty's question held a knowing, but it wasn't forceful. Just her way of trying to know Bailey better.

A long sigh came from Bailey and she bit her lower lip. "I just . . . I didn't want to look at him anymore."

"Does Brandon know about Cody?" Sara uncrossed her ankles, but kept her pretty red shoes neatly together.

"He does . . . they know about each other." She felt a well of sadness rise within her. "Cody has someone else now . . . he doesn't think about me anymore."

"Hmmm." Barbara didn't look sure. "How long did the two of you date?"

A sad laugh came from her. "Not long, really. A few months." There was too much to the story to tell it all now. "We grew up together. We had feelings for each other long before we started dating."

"I doubt he's moved on. Not entirely." Barbara sat back, unconvinced. "Look at you, Bailey. You're beautiful from the inside out. A guy would be crazy to miss that."

Bailey wanted to think so, but lately she doubted everything about herself. She wasn't Cheyenne — it was that simple. And she wasn't one of the Hollywood starlets who vied for Brandon's attention. She believed him that he wasn't interested in anyone else, but still . . . "I guess . . . if I had to answer the question, I'd say Brandon Paul is the one in my heart now. He wants to have a relationship, but I don't know." She looked intently at each of them. "How do you know? I mean . . . how were you sure about the men you married?"

Betty was the first to answer. "The picture of you and Cody?"

"Yes . . ." Bailey wasn't sure where she was going with this.

"When it's the right man . . . you'll have the look in your eyes that you have in *that* picture." She angled her head, sympathetic to all Bailey was feeling. "I've heard you talk about Brandon . . . but I haven't seen that look in your eyes. Only in the picture."

The conversation shifted to the Bible, and 1 Corinthians 13. The women planned to spend all summer looking at the chapter most famous for its teaching about love. Today they talked only about the first verse: "If I speak in the tongues of men or of angels, but do not have love, I am only a resounding gong or a clanging cymbal."

"That's why we must not only be vocal and visible," Barbara pointed out. "We must love most of all."

"Amen to that." Betty shared a quick smile with her friend.

When the study was done, Bailey thanked the women and hugged Betty. Then she returned to her room and found her journal, the new one her mom had given her for the move to New York. She wrote about the women — Betty and Barbara, Sara and Irma, of their love for their God and their families, and their nearly two hundred years of combined marriage.

I want that kind of love one day, she wrote *. . . Is Brandon the guy who I can love like that . . . the one who will love me fifty years from now?* She hesitated, reading over what she'd written. *Please God . . . lead me to that kind of love. Until then, help me to know* *that You are enough.*

She also wrote down Sara's admonition to be strong, and she jotted a few sentences that had come up that day — how the idea of being strong and vocal was only possible or effective when it was set against the backdrop of love.

"Soaked in love," Sara had said.

Bailey liked that. It reminded her of her place with the cast of *Hairspray.* Everything about her job was still new, the people still a little intimidating. But they needed God's love as much as anyone. Maybe more. If she were going to truly shine on Broadway, she would need to find a way to be strong and vocal. But absolutely soaked in love.

And finally she wrote the thing that stayed with her most, the part Betty brought up. She remembered her night on the Empire State Building, and the quote Brandon had brought up. How the eyes were the window to the soul.

Take more pictures with Brandon, she scribbled on the next line of her journal. *See if my eyes have that look.* Yes, that's what she needed. More pictures of Brandon and her — so she could analyze her eyes.

Maybe that was the real reason Bailey had moved the photo of her and Cody from her desk. Because deep down she knew that

what Betty had said was true. Real love . . .
true love . . . the kind that could last a
lifetime would require a guy who loved God
more than life, a guy who could lead her
and laugh with her and listen to her. And
with all that, Bailey would know he was the
right guy for one very simple reason.

Her eyes would look like they did in the
picture of her and Cody.

TEN

Ashley's phone call with Jenny Flanigan was exactly what she needed that Wednesday morning. Jenny had a way about her that reminded Ashley of the truth — no trial was beyond the reach of God.

For nearly half an hour Jenny let Ashley talk about Landon's health, his lung trouble, and the looming possibility of a disease too terrible to imagine. Jenny had to have been busy. Midway through June her boys would be clamoring for her attention for sure. Yet she had taken this time . . . something that touched Ashley deeply.

"Your family's been through this before." Jenny's voice emanated calm. "You've always relied on each other, reminded each other that you could do anything with God's strength." Jenny hesitated. "Remember . . . when you can't take another step, God will carry you."

The thought filled in the gaping holes in

Ashley's confidence. When she couldn't take another step . . . God would carry her.

The phone call ended, and even as Ashley rounded up the kids and called for Landon, she remembered to pray. Because today might just be one of those days when she wasn't sure she could walk.

"Landon!" She had Janessa in her arms. Cole and Devin were already out in the car. "We're going to be late."

"Coming." He didn't sound enthusiastic, not that she could blame him. All of their testing, every cough and asthma attack, all the concern from Landon's doctors would culminate in a single test in an Indianapolis clinic two hours from now. After that they would have their answer — one way or another.

She headed for the garage, buckled Janessa into her car seat, and was fastening her own belt when Landon finally joined them. She watched him, studying him. What was the look on his face? It wasn't fear . . . not quite. But it wasn't the joy and peace she'd always known from him, either. He'd been off work nearly six weeks now, and in some ways he'd been busier than ever. He had trimmed every shrub and bush in what used to be her mother's garden, and he'd planted a plot of vegetables. Turning over the dirt, cultivating it, mixing in mulch . . . planting seedlings. The boys had helped some, but he'd done most of it.

"Sorry. I was looking at something." He didn't turn to her, didn't make eye contact.

Ashley watched him, not sure whether she should feel frightened by this new Landon, or sorry for him. Months ago when Devin had assigned everyone roles in his pretend circus, Landon had told her to lighten up. She couldn't stop living just because he was sick. And she agreed. But now what was he thinking? Did she need to remind him of his own advice, or was it better to wait?

She sat back and stared out the window. From behind her, Devin kept up a stream of chatter about his future circus. Ashley had to admire his tenacity. He hadn't once veered from the idea of running a circus — not since the notion first hit him back in January.

"I have a plan, 'kay, Cole?"

Cole had a handful of baseball cards and he sorted through them without looking up. "What's your plan, Dev?" The kids were staying at her sister and brother-in-law's house — Kari and Ryan's place — and Brooke was bringing her two girls over also. Which meant Cole would hang out with his favorite cousin, Maddie. The two had always been fiercely competitive, but lately they shared a love of baseball cards. Not a surprise since Maddie's tomboy stage still persisted.

"Here's the plan." Devin talked fast when he had an idea, and his words ran into each other as he tried to get his thoughts out. "I think asides my 'magination machine, my circus might need a time machine too, and if it does then I think you should run it, Cole." He paused only long enough to refuel. "Can you live with that?"

Despite her nerves about the day's possible outcome, and her concerns over Landon's attitude, Ashley laughed quietly in the front seat. This was Devin's newest thing . . . asking people if they could live with something. She had no idea where he'd gotten the phrase but it made her laugh every time he used it.

"I can live with it. Sure . . ." Cole didn't sound even a little bit interested, but at least he responded. "I'll run the time machine."

Ashley turned in her seat so she could see her kids — all three of them in the row behind her. Janessa sucked her thumb — a habit they were trying to break. But she was perceptive — and if she needed a little extra comfort today, Ashley could forgive her. She turned to Devin. "Why a time machine, buddy?"

"Oh, Mommy, a time machine's the best machine of all." His eyes grew so wide she could practically see the whites around them. "A time machine means people can climb inside and then *whirrrr!*" He made one of his crazy noises, signifying some push of the button or flip of the switch. He tried to snap his fingers, but the movement fell short. "Just like that, Mommy. You get transpo'ted to the bestest moment in your whole livelong life." He glanced at Cole and then back at her. "Cole's gonna run it and you can . . . well, you can sell the tickets."

"Will I still wear my red shirt and my American flag tights?"

"Yes . . . 'cept this time you will also have big blue sunglasses and a loud voice so you can tell people all over the circus to come and get into the time machine." Another quick breath. "Can you live with that?"

She swallowed another laugh and nodded. "Yes, . . . I think so." She looked at Landon, his eyes locked on the road ahead. "What do you think . . . can I live with that?"

Landon hesitated, and then gave her a double take. "What?" He looked forward again. "Sorry . . . were you talking to me?"

A ripple of panic stirred the waters in her mind. Who was this, sitting beside her? The man she'd married never would've tuned out a conversation like the one between Ashley and Devin. She lowered her voice, but kept her tone upbeat. So the kids wouldn't think there was something wrong between them. "It's okay, Landon." She put her hand on his knee. "Never mind." She turned back to Devin. "Okay, so the time machine sounds like a great idea, but what about you? What moment would you go back to?"

Devin scratched his head, thinking hard. Suddenly his entire face lit up. "Last night. Cole and me were out back looking for frogs near the pond, and Cole told me I was the best brother he ever had." He grinned at Cole, satisfied with his answer. "That's where I'd go." He turned curious eyes to her. "What about you, Mommy?"

Ashley's throat felt tight. The question hit her in a way she hadn't seen coming. If a time machine could take her back to any moment, what would she choose? Memories came rushing at her and she could see Landon standing before her on the front yard of what had been her parents' house — the Baxter house, where she and Landon lived now. And he was touching her cheek and promising her that he'd never leave her again . . .

But before she could claim that as the moment, another memory filled her mind, and she could see Landon in his tux at the front of Clear Creek Church, and her mom was still alive and in the front row, and Ashley was dressed in her wedding gown, and she knew as long as she lived she would never forget the way she felt or the look in Landon's eyes . . . or maybe the moment in the hospital when they first laid Devin in her arms . . . or the time when Landon had stood beside her while their first daughter, Sarah, had died in their arms. The love between them, the support of their family, no matter how sad it had been . . . she was certain. She would pay to find her way back to that moment.

Or the time when Janessa joined their family, and the faithfulness of God was made real in the feel of Landon's fingers intertwined with hers. Any of those moments or a million others . . .

"Mommy? It's taking you a long time to think of an answer."

"Well, buddy." Cole looked up from his baseball cards and smiled at Ashley. "Mom has a lot of good times to think about. It's not that easy deciding where she'd go back to. Right?"

There was no way to express how much

she loved her family, but her love for Cole would always have its own special place. Long before Landon, life had consisted of just the two of them. She wouldn't have minded a trip back to one of those days either. "That's right." She leaned the side of her head against the headrest. "Hmmm . . . It's a hard decision."

"It's a time machine, Mommy!" Devin tossed his hands in the air and giggled. "You can go back to all of them if you want."

"True." She laughed and looked at Landon again. Like before, he was nonresponsive, as if he couldn't hear a word they were saying. Her smile dropped off and she withdrew her hand, folding her arms in front of her instead. "The truth is, I'd go back to just about any happy time with all of you. Because you're the people I love the most."

"Mommy!" Devin laughed at her, as if to say she was the silliest person in the car. "That would be our whole life." He shrugged big. " 'Cause our whole life is a happy time."

"Yes," she grinned at Devin. "You're right, buddy." But she couldn't help but think that just maybe those happy times were in the past. Before Landon got sick . . . before he had to quit doing the job he loved. She kept her feelings to herself. She could forgive Landon if he was distracted today. Her fear wasn't for the quiet ride to Indianapolis, but the ride home. And every day that might follow.

"I can think of a few baseball games I'd like to go back to." Cole laughed, like he was starting to enjoy the idea of Devin's time machine.

Ashley faced the front of the car again and let the boys continue the conversation. They reached Kari's house, and Landon helped her get the kids and their things to the front door. "They'll be fine." Kari crossed her arms and anchored herself against the door-frame. When the kids had bid them good-bye and hurried into the house, Kari looked long at Ashley and then Landon. "We'll be praying."

"Thanks." Ashley looked at Landon, but he only mumbled a quiet thank you and then looked at the ground. Ashley shot her sister a helpless look. "The kids are thrilled . . . a day with their cousins." She moved to the spot next to Landon. "What's on the agenda?"

"A water balloon contest . . . and maybe a little Dance Dance Revolution. The older kids love that."

"Perfect." Ashley wished with all her heart

that this was a different sort of summer day, and that she and Landon could stay and take part in the fun. That they weren't driving to Indianapolis to find out the verdict on what could be a lifelong sentence for Landon. Again Ashley gave her sister a knowing look, as if to say she couldn't really talk. Not now. "You'll have to tell us all about your day when we get back."

"For sure." Kari stepped out onto the porch, glancing over her shoulder to make sure the kids were far enough in the house that they couldn't hear her. "Will you know the results today?"

"Yes." Ashley looked at Landon. He still had said barely anything. "Dad talked to the doctor. I guess the test is usually pretty definitive." She felt like screaming at Landon . . . Didn't he think this was hard for her too? She exhaled, keeping her focus. "They attach needles to a bunch of muscle nerve endings, and then they flip a switch. Diseased muscles make a series of noises. I guess the doctor can tell what disease a person might be dealing with by the pattern of the sounds."

Kari's face grew a shade paler, and her expression looked stricken. "Polymyositis isn't just in the lungs?"

"It's a muscle disease." Landon finally

201

spoke up. His face was grim, his expression almost angry. "I haven't felt weakness anywhere else, but that doesn't matter. It doesn't follow the same pattern every time."

Kari seemed to sense that Landon really didn't want to talk about polymyositis or any other lung disorder. If he was going to fight fires again, he needed his lungs more than the average person.

"Okay." Ashley interrupted the awkward silence that hung between the three of them. "Thanks for watching the kids."

"Absolutely." Kari stepped back inside the house. She waved once as Ashley and Landon turned and walked back down the sidewalk to their van. Ashley heard her close the door as the two of them climbed back inside and Landon started the engine again.

Ashley understood Kari asking about Landon. She hadn't kept her sister up to date with every detail of Landon's condition. For that matter, she hadn't kept most of their extended family up to date. Only her dad, really. And then only because he was a doctor — he understood how serious things were with Landon.

The bottom line was, Ashley hadn't wanted everyone to know the seriousness of Landon's struggles. Until they had a diagnosis there was no reason to talk about it.

Clearly he was sick. He'd almost died in the fire six weeks ago — all of them knew that much. In fact, his lung damage from the recent house fire was the reason the doctor had wanted him to wait until now for the electromyography. Damaged muscles could give a false reading.

They were halfway to the highway when Ashley turned and studied Landon. He hadn't said a word since they'd gotten back in the car. "Are you okay?"

He gave her the same sort of look he'd given her earlier. Like he had forgotten until that moment that she was even in the car with him. "Me?"

"No, Landon. The kids in the backseat." She clenched her fists and tried to find the right approach with him. "You're the only other person in the van. Of course I'm talking to you."

He clenched his jaw and for a long moment he said nothing. Then he glanced at her, a hint of anger written into the fine lines on his forehead. "You want to know if I'm okay?" The sound that came from him fell short of being a laugh. "I'm headed to the city for a test that will probably confirm the fact that I have some rare lung disease . . . something they're finding more commonly in people who worked at Ground

Zero." He looked at the road again, his knuckles white from the way he gripped the wheel. "If I have it, I'm done fighting fires. Everything I've worked for . . . all of it . . . behind me. Finished." He paused, and his voice sounded strained, like he was fighting tears. "They can put me on a donor list, and if . . . if a donor comes along I have a one-in-five chance of living another ten years."

Ashley knew all of it, every frightening thing he said. But hearing him compile the situation into a handful of sentences made her heart skip a beat, and then stumble into a strange and unrecognizable rhythm. Ten years . . . was that really a possibility? That she might not have more than a decade left with him? Cole would barely be out of college by then . . . Devin still in high school. And Janessa . . . she would hardly be old enough to remember him after he was gone.

Nausea welled inside Ashley and she wondered if she might get sick right here in the car. She needed air, lots of air. Because this couldn't be happening to them . . . not after how long and hard they'd worked to get to this point. And worse . . . it wasn't just the situation they were facing, but the way Landon was handling it. He had always been strong for her, always been ready to tackle whatever came their way. But this time it was like he had become someone else, a different person. She didn't know if he was angry or afraid or both, but she couldn't take another minute of it.

"Listen," she raised her voice, but managed to keep a slight hold on her control. "I don't know what lies ahead for us, and neither do you. But I know this . . ." She was shaking. She turned and pressed her back against the side door, keeping as much distance as she could between them. "I know . . . I can't live another day with . . . with your attitude, Landon. You're the one who told me I couldn't stop living just because you were sick, and now —"

She had more to say, about the kids and how they were picking up on his mood and how tragic it would be if Devin stopped thinking they were always happy whenever they were together. But her voice caught, and a rush of tears took her by surprise.

"Ash . . ." For the first time in a week, the mask of anger or indifference that had made up Landon's face cracked.

"I can't do this, Landon." She began crying so hard she wasn't sure he could understand her. "I'm scared too. But we can't shut each other out." She waved to the place where he was sitting. "I watched you earlier and all I could think was, 'Who is this guy? And what . . . what happened to the man I married?' "

Grief flooded Landon's face, and without waiting another moment he checked the rearview mirror, glanced over his shoulder, and then pulled the car into the parking lot of an abandoned gas station. Landon killed the engine and turned to her. For a long time he said nothing, only hung his head like he was trying to gather his thoughts.

When he looked up there were tears in his eyes, tears for the first time since his initial asthma attack . . . since his doctor first began to believe something might be seriously wrong. "I'm sorry . . ." His hands shook as he took hers. "I've . . . I've never felt like this, Ash. I've always . . . been strong for you."

"I know . . ." A sob slipped from her throat. "That's why I'm freaking out here . . . I know something's wrong with your lungs, Landon. That kills me . . . of course it kills me." She spread her fingers over her chest. "But I can't go through this if something's wrong with your heart too. If you stop . . . stop loving me."

That was all she needed to say. Landon's tears came harder, and he pulled her close, hugging her so hard she couldn't move if she wanted to. "I'm sorry, Ash . . . I keep . . . I keep thinking I won't be any good for you."

"What?" She squirmed her way free and stared at him, shocked at his words. "Not good for what?"

"For working! Making a living for you and our kids. You can't . . . you can't count on me anymore. Have you thought about that?" His voice was loud with what sounded like anger, but Ashley knew better. Landon was afraid. Raging fires didn't scare him. He could run into a burning building and never once flinch. But this? The idea of being useless to her? That made him afraid like nothing else had. It terrified him. Scared him to death about what the future held.

She felt the slightest calm cut its way through her sorrow. "Landon . . ." a few quiet sobs shook her body. "I could never . . . ever love you . . . more than I do right now." She took his hands in hers and held them as tightly as she could. "I don't love you . . . for what you can do for our family. For the money you make or . . . or the work you do." She touched the place over her heart and then pressed her hand against his chest. "I love you for who you are . . . inside."

Her sobs subsided and she reached for a tissue in the glove box. "I just . . . I feel like you've been a stranger since you came home." She sniffed and wiped her tears. "Like I don't know you."

The fight was gone from him. He slumped against his door and looked at her, just let his eyes get lost in hers for the longest time. "I don't know how to do this . . . I . . . I don't know how to be weak."

"You're not weak!" She leaned closer, imploring him, her voice ringing with passion. "You could never be weak to me." With everything in her she prayed he could see how deeply she meant this. "You're the strongest man I know, Landon Blake." Fresh tears filled her eyes. "You taught me how to love, remember?" She settled back in her seat. "The strength it took to do that? It's still in you. It'll always be there . . . no matter what happens with your lungs."

The uncertainty in his eyes, the doubt and fear were emotions Ashley had rarely seen in her husband. But he adjusted their hands so he was in control, so his hands were holding hers, and he tightened his grip. "You mean that? You really do?"

"Of course." She laughed, but it came out as another series of sobs. Her arms came around his neck and she held on, willing life into him, praying with every heartbeat that they might be handed a miracle today, that he wouldn't have a fatal lung disease. When she drew back she searched his eyes, and a smile lifted her lips ever so slightly. "Devin told the whole family, remember? You're the strongest man in the world."

He smiled, and again tears gathered in his eyes. "I've been such a jerk. To you . . . to the kids." He shook his head. "I'm sorry, Ash. I just . . . I didn't know how to handle it . . ." He waited, gathering control of his tears, his emotions. With the shoulder of his navy short-sleeved shirt he wiped his face and breathed deep. Then he put his hands on her shoulders and looked at her the way he used to look at her. Before he fell sick. "I love you, Ashley . . . I don't want to lose you. We have to pray."

"I am." She ran her hand alongside his face and gently she leaned in and kissed him. "I'll give you a lung myself, if that's what it takes. I'm not ready to say good-bye."

"I won't hide my feelings from you . . . never again." He kissed her this time, and the moment lasted longer than either of them expected. Long enough that their tears mixed together and she could taste them on her lips. His intensity told her that whatever way he'd given up, he was back in the fight, ready to trust God for whatever the next few hours . . . or the rest of their lives might bring.

With that certainty, he wiped his face once more and she did the same, and they continued their drive to Indianapolis. They drove in silence, but they held hands the entire way, and Ashley could sense a dramatic change in him. Landon was back. At least he seemed that way for now. After today, there was no telling how the diagnosis might affect him.

The doctor's office was at the top of a ten-story medical building, and they waited nearly an hour before he could see them. He entered the room with a rush of activity, apologizing for being late and explaining that a procedure had taken longer than he'd expected. He looked at Ashley. "You must be Mrs. Blake?"

Ashley sat stiffly in a chair in the corner of the room. "Yes." She wondered if the man realized what was at stake today. He probably performed electromyography tests all day long. Every time much was on the line, no doubt. But today's diagnosis was a matter of life or death. She held her purse tightly against her stomach and waited.

The doctor turned to Landon and explained the test process — nothing new, just what they'd heard before. The needles, the placement, the machine that would determine the disease level of the muscles. "The needles look pretty lethal, but they won't hurt. They're so fine they make very little impact."

Please, God, please . . . we need a miracle.

I am with you, daughter. I have loved you with an everlasting love.

Ashley felt her anxiety ease. *Still, God, we need more than Your love today . . . let the doctors be wrong . . . let Landon's muscles be fine . . . please . . .*

The doctor began positioning the needles. From his place on the examination table, Landon looked at her and again relief flooded her being. Because this was Landon looking at her, not some shell of the man she'd married. Whatever the results, they would have each other. However long that might be.

It took less than five minutes for the doctor to get the needles into several dozen locations on Landon's arms and legs. If he had polymyositis in his lungs it would show up in his other muscles. The doctor checked over each needle, making sure of its placement.

Landon looked like a human pincushion.

But his eyes told her he was no longer afraid . . . he wasn't anything but hers. Hers and His. *Here we go* . . . Ashley held her breath. The next minute would determine Landon's health from this point on, for the rest of their days. *Please, God . . . be with us. . . . Thank You for being with us.*

"Alright, looks like we're ready." The doctor stepped back and crossed the room to the machine. He pushed a series of buttons and then flicked a small lever.

Ashley had no idea what to listen for. Her dad had explained that the series of beats in a diseased muscle would be different depending on the disease. She only knew that after a minute of listening, the doctor would have the final diagnosis. But for some strange reason the room was silent.

She slid to the edge of her chair, her eyes on the machine and then the doctor and back again. *What's going on?* she wanted to ask. But she couldn't speak or breathe or move or do anything but wait. *Please, God . . . please . . . not Landon.*

"Funny," the doctor adjusted his glasses and squinted down at the machine. "It's working." He checked his paperwork again, and once more looked over the needles sticking out from all over Landon's body. "Let's try it again." He ran through the series of buttons once more, and again flipped the switch.

They all waited, but again the only sound in the room was silence. Ashley exhaled.

Was it possible that this . . .

Was the silence proof that he might be . . .

She couldn't finish her questions, couldn't ask them or imagine them. The doctor tried a third time, running through the routine exactly as he had before. Again the room screamed with silence. Finally he flipped off the machine and extracted each needle from Landon's arms and legs.

A minute passed, a minute that felt like an hour or a week, even. But finally when he'd removed every last needle, the doctor shook his head. "Your muscles are absolutely fine." He smiled big, the thrill of this diagnosis both sincere and complete. "That sound you heard . . . that beautiful sound of silence? It means you don't have polymyositis, Mr. Blake. Absolutely not."

Shouts of joy went off inside Ashley, and she wondered if she could hold herself together on the chair. *Thank You, God! It's a miracle. You gave us a miracle! Landon isn't going to die from this . . . he has more to do here still. Thank You, Father.*

The doctor was going on about how rare it was for a person to have polymyositis in the lungs, but that the diagnosis would've been grim indeed. "I'd say you dodged a bullet." He gave Landon a hand and helped him sit up.

"It's a miracle." Ashley couldn't stop herself. She hated the idea of chalking this moment up to some random gift of fate. "We prayed, doctor. Every other test showed he might have the disease."

"Very well," the man smiled at her — not quite believing the idea, but not wanting to come against it either. "A miracle it is."

Landon's expression was frozen, as if he still couldn't believe what the doctor had said. "If I don't have it, then . . . does that . . . does it mean I'm going to be fine? That . . . that I can return to work?"

Ashley felt her elation take a dive. Did he have to ask about that now, when they had so much to celebrate? Her dad had already told her that even if Landon didn't have polymyositis, he had something wrong with his lungs. She wondered if this doctor was aware of that.

The man looked at Landon's chart, at the notes that had obviously been handed to him from Landon's other doctors. "From what I can tell, you're on a permanent disability from fighting fires." He looked up. "Is that what you've been told?"

Ashley closed her eyes and felt her stomach drop to her knees. *Dear God, . . . not now. Please . . . it's so much for him to deal with. Help him, Lord.*

Of all the verses that might flash in her mind, Ashley was certain this was the only one that could've breathed hope into her once again:

I know the plans I have for Landon, daughter . . . plans to give him a hope and a future.

God still had plans for Landon here on earth — definitely. But across the room the doctor was assuring Landon that since he didn't have polymyositis, he definitely had some form of chronic obstructive pulmonary disease.

"COPD, it's called." His expression was more matter-of-fact than regretful. "You can most likely return to work, but it'll be at a desk, Mr. Blake. One fire like the last one you were in and you might not make it out."

The reality made Ashley dizzy. Landon might not have a fatal disease, but his career was dead. He would never fight fires again. Ashley felt the oxygen leave the room, felt an oppression squeeze in around them. They thanked the doctor, and Landon dressed again. This time he didn't put up a cool front, or pretend not to care. As they walked to the car, he slipped his arm around

215

her waist and leaned on her, drawing strength from her.

When they reached the van she saw that his tears were back — the man she had only seen cry a handful of times in her entire life was crying for the second time today. Sure he was going to live — and for that he was certainly grateful. But Landon was a firefighter. It was the job he felt born to do, the job he loved. But with today's appointment, something he had only dreaded was confirmed true.

His days of fighting fires were over.

Ashey offered to drive, but Landon shook his head. The look in his eyes was clear. He couldn't fight fires, but he could drive her home. At least that. She didn't say anything. She didn't need to. She remembered what Jenny Flanigan had told her earlier that day. When God's people couldn't take another step, He was there to carry them. The truth soothed the broken places in her heart and soul, and as they pulled out of the parking lot, Ashley was convinced of one thing: If she could've looked back at their path from the medical building to the van, she wouldn't have seen two sets of footprints leading to their van.

She would've seen one.

ELEVEN

Cheyenne was making tremendous strides, so much so that through the first month of summer Cody was consumed with gratitude. Her cast was off her leg now, and tonight — after a full five days of tough football practices, Cody was doing something he'd wanted to do ever since Cheyenne was released from the hospital.

He was taking her out on a date.

She still had her walker, so he didn't want to take her anywhere that might cause an issue with her mobility. He settled on a movie — a romantic comedy the media was talking about. It had been out for several weeks, so when they arrived at the theater just outside Indianapolis, they didn't have to fight a crowd.

They walked slowly toward the theater. It was the last Friday in June and the night was comfortably warm. Still too early for the humidity to come. As they finally reached the front doors she gave him an apologetic look. "You're patient."

"Don't be silly." He slipped his arm around her shoulder. "You're like a marathon runner the way you've gotten through rehab. No one thought you'd be walking yet."

She paused, her eyes shining with the reflection of the light from the marquis. "You did."

"True." He sensed that she was feeling more emotional than usual, but the idea scared him a little. He worked to keep things light between them. "But that was only so I could get you out to a movie. The guys on the team wouldn't see this movie if you paid them."

Laughter filled the slight spaces between them as Cody bought the tickets and helped her inside. They sat in the front row of the upper section in two handicapped-accessible seats. "I take longer, but I get there . . ."

Cody remembered when the same could be said about him, after his time in Iraq. His leg had required all of this rehab and more. Again it was another reason he felt close to her, because they shared the hardship of the climb, the overwhelming determination to come back from something that had nearly killed them. He stayed at her side

218

until she was seated, then he bought popcorn and water bottles and took his place beside her.

The movie was a chick flick, for sure, but it held his attention. More than the film he enjoyed being with her. This was the first time their evening together had been less about her progress, her needs, her schedule of workouts — and more about the two of them having fun together. Cody let his arm brush against hers. She smelled nice — the same way she always smelled. Cinnamon and vanilla, and something else . . . the freshness of her shampoo, maybe.

Whatever the combination, it filled his senses and reminded him of the question he didn't always stop to ask himself. Where was the line between friendship and something more? And how close were they to stepping over it? The last scene of the movie showed the main characters — two best friends — realizing for the first time that they'd been fooling themselves. They were not in love with the other people they'd been seeing. Not at all. And at the last moment — when they might've gone off with the wrong people, they admitted their feelings for each other and fell into each other's arms.

Another happily ever after.

Cody tried not to think of Bailey as the

movie ended, but there was no way around it. She'd been his friend too long to not make the comparison for a few seconds. Cheyenne dabbed at happy tears as the credits rolled. "Best movie I've seen in a long time."

Cody dismissed his guilt along with thoughts of Bailey. "It was good."

"That's the crazy thing about you, Cody." She studied him, in no hurry to leave the theater. "Big, tough football coach . . . Army hero . . . rock of faith kind of guy." She wrinkled her nose and giggled. "But you'll sit through a movie like this."

He chuckled. "You could sort of predict the ending."

"Yeah," she grinned at him. "But still . . ."

The mood between them stayed light as they made their way back to his pickup and headed for the coffee shop across from the theater. Cody had looked forward to this part of their date almost more than the movie — the chance to talk to her outside of the crisis of her accident, and the constant need to help with her rehabilitation. He ordered straight coffee for himself and a cappuccino for her, and they took a quiet corner booth. Cody parked her walker off to the side, and once they were settled she took a deep breath. "Wow . . . I can't believe we're here. Out like this."

"It's a celebration! You got your cast off — one step closer to walking on your own."

"A few more weeks." Her personal schedule was more aggressive than the one the doctor gave her, but then that had been true since she regained consciousness after her accident. She rested her elbows on the table and folded her hands, watching him, her expression thoughtful. "I have a question."

"Ask it." He leaned back. "Whatever you want to know."

"Why, Cody?" A soft smile lifted her lips. "Why are you doing this?"

He expected she might ask questions about his background or childhood, his time in Iraq, maybe. But this one made him hesitate for a few seconds. "I care about you . . . I told you. I won't leave."

"But I'm almost better." She nodded to his place across from her. "And you're still here." Her smile wasn't flirty or frantic or anything but curious. "I just wonder why?"

"Well . . ." Cody spoke the words as they hit his heart. "I wake up every morning wondering how you are, whether you're in pain, or if your headaches are still there after a full night's sleep." His answer came slowly, as if he were explaining the situation to himself as much as to her. He looked at her more intently. "And at practice, I catch myself looking at the sidelines wondering when you'll be well enough to come out on your own . . . like you used to."

"So . . ." Her honest eyes touched his soul, her heart as transparent as the wind. "This isn't you feeling sorry for me?" She held no self-pity in her voice, no weakness. If anything her confidence was incredibly attractive. She might as well have told him that though she cared, she didn't want him to do her any favors. She would be fine either way. "I mean . . . I don't want pity. I just want to know."

"Pity?" His laugh was more a sound of disbelief. "Absolutely not." He thought about reaching across the table and taking her hands, but he changed his mind. Not now, when even he wasn't sure he could explain his actions. He hoped his smile would soothe her doubts. "It's my choice. I like being with you, Chey. You've become very special to me. You have to see that."

Cody had spoken exactly what was on his heart, but he wondered if she was replaying his words the way he was. The fact that he *liked* being with her, or that she was *special* to him . . . or how he *thought* about her. All very true, very nice sentiments . . . but clearly he wasn't admitting to anything more than a deep friendship.

She didn't ask, and he was glad. It was enough that she was convinced about his motives, that he wasn't here because he felt sorry for her. Cody studied her and realized he wanted to know more about her past, more about what had shaped her into the woman she was today. "Tell me more, Chey, . . . about you, your life."

She sighed and took a long sip of her coffee. "It's not a happy story."

Cody gave her a crooked smile. "That's true for a lot of us."

A depth filled her face and she stared out the coffee shop window for a long time. "My mom left when I was little . . . four years old. I think you know that part."

"I do."

Her eyes found his again, and her smile was tinged with a sorrow that had been there for a long time, a sorrow she was clearly comfortable with. "We didn't hear from her for a long time. But just before I met Art I got word from a friend of my grandmother's . . . my mom's body was found in a dumpy apartment in downtown Chicago. By then my daddy was already in prison. Life sentence for armed robbery. His third offense." She let her eyes linger on Cody's.

He wondered if she knew how strongly he could relate. He would tell her later. For now he didn't want to interrupt her story.

"In the end it always came down to the drugs. For both of them." She shrugged one slim shoulder. "I guess I always hoped it was the drugs . . . and not me. A mama doesn't leave her little girl unless something's wrong with her mind."

"Yes." Cody felt the familiar heartache well up inside him. "You're right about that."

She nodded. "And a daddy doesn't grab an automatic rifle and hit up a liquor store if something isn't screaming inside him." Peace radiated from her. "I always took it as a blessing. That they didn't choose the single life . . . the criminal life over loving me. Their addictions just gave them no other way out."

The admission reached deep into Cody's soul, touching him to the core. "Wow." He sat back, amazed. As she told her story he realized he hadn't shared much of his either. "I haven't told you about my mom."

"No." Cheyenne looked puzzled, like she was surprised she hadn't thought about the question before. "I guess I assumed she lives in Indianapolis."

"She does." Cody didn't break eye contact

with her. "In the women's prison." He paused. "Serving time for dealing drugs."

Surprise quickly turned to sympathy and without hesitating she reached across the table and slowly took his hands. "I'm sorry."

"Me too."

She looked at him for a long time, letting her eyes do the talking. "What about your dad?"

"He left when I was little. One or two . . . my mom can't remember." He smiled sadly. "We haven't heard from him since."

Cheyenne tightened the hold she had on his hands. There was nothing awkward about the moment. They were simply two broken kids who had grown up without families — without a mom doting over their math homework, or a daddy tucking them in at night. Two hurting people who hadn't known the magical warmth of Sunday dinners or the smell of turkey cooking in the oven on Thanksgiving Day.

It was why Cody never thought he was good enough for Bailey. His past was so different from hers, so broken in comparison. She deserved someone who could help her carry on the traditions of family and faith she'd been raised with. Cody . . . well, he wasn't sure how to do any of it. All of life — every stage from high school till today

225

and long into the future would be him trying to invent what he'd missed out on.

Same as it must've been for Cheyenne.

She took another sip of her drink, her eyes
distant as if she might be lost in a montage
of painful memories. Finally she breathed
in slowly, as if she were clearing her mind at
the same time. "I decided I needed an addiction too." The pain lifted some. "When I
was sixteen I found a relationship with
Jesus. I lived with my grandma by then. She
was too sick to help much, but I had friends.
They took me to Young Life meetings and
to church on Sunday." Her smile grew, and
the light shone in her eyes again. "I realized
I could have as much Jesus as I wanted. He
was the only addiction that would make life
better. I met Art the year after that — at
Bible study."

"Jesus is faithful." Cody nodded slowly. "I
learned that living at the Flanigans."

A curious look danced in her expression.
"The Flanigans?"

For as much time as he'd spent with
Cheyenne, he still hadn't told her about
Bailey and her family. Before the accident,
he and Cheyenne had just been getting to
know each other. And since then they'd
been consumed with her rehabilitation. He
sucked in a quick breath and stared at his

coffee for a long moment. Where could he begin? "I didn't find Jesus as quickly as you did." He hated this part of his story, . . . but there was no way around it. "I began drinking in middle school. My mom actually taught me how to make mixed drinks."

"See?" Cheyenne still had her hands intertwined with his. And now she ran her thumbs over his. "Alcohol's a drug. Only drugs would make a mama do that."

It was true. Cody nodded, and drew his hands gently from her. He rubbed the back of his neck and looked for a way to tell the story quickly. "By the time I was a junior in high school I was an alcoholic. Binges . . . blackouts . . . the whole thing." He kept his eyes down at the table, somewhere near his paper cup. Moments like this he was back there again, standing on the football field with Jim Flanigan confronting him. "I smelled like alcohol at practice, and my coach, Jim Flanigan . . . he realized my situation." He uttered a regretful laugh. "By then my mom was back in prison, and I lived alone. Coach Flanigan . . . he invited me to live with his family. I lived with them until I left for Iraq." He smiled, not wanting to talk about the Flanigans now. "At one point I nearly died from drinking."

"While you lived with them?"

"Yes. I had to be hospitalized." His tone held the shame he still carried over that time. "After that they helped me see what you just said. We all have a hole in our hearts. We can try to fill it with a lot of things . . . but in the end only Jesus fits."

"Yes."

"So that's my story." He hoped his smile made her see there was nothing more to the story. But in every situation, Cody had found Cheyenne to be perceptive, and this was no exception.

She narrowed her eyes slightly. "There's more to the story." It wasn't a question. Cheyenne simply knew. "Do they . . . do the Flanigans have a daughter?"

It was like she could read his heart, like everything he'd done or felt was so clear to her she didn't need to ask. She already knew. He hesitated, but then he nodded just barely, only enough so that she would know she was right. "Yes . . . they do."

"So that's it . . ." She eased her hands from the table back to her lap. Her careful smile told him she wasn't hurt by his revelation. Rather it was like the pieces finally fit. "I knew someone had a hold on your heart, Cody Coleman. I wondered when you might trust me enough to tell me."

He wasn't sure what to say. Not once had

228

he intended for this date to involve a discussion about his past. But now that's exactly where they were headed, and Cody wanted to divert the conversation — any way he could. Tonight was about Cheyenne, and the celebration of her life. Not about Bailey and him.

But she was still searching his eyes, the understanding still dawning within her. "What's her name?"

He sighed, and leaned against the padded side of the booth. "Bailey. Bailey Flanigan."

"You still care about her." Again it wasn't a question. But her tone politely asked for more details.

"Yes. Always." Cody understood why this mattered. If he wasn't here out of sympathy, and if he enjoyed being with her . . . then what about his past might stop her from letting herself have feelings for him? She had a right to know. "Things changed between us. At the end of last year." He explained how he and Bailey had allowed their friendship to turn into a dating relationship, but only for a short while. "My mom went back to prison, and Bailey was busy making a movie with Brandon Paul."

Cheyenne's mouth opened, and she sucked in a quiet breath. "That's where I've heard her name. She's in *Unlocked.* I've seen the trailer a hundred times on TV."

"Yes." Cody couldn't help but feel proud of her. "That's her. The world doesn't know it, but she and Brandon are dating now." He faced forward again and rested his forearms on the table. "It's been over between us for many months."

"Mmhmm." She nodded, but her eyes told him she wasn't quite convinced . . . that the situation with Bailey Flanigan was a red flag on the panel of her heart, and after tonight she would have a reason to take things slowly.

That was fine with Cody. He didn't want to move quickly, anyway. Cheyenne was still building up her strength. She didn't need a serious relationship to complicate her life right now. "Well . . . we know each other a lot better now." He laughed, and though it sounded a little nervous it broke the heaviness between them.

By the time they walked back out to the truck they were both laughing about something from the movie. He put his arm around her shoulders again, and as he folded up her walker and helped her into his passenger seat he recognized the obvious: He felt more than friendship for her. "Hey . . . I have an idea." He turned the key in the ignition. "How about we take a drive to Lyle? The uniforms were delivered, and Ms. Baker asked me to count them in." He liked the idea . . . the two of them alone in the quiet emptiness of the high school. More time to talk. "Are you too tired?"

"Not at all." She laughed. "Just don't ask me to try anything on. I'd disappear in a football uniform."

His laughter mixed with hers. "Don't worry . . . just the helmets and face masks. That's the only part you'll have to try on."

On the drive out, they listened to Tim McGraw and Tyrone Wells and talked about her nursing program. The teachers were going to work with her, so she could make up most of last semester's units online over the next few months. Once they reached the school, he let them in with his keys. No one was there, but still they talked in whispers as they walked the short distance from the back door of the athletic complex to the equipment room. Cody found a chair for her and he handed her a clipboard. "I'll count, and you write down the numbers." He grinned at her. "Sound good?"

"Better than trying on helmets." She grimaced just a bit as she situated herself.

"You're hurting." He would've done anything to make her feel better. "Want a different chair?"

"No." Her expression eased. "It's not as bad as it used to be."

Cody started with the jerseys. He was halfway through the count when he heard footsteps in the hallway outside. He stopped and saw that Cheyenne heard the sound too.

At nearly eleven on a Friday night the janitor couldn't be here. He held his finger to his lip, urging her to be quiet. Was it kids maybe? Someone about to vandalize the school? He moved quietly to the door, and as he opened it he heard the unmistakable sound of someone running down the other hallway, the one that led to the gym.

The flashes came at him with lightning speed, like a series of rapid-fire gunshots. Bright bursts of images . . . him and Art running for cover across a pock-holed desert floor. "Run!" someone screamed. "Get low!" Cody blinked, fighting the pictures in his head, resisting the urge to obey the long ago commands. Another image and another. Flashes snapping like broken tree limbs in the forest of his complicated mind.

And beside him — right beside him — one of his buddies was hit in the face. His whole face gone in an instant as he crumpled to the ground. Dust and blood and gunfire. More gunfire. "Get down."

"What?" Cheyenne gave him the strangest

look, her voice quiet and panicked. She glanced toward the sound of the running feet and back at him. "Get down?"

"No." Cody's voice was an intense whisper, a command to himself. "Not that. Sorry." *Help me, God . . . Cheyenne needs me. Someone's here . . . I have to think clearly. Please, Father . . . please . . .*

In the time it took him to breathe out, the images were gone. Sweat gathered across his forehead and the back of his neck and he shook like he hadn't in weeks. Cheyenne slid to the edge of her seat, clearly concerned. "Cody . . . what is it? Flashbacks?"

He nodded, hating himself for this weakness. Iraq was behind him. He had no reason to get lost in yesterday at the simple sound of running feet. He wiped his forehead and sucked back a few quick breaths. He wasn't armed . . . had no way to protect himself. But if he had to fight someone he wasn't worried. Cody could handle the situation. He was trained in hand-to-hand combat, and more than once at war he'd had to prove himself. He was one of his division's best fighters. "Stay here," he whispered. "I'll call you if I get in trouble."

The sound of the footsteps faded, getting farther away. He set off down the hallway running, and at the end of the hall he turned right. Ahead of him in the distance he could see the shadowy figure of someone trying to leave the building. A guy . . . tall . . . dressed in dark clothes. Whoever it was, he didn't have legal access to the building. And the fact that he was trying to escape told Cody he'd probably done something wrong.

Speed wasn't a problem for Cody — even since his injury. He had competed in marathons and triathlons since coming home from Iraq, and he still did speed training. Times like this he was grateful. He intensified his run, pushing through the school doors and across the back courtyard between the administration building and the athletic complex. "Hey . . . stop!"

He ran faster . . . holding the flashbacks at bay . . . focusing on the figure in front of him. Faster and faster but just before he might've made a dive at the trespasser, the guy turned around, gasping for breath, his eyes wide, terrified.

Cody stopped short, his breathing hard and fast. "DeMetri?"

"Coach, . . ." DeMetri Smith sank down in a crouched position, too shaky to stand. "You scared me to death."

"Yeah." Cody doubled at the waist and exhaled hard a few times. "Me too." He straightened and looked hard at the kid. "Why are you here?" Cody felt his heartbeat finding normal again. "You should be at home in bed . . . we have practice tomorrow."

DeMetri rose to his feet. "I . . . I don't have anywhere to stay." The kid didn't want to cry, that much was evident. He clenched his jaw, fighting his emotion. "My mom got arrested . . . they evicted me."

Cody wanted to drop to the ground and cry right beside his player. Another kid? Another mother like his and Cheyenne's? How many other teenagers tonight weren't sure where to sleep? How many parents were in prison while their high school sons or daughters tried to dodge the embarrassment and figure out a way on their own? He took a few slow steps to DeMetri. "Smitty, . . ." He put his hand on the player's shoulder. "I'm sorry."

DeMetri was still breathing hard. With Cody's understanding, he lost the battle with his tears. "It's okay. The school's fine."

Dawning hit Cody again. "You've been staying here . . . sleeping here?"

"Yeah," he stuck his chin out, like the situation was fine, as if he didn't want any sympathy from Cody or anyone else. "It's okay. I have some stuff in a closet."

"Where?" His heart broke for his player. "Where do you stay?"

"The wrestling room." He blinked, and for a few seconds he looked more like a kid than the adult he was being forced to become. "It's fine, Coach. Really."

"It's not fine." He felt a gust of anger toward DeMetri's mom, and all those who didn't fight harder to be parents. "You're coming home with me."

DeMetri blinked. "With you, Coach?"

"Yes." Cody's roommate was gone this weekend. Besides, they had an office, a third bedroom that neither of them really used. He could work out the details later. De-Metri wasn't going to spend another night living in the Lyle wrestling room. His tone softened. "Come on. Let's get you home."

He finished counting the uniforms, and he and Cheyenne and DeMetri drove home. They dropped Chey off first, and he got out of his pickup only long enough to help her up the stairs and inside. From there she assured him she had it, and even before he could tell her goodbye, Tara appeared in her bathrobe. "You two okay out here?"

"Yes." Cheyenne gave Cody a knowing smile. He hadn't said much since he'd brought DeMetri back with him to the equipment room. He didn't need to. Everything that might be said on the subject had already been said over coffee earlier that night. If anyone would understand Cody taking DeMetri home with him tonight, she would. It was one more thing they would share, one more bond between them. Chey looked at Tara. "We were just saying goodnight."

"Well, then." Tara waved her hand in the air and spun back toward her bedroom. "Don't let me get in the way!"

Cody and Cheyenne laughed quietly, and he appreciated the understanding in her eyes. He hugged her, and let his face linger near hers. "I had fun tonight."

"Me too."

"Goodnight, Chey." He hugged her once more, gingerly because he didn't want to hurt her. Not now or ever.

"Goodnight." She looked back at the truck. "Go take care of that boy."

"I will."

Cody waved goodbye once more. Then he headed out to his truck, to a high school boy whose skin color might be different, but who in this moment looked a whole lot like himself at that age. Frightened and determined, trying to find a way through life on his own. And as he climbed in the truck, he committed to God to do whatever it took to help DeMetri, to be there for the young man.

The way Jim Flanigan had been there for him.

TWELVE

Jenny sat on the front porch and listened to her oldest son Connor sing his heart out. He was trying out for *American Idol* at the end of the summer . . . something he'd decided just a few weeks ago. The show was making a stop in Indianapolis, and though ten thousand people were bound to show up for the audition, Connor wanted his chance.

"God only opens doors we knock on," he had told her when he made up his mind. "I have to try."

She loved that about her kids, that they were willing to go after their dreams. It was a bittersweet joy, because in time their dreams were bound to take them to vastly different places. Bailey already in New York, and now Connor. If he gravitated toward a singing career he would live in Nashville eventually, or maybe Los Angeles. Certainly not here in Bloomington. She smiled to herself. *American Idol* was a long shot, no matter how great he sounded singing at their family's piano.

But the possibility that Connor's dreams would take him far away was very real.

She had a five-page document in her hand, her latest article for *Christian Family* magazine. This was her newest writing position, and she liked it better than the other magazines she'd worked for. This one allowed her to talk about the things most dear to her, the challenges of adoption, the task of raising kids who would develop a strong faith of their own, the importance of laughter around the dinner table. Today's article was on another topic close to Jenny's heart: the decision to have an open door to the people God brought into their lives.

Jenny smiled, remembering the many kids who viewed the Flanigans as their second family. None more so than Cody Coleman. She focused on the first paragraph of the article and began to read. But she wasn't halfway down the page when she heard a car coming down the hill. She looked up and squinted. It was the last day of June, and the heat was getting intense, the humidity causing a buildup of clouds along the horizon. The glare of the sun made it hard to see, but as the pickup grew closer, as it

240

slowed and turned into their driveway, she had no doubt whose it was.

"Cody Coleman," she whispered out loud. How long had it been? She watched him park, and as he climbed out of the truck and walked closer, Jenny felt her heart hurt at the way she'd missed him, the way they'd all missed him.

He saw her, clearly. His hands in his pockets, he made his way up the porch steps and over to her before he said a single word. She stood to meet him, and they came together in the sort of hug usually reserved strictly for family. A hug that held on and gave absolute unconditional certainty that love once here, was still here now.

She stepped back and they sat down on the porch swing.

"Hi." He smiled as he spoke for the first time. With the Flanigans, he already knew he didn't need words. "It's been a long time."

"Too long." She set her document down beside her. "You look good."

"I am." He nodded, confident. His face looked older in a good way, more mature than before. "I'm coaching and teaching . . . at Lyle High . . . halfway to the Ohio border."

"Yes." Jenny smiled at the irony. Cody

here beside her when she'd just finished an article about having an open door. "Ryan Taylor told us."

"I thought he might." He looked uncomfortable for a moment, like maybe he felt guilty for not calling. "I thought I'd come by and talk to Coach . . . see if he had any advice about summer camp. I've never run one before and . . . well, it's coming up. I have a lot to learn."

"He'll be home soon." She smiled, hoping to erase any awkwardness he might feel. Especially in light of the situation with him and Bailey. "He'd love to help you."

"I figured." Cody relaxed. "I miss him . . . I miss all of you." His eyes held an aching that made Jenny feel good. Like the time he'd spent with their family mattered to him. Even if he hadn't been in touch lately.

"I heard about the car accident . . . your friend." She wanted him to know he could talk about his life. How he had moved on. "What's her name?"

He hesitated, and for a moment he looked across the expanse of their front lawn, the sun on his face. "Cheyenne." He turned back to Jenny. "She's doing much better. We . . . we spend a lot of time together." Again he looked slightly out of sorts. "I guess you know . . . I haven't talked to

Bailey since she left." He turned slightly so he could see her better. "How's she doing?"

"She loves the show." Jenny had to be careful. Bailey wouldn't want her saying too much. If Cody wanted to know about her life, he could text or call her. She'd told Jenny that a number of times. "She's keeping busy."

"Her and Brandon?" Cody almost winced, and there was no denying the fact that he didn't really want to know the answer. "Are they . . . are they together?"

"I'm not sure they have a label." Jenny studied him, how right it felt that he was back. "Brandon's a part of her life."

"Yes." Cody set his jaw and nodded. "I'm glad she's happy." He stood and took a deep breath. "Well . . . are the boys out back?"

"They are." Her heart hurt at the look in Cody's eyes, the way he so obviously still had feelings for Bailey. But there was nothing she could say to help the situation, no advice or wisdom that would be appropriate. The relationship between Cody and Bailey was something only God and the two of them could figure out. "Come on." She grabbed her document and together they walked inside. "They'll be thrilled to see you."

Connor was first to notice him. He got up

243

from the piano and gave Cody the sort of hug usually reserved for the closest team-mates. "It's been too long . . ."

"I know." He nodded toward the piano. "Listen to you, man, . . . you sound amazing. You going out for *American Idol* this year, or what?"

Connor laughed. "Actually . . . yeah. This summer."

"No way!" Cody gave Connor an enthusiastic pat on his shoulder. "That's awesome, bro, . . . you'll blow 'em away."

Jenny watched from a few feet away. She loved this, how with Cody it felt like no time had passed. This was their reward for opening their home and hearts to Cody in the first place. He would always be a part of them — regardless of time passed.

"You gotta keep me posted." Cody shook his head, his grin reaching easily to his eyes. "You'll knock it out of the park. Seriously . . . you sing like that and we'll be watching you on TV."

They were halfway down the hall, Jenny tailing the guys and headed toward the kitchen when Ricky spotted Cody. "What?" He shouted the word and jumped up. Ricky seemed to grow taller every day, and now he lumbered up to them, all big feet and long legs. "I can't believe you're here!" He threw himself in Cody's arms and the two hugged and slapped each other's backs.

"What happened to you? You're huge!" Cody stood back and studied Ricky. "Don't tell me you're thinking of passing me up."

"He's six-foot-two." Connor laughed. "Crazy for a thirteen-year-old."

"Yeah," Ricky laughed, his expression proud of the fact. "You still have me beat by an inch, but not for long."

Cody raised his brow. "Not if you're this tall at thirteen."

"Come on . . . Shawn and Justin are playing football out back." Ricky ran ahead. "Wait till I tell them!"

Cody grinned at Jenny and Connor. "I guess I'm playing football."

"Me too." Connor ran for the stairs. "I'll change and be right down."

"Like old times." Jenny hoped he could see in her smile how glad she was that he'd come. "It's good to have you home, Cody."

"Thanks." He started toward the back door. "It's good to be here." With a quick step he jogged off to the backyard.

Jenny watched him go. Ricky gathered Justin, Shawn, and BJ, and like he'd never left, Cody organized them and threw the first pass to Ricky.

"And," Ricky shouted, "he catches it for a

first down!"

The other guys clapped, and Shawn began to run, his hand outstretched. "Hit me up, Ricky, . . . right here!"

Connor came running down the stairs dressed in shorts and a T-shirt and flew out the back door to join the others. Jenny couldn't pull herself away. The scene was like being back in the past, as if she'd taken a ride in Devin Blake's time machine — the one Ashley had told her about — to one of the happiest moments of her life: when Cody lived with them and growing up seemed like a lifetime away for all her boys. So much had changed, and now Connor was ready to take on his senior year, ready to head into the world and pursue his dreams. And the other boys were only getting taller and older, closer to the front door and the plans God had for them.

But for now, the boys out back reminded her of God's goodness, His ability to give her gifts like this when she least expected them. There was a sound behind her, and she turned to see Jim walk in through the garage door. "Hey," he grinned at her. "Is that Cody's truck outside?"

"It is." She turned and watched the boys again. "Like he never left."

Jim joined her and gave her a quick kiss

as he looked at the game of catch going on outside. "He looks good."

"He's growing up." Jenny leaned her head on his shoulder. "He wants to talk to you. About football."

"Really?" He looked touched by the fact. "Sometimes enough weeks pass I wonder if he even remembers us."

"Jim . . ." She raised her eyebrows at him, her voice softer than before. She tapped his chest a few times. "You know deep inside here that could never be true. Cody won't ever forget us."

He looked past her to the boys once more. "You're right." He smiled. "I'm glad he came by."

Jenny set about making dinner — leftover chicken and rice. She'd made enough that she easily had plenty for Cody to join them, and once it was heated up she called out to them. She lingered at the doorway, enjoying once more the look of her boys laughing together with Cody, the way they slung their arms over each others' shoulders and laughed while they headed inside with the football. She looked at Cody as the boys filed past. "Stay for dinner?"

He hesitated, but only for a few seconds. "You have enough?"

"Always enough for you." Ricky put his

arm around Cody's neck and gave him a light punch in the arm. "Even if I caught more passes than you."

"He was easy on you, bud, . . ." Justin grinned. "Don't get a big head, now."

The boys made their way to the back bathroom to wash up, and Cody spotted Jim in the other room reading the newspaper. Cody went to him and immediately Jim set his paper down and hugged him, much the way Jenny had. Like Cody was their long lost son — which after this much time, was close to the truth.

They ate dinner then, laughing over stories from Clear Creek High. "We miss you on the field." Connor took a forkful of rice and waited until he had swallowed it. "No one coaches us quarterbacks like you, Cody. Coach Taylor's too busy with the rest of the team."

"He's a very good coach." Cody looked from Connor to Jim. "I keep thinking how lucky I am to have played for you . . . and to have coached with Ryan Taylor. It's amazing how much I learned." He raised his fork in the air. "And how much I still have to learn."

Jenny watched Jim to see if he might say anything about Ryan Taylor and the possible promotion he might be getting. But when Jim said nothing, Jenny kept quiet too. The Colts were looking to bring in a new coach. Ryan was a former NFL player, with state play-off success at the high school coaching level. He was definitely being considered for the position. Something even Ryan didn't know.

Like always, the kids made short order of dinner, and the cleanup began with all the Flanigan boys working together. As they did, Jim and Cody headed to the game table in the family room. Jenny couldn't hear everything they said after that, but Jim pulled out paper and pencils and for an hour the two of them talked intently — taking turns drawing up what must've been plays and drills, ways Cody's summer camp could be productive and effective.

Jenny took a spot at the kitchen bar where she could keep them in view. How would Bailey feel about how easily Cody had fit back into their lives? If only for a day? Once he was gone Jenny planned to call her. She would be on stage still at this point, but later they could get on Skype . . . talk face to face.

As Jim and Cody finished their talk, as they laughed together and put their heads together, and dreamed about football side by side, Jenny prayed for Cody. That God would continue to bring him back, and that Cody would work things out with Bailey. So that at the very least they might be friends. Because of all the things Jenny could imagine about the future, there was one thing she couldn't think about.

The idea of never seeing Cody Coleman again.

THIRTEEN

Bailey was dancing so hard she could feel the sweat on her back. It was the last number of the show, the last performance of June, and as she finished the final lines of the song, she felt a sense of elation well up within her. She was doing this! Finally . . . after two months she was keeping up.

The number ended and the cast took their bows. Bailey tried to sense whether any of her castmates noticed the difference. Two guys who took curtain call with her smiled in her direction, a little bigger than usual. Or maybe it was her imagination. As they stepped off stage, one of them, Gerald Gear, touched her elbow.

"Ella, . . . great work tonight." Gerald's expression held the familiar arrogance despite his smile. "You looked like . . . like you belonged."

Ella. Her character name in the movie *Unlocked.* The compliment went down like dry bread, but Bailey smiled in return. Gerald's buddy Stefano was watching, and she didn't want to give either of them a reason to see her as easily offended. "Thanks." She couldn't let the hurt show, not now.

Gerald and Stefano walked off together without another backward glance at Bailey. A sigh rattled from her and took with it all the good she'd been feeling about her performance. What would she have to do to be accepted by the cast, to make them see she wasn't here only because of her movie credit? She grabbed a towel from her bag and wiped her neck. She was about to change out of her costume when she heard someone come up behind her.

"Bailey."

The voice belonged to Francesca. Bailey turned in a hurry, surprised. The director rarely sought them out after a show. "Yes?"

"Get dressed and then find me in my office." Her smile was flat. "We need to talk."

Bailey's throat went dry, and her heart flipped into an unfamiliar rhythm. "Yes, ma'am." She turned back to her bag but she couldn't help but wonder. How many of the girls in the dressing room had heard Francesca's request? They had to be thinking the same thing she was: That somehow

— even on a night when she thought she'd nailed it — she'd done something wrong. Her performance hadn't measured up to the others.

She dressed and put her costume on the appropriate hanger. As she did, the dressing room fell quiet. The girls didn't talk to her or to each other, which left an awkward silence thick over the room. Bailey tried to stay brave. *Dear Lord, I don't know what I did wrong, but there must be something. Help me . . . give me courage to hear whatever Francesca has to tell me. Please, God.*

Bailey gathered her things, left the dressing room, and headed for Francesca's office. Along the way she thought about taking a minute to pray longer, to check her Bible app on her phone for a verse that would give her strength. But there wasn't time. Instead she prayed once more, asking God to be with her, and like that, she was knocking at the director's door.

Francesca waved her inside. "Have a seat." Again her smile felt more polite than purposeful.

Bailey's hair was still damp from the show, and now that she was here — face-to-face with her director in the air-conditioned office — she felt a chill run from her neck down her body. She resisted the urge to

253

shiver. "You . . . wanted to talk?"

"Yes." Francesca folded her hands and planted her elbows on the desk in front of her. She leveled her gaze at Bailey and held it for a few long seconds. "You were very good tonight."

Relief washed over Bailey, but she didn't let it show. She was a professional. She was supposed to be good. "Thank you."

Francesca breathed out, and the sound was filled with ambiguity. "I have to be honest. Until this week, I was planning to let you go this Friday." Disappointment colored in the lines around her eyes. "I expected so much more from you, Bailey Flanigan. But maybe you're too young. Most of our cast is in their midtwenties or older."

Bailey heard the sound of her heartbeat in her eardrums. Francesca expected more? And she seemed too young for the job? How was this happening? If the director hadn't been happy with her, why hadn't she said something sooner? She squirmed in her seat, not sure what to say. Sure Francesca had been tough during rehearsals, sometimes singling her out to work harder on a certain move or sing the words of a song more clearly. But she'd never led Bailey to believe she wasn't making the grade, that her job in the *Hairspray* cast was in jeopardy.

The director didn't wait for Bailey's response. "You must know that we didn't hire you only because you could dance and sing. Your name, your involvement in the movie *Unlocked* — all made us believe you could fill seats." She made a noncommittal face and tilted her head slowly from side to side like she was weighing the reality. "It's possible. Our numbers are up a few percentage points. But not like we expected."

The news hit Bailey like successive bricks, each one bigger than the last. She had been on the verge of being let go? And only her performances this week saved her? Even at that, the seats weren't as full as they needed to be, so what was this meeting for? The chills from earlier were gone. Instead heat flooded her cheeks. Worst of all the grumblings she'd heard from the cast were true. She'd been brought in because of *Unlocked*. She fought against a rush of anger. The director could've told her. At least then she wouldn't have been under some delusion that she'd earned her way. "I'm sorry." Humiliation dimmed her voice. She still felt like she was asleep, stuck in some nightmare. "I didn't know."

Francesca waved her hand around, like the entire situation frustrated her. "That's my fault." Another loud breath. "I've tried to bring your stage abilities to another level in practice. But, well, until this week I wasn't seeing it." She lowered her hands and picked up a document on her desk. "You signed a year-long contract, but frankly . . . we might not be in business a year from now. And as you know," she gave Bailey a pointed look, "your contract can be cancelled if you're not getting the job done."

"Yes, ma'am." *So what about today?* She wanted to ask. Was her position on the cast sure? At least for another few weeks if not for the remainder of her contract? A year felt like a long time in light of Francesca's talk. Bailey tried to look calm. *Be professional,* she told herself. *Stay professional.* But she felt like running or crying or calling home and booking the next flight back to Indianapolis. She was doing her best, and that hadn't been good enough. No wonder she'd doubted her abilities.

A handful of seconds passed, and Francesca sat back and folded her arms in front of her. "I want you to go home for the holiday weekend. Spend the Fourth with your family or friends. And while you're there I want you to think about whether or not you belong here." Her words came sharp and fast like automatic gunfire. "Whether you want to belong here."

"I do." Bailey couldn't stop herself. She sat up straighter, her shock and defeat forgotten for the moment. "I mean, I do want to be here." Now that she'd started, she couldn't stop herself. "I'll work hard. I know what to do now, and I'll keep doing it better. I promise."

Francesca's expression didn't change. "You'll have to prove that. After you take a few days off." She went on to explain that the cast would use on-call dancers to fill her spot. "Think about how hard you'll have to work. Don't come back unless you're ready to give me everything you have, Bailey. Everything." She paused, sizing up Bailey the way a principal might look over a delinquent student. "I believed in you. But the only reason you're still on this cast is because of your performances this week. They were better." The director angled her head and thought for a few seconds. As if she was possibly doubting her earlier assessment and maybe Bailey wasn't actually better. But the moment passed and she continued. "When you return . . . if you return . . . I want much more from you." She exhaled, looking suddenly exhausted by the entire situation. She offered a tired smile that wasn't quite sympathetic. "Is that clear?"

"Yes, ma'am." Bailey remembered the

warning from Tim's girlfriend: Francesca was tough. But Bailey had no idea how tough until today. She refused the tears stinging the corners of her eyes. "I'll take the break, and I'll be stronger when I come back. I will."

"Very well." Francesca stood and opened her office door. "I will reevaluate again after the Fourth. Oh, and another thing." Her smile dissolved. "You aren't fitting in well with the rest of the *Hairspray* family. A few of them have talked to me about it." Her expression said she believed them. "They get the sense you're judging them."

"No, ma'am." Bailey stood and tried to keep her balance. "I care about them. All of them." She felt light-headed and dizzy, the reality of her shaky place on the cast still making its way to a place in her mind where she could fully grasp it.

"Maybe show that then."

Bailey could hardly believe what she was hearing. She felt embarrassed and humili-ated, unsure of how she'd let the director down or why people thought she was judg-ing them, and most of all why no one had told her this to her face before. As she walked out, Bailey looked around, but this part of the backstage was empty. How many of the cast had seen her walk into Fran-

258

cesca's office? They probably all knew this was coming — they knew even though she didn't. Because they were professionals and along with Francesca they must have seen the lack of experience in Bailey.

Her heart slipped another notch. No wonder some of her castmates whispered about her.

When she was on the other side of Francesca's office door, another thought hit her. She'd have to call home and tell her parents now, tell them that she wasn't making it on Broadway. That basically she had one chance left. The tears she fought earlier were back, and she closed her eyes to stop them. *I didn't see this coming, God . . . I really thought . . . I thought this was where You wanted me, but now . . .* She couldn't think about it. Not here. She pushed everything from her mind but the one detail that mattered. She needed to get out of here. No way she wanted to face anyone from the cast now.

She gathered her things and called the car service at her apartment building. Her ride would be there in five minutes. As she hung up, again the situation clouded her heart. She was practically failing at the one thing she'd felt driven to do, the one dream she felt sure God had given her. Bailey held her breath for a moment, drawing on a strength that wasn't her own. Whether she was alone in the building or not, she couldn't break down here. Francesca might see her, and then she'd know for sure Bailey wasn't ready for Broadway.

She turned the corner to the brick hallway that led to the stage door, but what she saw made her stop short. Chrissy was a dozen yards away, bent over and leaning against the wall. She looked pale, like she was about to pass out.

"Chrissy?" Bailey hurried closer and set her things down. She put her hand on her friend's shoulder. "Are you okay?"

"Yeah." She straightened and ran her hand through her hair. "Just tired . . . long night."

Francesca's words rang in Bailey's heart and mind. If she cared for the cast, she should show them. Bailey moved so she was directly in front of Chrissy. She put her hands on her shoulders and looked straight at her. "You need a doctor . . ."

"I don't." Again she looked weak, like she might not make it to the door. She tried to smile at Bailey but it fell short. Like she couldn't muster up the energy. "I was up late. That's all."

Bailey searched desperately through her options. Chrissy wasn't telling the truth;

that much was clear. She looked too thin and beyond tired. Makeup could hide the dark circles under her eyes on stage. But now, after a full show, there was no hiding the signs. "You're not okay." Bailey kept her tone gentle, but she hoped her urgency showed in her expression.

"I am." She drew in a deep breath and worked hard to shake off the struggle. "Some days are just harder than others."

A uselessness came over Bailey. Chrissy wasn't the only one of her castmates in trouble. A number of them were into pills and smoking pot. Whatever it took to relax after a performance, or stay thin enough to fit in the costumes. Bailey was young, Francesca had pointed that out. But she couldn't stand by and watch Chrissy hurt herself by not eating. She reached into her bag and pulled out a protein bar. "Here," she handed it to her friend. "Maybe if you ate something . . . you'd have more energy."

"I . . . I already ate." Chrissy stared at the cement floor for a long moment and then looked right at Bailey.

In that single instant Bailey could feel that they shared a tragic, terrible knowing. The fact that Chrissy wasn't going to eat, and the sad reality that Bailey could do nothing about it. "I know, Chrissy . . . what you're dealing with. You can't hide it." Bailey kept her voice soft, as unthreatening as possible. "Let me call someone. There are people who can —"

"Listen." Chrissy's tone was just short of angry, and her eyes shone with a sudden intensity. "I'm getting help, okay? I told you," she seemed to work to bring her voice back in check, "I'm fine."

Chrissy gathered her things, and though she walked more slowly than usual, the moment of exhaustion seemed to have passed. Bailey kept at her pace, and when they reached the door she saw her ride waiting for her. "Come on." She motioned to the car. "We'll drop you off."

Her friend lived a few blocks away in a shared flat, but usually she walked with a group of actresses. Tonight everyone else had gone ahead. Chrissy hesitated, as if maybe she didn't want even five more minutes of prodding from Bailey. But after a few seconds she shrugged and allowed a partial smile. "Okay. Thanks."

Before the driver let Chrissy out, Bailey made one last attempt. "I'll pray for you." Bailey watched her friend's eyes, but she kept them turned away. "If you're in trouble, Chrissy . . . I'm here."

Chrissy nodded slowly and lifted her face

to Bailey just briefly. "Thanks. See you to-morrow."

And with that she stepped out and hurried off. She looks stronger now, Bailey told herself. And if she was being honest, then Chrissy was already getting help. Still, Bailey wished there was something else she could do. The ride back to the apartment was quick, and the Kellers were asleep by the time she crept inside. When she reached her room and shut the door, she grabbed her journal.

Dear Lord, she wrote, *I feel like I'm failing at everything. My role on Broadway . . . my ability to help Chrissy . . . my impact on the cast. Nothing's working. And now I have to tell my mom and dad.* Bailey reread her words and a sick feeling came over her. They had gone to so much trouble to get her here, and they had believed in her completely. They'd even flown the whole family out to see her show.

She pictured how it felt, having them there, knowing that they were watching her perform the way they once watched her perform for Christian Kids Theater. They had all gathered around her afterward and told her how well she'd done. But even then — in the basement of her heart — Bailey had quietly doubted her abilities. As a

performer . . . as a friend . . . as a light for
God. Back then she wondered if maybe she
wasn't good enough.

Tonight she had her answer.

She wasn't.

FOURTEEN

Sleep didn't come easy after Francesca's warning and Chrissy's refusal to accept her help. But Bailey avoided talking to her parents or to Brandon. She was too embarrassed to know what to say. Anyway, that could come later. Now already she was back at the theater, ready for another show.

She walked toward the dressing room and stopped before she reached the door. Two of the actors from the show were talking, their tones sharp.

"I don't care who she is." The voice belonged to the girl who played Tracy, the show's lead. "She's only here because of her Brandon Paul connection. People loved *Unlocked* and now their curiosity brings them to New York to see if Bailey can perform on Broadway."

"Which she can't." The other girl laughed. Bailey couldn't make out her voice.

"Well," the first girl chuckled. "Let's just

say there are a hundred Broadway dancers who could take her spot. People who could use the money."

"Exactly." The girl clucked her tongue. "I hate the trend in New York, producers bringing in actors with no Broadway experience just because they have a name. Let her work for it like everyone else."

Bailey intentionally dropped her dance bag. At the sound, the conversation on the other side of the wall stopped. She grabbed her gear and hesitated before walking in. "Hey." She smiled at them, determined that they wouldn't see the way their remarks hurt her.

"Hey." They answered her in unison and quickly fell quiet, turning their attention to preparing for that night's performance.

Bailey couldn't imagine how hard she'd have to work, how much better she'd have to become on stage before she had their respect. But combined with Francesca's comments from last night and the whispers she'd heard since she started, she felt like a pariah.

The thoughts plagued her then and that Saturday morning as she headed to La-Guardia by herself, and even as she shared a happy reunion with her family at the Indianapolis airport.

266

Bailey figured she'd wait until the picnic to talk to her mom more in depth about the way things were falling apart back in New York. So far she hadn't told anyone about the situation, and only Chrissy had noticed there was something wrong with her the last few days. Brandon was overseas for a week as part of the shoot for his current film. He planned to call when he could, but they hadn't talked since Wednesday.

Now it was the morning of July Fourth, and as Bailey woke up in her old bed and stretched out her legs, she felt a peace that had eluded her most of the week. With all that was happening, she wasn't sure she ever wanted to go back. She sat up and stepped onto the thick cushion of carpet. Her room still looked just like she'd left it.

She walked to the window and looked out across their manicured front lawn, the winding drive, and the full trees that lined either side. She had a million happy memories from past July Fourths. She and her brothers chasing each other across the grass with squirt guns, or her parents hosting a barbecue for all their friends.

But the only memory that played in her mind, the one she woke up thinking about was last July Fourth. Her family had gone to Lake Monroe with the Baxters. Bailey had broken up with Tim Reed by then, but she hadn't told Cody. When he showed up at the picnic, she wasn't sure if they'd have a moment alone to talk, but they'd taken a walk around the lake and along the way everything changed.

They admitted feelings they'd had for years, and in a moment she could still remember in vivid detail, Cody had kissed her. When they returned from that walk, the pretending was over. Everything they felt about each other was out in the open and there would be no looking back. At least that's the way Bailey felt about it. But only a few months later Cody was back to being distant, pulling his usual running act. The one that had finally and completely separated them.

Bailey sighed. *Dear Lord, I can't do this to myself . . . not every Fourth of July.* Bailey let the prayer echo in her heart for a few seconds. A sad laugh came from her. It wasn't only the Fourth of July. She thought about him every day. Or most days, anyway. Every time she was on Facebook, and when she walked into her room at the Kellers' — always aware of the framed photograph on the floor under her bed, right against the baseboard, getting dusty.

She sat up and stretched as her mom

knocked on the door and opened it. "Good morning." She smiled. "Another Fourth."

"Yes." Bailey yawned and pulled her knees up close to her chest. She patted the spot on the bed beside her. "Come talk."

Life had been so busy lately, between shows and rehearsals and her mom's schedule with the kids and her writing. They hadn't talked for more than five minutes in a week. Her mom stepped inside and took the spot next to Bailey. She breathed in deep and looked out the window. "Should be a hot one."

"Always." Bailey smiled.

"I was hoping you were awake." Her mom turned to her. "I haven't had a minute to tell you, but . . . Cody stopped by last week. Didn't call . . . just drove up." She smiled, and the sadness in her expression was clear. "It was nice seeing him again."

"He stopped by?" Bailey sat up straighter. "That's sort of a big deal."

"I know." Her mom managed a sheepish shrug. "Seriously every time we talked I didn't think about it until we hung up. I hate that part about you living so far away. The everyday stuff falls through the cracks." She angled her head. "I figured we'd talk longer this weekend, but now you're here."

The sick feeling hit her instantly. This was

the day she needed to tell her mom the reason she was home. "Yeah. I have things to tell you too." She tried to picture Cody dropping in. "So why'd he stop by?"

"He wanted to talk to Dad. About football and camp, drills . . . that sort of thing."

"Hmmm." Bailey's heart felt raw and maybe a little jealous. "What about the boys? Did they see him?"

"They did. They played a little football out back, and then Cody stayed for dinner and he and your dad talked after that."

Bailey hugged her knees a little closer and wrestled with her emotions. "Was he nice?"

"Very." A sigh eased from her mother's lips. "He misses the boys and us. And he misses you, Bailey. You have to know that."

"Not really." Bailey didn't feel bitter, but she had to be honest. "He hasn't called or texted." She raised one shoulder and let it fall again. "How much could he miss me?"

"He asked about you."

Bailey hated the way her heart jumped. "What did he ask?" She kept her tone neutral. Not that she wanted to hide her feelings from her mom. She wanted to hide them from herself.

"How you were doing, how the show was going." Her mom smiled big, her eyes kind. "I told him you were doing great. The best dancer on Broadway."

The sick feeling grew, and her mind raced. Cody had been here, at her house? For most of an evening? And he'd asked about her? She should've been here instead of making a fool of herself on Broadway. Then they could've taken a walk and figured out what went wrong. What really went wrong. Bailey waited. She didn't want to ask her next question, but finally she couldn't stop herself. "Did . . . he talk about Cheyenne?"

"The friend in the car accident?"

"His girlfriend, Mom." Bailey's voice was even, without a hint of sarcasm. "Did he mention her? Or did you ask?"

"I didn't ask."

"So he mentioned her." It wasn't a question.

"Not really." Her mom's tone was gentle. "He told me they spent time together. That's it." Her mom had hesitated. "He asked about you and Brandon."

Bailey felt her breath leave her for a second or two. "Okay." She paused. "What did you tell him?" She didn't like the idea of her mom talking to Cody. After how he'd treated her, she felt like she needed her mom on her side. There wasn't room in the situation for her mom to be both Cody's ally and hers.

"Don't worry." Empathy shaded her expression. "I said Brandon and you talk. Nothing more."

"Good." Bailey felt relieved. Of course her mom understood. "He could reach me if he wanted to."

"You're right." Her mom looked like she wanted to say more, but she hesitated and the change in her eyes said she was switching topics. "So what's new in New York?"

Bailey felt her heart drop to the floor. She'd dreaded this since Francesca's talk with her, but now there was no better time to break the news. She exhaled and searched her mom's eyes. "It's not good."

Her mother showed no obvious reaction. She clearly didn't worry that Bailey had made some tragic decision, or gotten into trouble. Instead she put her hand on Bailey's shoulder. "Okay. I'm listening."

"Well," Bailey hadn't thought she'd cry, but suddenly her emotions turned to liquid and filled her eyes. "Francesca pulled me aside . . . and told me I wasn't cutting it. I need to get better or . . ." Her voice cracked and she hung her head.

"Bailey . . ." the shock in her mom's voice was genuine. "What are you talking about? You're wonderful on that stage."

She shook her head. "No. Not . . . not like

I need to be."

"Oh, honey." Her mom took her in her arms and hugged her. "That's ridiculous. You won the part over hundreds of dancers."

A quiet sniff came from Bailey, and again she shook her head. Her throat was too tight to speak.

"You did . . . I was there, sweetheart." She ran her hand along Bailey's back. "The director's just being tough on you. She has a reputation for that."

Bailey wiped at a few tears on her cheeks. "It wasn't that." She wanted to cry for an hour, let out all the feelings she'd bottled up over the last week. But she had to explain. "I didn't tell you before, but . . . I had a feeling I wasn't keeping up. Like . . . I don't know, like the level was over my head."

Her mom's body tensed, and for a moment Bailey thought she might disagree again. But instead she waited, letting Bailey finish.

"They were going to let me go." She drew back and searched her mother's face. "Last week would've been my last if," she sniffed again, "if I hadn't found another level."

The surprise and shock hit her mom then. "I can't believe that."

"I can." That was the hardest part. Bailey

had wondered if she wasn't quite where she needed to be, but when no one told her so, she figured she was at least good enough to stay.

"I guess, I don't get it." Her mother folded her arms, clearly baffled. "You won the part over so many girls."

"No." Bailey shook her head. Her tears were under control again, but the heaviness in her heart remained. "They hired me because of *Unlocked.* Because of my connection with Brandon. That's what Francesca said."

A soft groan came from her mom. "Oh, Bailey, . . . I'm sorry."

"It's okay." She tried to find a smile. "I'm doing my best. I rehearse longer than anyone, and I feel like I'm getting better. But that's why I'm home. She wanted me to take a break and think about how badly I wanted it."

Resignation came over her mom. "And?"

"I still want it. But I have to get better. Francesca told me that."

Again her mom leaned in and hugged her, longer this time. "If you want it, then you'll get it. I know you." When they pulled back, her mother put her hands on either side of her face. "God has good plans for you, honey . . . if Broadway isn't what He has in mind, He'll show you."

"I know. Thanks." They were quiet for a few seconds, Bailey still wrestling with the embarrassment of her director's words. But that wasn't all. "The cast is still acting weird. Not really talking to me . . . But at least I know why."

"The *Unlocked* thing?"

"Exactly. It's like they all know I'm not good enough, and that I won the part because of the movie." Bailey stood and opened the window. Immediately a breeze drifted into the room and with it the sound of finches and robins outside. Bailey turned and leaned against the windowsill. "And I'm still not making even a little impact on anyone else."

Bailey told her mom about Chrissy and the dancers who did drugs or drank. "Chrissy's anorexic. I'm almost positive." Bailey felt tired imagining going back to New York on Tuesday. "She says she's getting help, but what if she's not?"

Her mom was slow with her answer. "If people don't want help, we can't force them." She stood and joined Bailey near the window. For a long time she waited, like she was thinking through the options, any way Bailey might've actually been able to help Chrissy. "You could tell Francesca your concerns."

"Yeah." Bailey wasn't sure. "She leads rehearsals. You'd think she could see for herself."

Again they were quiet. "Keep praying . . . God will make your purpose clear in His time. He really will." Her mom gave her another long hug. "You'll be fine. It's okay if you have to work hard to keep your spot."

"That's what I told Francesca. I'll work harder than anyone."

Her mom checked her watch. "Come down and help me with the picnic when you're ready." She smiled. "Be in the moment, Bailey. We're all glad you're home."

"Me too. Thanks for understanding." For the first time that morning the sadness eased. "You really are my best friend, Mom."

Her mother's smile said what no words could. "Oh . . . and Brandon Paul sent a fruit basket . . . wished us all a happy Fourth." She raised her brow and uttered a quiet laugh. "That boy doesn't miss a beat."

As her mom left the room, a smile played on Bailey's lips for the first time that morning. A smile because Brandon had a way of making her troubles seem small and insignificant. She missed him more than she realized until now. A fruit basket? How thoughtful was that? Today — instead of worrying about her role on Broadway or thinking about the texts and calls she wasn't getting from Cody — she would focus on something she did have.

The friendship and attention of Brandon Paul.

Bailey dressed and then jogged down the stairs where she found her mom and Justin working to finish a batch of deviled eggs. Bailey jumped in, glad for the distraction. Her mom smiled at her. "You look pretty."

"Thanks." Bailey elbowed Justin lightly. "I was just going to say how buff this brother of mine is getting."

"I have a long way to go." Justin flexed and laughed, humble about his solid physique. "NFL players my height have forty pounds on me."

"And seven years." Their mom waved her spoon at him. "You're on your way, Justin. Bailey's right." Their mom raised her eyes in Bailey's direction. "Your dad has the boys on a strength and speed training series for the summer. They're all bigger and faster than when you left."

Bailey smiled at the idea, but it made her sad too. Her brothers were growing up without her, while she was fighting to make a name for herself in New York City. And for what? She looked at Justin and then she glanced around the house. One day everything here, everything she could hear or see or know would be gone. And in these final seasons of life as she'd known it, she spent her time alone in Manhattan ineffective in every possible way.

The day stretched out sunny and beautiful — like almost every July Fourth Bailey could remember. Ninety degrees and a light breeze, with only some of the humidity that was bound to hit full force any day. She played frisbee on the shore with her brothers and tried not to remember how last year at this time she was playing catch with Cody. Tried to forget the way they'd both wound up in the lake trying to grab the football at the same time.

Bailey stepped away from the game long enough to catch her breath, and as she did she surveyed the group around her. The Baxter family was doing great — all of them here with their families. Landon Blake looked thinner than usual, and she remembered that he was struggling with some problem in his lungs. But otherwise, he and Ashley looked happy.

Even Katy and Dayne and their little girl Sophie had made it back home for the annual picnic. The laughter and joy among the group was again enough to make her want to forget ever going back to New York. She had nothing in common with the cast, and if there were more qualified dancers who could take her spot, then so be it. But here was the thing. She couldn't give up that easily. Not after spending a lifetime dreaming about performing on Broadway. God had opened this door, Bailey was convinced. Now she would have to work harder than anyone else to keep her spot.

She sat on the edge of an open picnic table and watched her brothers. She was about to join them again when Katy Hart Matthews took the spot beside her. She was tanned — probably from her time in Los Angeles — and breathless from racing her little girl around the beach all afternoon. But now her husband, Dayne, had Sophie by the hand. "Whew . . . it's getting hot."

"It is." The breeze had let up, and the sun was hot on their shoulders. She welcomed the partial shade of the trees that lined the picnic area.

"So," Katy caught her breath and grinned at Bailey. "How's New York?"

Bailey wondered how much she should say. Katy was her first drama instructor, after all. The person whose belief in Bailey was second only to her parents and Bran-

279

don. "Not great. Not really."

"Bailey . . . I'm sorry." A troubled look quieted Katy's tone. "I feel so out of the loop spending most of my time in California."

"It's okay." She sighed, glad there were no traces of this morning's tears. "At first glance everyone looks so happy, dancing and singing about the sixties."

Katy nodded. "New York can be a tough place."

"So hard." She sighed, her eyes on the blue sky ahead. The story about Francesca spilled out, how Bailey wasn't making the grade no matter how hard she tried. "There's more. One girl is anorexic, and lots are on drugs. And so much homosexuality."

"In Los Angeles too." Katy's expression held no judgment, just a deep sorrow. "Our culture celebrates it these days."

"Exactly. If someone asked me what the Bible said about it, and if I told them the truth, I feel like they'd shoot me." She squinted against the sharp afternoon sun. "You know?"

"I do. It's hard to be a light in the entertainment industry." Katy smiled, and a peace resonated with her. "But it's possible. Otherwise, God wouldn't have put you there." She was quiet and the laughter and voices of their families filled the air around them. "Maybe God's closing the door on Broadway." Her tone was easy. "If you ever want to do movies, Bailey, . . . you could live with Dayne and me." She slipped her arm around Bailey's shoulders and hugged her. "Just so you know."

"Thanks." Bailey leaned her head on Katy's shoulder. The offer meant more than Katy could ever know. But even so the timing felt wrong. She stood and grabbed the suntan lotion from the table. Her shoulders were getting burned for sure. "I mean, I can handle it in New York, and I'm willing to work harder. I guess I'm not sure I'm doing all I can to help the cast, to make an impact. Or even to keep my job." She poured the lotion into her hand and worked it into her left arm. "Like maybe God's disappointed in me."

"Bailey," Katy looked straight at her. "God's not disappointed in you. He's just not finished with you. That's all."

The sound of that soothed Bailey's uncertain soul. "Just pray for me . . . that I'll hear His voice . . . do whatever He wants me to do." She finished putting the lotion on her other arm and set the bottle back down. "Thanks again . . . for the offer. That means a lot." She thought about Brandon, how happy he'd be if she moved to LA and focused on film. A smile started in her heart and made it to her eyes. "I'll pray about it. You never know."

They talked a little while longer about the cast, and Bailey's frustrations. "I think my faith bugs people. Which is okay . . . it's just sad."

"What makes you think that?" Katy didn't sound surprised, just curious.

"I told Chrissy I pray about my performances." Bailey sat back down beside Katy on the picnic table. "I've talked with her a few times about God, and then last week . . . she told me the rest of the cast knows."

"About your faith?"

"Yes." Bailey had never experienced anything like this, the way she felt like an outsider because she loved Jesus. "They have such a bad view of Christians. They think we're all hateful and judgmental. That's the vibe I get anyway." She thought for a moment. "I mean, I can see it in the eyes of half the guys when they walk past me, like they're mad at me for something I haven't even done."

"Hmmm." Katy's tone held a wealth of understanding. "They see God in you — even though you're not perfect. And God

282

scares a lot of people. They aren't used to being around someone who loves Jesus. It's completely foreign."

Bailey looked at the ground, fighting the defeat that clouded her soul. "My dad told me to shine for Jesus on Broadway." She sat a little straighter. "How can I do that when almost everyone I've met doesn't seem to believe in Him?"

"It's a tough question." Katy smiled, thoughtful. "But Bailey, honestly . . . have you actually talked to them? Or does it just seem that way?"

The question hit her straight at the center of her soul. Katy still knew her so well. "I've kept pretty quiet."

"That's understandable." She smiled. "It's why you still have your spot in the show. God wants more from you."

The possibility seemed pretty right on.

Katy glanced at her. "I'm not sure I have the answers. But the Bible says to love . . . if we love people, they'll know we are Christians and they'll want what we have."

"True." Bailey still wasn't sure what that would look like. How was she supposed to love people who didn't like her? People who understandably doubted her talent and maybe even resented her place on the cast? "Pray for me . . . that I'll be bolder."

"I will." Her eyes only accentuated her promise. "So what's this about Brandon Paul? We run into him now and then. He's a nice guy . . . totally different from what everyone says." Katy grinned. "Because of a certain someone's influence in his life."

"I didn't do much." her heart felt lighter as she said the words. "I like Brandon. He's fun. He makes me laugh all the time."

"And Cody?" Katy knew more about Cody than anyone outside her family. After all, she lived with the Flanigans in the same season Cody lived with them.

"Nothing." Bailey couldn't hide her sorrow in her voice. "He doesn't talk to me at all."

"Guys . . ." Katy frowned. "He still cares, Bailey. No matter how distant he seems. I know him that well, at least." She waited, letting her statement settle for a few seconds. "God will make it all clear in time." She stood and shaded her eyes. "Better go help with dinner. Smells like the barbecue's ready."

Bailey thanked her again and Katy ran off to be with Dayne and Sophie. After a few minutes, the boys stopped playing football and the Flanigans worked together to get their own barbecue on the table. The smells and sounds, the feel of everyone together on the Fourth. All of it made her think about Cody, and how they'd been last year at this time. Happy and together. Why would he stop by her parents' house, hang out with her brothers and visit with her mom and dad — and yet make no effort whatsoever to contact her? Okay, so he had a girlfriend . . . and she had Brandon. But after so many years could he really pretend she'd never existed?

Sure, she could text him . . . make the first move. But she'd done that last time — when she drove to Indianapolis and found him at the hospital with Cheyenne. She'd even given him the box of things he'd left at her house. So if he was interested, it was his turn to reach out. Like her mom had said a few months ago . . . next time around, he'd have to pursue her like a dying man needing water in the desert. And no matter how she wanted to enjoy this July Fourth, no matter how much she loved the time with her family and the talk with Katy, there was no avoiding the painful truth when it came to Cody Coleman. He wasn't pursuing her like a dying man needing water in a desert. He wasn't pursuing her at all. Between that and the uncertainty of her place in New York City, Bailey could only hold onto the truth Katy had shared before dinner. Somehow, someway . . . God would make all things clear to her in time.

Even if that truth was hard to believe today.

FIFTEEN

The excitement throughout Lyle, Indiana, was so palpable Cody could feel it in the air . . . see it on the faces of the guys hanging out together in front of TJ's Hardware and Feed store on Main Street . . . hear it in the voice of Hank who pumped gas for Meijer's at the corner of Franklin and First. Already signs hung in the windows of the Curl and Cut and Sandy's Diner:

Go Buckaroos!

Look Out World . . . Lyle Football's Back!

Several stores had information at their front counters about today's barbecue, the official kickoff of the Lyle football season. From what Ms. Baker had told Cody, the barbecue had fallen by the wayside in the last few years. Coach Oliver hadn't thought it was important. Didn't see that a losing season was worth celebrating after the fact, and couldn't imagine anything exciting enough about the future to convince an entire town to come out for a barbecue under the sweltering July sun.

Cody disagreed. A few minutes talking with Ms. Baker and he had permission to reinstate the barbecue. "It's going to be a great year," he told her. "I mean . . . the kids are capable of big things. I really believe that."

Her smile told him much about the relief she felt with Cody in charge. "Thank you, Mr. Coleman. The kids . . . the town . . . we all appreciate your efforts. You may never know how much."

While he was in her office, Cody asked about Coach Oliver. Apparently the man was getting counseling for his anger issues, and feeling happier without the burden of coaching and teaching. "It was time for him to step down. A good move for everyone."

Now it was the day of the barbecue, and Cody had gotten out of bed at six in the morning, unable to sleep. He did push-ups and sit-ups and ran three miles through his neighborhood, and still made it back in time to whip up a batch of pancakes for De-Metri. As it turned out, his roommate moved back home for good a few weeks after DeMetri moved in. The rent was a little steep for Cody to handle on his own, but he'd worked out his budget. DeMetri needed to focus on school and football. And since the kid didn't have a car there was no way he could get a job. Instead he made it his personal goal to keep the apartment spotless. Together they were making it work.

Cody wasn't much of a cook, but he'd learned a lot this past year. Cooking was something he needed to know — especially since DeMetri's arrival. He could handle a few basic breakfast menus now — scrambled eggs, omelets, pancakes . . . and a small assortment of chicken and beef dinners. Enough for him and DeMetri to get by. He'd gotten the okay from Ms. Baker and the administration to have DeMetri live with him, and the boy's mom had signed over guardianship from prison a week ago. DeMetri was seventeen, but he was still a minor. The paperwork needed to be in order and now it was.

From the back room Cody heard DeMetri get up and make his bed. Again the situation reminded him of his place in the Flanigan house years ago. He flipped the pancakes and thought about the cycle of life. He wasn't doing much, really. Just giving DeMetri a place to live, a way to be safe and successful in school and sports.

He smiled to himself. All his life he had wanted to thank the Flanigans for what they'd done for him, the way they'd taken him in and showed him what it looked like to live a life for God . . . to work hard and be successful. Now he understood. The best way he could thank the Flanigans was to do that very thing for someone else. Someone like DeMetri.

Through breakfast DeMetri asked Cody about a number of plays they'd learned. They had playbooks now, and DeMetri had told him that the guys were more excited about football than they'd ever been. The kid was chatty, which Cody liked. So many high school boys didn't talk much. He had a feeling DeMetri would be a part of his life for a long time. His mother was serving a five-year sentence, and he had no one else.

They picked up Cheyenne on the way out of town, but Tara couldn't come. It was a Friday, and she was still at work. Chey took the middle seat, since Cody's truck didn't have a back row. Cheyenne was moving around easier now. The walker was gone, and she wouldn't need her cane for long.

As they set out, she situated herself and buckled her belt. "So this is a big deal, huh? The barbecue kickoff?"

"It used to be." DeMetri was still a little shy around her.

Cody liked DeMetri's maturity, how he

didn't blame the loss of the picnic on Coach Oliver. No reason to bring up the coach's name now — especially in light of the fact that he was suffering from a stress disability. He kept his eyes on the road. "Ms. Baker thinks the whole town will show up." The chamber of commerce had provided burgers, hot dogs, and a dunk tank.

"Sounds perfect." Chey seemed comfortable close to his side.

On the way there they talked about tomorrow's football camp. The team would meet at Lyle early in the morning and head for Butler University, where they would stay in dorms and compete with other high school teams from around the state. Butler was on the map lately because of its crazy successful run in the NCAA men's basketball tournament, and the football program was strong as well. It was another part of Lyle football that had been dropped during Coach Oliver's tenure.

"The guys are a little worried." DeMetri leaned over his knees, looking at Cody. "About camp. I mean, no cell phones? A lot of guys have a hard time with that."

"They'll be fine." Cody had every hour of their time organized. Jim Flanigan had helped him figure out the best drills and workouts for their time away. "Camp's always tough. But it'll be fun." Cody intended to live by the standards he'd set for the guys. No cell phones except for an emergency. Even where Cheyenne was concerned.

"I guess it's not really the cell phone thing." DeMetri sat back against his seat again. "They don't know how they'll do against the other teams. They don't wanna let you down, Coach."

The words hit Cody straight in the heart. That the guys cared that much now, from where they had started out when Cody took over . . . he was deeply touched. Somehow . . . despite his inexperience and the tough place the kids were in when he arrived, a change was happening at Lyle. They didn't show up expecting to lose. They actually cared.

"Well . . . thanks for letting me know, Smitty. I'll have to talk to them about that."

"Don't tell 'em I said so." He didn't want the guys thinking he had an advantage because he lived with Cody.

"I won't." Cody peered over Cheyenne at him. "You know me better."

"True." A grin spread across DeMetri's face. Cody captured the picture of the kid smiling, driving to the picnic with them. A few weeks ago he was living in the school's wrestling room. Now he was happy and a lot more adjusted.

Cody fell quiet for the rest of the ride, enjoying the feel of Cheyenne beside him, the presence of DeMetri. He'd learned something about himself these past months. He had a purpose again. His counselor agreed that was the reason the flashbacks had all but stopped. Between Cheyenne and DeMetri, he felt needed now. More than Cody had realized, he lived to help others. It was one more reason things hadn't worked out with Bailey.

She didn't need him.

He let that thought slide loosely around the floor of his heart. Okay, she might've thought she needed him, because she had feelings for him. But Bailey could have whatever she wanted. She had the perfect family, the perfect life . . . and now she had a dream job and a relationship with the nation's hottest young actor. What could she possibly need him for?

Enough time had passed, that he understood their breakup better. Subconsciously when he realized a few months ago that Bailey didn't need him, he'd withdrawn from her — blaming it on the situation with his mom. Sure, there was danger because of the drug dealer his mom had dated. But still

293

he could've stayed with Bailey . . . told her they needed to see each other less, and wait the situation out until the man was arrested. He didn't have to walk away from her the way he did.

But deep down he knew she didn't need him — and that had triggered his decision to run, which in turn led to his nightmares and flashbacks. Because without Bailey he had been without purpose.

He felt the urge to reach for Cheyenne's hand, but he held back. DeMetri had asked about her, whether they were dating . . . and Cody had told him no. It wouldn't set a very good example if he held her hand now — when they were supposed to be only friends.

The picnic was set up at the fairgrounds — since the football field wouldn't have been large enough for so many people. Cody guessed just about every retired guy in a ten-mile radius showed up to flip burgers and hand out hot dogs. He wasn't good at estimating the number of people in a crowd, but it felt like Ms. Baker was right — the whole town had shown up. Not only that, but they'd each brought a friend.

An hour after the picnic's official start time — just before dinner was served — the Lyle mayor took his place on a makeshift podium and asked everyone to move to one side of the field. "It's now my pleasure to introduce to you this year's Lyle High football team!"

The entire crowd broke into loud applause and cheers, a show of support that amazed Cody and continued through the introduction of every boy on the team. When Cody's name was announced, the crowd grew louder still. The mayor also welcomed two teachers — Mr. Schroeder and Mr. Braswell, both of whom would assist the Buckaroos this year.

When the team was lined up, facing the crowd, the mayor asked for another round of applause. Cody blinked, not quite believing the response. How had God been so good to bring him here and allow him to take over a team with so much love and support? He had a feeling that they could win one game this year and the town would be thrilled. Ready to welcome them back at the barbecue next summer.

"These boys leave tomorrow morning for camp," the mayor told them, his voice rich with hope. The sun beat down on them, and sweat beaded up on the man's bald head. He didn't seem to mind. "So now I'd like everyone to bow their heads and join me in a prayer for our team. That they'll find

something special while they're at camp."
He paused. "Something that's been missing
for a few years."

That was as close as the mayor came to
talking about the dismal winless seasons
Lyle had recently suffered. Cody watched,
mesmerized as the entire crowd quieted.
Men and boys removed their baseball and
cowboy hats, and everywhere he looked,
families and small groups held hands as
they bowed their heads. When the mayor
was satisfied that the picnic crowd was
ready, he began, his voice booming across
the fairgrounds.

"Dear Lord, we bring to You our Lyle
High football team, and we ask that You
bless their efforts while they're at camp."
His voice rang with unabashed sincerity.
"This team is capable of much . . . and our
town believes in them. Now, Father, we ask
Your blessing not only on their time at
camp, but on their season . . . May they
dedicate every game to You out of gratitude
for how You've blessed us all. And may
Lyle's season be so successful that people
everywhere would know about us, and how
at least here You still reign in small-town
America." The mayor's prayer was as simple
as it was profound. It was met with a roar-
ing applause that was greater than anything

yet that afternoon.

Cody felt a shiver of awe run down his spine. Did they know what they had here in Lyle? How out of the ordinary it was that a small-town mayor might rally his people to pray for the football team? The mayor was going on, talking about the upcoming season and how he hoped to see the stands packed for every game.

He caught himself gazing down the line at his team, the ragtag group of guys who hadn't believed in themselves whatsoever until a few months ago. Yes, they struggled with grades and girls, and the sort of partying that had nearly destroyed Cody when he was that age. But one by one, Cody was meeting with the guys, talking to them, and confronting them with evidence and alternatives. For many of them he'd issued ultimatums: Quit partying . . . quit climbing through windows at girlfriends' houses . . . get the grades up. Otherwise they would lose their place on the roster. And the guys were responding better than he'd imagined.

Dear God, . . . I'm not worthy of the challenge ahead, he prayed silently. *But with You . . . with You all things are possible. So let us play for You this year . . . like the mayor said. And let everyone, everywhere know that where Your name is called upon, Your people can win battles they never should've won. Thank You, Father . . .*

I am with you, son. You will do great things this year in My strength . . . watch and see . . .

Thank You, Father . . . if that's You . . . thank You. Despite the muggy heat of the late afternoon, a chill ran through Cody again. He liked to think in moments like this that the voice he had heard in his heart was really that of the Lord. But it seemed hard to believe that he might take the Buckaroos from two winless seasons to anything truly noteworthy in his first year as head coach. A few wins, yes. A better attitude, of course. But great things? He tried to believe the possibility.

All around him people were crossing the field, coming up to him and the team. "Coach, . . . we're pulling for you." And, "This is your year, Coach." Cody shook more hands than he could count and held the same conversation over and over again. The townspeople wishing him well, and Cody thanking them for their support.

Cody must've held a hundred conversations like that before he saw Cheyenne walking his way. She used her cane, but she walked faster than she had last week. Their eyes met over the crowd, and she smiled, as if to say she was proud of him. When she reached him, she waited nearby until every townsperson had welcomed him, and when they had returned to their picnic blankets and lawn chairs, she walked up and gave him a quick hug. "Wow . . . I didn't know you were famous."

"Faith, family, and football." Cody slid his hands in his pockets and chuckled. "That's Lyle — the town and the school."

"I love it." Cheyenne walked beside him as they returned to their chairs — set up near the barbecue tent and close to the players. "I didn't think there were still places like this."

"Me either." He breathed in deeply through his nose, imagining the challenge ahead. "I hope they're this supportive if we don't win a game."

"I get the feeling it's not about winning for these folks."

"Oh, they care." He chuckled, remembering what a few dads had told him. How the town had its hopes on Cody. "They think I can rebuild what they once had."

Her eyes told him she had no doubts. "Maybe you can."

"We'll see." They stood in line for burgers and then found seats. When the meal was over the guys gathered round and talked him into playing catch on the adjacent field.

Cheyenne watched and after an hour, when Cody's T-shirt was damp with sweat, Cheyenne called him over.

"Time for the dunk tank." Cheyenne took his hand. She whispered close to his ear. "The mayor put me up to it. Bribed me with one of his wife's homemade cupcakes."

Cody laughed. "Oh, really." He noticed the rest of the football team falling in around them.

"Come on, everyone," his quarterback Arnie Hurley shouted above the sound of the crowd, waving at the people to follow them. "Coach is getting in the dunk tank!"

It took a few minutes, but most of the picnic goers moved to the place where volunteers had set up carnival games and a classic dunk tank. Once again the mayor took the microphone. "Just so you know, we asked Miss Betty from the Chamber of Commerce to toss all the extra ice in the dunk tank water!"

A cheer came from the crowd, and the players hooted and hollered. "Yeah . . . you're going down, Coach!"

Cody laughed and gave Cheyenne an exaggerated look of helplessness. Then he turned to the crowd and shook his head — playing with them. "No dunk tank," he shouted. "I hate cold water."

That started a chant from his players. "Dunk tank . . . dunk tank . . . dunk tank . . ."

Finally when Cody had gotten them appropriately worked up, he waved them off. "Fine . . . you got me!" He threw both arms in the air in mock surrender and walked to the tank. The mayor met him there and helped unlatch the top chamber.

"You're a good sport." The mayor's eyes were kind, his words this time for Cody alone. "Breath of fresh air for this town. A real answer to prayer."

"Thanks." Cody hesitated long enough to look at the man's eyes. He wanted the mayor to know how much his words meant. "I'm glad I'm here. I love these kids."

"The feeling's mutual." The mayor laughed. "I haven't seen this much excitement in Lyle for a long time."

"Well . . ." Cody grinned and looked at the ice water below him. "I guess that means there'll be a long line of people trying to dunk me."

"Yes." The mayor raised his brow. "I don't think it'll take long."

A few of the players went first, and the mayor took the mic again. "Rise to the challenge, men," he shouted. "Back up ten yards. Take the high road."

But not one of them hit the target hard enough to knock Cody into the water. It was Cheyenne's turn, and the mayor moved her up to the line where most people would throw from. She set her cane down as the team gathered around, cheering her on.

With the softball in her hand, she looked at the crowd, clearly enjoying the moment. Then she reared back and threw the ball dead on target. Cody caught a quick breath as he plunged into the ice-cold water. His laughter came so hard and fast he barely noticed the shock to his system. In a hurry he scrambled back to the trapdoor and down the ladder, where he made a grandiose bow for the cheering crowd. He caught Cheyenne's full-faced grin, the way her eyes held his, and he wondered if his racing heart was because of the ice water . . . or because of his feelings for the girl across the field.

Long after the picnic was over, after he had taken Cheyenne home and brought DeMetri back to the apartment so they could finish packing for camp, Cody replayed the day in his mind. Every wonderful detail about it. The way the town supported him and the team, the look in Cheyenne's eyes . . . and the quiet words of support from the mayor.

You're a breath of fresh air for this town. A

real answer to prayer. Cody felt the man's approval to his core. Like his counselor had told him a week ago, the position at Lyle was better for him than any therapy. Whereas Bailey no longer needed him, as coach at Lyle High, Cody had a purpose. The kids needed him and Cheyenne needed him. And somewhere in his brain those single truths caused his time in Iraq to be worthwhile. Which meant he didn't need to think about the past or dwell on it or relive it. Very simply those days had led him to this.

Where maybe God had planned for him to be all along.

SIXTEEN

Her performance wasn't halfway finished, but Bailey wondered how she could feel so miserable dancing on Broadway. She hoped no one in the audience could tell what she was thinking while she danced and sang and smiled her heart out alongside her cast-mates. They were almost finished with "Welcome to the Sixties," but all Bailey could think about was Francesca, and how somewhere in the dark recesses of the theater, the woman was watching her, judging her, evaluating whether she would stay another week.

Before she went on stage, Bailey sought out the director and explained that she had signed up for private dance instruction. The idea of training had come to her on the flight back from Indiana. Something she could do to show she was serious about "Four mornings a week I'll work on my technique."

Francesca said nothing, just looked at Bailey like she was weighing the worth of the effort she was making. When the space between them remained silent, Bailey forged ahead. She'd come up with the plan on the flight home from Indiana. And she also wanted to let Francesca know her concerns about Chrissy.

"I think she's anorexic." Bailey didn't hint around, though she'd kept her tone quiet. "She says she's getting help, but . . . I wanted someone else to talk to her. Just in case."

Francesca's response was the reason Bailey usually kept her distance from the woman outside rehearsals. She lowered her chin and raised her eyebrows. "About the dance instruction . . . it's about time." She barely paused. "About Chrissy . . . like I already asked you . . . mind your own business. Don't judge the cast."

The conversation played again in Bailey's mind as they finished the number. Chrissy was dancing beside her, and she seemed to work harder than usual. She was thinner than she'd been a few weeks ago — but only Bailey seemed worried. Before they stepped on stage earlier that night, Bailey caught Chrissy taking a small fistful of white pills.

"Why do you do that?" Bailey tried to

keep her tone kind, not accusing. "I mean . . . aren't you afraid of what they might do?"

"They give me energy." Chrissy smiled in a way that was more condescending than kind. "You wouldn't understand."

"Of course I would." Bailey hated that her friend thought she didn't struggle. "I'm not as good as you. Which means I have to work harder." She kept her voice to a whisper since they were in the wings, ready to perform. "Of course I get tired."

"Not like I do." Chrissy's expression told her the conversation was over. "It's a hard business for most of us." Her smile held a sadness that she had never quite talked about. "My resume doesn't have a movie credit with Brandon Paul."

"Chrissy . . ." Bailey felt like crying. "Can we get past that? Really?"

Her friend's eyes held an apology for the first time Bailey could remember. "I'm sorry." She released a shaky breath. "It's not your fault. You've lived a charmed life, Bailey. That's not how it is for me. It's a fight, that's all. Life. All of life."

Bailey had thought about giving Chrissy a Bible verse, something from Philippians or James or Ephesians that might help her hold onto the reality that with Christ there was peace and hope, that the battle of life didn't have to be fought alone. But as soon as she opened her mouth, she changed her mind. She took a step closer. "Is there . . . anything I can do?"

Even as Bailey asked the question she could feel the Lord prompting her: *Daughter, take her hands . . . pray with her. If you don't pray with Chrissy, who will?*

But again she pushed the thought away. She couldn't talk about God too much to Chrissy, couldn't host a Bible study with the cast, or any such thing. Not yet. Otherwise they would only push her away. Then they'd never be open to hearing about Jesus.

The music played loud and fast. It was the most difficult part of the song, the section Francesca rehearsed often. The beat was intense, the words of the song rapid fire. Only dancers in great shape could dance like this and still belt the words. *Push through,* she told herself. *Sharper movements . . . a bigger smile. Francesca was watching. God, . . . let me shine for You. I can only do this in Your strength . . .*

The audience was fairly full, better than usual for a Friday night — especially in the last few months. The music rose a notch: "So let go, let go of the past now . . . say hello to this red carpet life . . . welcome to the sixties." Bailey sang for all she was worth. The stage was hot from the heat of the dancers and the sweltering humidity that had fallen over the city that day. As the song played on, Bailey caught another glance at Chrissy. She looked less able to keep up, and at one point she nearly stumbled.

Bailey tried to stay in character, but her eyes darted to the wings. Did the stage manager know something was wrong with one of the dancers? She looked back at Chrissy, and saw that her face was pale . . . gray even. Bailey danced closer and — her smile intact — she whispered, "Are you okay?"

But before Chrissy could answer, her knees buckled and she collapsed.

"Chrissy!" Bailey dropped to the floor beside her friend. Then she yelled to the wings. "Hurry! Someone help!"

For a few seconds the music played on as the orchestra realized what had happened. Then very quickly the theater fell quiet and a gasp came from the audience. Bailey was still crouched at Chrissy's side and now the others gathered around, sweaty and breathing hard from the performance. Bailey looked at Chrissy, and then at the stagehand running in from the wings. "Call 9 – 1 – 1!"

Bailey barely finished her sentence when the velvet curtain came crashing down, creating privacy for her and the rest of the cast as they circled the fallen dancer.

"Chrissy, can you hear me?" She took her friend's hand, but the girl was nonresponsive. She looked closely and it seemed that Chrissy was breathing. Her chest still rose with every breath, but she looked very sick. "She needs paramedics!" Bailey stood, searching the wings once more for someone who might do something. "Hurry . . . I'm not sure she's breathing!"

The stage manager ran onto the stage, a cell phone in his hand. He ordered the cast to quiet down, and he gave Bailey a stern look. "Never . . . never talk about 9 – 1 – 1 when we have a full house!" He knelt down next to Chrissy and as he did, another production assistant ran out with what looked like a cold washcloth. The stage manager pressed the cloth to Chrissy's head and motioned to the rest of the cast. "Take five . . . drink some water and get back out on stage. The show will go on."

"Is she breathing?" One of the other dancers looked as worried as Bailey.

"Of course she's breathing." The stage manager waved his hand around angrily. "It's heat exhaustion. Nothing more." He waved the cast back. "Everything's fine."

Even as he said the words, a booming voice assured the audience that they were experiencing a cast issue, but that everything was okay. "Please, ladies and gentlemen, use this brief intermission to visit our lobby or the restrooms. The show will resume in ten minutes."

Ten minutes? Bailey could hardly believe what was happening around her. Chrissy was still motionless on the stage floor, but most of the cast followed the manager's direction and disappeared into the wings for water.

"Chrissy." The man brought his face close to hers. His tone softened considerably. "You're okay, Chrissy . . . we're getting help for you."

Bailey thought Chrissy's complexion looked worse — blue around her lips even. "Have you felt for her pulse?" Panic coursed through her. What if this was more serious than the stage manager thought? Bailey had missed the chance to pray for her earlier, so she wasn't going to miss this one. Not caring about the other cast members still gathered around she closed her eyes and put her hand on Chrissy's shoulder. "Lord . . . be with our friend. Help her, Father. Touch her with Your healing hand,

and let her feel Your presence. Please, God . . ."

"Bailey . . ." The stage manager sounded slightly more tolerant. "You need to get out of the way. The paramedics are here."

She opened her eyes and saw two men walk on stage carrying a stretcher. Did the people in the lobby buying popcorn know how serious things were for the blonde dancer? She stepped back, silently praying, still asking God to spare Chrissy . . . to allow more time so Bailey could do what she should've already done: start a Bible study . . . invite Chrissy . . . offer to pray with her.

Please God . . . I need more time . . .

The paramedics raced through an initial check, talking quietly and urgently between themselves. Bailey couldn't hear everything they said, but certain words stood out . . . phrases that terrified her. *Irregular heartbeat . . . shallow breathing.* When they lifted her onto the stretcher, the face of the one in front was lined with concern. "Be ready to start CPR in the ambulance."

CPR? Bailey felt dizzy, terrified at what was happening. This was much more serious than the stage manager thought. Suddenly she remembered the pills, the bottle Chrissy had put back in her purse. "Hold

311

on!" She ran after the paramedics. "She took pills. Before the show."

They were rushing her to the ambulance, making it hard for Bailey to keep up. By then a police officer backstage was talking to a few of the cast members, writing down notes. "Tell him," one of the paramedics shouted. And with that they hurried out the side stage door with Chrissy motionless on the stretcher.

This couldn't be happening . . . Bailey's heart thudded hard inside her as she ran back to the girls' dressing room and searched under the table. Most of them didn't lock up their things, so it took only a few seconds to find Chrissy's purse. The bottle of pills was still there near the top, and Bailey grabbed it, running it back to the green room where the police officer was still taking notes. "Here." She handed the pills to the man, breathless. "She took these. Several of them . . . right before the show."

He glanced at the label, and then he hurried from the room. Before he left he looked back over his shoulder and spoke straight to Bailey. "Thank you . . . for saying something." With that he was gone.

Bailey stood alone at the center of the room, the rest of the cast looking at her, ogling her with glances of disdain. She couldn't tell if they were angry because she'd betrayed Chrissy's secret . . . or if they were afraid because maybe she knew secrets about them. Secrets she might tell the police officer if he came back around. Or maybe they were disgusted with her because she hadn't said something sooner — the way she was disgusted with herself.

Whatever it was, she didn't have time to think it through. Before anyone could say a word, the stage manager appeared and clapped his hands. "Hurry people . . . places . . . let's pick up at the top of the number."

And like that, they were herded back on stage, smiles ready, waiting for the music to begin. Bailey felt horrified. She wanted to run outside and grab a cab to the hospital — whatever hospital they were taking Chrissy to. What if she wasn't okay? What if they couldn't get her heartbeat right? She might need someone beside her, someone to help her through. Bailey concentrated, trying to remember the steps to the dance, the words to the song.

The music began and the warm announcer's voice assured them the issue with the cast had been dealt with. Everything was fine. With that, the curtain lifted, and Bailey scanned the audience. Men and women, children . . . all were back in their seats, fresh candy and drinks in their hands. As if it were an everyday occurrence to see a dancer collapse midshow at a Broadway performance.

Bailey couldn't remember a moment of the show after that. She slipped into a sort of autopilot, the whole time praying for Chrissy. Not until the show was over did a handful of the cast share the fact that, yes, they were frightened for Chrissy.

"She's been taking those pills for almost a year." Stefano's tone was grave. "Who wants to come with me to the hospital?"

"I will." Gerald was quick to jump in. He grabbed his backpack and swung it onto his shoulder. "She didn't look good. Her color."

Bailey ran a few steps toward the dressing room. "I'll come too." She grabbed her bag while Stefano and Gerald rounded up another dancer. "I have the hospital address." Gerald handed it to the driver. "Hurry, please."

They rode in silence, and when they arrived at the hospital Bailey noticed the looks they got as they rushed into the emergency room. Only then did she remember they were still in costume and full makeup. Stefano explained to the man at the front desk that they were friends of Chrissy's, the dancer who had been brought in an hour earlier.

Bailey tried to read the man's expression, and she was almost sure she saw a shadow fall across his eyes. "Does she have family here . . . anyone related to her?"

Again Bailey realized how little she'd invested in her friend. She had noticed the girl's thin body, the way she seemed to struggle with anorexia — yet she had never asked about Chrissy's home life. Was she from New York? Did she have parents or siblings? Bailey had no idea, and as she looked at the other dancers with her she saw that they shared the same blank look.

Gerald answered for all of them. "I'm not sure."

"Very well." The man at the front desk pursed his lips.

"We can call our director." Stefano nodded at the others, his tone panicked. "Someone should know."

The man nodded. "I'd appreciate that." He stood. "Now, if you'll excuse me. I'll . . . let you know if I hear anything about your friend."

They sat back down and Bailey did what she should've done earlier that day. She looked at the dancers in the small circle around her and held out her hands. "Let's pray . . . she needs us."

The three cast members looked at each other and then at Bailey, and with a sort of confused reluctance, they did as she said. They linked hands, and let Bailey lead them in prayer. Every word felt forced and stilted, because while she prayed she couldn't get past the fact that it was too late. She'd had her chance with Chrissy and she'd missed it. "Please God . . . we want more time with Chrissy . . . help her, we ask You."

Bailey had no idea how long they sat there. After half an hour several other cast-mates joined them, and eventually the stage manager arrived. He had Chrissy's file and he gave the man at the front desk the information he wanted. Her family was from Montana. There was only one phone number listed in her emergency contacts, and no one was answering.

But in the end, the details didn't matter. A doctor came into the waiting room and asked if he could talk to anyone who was there for Chrissy Stonelake. Bailey realized then that she hadn't even known her friend's last name. In her worry about fitting in and trying to blend with her cast, and because of her own hurt feelings from the way she felt she was being treated, she hadn't even cared enough to ask that single crucial detail: Chrissy's last name.

The doctor's look was stonelike, and as they followed him into a small room, Bailey already knew. She knew with everything in her. When they were all in the small waiting room, the doctor shut the door and for what felt like a long moment, he looked at them, at each of them. Then he sighed and shook his head. "I'm sorry . . . we weren't able to save her."

"What?" Stefano screamed the word. He grabbed at the doctor's white coat. "That's crazy. She fainted . . . she's going to be fine!"

The stage manager put his arm around Stefano and drew him away from the doctor. Around the room several of the cast started to cry, hands to their faces, the shock hitting them full force. Bailey felt sick to her stomach. She turned toward the wall and let her head rest against the cool plaster. This wasn't happening . . . it couldn't be happening. She'd missed her chance with Chrissy. More than that she'd prayed with her castmates, and Chrissy had still died.

Bailey wasn't sure how she stayed on her feet, how she kept from running into the bathroom and throwing up. Chrissy was dead? This couldn't be real . . . it was a nightmare. That had to be it. The doctor was saying something about the pills . . . the white pills . . . and Bailey tried to focus, tried to understand him. Because Chrissy wasn't the only one taking the pills. Bailey had seen other girls popping them. Or something similar to them. She turned around, still leaning on the wall, and clutched her stomach, her eyes on the doctor.

"We see this with dancers once in a while." He pressed his lips together, his expression grave. "Chrissy was taking an amphetamine, an upper. A diet pill, basically. From the tests we ran, she didn't have proper nutrients for her heart to function — not in quite a while. We aren't sure how many pills she took, but without food in her stomach they created a deadly effect."

"So . . . was it . . . heatstroke?" The stage manager looked worried. Bailey hated the possibility, but there was no way around it. The man was clearly trying to determine if the theater company was at fault.

"This wasn't caused by heat." The doctor looked grim again. "The stimulants caused her heart to go into an arrhythmia, a rhythm too fast to move the blood through her body. Someone else might've handled it, but Chrissy's anorexia complicated things. In effect, when the heart is pumping that fast it's only fluttering. She died of heart failure."

Around her several of the girls were softly crying . . . Gerald and Stefano too. A couple of the guys folded their arms and stared at the floor. The doctor apologized again. "Take a few minutes. We don't need this room for a while." When he left, a few of the girls wailed their grief out loud, shouting that it wasn't possible, that she couldn't be dead.

But she was, and the reality shook Bailey like nothing in her life ever had. God had prompted her to talk in more depth to Chrissy, to pray with her, and now it was too late. She had let Chrissy down . . . let God down. Her troubled friend, the one so defeated by the fight of life was no more. The tears began to fall for Bailey, and slowly she dropped to the floor, pulling her knees to her face. She sat there weeping. *Why, God? Why didn't You give Chrissy a second chance? Is it all my fault? Because I didn't pray with her?* Bailey shook with grief, furious with herself and desperate to have Chrissy back. But that wasn't going to happen. Chrissy was gone, the girl whose heart had shouted for help every time Bailey saw her.

The truth was as painful as the loss of

Chrissy. Bailey had cared more about fitting in than speaking truth to a girl who desperately needed it. *God, I've failed You . . . I failed Chrissy. What am I supposed to do now?* She had failed at the biggest God assignment of her life, and now Bailey could only let her tears fall, let the sobs overtake her. Chrissy was gone . . . there would be no second chance, no time to pray for her or invite her to a Bible study. Bailey cried as she had never cried before. For a girl who had tried to take on the rigors of Broadway and failed. A girl who had starved for love — the sort of love Bailey could've told her about. The only love that could ever truly satisfy: God's love. But Bailey hadn't prayed with her or told her about the Bible or asked her the deeper questions. Her heart felt like it lay in a million pieces on the floor, because Chrissy was gone. And on top of all the ways she hadn't told Chrissy about God's love, she had missed something else too.

She hadn't even remembered the girl's last name.

SEVENTEEN

Butler University was situated on one of the most scenic campuses in all of central Indiana. But more than that, it was outside Indianapolis far enough that it felt isolated among the cornfields and sweeping panoramas. Cody took in the view as the bus pulled into the school's parking lot. This week would be about football, yes. But if God had His way, it would be about a lot more than that.

"Okay, men . . . let's wake up." Cody stood and his voice boomed all the way to the back of the bus. They'd left Lyle an hour ago at seven in the morning, and most of the guys had fallen asleep. But registration was in thirty minutes. "Come on . . . let's go . . . welcome to football camp. Wake up, men . . . hustle!" His assistants, Coach Schroeder and Coach Braswell, helped round up the guys, and together they gathered gear and plodded their way across the parking lot.

This early in the morning the heat hadn't set in, but already the day promised to be sweltering. Cody had plenty of powdered sports drink, and three five-gallon containers which they would keep full for the guys. He didn't want his guys dealing with dehydration. "This way." He took the lead. He'd been here a week ago to scout out the campus. He knew the layout of the university, where their dorms were, and the path from the dorms to the field — where registration would take place.

As the guys climbed the stairs to the dorms, they seemed to wake up a little more. Only a few of them were seniors, old enough to remember the coaching era of John Brown, back when the players still believed in themselves. That was the last time the Lyle Buckaroos had been to football camp. Cody felt sorry for Coach Oliver, because the man had missed this experience.

"Man, look at this." Marcos Brown walked with a few players just ahead of Cody. "This place is sick . . . I didn't know college was this nice."

The comment was poignant. If something didn't change for Marcos, his grades were so bad outside football camp he wouldn't set foot on a college campus. *We can't have that,* he told himself. *God . . . give me more than the X's and O's this week. Please, Father . . .*

I have all this figured out, my son . . . I know what you need before you ask it.

Cody felt himself relax under the certainty of the response. God knew what he needed before he asked for it . . . that was the point of the Bible verse he and DeMetri had read this morning before they headed out to Lyle.

"Alright," Cody read from a clipboard as they reached the second-floor dorms. "Room assignments are set, so don't look to switch and don't complain." He had to be stern, had to get them focused. "Listen for your name, take your gear, meet up, and find your dorm room."

The guys had come a long way since Cody took over, but they still weren't a team. It was something Cody had noticed yesterday at the barbecue. After the dunk tank excitement had died down, the guys hung in cliques of twos and threes. Cody thought it strange, because these kids had grown up together. Probably since kindergarten. But then, no one had ever required that they be a team.

Until this week.

When everyone was situated, Cody led the

guys down to the field where they would check in. He met up with the coach from the college at registration. "Lyle High School, checking in, sir."

"Lyle." The man looked up, a twinkle in his eye. He gave a shake of his head. "So you're the brave kid who took over for Oliver."

Cody wasn't offended. "Yes, sir." He reached out and shook the man's hand. "Cody Coleman."

"Brave." The man chuckled and marked something down on the list in front of him. "People have all but forgotten about Lyle."

"Yes, sir." Cody felt a rustling of anger stir inside his heart. These were his players the man was talking about. "That was the old Lyle."

Cody's tone must've gotten the man's attention. He looked up, squinting at Cody against the bright morning sun. "Okay, then." He nodded to a man who was probably his assistant. "Coach here has a welcome packet for each of your players."

And with that the camp experience began in earnest. Inside the packet each guy received a T-shirt and a folder, to track progress made over the week. Sixteen teams were registered for camp, and half an hour later the college coaches in charge gathered them at the fifty-yard line.

"This will be one of the toughest weeks of your life." The head coach, Liam Henry, was a veteran, a stocky man with a big growly voice and a reputation for winning football games. "You'll have mandatory group training sessions, and time with your teams." He explained where the various fields were located. During their appointed sessions, each team would have access to half a field.

The camp was organized. Cody loved that. It left him time to think about his players, what they needed to gain this week to be successful. If they were going to leave here a team, the work ahead was daunting.

Coach Henry wrapped up his talk and allowed five minutes for water and dressing out. The Lyle team wore matching T-shirts, navy and white, the Buckaroo colors.

"Come on, guys . . . get a drink. Let's be first on the field." Cody stayed with them, encouraging them. He looked for signs that they cared about each other, and again he didn't see any. Still, they managed to be third on the field after the break.

Better than last, Cody told himself.

Stretches came first. Coach Henry walked the lines of players shouting truth at them. "Being limber and warmed up is crucial.

325

No one ever took football seriously if they didn't know about stretching." He had them pair up and work together, helping each other stretch their hamstrings and back muscles.

Stretching led to footwork, monotonous movements that caused Cody to watch his players closely. Were they on board with Coach Henry's aggressive approach? Were they listening? The coach was going on, telling them about the daily competition. "Every day we'll award points." He stared them down. "The team with the most points wins first place for that day."

The glare of the sun made it hard to see, but Cody squinted at his guys. A few looked down, as if they weren't even here. Arnie Hurley whispered to Joel Butler, a lanky wide receiver from the junior class. Joel's parents were in the middle of a messy divorce. Other than DeMetri and a few others, Cody's team treated this opening session like a morning biology class.

High school coaches were allowed to walk the lines, casting glances and keeping their players in order. Cody headed toward Arnie and Joel, and the boys noticed him. Immediately they paid attention. The other players seemed to pick up their pace.

Even still, by morning break — after their

first team session — Cody wasn't impressed. "Listen up." He called his guys over, and when they didn't run, he blew the whistle around his neck. The sound got their attention and most of them hurried into place in front of him. "Listen." He didn't want to get angry. But if they didn't find something special at camp, the time would be a waste. "This isn't the picnic. We have to be serious."

He called his assistants over. "Everyone knows their playbook, right?"

A murmur of *yes*'s and *sort of*'s came from the crowd. Cody tried to keep his patience. "We will know our playbook by tomorrow. If we don't, we will use every minute of our team time to run the perimeter of the college." He looked over the players, catching the surprise in some of their eyes. He hadn't been this strict with them before. There had been no need. "Does everyone understand?"

Again the response was weak and mumbled. DeMetri shot an angry look at his team. "Did you hear, Coach? That's not how you answer, y'all. Understand?"

Cody swallowed the smile that played in his heart. DeMetri was a leader. He needed several of those — but this was a start. The sort of beginning his team would need if the week were to matter. "Smitty is right!" Again Cody's voice boomed. He remembered Jim's advice. *Take charge . . . let them know you're in charge. They have to know what you expect.* Cody lowered his clipboard. "When I ask you a question, you respond as a team. You say, 'Yes, sir.' Is that understood?"

The response was better than before, but nowhere near where Cody wanted it. He raised his voice again. "I said . . . is that understood?"

This time most of the team figured out what they were doing wrong. Their voices came together again in a fairly loud chorus of "Yes, sir," and "Yes, Coach."

Cody caught the satisfied nods from his assistant coaches. They were making progress. "Good. Now let's get to work."

The afternoon teamwork was long and arduous, and temperatures hovered in the high nineties. Cody gave them numerous water breaks, and at the last one DeMetri approached him. "Guys are going through the motions." He looked ready to cry, sweat pouring down his face. "I've been praying for this team . . . for you . . . for all of us for such a long time." He kicked at a clump of grass and put his hands on his hips. "They need to care more."

"They will." He winked at his player . . . the kid who had become like a younger brother. "Keep praying, Smitty."

DeMetri didn't look sure. He pursed his lips and blew out hard, sweat spraying. Anger played out in his expression, and he shook his legs, trying to stay loose. Finally he nodded, his intensity stronger than before, but more controlled. "Yes, sir. I'll pray."

"I'll count on that."

Cody watched him return to the others, his shoulders back, his purpose clear. During the last set of drills, Cody let DeMetri and two other guys lead the team. He called the other coaches over and the three of them huddled off by themselves. "I need to know about the players . . . whatever there is to know."

The two assistants looked at each other and then at Cody. "You would know more than us." Schroeder took his baseball cap from his head and smoothed his hair back, clearly at a loss. "We only just started coaching."

"Not about their playing ability." Cody kept his voice low, between just the three of them. "About them as people. Who's struggling with what . . . where the challenges are . . . that sort of thing." Cody explained what he knew. "DeMetri's mom is in prison again . . . he's living in the guest room of my apartment." He paused, making sure they understood. "Arnie's sleeping with his girlfriend . . . talk is she could be pregnant even now . . . that sort of thing."

The men nodded, and Coach Braswell took the lead. "I've been teaching at Lyle for six years. I've watched these kids grow up. Wells and Bronson . . . their dads are out of work. The bank's trying to foreclose last I heard."

"Larry Sanders' little sister has bone cancer." Coach Schroeder's eyes softened. "His home life's a mess."

"And Terry Allen's house burned down last month. The whole family's living with his grandpa." A knowing filled Braswell's eyes. "For the most part the kids don't have a clue what the guy next to them is going through. It's a small town, but people are very private. No one talks . . . no one complains." He nodded slowly. "I see what you mean."

Cody felt satisfied. This was what he figured — the guys were each dealing with something. Same as any teenager on any other football team. "Alright . . . this is what I'm talking about." He looked over his shoulder at the guys on the field. "If those guys knew these things about each other, they'd stop feeling like a bunch of individuals from Lyle. And start feeling like a family."

Slowly the idea began to make sense. Cody watched the change happen in the faces of his assistants. Schroeder nodded big. "I get it. Like maybe they need a reason to care."

"Exactly." Cody stared at the players running drills on the field. "Now all we need is a plan."

That afternoon he called Jim Flanigan. "I heard one of the guys on the Colts has a foundation to help high school football teams with small budgets. Is that right?"

"Absolutely." Jim explained the player and his charity. They talked for fifteen minutes before Cody's idea fully came together. After another half hour and a series of phone calls, Cody couldn't have been happier.

Now it was a matter of praying that his idea would work.

EIGHTEEN

That night after dinner, when the guys were exhausted from another group session, and still one more team practice, Cody called a meeting. With everyone in a room on the first floor of the dorms he set his plan in motion.

"We have a chance to help someone." He looked around the room, studying their eyes. Only a few of them showed even a slight bit of interest. Cody reminded himself to be patient. They were tired, but that didn't matter. They needed to respond when they were tired or they'd never respond at all. "I didn't hear your answer."

The guys rallied, pulling together a mediocre, "Yes, sir."

"What?"

This time they were louder, more together. "Yes, sir!"

"Okay, then . . . here's the deal." He shared a quick look with his coaches, both anchored against the wall near the door, their arms crossed. They believed in his plan. It was their job to watch for dissenters — since it only took one for the plan not to work. "There's a football team in central Indiana . . . the coach wants to keep their name anonymous." Cody had rehearsed this part. He kept eye contact, his tone intense. "These guys have been hit by so many problems they're thinking of not playing this year. They aren't sure they'll have a team."

The guys shifted, curious and maybe even slightly irritated. DeMetri raised his hand. "Do we play this team, Coach?" He looked at Arnie and Marcos. "I mean, are we supposed to help the competition?"

"No." Cody shook his head, adamant. "They're not on our schedule."

Again the guys shifted, wary, their eyes on Cody.

"Every day we'll have a chance to win three-thousand dollars for one of the players on that team — money that could make the difference for whether that player stays with football or not." He paced to the other side of the room, looking each guy straight on. "The prize money is being put up by a player from the Indianapolis Colts, and it involves only our team." He stopped and folded his arms. "Here's the catch. We can only win the money on one condition — we have to take first place that day here at camp. Every day Coach Henry picks Lyle as the number one school, every day Lyle has the most points for the day — we'll earn three-thousand dollars for one of the players' families on that Indiana team."

The indifference on the guys' faces confirmed Cody's fears about this stage of his plan. Why should they care about some other team . . . or the problems of a group of guys they didn't even know? Cody took a deep breath and made it more personal. "Tomorrow we raise money for an eight-year-old girl with bone cancer." Cody paused. "She has already lost most of her right leg, and now the cancer has spread."

He was careful not to stare, but out of the corner of his eyes Cody saw Larry Sanders hang his head. "This little girl's family needs three-thousand dollars for an experimental medication that might . . . it just might save her life." He paused, his voice ringing through the room. "Imagine if that little girl was your sister. Missing school . . . missing time on the playground with her friends . . . struggling with crutches and hoping to see another summer." His voice fell, and he struggled with his own emotions. "Three-thousand dollars, men. You can win that money for her tomorrow."

Suddenly, with the slow certainty of a sunrise, Cody watched the message begin to sink in. The guys stood straight, their expressions intense. A few of them even had tears in their eyes. "Are we ready to win this thing tomorrow? For that little girl?"

The guys shifted, restless, like they were ready to get started. "Yes, sir!"

Their voices came together in a resounding response that caught even Cody off guard. He clapped a few times. "Alright . . . let's bring it in." They gathered around him more quickly than they had at any time that day, their hands high at the center of the circle. "Dear God . . . use us. Bring us together and use us. That's all we ask, Lord. In Jesus' name, amen." He paused briefly. "Whose way?"

"His way!" The guys were loud . . . intense because of what they now knew about the girl with cancer.

"Whose way?" Cody's voice boomed out from among them.

"His way!"

"Three thousand . . . on three . . ." Cody didn't let up. "One . . . two . . . three . . ."

"Three thousand!" The words were a cry, a shout that echoed against the walls of the room.

Cody could see the smiles on the faces of his coaches. "Alright, men, let's get some rest. We have a big day ahead of us."

After praying much of the night for his guys, the next day was like a scene from a feel-good movie. From the moment the Lyle guys began stretching drills after breakfast until the last play of the afternoon scrimmage, his Buckaroos played with a heart and desire Cody had never seen. Arnie threw passes even he hadn't known he was capable of, and Marcos blocked like his life depended on it. Only a few times did Cody have to call the guys together and remind them, saying things like, "She'll never run like the other girls . . . but at least she has a chance to live. It's up to you, men. Help her live! One . . . two . . . three . . ."

"Three thousand!" Fire filled the guys' expressions, and their eyes shone with a determination nothing could thwart. They were playing their hearts out for a little girl they didn't know. The other players at the camp had no idea what had gotten into the Lyle guys, but as Coach Henry announced the winner for the day no one was surprised.

"Our first place team is Lyle High." His gruff disposition was gone, and a mix of humor and bewilderment filled his voice. "Not sure if maybe you Lyle boys got things mixed up . . . this isn't the state play-offs."

A round of lighthearted laughter came from the players — even the Buckaroos. Marcos Brown walked to the front of the group to accept the Sunday trophy. He held it up and there was no mistaking the glimmer in his eyes. Marcos was fighting back tears. Cody understood why. Lyle wasn't a wealthy town . . . none of the football players had ever made that much money . . . or even imagined it. But together they had done what might've felt impossible just twenty-four hours earlier. They'd raised three-thousand dollars for a sick little girl, the sister of a football player they didn't even know.

That night, when the celebrating had let up, Cody told them their next assignment. "There's a guy on that team, his house burned down. Family lost everything." This time it was Terry Allen who briefly hung his head. But he looked up quickly, intent about the task at hand. "Habitat for Humanity is going to rebuild their house . . . but they need money for supplies. Three-thousand dollars, men. That's what it will take to get them started, to make sure this football player and his family have a roof over their heads as winter hits in a few months."

This time the guys rounded up more

quickly, and their voices rang with a pride that hadn't been there the day before. Because now they knew they were capable, and the same was true the next day as they intensified their efforts for every drill, every session. "A roof for the winter . . . come on, men," Cody yelled a few times throughout the day. "One . . . two . . . three . . ."

"Three thousand!"

No one was surprised when Lyle again took the Monday trophy, and so the pattern was set. Tuesday and Wednesday they played for the family of a football player who needed three-thousand dollars to make back payments and keep their house from being taken away. "They can be homeless, or they can keep their houses." Cody kept finding new levels of passion for the work at hand. "It's up to you, men!"

The Lyle team worked harder. Tuesday's trophy and Wednesday's trophy, and on Thursday they won the money for a kid whose mom was in prison, a kid with no clothes, and no way to take the weekly trip to visit his mother behind bars. "Bus money so a football player on this team can talk to his mom once a week!" Cody allowed the incredulousness to slip into his tone. "Can you imagine that? Not having your mom there when you get home from school? We can do this, men . . . we can."

By the time Friday rolled around, the guys were thicker than brothers. Not only because they'd found new levels of effort and because they'd won a combined fifteen-thousand dollars for the families of a bunch of football players they didn't know. But because other teams were rising to the challenge, doubling their efforts, doing whatever they could to take the last day's trophy away from Lyle. This time the prize money would go to counseling for a handful of players whose grades were too low to get them into college.

"These are guys who have no chance without a college education . . . and no chance at college unless they get some help." Cody paced in front of the guys that morning before stretching drills. "Someday you might find yourself getting a home loan or a doctor's appointment, and the guy helping you will be standing there — not homeless on a bench somewhere — because of what you men do today." He was talking loud, underlining the importance of their efforts. "Do you understand? How important this is?"

"Yes, sir!" Their answer was crisp and bellowing, in complete unison.

"Okay . . ." Cody stifled the smile bursting through him. "One . . . two . . . three . . ."

"Three thousand!"

That day the competition was closer than it had been all week, and what Cody saw made him and the other coaches watch in silent awe. The guys pushed each other on, refusing to let one of them lag behind. "Come on," DeMetri shouted at Arnie. "Don't give up. Those guys are counting on us!" It was a scene that was repeated throughout the day even as Burton High made a serious run at the Friday trophy.

But when Coach Henry took the platform that night, he only shook his head, dazed. "I've been running this camp for more than a decade." He looked across the sea of football players. "I've never seen anyone play with more intensity than Lyle High played this week. For the first time in the camp's history — first place goes to the same school all six days. The winner of the Friday trophy is the Lyle High Buckaroos!"

The guys looked back at him, and Cody understood. He nodded his approval, and the entire group ran to the front to accept their prize. As they jumped around, holding the trophy overhead, their faces lit up with smiles and cheers, only Cody and his other coaches understood what they were celebrating. Not until that night did Cody call a meeting in the same room where they'd met six days ago.

"I'm very . . . very proud of you, men." Cody choked up as he faced them. "You proved what you're capable of . . . and you proved how much you care." He paused, hoping he could get through the next part without breaking down. "I want to tell you something about that team, the team you've been fighting for and playing your hearts out for all week long."

The guys were seated on the floor, a camaraderie between them that hadn't been there when they arrived at camp. They looked interested, but not overly so. It didn't matter what team they had competed for . . . but only that they had done so. A group of lives would be changed because of their efforts this week. That was the important thing. Cody could see that in their faces. Clearly they had no idea what was coming.

"That team . . . the one you won eighteen-thousand dollars for . . . they're here at camp this week."

Cody's players looked slightly baffled, and a whisper of voices came from a few of them as they tried to guess which team here at camp might've struggled with so much adversity. When he had their attention again,

Cody dropped his voice — low enough so the guys had to strain to hear him. "What's amazing about this team, is that only the coaches knew about their troubles. Guys were seated next to each other this week, blocking tacklers side by side . . . throwing touchdown passes to guys they didn't know were struggling."

He shrugged, never breaking eye contact. "The team was on the verge of collapse . . . guys ready to give up. But no one knew." He let his voice rise a little. "You know why? Because they weren't a team. They were a bunch of guys who wanted to play football. But they didn't talk . . . didn't share . . . didn't care at all about the man on their right or their left."

The room was dead silent, each player waiting to find out which team they'd competed against that week that might've been so unaware of their own struggles. Finally, when Cody couldn't wait another minute, he looked at each of them and nodded with a certainty that hinted at what was to come. "That team is you, men. It's you."

"What?" DeMetri's question summed up the expression on all their faces. They couldn't have looked more surprised if Cody had told them they were going to grow wings. Their mouths hung open and a few of them looked down: Larry Sanders and Terry Allen . . . Wells and Bronson. Guys who had known they were up against the same struggles someone else was facing, but who'd never imagined the team with all those troubles was their own.

"Look around the room, men." Cody's voice was loud with concern, his tone a reflection of how much he cared. "Sanders!" He walked to the tight end and helped him to his feet. Then he put his arm around the kid's shoulders. "Tell the guys about your sister."

Tears spilled onto Sanders' cheeks, and he rubbed at them with his fist for a few seconds. His face was red, but when he had control he looked at his teammates. "She . . . she has bone cancer. She needs a new medicine."

Around the room several of the guys were quietly crying, not the type of crying that showed weakness, but the kind that proved commitment and concern. Sanders sniffed loudly and nodded. "Thanks guys . . . the money . . . it might save her life."

Before Sanders could sit down, the other guys rose, clapping for their teammate. They surrounded him, patting him on the back and hugging him around the neck. The message didn't need any words. Whatever

Sanders and his sister were going through, the team was there for him. By the time Sanders sat down, he was no longer among fellow football players.

He was among brothers.

"Terry Allen . . . come here please." One at a time Cody brought up the players and allowed them the chance to explain their situations, a chance to thank their teammates for raising money that might mean they would keep their homes or have a warm place to sleep that winter, money that would keep them in school and give them a chance at college.

When he called up DeMetri, the junior was already crying, his voice too choked to talk right away. The others came close, supporting him, surrounding him. As soon as he could speak, he shook his head. "I'll find a way to see my mom . . . I'm not worried. I can work." He looked at Cody and no words were needed. The message in his eyes was unmistakable. He had a place to live, food to eat. He would be fine. DeMetri looked at Sanders. "I'd like my money to go to your sister. So she has plenty to help her . . . to help her get better."

With that, Sanders broke down, and again the guys came together in a huddle that left no spaces, no distance. In the midst of the emotion, Cody put his hand high over the huddle. "Whose way?"

"His way!"

"Whose way?" he yelled.

"His way!" The room shook with the love of a group of teenage guys who had never cared more. Guys who understood only God could've brought them to this point.

Cody stepped back and stood beside his assistant coaches. All of them had tears in their eyes too. The plan had worked. God had met them here at Butler University, and not only had they raised money for the hurting among them, but He had answered Cody's prayers that these boys might become a team. They would go home caring deeply for each other, aware of their struggles individually and as a whole, tight enough to take on any opponent. They had come here a group of individuals, each one concerned only for himself. But as they headed home that Saturday morning, the bigger miracle was that Lyle High's football players had become more than a team.

They had become a family.

NINETEEN

The memorial for Chrissy Stonelake was held the morning of Friday, July fifteenth, a week after her death. For Bailey it was one of the saddest moments in her life. Chrissy's mom and dad flew in from Montana, collected her ashes, and hurried home without talking to Francesca or the cast, so they weren't there. From what Bailey had heard, Chrissy's parents had never wanted her to perform on Broadway. They'd seen her health decline, and they guessed she was taking pills.

But they had been helpless to intervene, counting on the people around her to reach her — something that never happened.

Every member of the cast was in attendance that morning, gathered in the drafty J. Markham Theater to sing a few songs and remember the girl who had danced among them . . . the girl who had died among them. Bailey sat in the back

346

row, isolating herself from the others. The cast wasn't to blame this time. Since Chrissy's death, the dancers she worked with seemed kinder — even toward her. But that didn't change Bailey's responsibility in the matter, the way she held herself accountable for her friend's death.

Bailey had talked to her mom about Chrissy every day since she died. Her mom was adamant — Chrissy's loss wasn't Bailey's fault. Still, Bailey couldn't get around the obvious truth. She had been in a position to help, but she'd kept to herself. Even when she felt the Lord talking to her, telling her to step in and pray or share a Bible verse, Bailey had done nothing.

Now she held a single folded sheet of paper with Chrissy's picture and her name. Her first and last name — neither of which Bailey would ever forget. She watched quietly, tears on her cheeks as one cast member after another took the stage and shared about Chrissy. Like before, Bailey could hear the Lord speaking, feel Him prodding her into action:

This is your time, daughter. Your chance to speak . . . take courage, and be strong. Don't be afraid.

Yes, God . . . I hear You.

Bailey had never been more afraid in all

her life. No matter what happened before, regardless of the consequences, she still wasn't convinced. Did she really have the strength to speak up for God here? Among the dancers and actors who made up the *Hairspray* cast?

A verse from Deuteronomy 20:1 played over and over in her mind. *When you go to war against your enemies and see horses and chariots and armies bigger than yours do not be afraid. For the Lord your God who brought you up out of Egypt will be with you.*

God would be with her . . . whatever He was calling her to do He would stand beside her and give her the words. Even here when she felt absolutely incapable of making a difference. She'd been quiet with Chrissy — when speaking up might've mattered. When she'd finally prayed very publicly for Chrissy after her collapse, Chrissy had died. What reason would her castmates have for believing in God now?

When you go to war against your enemies and see horses and chariots and armies bigger than yours . . .

Bailey's mouth was so dry she could barely swallow. Francesca was on the stage, looking at them, sizing up the emotion in the room. It was the first time Bailey could remember that the woman had nothing

348

snide to say, nothing sarcastic. She was as broken as everyone else. "Several of you shared wonderful memories, beautiful sentiments about our friend Chrissy Stonelake." She folded her hands. "We have time for a few more."

Gerald went next. He talked about how Chrissy had understood him and encouraged him to perform. "My family doesn't want me here . . . same as hers." He hung his head for a moment. "But Chrissy . . . she believed in me. She was an encourager." A sad smile brightened his face. "She told me I couldn't quit performing or she'd hunt me down." His smile fell, as if he was realizing again that Chrissy was gone. She would never again encourage him to stay on stage, using his talents.

When Gerald finished, a silence filled the theater. *Go, daughter . . . you know what to say . . . I am with you.*

Father, I'm afraid . . .

I am with you . . .

What if they don't listen . . . what if they laugh . . . Bailey's heart pounded so hard she could hear it above the sound of her shallow breathing. She grabbed a water bottle from her purse and drank down half of it. *I don't know if I can do this, Lord . . .*

You can do all things through me . . .

because I give you strength, daughter.

It was those words that finally pushed Bailey up and out of her seat. The words on the promise ring she'd given Cody Coleman before he headed off to war. If Cody could lean on that Bible verse as he left for Iraq, she could let them hold her up as she took the stage now, in front of her peers. She swallowed, gripping her Bible and searching for her voice as she moved slowly up the steps and turned to face them. Nothing gave her the right to be here. She had already failed God's assignment where Chrissy was concerned.

But just as she was about to turn back, run down the stairs and out the building away from their looks and quiet whispers, she remembered the Deuteronomy verse. *When you go to war against your enemies and see horses and chariots and armies bigger than yours . . .* It was the perfect description of this moment. These people didn't like her, they didn't like her God or her background or her lack of experience. But there was a truth that mattered more than any of that.

God was with her.

Bailey stood a little straighter and looked at her castmates, really looked at them. Past the walls of indifference and arrogance and humanism. Deep inside where it mattered, where they were all hurting as much as she was. They had failed Chrissy, same as her, and they needed hope. They all did. The sort of hope only Christ could offer. She breathed in slowly and asked God for the right words, the right tone.

"In the days before Chrissy died . . . I knew she wasn't okay." Bailey worked to speak despite her dry throat. "I saw the pills . . . I noticed how thin she'd become. And I heard God . . . ask me to talk to her."

A couple guys in the middle seats rolled their eyes and looked down at the floor. Bailey pressed on. "I know . . . that might sound strange to you. But I have to take this chance . . . I'm not willing to disobey God this time."

"We don't need a sermon," one of the guys at the end of the middle aisle called out to Francesca. He threw his arms in the air, disgusted. "This is Chrissy's memorial, not church."

Bailey expected that would be the end of her moment on stage, and that Francesca would hurry her back to her seat. But the director only shook her head, her face masked in a peace that she had never once displayed before this. "Bailey may continue. Keep in mind these are her opinions, her feelings. And she's entitled to them." She glanced around the room. "That's what a memorial is. A chance to share our thoughts and feelings."

The guy who had shouted out slumped down in his seat, clearly disgusted.

Bailey hesitated, practically paralyzed with fear. *They hate me, God . . .*

When you go to war against your enemies . . .

The verse played in her mind one more time and she felt herself grow stronger. "Anyway . . . in honor of Chrissy, I'm starting a Bible study. We'll meet Friday mornings in the rehearsal space." She looked at Francesca. "I've already secured it." Her heartbeat was so loud it was distracting. "I'd like permission to hold the first Bible study here . . . when we're dismissed . . . for whomever would like to stay."

Francesca had the right to say no, and clearly she was considering making such a pronouncement. But instead she stood, her expression slightly favorable. "Tell everyone what you mean, Bailey. A Bible study . . . what would that look like?"

Adrenaline surged through her . . . God was moving walls, opening doors. She blinked, trying to stay focused. "No one has to know all that much." She shrugged. "I

352

don't know that much." She held up her Bible. "We can look at Scripture by topic . . . addiction . . . loneliness . . . rejection. Just see what the Bible says and then . . . you know, talk about it."

"This is ridiculous." It was the same guy who had shouted out before. "Francesca, you can't be serious."

"You don't have to attend." The director's answer was sharp, pointed. "This is something Bailey wants to do in honor of Chrissy." She gave a single nod. "I'm going to allow that."

A burst of sunlight exploded across Bailey's fearful, anguished soul. God had pushed her up here on stage, and now He had done just what He'd promised. He had delivered her from her enemies. At least for now. She thanked them for listening, and explained that at the end, she'd wait for anyone who wanted to stay.

Francesca closed them with a sweet story about Chrissy, how she had been so nervous her first day with the cast that she had found Francesca and asked for something unconventional, something no other dancer had ever asked for before or since. Francesca's eyes glistened. "She asked me for a hug." The director smiled, fighting her tears. "She always got a hug from her mom on the first day of school . . . and working here with all of us . . . it felt like a classroom to Chrissy." Francesca smiled at Bailey and then at the others. A tear slid down her cheek. "So I hugged her. Like she was my own daughter, I hugged her." A slight sob shook the director's composure, and her smile faded. "I will remember that hug . . . and I will miss her."

Bailey wondered if Francesca blamed herself for not taking action regarding Chrissy's anorexia. So far the director hadn't said anything to Bailey about it, but several times Bailey remembered Francesca's admonition the day of Chrissy's death. The girl's anorexia was being dealt with. Bailey should mind her own business.

Watching Francesca now, Bailey was almost certain the director regretted her attitude that day.

The memorial was over and most of the cast filed out in groups of twos or threes, several of them whispering among themselves. Bailey stayed seated, her eyes on her Bible. They were whispering about her, she was sure. She even heard her name from a few of them as they left. But she didn't look up, didn't want to see the fact that not one person was likely to join her in reading the Bible.

They don't care, God . . . You had me go out on a limb up there, and for what? Now they'll never talk to me, and so how does that help them to know You . . . to feel Your love, Lord?

Daughter, be still and know that I am God.

The answer caught her by surprise. She felt instantly sorry. No matter what happened here in the next hour, even if she stayed in the empty theater by herself, God had a plan. It wasn't her place to question what He was doing, or why He had prompted her to act. She was only responsible for one thing: obeying His voice. Just when she was sure every last actor had left the theater, she heard the sound of footsteps.

She looked up and saw three girls and Gerald, walking toward her. They looked nervous and uncertain, but they came anyway. Gerald took the lead. "You're brave, Bailey . . ." He looked back at the others. "The truth is, we're curious. We've never read the Bible."

"That's okay." Again Bailey's heart raced. How could she do this? "We'll take it slow, for sure." Her hands shook so hard she wasn't sure she could read the text. But she opened her Bible anyway. As she did, panic seized her. She had nowhere near enough experience to lead a study like this. *I can't do it, Lord . . . I'm not good enough . . . not smart enough . . . not —*

Obey, daughter . . . I will meet you here . . . you will not have to fight this battle.

Peace put its hands on her shoulders and she felt a surreal calm. Like with Chrissy . . . or when she walked up on stage a few minutes ago . . . God didn't call her to be intelligent or wise or particularly gifted. He simply called her. It was a truth she was learning even now. *You can do this, Bailey,* she told herself. *You can obey.*

And with that she asked them to follow her on stage. They sat in a circle, cross-legged, and Bailey let them talk first. "Tell me why you stayed . . . why you're interested in learning the Bible."

Each of the girls had a different answer. One of them had come from a family that believed in God, but after her parents' divorce when she was nine years old, they stopped going to church. "How do I know God is real?"

Bailey nodded. "That's a great question . . . we can look at that."

Another of the girls wanted to know why Chrissy had died, if prayer works. "I heard you pray for her." The dancer's eyes were dark with doubt. "What's the Bible say

356

about that?"

Again Bailey promised they'd take a look at that topic in the coming weeks. Even as she spoke she had no idea how she would deliver on that promise. But between her parents and the Kellers and the Bible in her hands, God would give her the wisdom, show her how to help build the faith of her peers.

Gerald was last. "I struggle with my sexuality." He looked embarrassed about the fact.

One of the girls put her hand on his shoulder. "You have a right to be yourself."

Bailey cringed. *God, I need Your help . . . how do I help them see the truth without turning them away?*

Lean not on your own understanding . . . I am God.

Okay. Help me do that, Father . . . help me. Again peace silenced the fear in her heart. "The Bible talks about that too, Gerald. We'll look at it a little later, okay?"

"Okay." He shrugged, still nervous. "Here on Broadway it's no big deal." He laughed, but the sound held no humor. "Most of the guys are gay. I get that." His eyes clouded with pain. "But my uncle's a preacher. He told me being gay's a sin, and that I could go to hell over this struggle." He hesitated, slumping a little over his knees. "I guess I want to know if that's true."

Bailey gulped, but she didn't look away, didn't break eye contact with Gerald. "There are a lot of sin struggles . . . the Bible talks about that." The strength in her heart wasn't from her. "We can look at that too."

"Let's look at that today." Gerald clearly wanted answers. "I mean, my uncle acts like he knows everything. He makes me feel like an outcast. A pariah."

This was how Christians had fallen under the umbrella of being judgmental and narrow-minded. The idea that one sin could be singled out as the worst, the area God disliked most. She would've liked a few minutes with Gerald's uncle to show him what his comments had wrought on the kindhearted guy sitting in the circle with her.

"Let's start there," one of the girls chimed in. "It's everywhere in New York City . . . People talk about whether gay is okay or not." She gave Bailey a pointed look. "What do you think?"

Bailey knew she was being tested, but she was no longer afraid. She would let the Bible talk, and with a deep breath she searched out a few verses on homosexuality.

She read them, trying not to wince at the harsh way they probably sounded to the dancers seated in the circle. The test was intense, but God was with her.

"This is what the Bible says in First Timothy . . ." She read the section of Scripture that dealt with groups of people who were considered lawbreakers and rebels . . . ungodly, unholy and irreligious. *"People who kill their fathers or mothers, murderers, the sexually immoral, those practicing homosexuality, slave traders, liars and perjurers . . . and for whatever else is contrary to sound doctrine . . ."*

The list felt exhausting, and as Bailey reached the end of the verse she caught the defeat on Gerald's face. "So gay people are listed right there with murderers?"

"And liars." The answer came too quickly for Bailey to take credit for it. "See, Gerald . . . God doesn't have something against people who struggle with homosexuality. We all struggle with one of those sins, and no sin struggle is worse than another. All God asks is that we keep struggling — especially since Jesus died to set us free from our sin struggles. Whatever the sin."

Anger flashed in Gerald's eyes. "But I was born this way, Bailey . . . don't tell me God would make me this way and then doom me to a life of sinning."

Bailey didn't blink, didn't look away. "We're all born with some kind of bent toward sin." Her words were kind, her response slow and even. They were listening . . . when they might've gotten up and walked away, they were definitely listening. "I fight against pride . . . wanting everyone to like me and ignoring God's voice over my own."

She turned to another section of Scripture and read from Proverbs 8. "See, here God says He hates pride. He hates it." She lowered the Bible to her lap. "That means I need to ask God's help every day so I don't let my own pride win. Every day."

The circle was quiet, her castmates taking in this possibility. Bailey pressed on, her tone gentle and kind. "God doesn't want me to say, 'Oh well . . . I'm prideful. I was born this way, and I'm going to stay this way.' "

Gerald hugged his knees to his chest, his eyes less defensive than before. "Same with liars . . . or murderers?"

"Exactly." Bailey felt like she was on a tightrope. One wrong word or tone or glance and the group would leave and never come back. But God was holding her up, and so she continued. "The person who kills isn't supposed to say, 'I'm a killer . . . God made me this way, so therefore it's okay if I kill.' And the liar isn't supposed to say, 'I struggle with lying, so I'm going to stop struggling and go ahead and lie. I'm a liar . . . God made me this way.' " She paused, and in their eyes she could see that what she was saying made sense. She pressed on. "It's the same for people who sleep together and aren't married. That kind of sexual sin is in the same category. We're all going to struggle with one of these . . . but we're not supposed to give up and say the fight is over. Does that make sense?" She hesitated, letting the thought sink in. "See . . . God loves all of us, whatever our struggles. He knows life is hard for us . . . so He promises to be with us, and He asks us to come together like this. To encourage each other and keep fighting against whatever sin has a hold on us."

For a long time none of them said anything. Bailey noticed that tears had fallen from Gerald's eyes. He used his shoulder to wipe at them and after a while he nodded. "Thanks . . . I guess . . . I never looked at it that way."

"Christians haven't done a great job with the topic." Bailey understood this better now than ever before. "We've either been judgmental and critical, like homosexual sin is the worst sin . . . or we've been too complacent. Using the banner of love as a way to excuse sin — when God clearly has an opinion about it. We fear we'll offend, so we veer from the truth."

"Wow . . ." Gerald lowered his legs. He looked at the girls and then at Bailey. "That makes complete sense." He looked lost in thought for a moment. "I might struggle with this all my life . . . but the point is I have to keep fighting. Like the liar or alcoholic or whatever."

"Exactly." Bailey felt her heart rate return to normal. She took a deep breath. "There's hope for all people . . . whatever they battle." Bailey knew this from personal experience. She wouldn't be here leading a Bible study if it weren't so. "God gives us strength beyond what we are capable of. He died on the cross to set us free from the sins that chain us. We won't have to battle forever — because He's already won the victory."

There wasn't much more to say on the topic. Bailey closed by looking at a verse from Ephesians chapter three telling the small group that they should all pray to know how wide and long and high and deep was the love of Christ. "He loves us so much . . . I guess that's what I wanted to tell Chrissy."

And as the Bible study ended, they held hands and Bailey prayed, and even as they hugged each other and set out to whatever their days held, Bailey felt keenly aware of two things. First, whatever trouble she had with the cast before would pale in comparison to the way most of them would see her now. But she had done what God asked her to do. In honor of Chrissy Stonelake, and out of love for her peers. And because of that, the second point was all that mattered.

Whatever happened from here, she had obeyed God.

TWENTY

Their first football game was three weeks away, and Cody could hardly wait. The team continued to come together in the weeks since they returned from camp. Sanders' sister was getting the new treatment, and so far she was responding brilliantly. Their dad had come to practice one day, and with a barely composed voice he had personally thanked the team for raising the money.

Everyone in town talked about the difference in the football players. People even whispered about the possibilities that lay ahead. If Lyle High could do what no other group of football players had done — win every single day at the Butler camp — then maybe they might be on to something. Maybe a winning season was possible. Cody loved the support. Even Cheyenne noticed a difference in the team. She was well enough to drive now, and though at first she admitted to being nervous, she had driven out a few times in her new Honda to watch practice.

Today, though — the third Saturday in July — Cody and DeMetri and Cheyenne had all come to practice together, and now that it was over, none of them wanted their time together to end. Marcos Brown had nothing to do either. It was Chey who mentioned the zoo first. A thunderstorm had come through the night before and cooled temperatures, easing the humidity. "The animals will be moving around for the first time all month." She smiled at the idea. "Let's call Tara. She'd love a day at the zoo."

DeMetri's expression looked slightly puzzled, and he shared a glance with Marcos. "You ever been to the zoo?"

"No, man." Marcos laughed. "Camp was the most days I've ever been out of Lyle."

Cody stared at the boys, amazed. They had so much to learn, so much of life ahead. He felt honored that God would trust him with this season of the boys' lives. Even if that meant sharing a day at the zoo.

As it turned out, Tara was available. She met them at the White River State Park in downtown Indianapolis. The zoo was located on the grounds there, and was known for its beautiful gardens. From the moment they arrived, DeMetri and Marcos looked like a couple of little boys on Christmas morning.

"Real live elephants, man." DeMetri had to hold back from running ahead. He motioned for the group to hurry. "I mean, seriously! Real live elephants!"

Tara kept the boys company, staying with them even when they hurried ahead. That allowed Cody to stay at Cheyenne's pace. She didn't need the cane anymore, but she still moved slowly. Cody held out his arm, allowing her to lean on him for support whenever the trail was a little uneven.

"This was a great idea." Cody no longer felt guilty for enjoying Cheyenne's company. They were together nearly every day, and after going through her recovery after the accident, they were as close as most married couples. Cody understood that . . . and he knew one day soon he'd have to examine his feelings, figure out if he was ready to take things to the next level with her.

A few times they let Tara and the boys get far enough ahead that they felt like they were alone. Once Cody stopped at a more secluded exhibit. He and Chey leaned against the railing, their arms touching, and watched what was easily the biggest hippopotamus Cody had ever seen.

"Looks relaxing, wallowing around in the

mud all day," Cheyenne laughed. "I think I'd get bored, though."

"You would." He turned and faced her, struck by how completely she had recovered. No one could've guessed the ordeal she'd been through earlier that year. His eyes held hers and like a number of times before, the rest of the world faded way, leaving just the two of them and a sense of desire that seemed to catch them both by surprise. "You look beautiful . . . have I told you that lately?"

"Not enough."

For a few seconds Cody wanted to pull her close and kiss her, explore whether his feelings were real. But that wasn't his style, not since his rebellious high school days. If he cared enough about Chey to kiss her, then he cared enough to wait until she was officially his girlfriend.

"You're thinking something . . ." She squinted, her eyes soft and vulnerable. "Tell me."

"Hmmm." He put his hand alongside her face and looked deeper, to the beautiful soul within her. "About us, I guess . . . where this is going."

She didn't say anything, but her eyes told him she felt the same way. Had they found forever . . . or something that was only just for now? "I don't have any answers." Her words were simple and profound, and they took him by surprise. He had thought she was looking for a relationship with him. But she didn't know whether she wanted that any more than he did.

"I can say this . . . I care for you very much, Chey. I think about you every day."

Her smile lightened the moment. "I'm glad." She stepped away from him and took his hand. "Come on . . . they'll be looking for us."

They met up with the others, and the day turned into one of their favorites of the summer. The subject of the two of them as a couple didn't come up again until they were seated around Tara's dinner table. She had made sloppy joes the night before, and had plenty of leftovers. Marcos and De-Metri couldn't have been happier. "No one's ever cooked like this for me." De-Metri was downing his second sloppy joe. He stopped mid-bite and shot a quick look at Cody. "I mean, you try and all, Coach. But this is something else!"

Tara glowed under their compliments, and Cody imagined how she must feel. Art had been her only child, and after he was killed at war she loved opening her house to his buddies. But this would've been the first time she'd had teenagers in her home — the first time since Art was this age.

At one point Tara cleared a few dishes and disappeared into the kitchen, leaving the boys and Cody and Cheyenne at the table. Marcos was more outspoken than DeMetri, more of a jokester. He leaned back in his chair and sized up Cody and Cheyenne. "Okay," he waved his finger at them. "What's the story with you two?" He raised his brow at Cody. "I'd say it's time to make this little love affair official." He elbowed DeMetri. "Right, bro?"

"Right." DeMetri gave Cody an exaggerated look of innocence, as if to say this idea hadn't been his. But now that the matter had been broached . . . "You do spend a lot of time together." He gave a happy shrug. "Just saying."

Cheyenne giggled and hung her head for a minute, obviously embarrassed. Cody cleared his throat and gave the boys a look that was half teasing. "You'll be the first to know, boys . . . whenever we have anything official to announce."

"Which better be soon, Coach." Marcos raised his hands and let them fall back to the table. "I mean, come on. A girl can only hang around waiting for so long. That's what my aunt says about my older cousin.

He's been dating the same girl forever."

The conversation was probably about as much as Cheyenne could take — even though she was still laughing. She stood and looked straight at Marcos. "You boys can carry on without me." She grinned at Cody. "I'll be in the kitchen."

As she left, both boys gave him a pointed look, and then burst into laughter. "Sorry, Coach . . . that was awkward." They laughed so hard they could barely talk.

"I couldn't wait another minute. I mean, Coach, I had to say something." Marcos was all brash and happy confidence. "Come on, I mean, she'll say yes. You don't have to worry."

Cody chuckled, playing along. But the comments from the boys only underlined the fact that he needed to deal with the situation. If Cheyenne would indeed say yes, then he needed to ask her, right? She needed him, after all. He twisted the ring around his right hand, the one on his pointer finger.

The friendship ring from Bailey Flanigan. *He could do all things through Christ who gave him strength.* That was the message on the ring, but what about this? Asking Chey to be his girlfriend would mean taking one more step away from Bailey. The idea rattled around in his heart. What would one more step matter? Bailey had already taken that move, already gone on without him. So maybe Marcos and DeMetri were right.

Maybe it was time for him to do the same.

Cheyenne could hear the quiet sobs from Tara even before she stepped into the kitchen. Her heart sank as she rounded the corner. Tara, usually so strong and happy, so sure that God worked out all things, clutched the kitchen sink, her head hung, crying as if her heart had just been broken in half.

"Tara . . ." she kept her voice low. The kitchen was far enough away that the guys couldn't hear Tara crying. But she wanted this moment to be private, between just the two of them. She came to her, and put her hand on Tara's shoulder. "Are you okay?"

She nodded, unable to talk. Then she turned and for a few long seconds she pulled Cheyenne into an embrace, one filled with the desperation that could only come from very great loss. "I thought . . . I thought I could handle it."

Cheyenne understood. She had wondered how Tara would get through the day and the dinner, especially when the banter had to remind her so much of Art. "I know,

Mama, I know." Cheyenne whispered to her, still in her arms. She stepped back and framed the older woman's face with her hand. "I miss him too. So much."

"It's supposed to get easier." She sniffed and turned, reaching for a tissue. "But those boys." A sound more laugh than sob came from her. "Those wonderful boys took me back to how it used to be, and . . . for just a few minutes it was like I was looking right at my Art. Like he was here again and I could hear his laugh, and smell that teenage mix of cologne and sweaty armpits." She released a sob and covered her face with her hands. "Dear God, I miss him."

If Cheyenne was honest with herself, this was why she had left the dinner table. The guys didn't mean anything by their teasing, but the idea of she and Cody being a couple . . . it made her feel the same way Tara felt. Like all she wanted was to have Art back here. Where he belonged.

"Ugggh." Tara blew her nose and shook her head. "I'm sorry, baby." She brushed her fingers against Cheyenne's forearm. "I didn't mean this to happen. I'm happy for you and Cody . . . and I'm glad the boys are here. All of it . . . I'm so happy." She blinked back another wave of tears. "I just want to hug him one more time."

Chey's own eyes were blurred with sadness. "Me too." She looked deep into Tara's face, because if one person in the world could understand how she felt it was Art's mother. "I think . . . I think I'm falling in love with Cody."

"I know, baby." There was no denying the joy in Tara's eyes. "That's what I wanted. It's why I introduced you two. Because God saved that young man for you." She looked almost stern . . . her adamant belief that strong. "It's the right thing."

"But, Mama . . . I'm not sure I can ever love the way I loved Art." She kept her voice low. She would've been horrified if Cody heard her, but she had to be honest. "Not even Cody."

Tara nodded, the tears having their way with her again. She could barely speak, but she managed to eek out the words. "I understand, baby . . . everything takes time." They hugged again. "I understand."

Something about their moment in the kitchen relieved a tension of sorts in Cheyenne, like she no longer had to doubt herself for the ambivalent feelings she had for Cody. She missed Art, and so did Tara. They always would. But he was gone, and Cody was here. Cody who cared for her and made her laugh and who looked at her in a way that melted her heart. Cheyenne had a feeling tonight was a turning point. Because after that evening and her talk with Tara in the kitchen, she could freely admit the truth to herself. She would miss Art Collins for the rest of her life, but something had happened over the last few months.

She had fallen in love with Cody Coleman.

TWENTY-ONE

The weeks of summer training passed quickly, one blazing hot humid day blending into another until the first part of August when two-a-days began. This was the most intense part of practice for most football teams, but Cody's Lyle players seemed to take it in stride. After the breakthrough they'd made in camp, Cody could've asked them to walk across fire for each other and they would've done it.

Two practices a day was a walk in the park.

Not only did they embrace the challenge, but they were committed to getting better. By the time their season opener rolled around on the third Friday night in August, Cody's excitement about his team was at a fever pitch.

Cody brought DeMetri a few hours early, and well before game time Tara and Cheyenne arrived. Cody had taught Chey how to take stats, so she and Tara found a comfortable spot at the top of the bleachers, and he watched her hover over the clipboard — no doubt filling in the stat sheets with the player names and numbers.

All around Lyle, excitement filled the air like electricity. An hour before game time the stands filled and people lined up along the sidelines with lawn chairs. Even the visitor stands were full of Lyle fans. Cody tried not to think about the people and their expectations. *This is for You, God . . . whatever happens tonight. You brought us together as a team. Now let us play for You. For Your glory.*

There was no answer, but Cody didn't need one. He reminded himself of the Bible story he and DeMetri had read that morning. It was from 1 Samuel, the story of David and Goliath. The team they were playing tonight wasn't in their league. Herron High was a powerhouse from the west side of the state, a 3A school with twice the enrollment of Lyle. Cody had no idea why Coach Oliver had scheduled the game.

But here they were.

He was headed into the locker room when something caught his attention from the sidelines. For a brief moment he turned and there . . . by himself with only a Lyle baseball cap to remind anyone of the position he once held — was Coach Oliver. He motioned for Cody.

What was this? Was the man going to rail at him, threaten him for taking over his team? Or complain that the guys had gotten too much attention for having not really proven anything? He jogged over, hesitant. But as he reached him, the older coach nodded slowly, his chin trembling. He pointed at the field, at the guys warming up. "You're the right man for the job, Coleman. I'm . . ." He removed his hat and held it over his heart. "I'm sorry. For how I treated you and the guys."

Cody was stunned. Of all the man might say, this wasn't even on the list. "Coach . . . that's very kind of you. I'll . . . I'll pass your words on to the guys."

"Do that. Please." He put his hat firmly back on his head. "I'll be cheering." He gave him a thumbs up.

Whatever counseling the man was getting, it must've been working. Actually, Cody knew better. Something kind and humble and deep in the man's eyes must've come from more than counseling. Like maybe he'd found the closer walk with God that he'd been missing. Either way, Coach Oliver was sorry. It was one more reason for

the Buckaroos to play their hearts out tonight.

With that he jogged to the sidelines and
rounded up the guys. He and his assistants
led them into the locker room for a final
talk. When they were seated, Cody looked
at them the way he might look at a room
full of sons. "The season begins tonight,
and look at what you've accomplished
already." Cody's voice rang through the
locker room, his tone rich with encouragement. "But tonight we start fresh. The good
we've already done is behind us." He
paused. "The season begins tonight, men."

"Tonight, y'all!" Marcos stood and
pumped his fist in the air. "Let's get it done,
boys!"

Several of them stood and slapped Marcos
on the back, adding their voices to his.
"Tonight's our night! Let's do this!"

Cody let the excitement build. He smiled
at Coaches Braswell and Schroeder. Here,
with the group of them shouting and hollering and encouraging each other, one thing
was for sure: They had become a team.

When they quieted down, Cody paced in
front of them. "The thing with life is you
get one chance." He held up his pointer
finger. "One chance to play like a team . . .
one chance to leave it all out there on the

field. To walk back in this locker room at the end of the night with no regrets. One chance to know you've played this football game His way. For all the right reasons."

"Let's do it!" Marcos was already on his feet, his fist raised high in the air again. With his other hand he urged his teammates up. "This is our time, y'all! Get up!"

The guys didn't need to be asked again. They surrounded Marcos and DeMetri, the team captains, and Cody and the other coaches pressed in from the outer edge of the huddle, all of them with their hands together at the center. "Let's show the world who Lyle football really is!" Cody shouted loud enough so they could all hear him, and a round of guttural responses and bellows of agreement followed.

"Whose way?" Cody stayed loud, intense, fitting for the moment.

"His way!"

"Whose way?" Still louder.

"His way!"

"Whose way?" The chorus grew and filled the locker room.

"His way!" Cody felt the thrill through his entire body. Something special was about to happen, he could sense it. "On three, team . . . one . . . two . . . three . . ."

"Team!"

With that the players broke free from the huddle and rushed for the door, some of them holding their football helmets high, others pumping their fists in the air. They pushed through the doors and stampeded out to the field, to the overflowing stands and the entire town of Lyle that had come out to support them.

Cody and his assistants jogged behind the guys, and before they reached the bench Cody was struck by how far they had come. His players believed God was at the center of everything they had done to this point, everything they would do from here. Tonight . . . with this Lyle team, anything was possible. Cody reveled in the wash of Friday-night lights that shone over the small-town high school field. It wasn't just that anything was possible tonight.

Everything was possible.

For a few seconds Cody looked at the packed stands and the crowd six and seven deep watching from along the far sidelines and panic squeezed in around him. Every single person who had come out to watch was counting on him. A handful of images from Iraq flashed in his mind. Himself, trapped in a makeshift prison cell, while his men waited for him to do something . . . anything to get them out. And the image changed and became a platoon of men following Cody into the desert, ready to take on the enemy . . . counting on him.

Sweat beaded up on his forehead just below the line where his baseball cap sat. But this time Cody took a deep breath and removed his hat. He wiped his forehead and forced himself to picture the scene in the locker room a few minutes ago. *Be with me, God . . . Please . . . this isn't Iraq. It's only football . . . they're not relying on me for anything more than a few hours of good times together. They're here to support me, not look for me to rescue them from anything.* He hesitated, waiting. The flashbacks were gone and he felt utter relief as he fixed his cap back in place. *Thank You, God . . . thank You for the truth.*

I am with you, son . . . always.

Yes. That was the greatest truth of all. He grabbed his clipboard and called for his assistant coaches. His focus became so great over the next minutes that nothing could've distracted him. But even so — with all the preparation they'd done and the way they'd come together and the strength of their belief in each other, after two quarters Lyle was down twenty-one to seven.

Quiet filled the locker room during half-time, and Cody wanted it to be that way.

The guys were outmanned for sure. Their smallest linemen were the size of Marcos, and they executed plays with machinelike precision. But with all that, Cody still believed his team could compete with Herron High. The guys were nervous, hurrying their plays, panicking. Trying to prove themselves too quickly.

When the team had gotten drinks and come together once more, Cody kept his talk short. "Nothing has changed, men. You are capable of great things if you relax." His tone rang with sincerity, but he didn't yell, didn't shout at them. That's not what they needed. "All summer we've asked one question. Whose way?" He hesitated, looking at the eyes of his men. "And what's the answer?"

"His way." They sounded discouraged, but still strong, still together.

"Okay then . . . let's not force anything. We have two quarters to prove that we mean what we say when we answer that question." He motioned for them to stand and as they did, they came together, arms around each other, a fresh determination dawning in their expressions. "Whose way?"

"His way!"

Cody walked alone as his team took the field. God was with them . . . regardless of the score. *Heavenly Father, these are Your guys.* He kept his pace slow, his eyes on the sky beyond the stadium lights. *Lord, they don't have to win tonight, but let them play the game Your way . . . please . . . until the final whistle.*

From the opening second-half kickoff, it was obvious something had changed. As the Lyle offense took the field, the guys carried with them a sense of strength and determination that was otherworldly. Arnie Hurley connected on passes to Joel Butler three plays in a row sending the Buckaroos to the Herron twenty-yard line in less than a minute.

The cheers from across the field were deafening, but Cody blocked them out. If he expected focused reliance on God from his players, he had to ask it of himself. Each play, every play breaker — all of it had to be thought out and carefully conveyed. The guys needed that sort of leadership for every series. By the end of the third quarter, Herron was up by just a touchdown, twenty-eight to twenty-one. Midway through the fourth quarter, Arnie found Larry Sanders for a seven-yard touchdown pass that tied the game and brought the entire Lyle offense into a celebratory huddle around Sanders in the end zone. Cody glanced up at the stands and found Larry's parents. They were holding up his little sister, the three of them celebrating. Cody loved this, the feeling of community in this small town. Larry had told them yesterday after practice that his sister was responding to the new medication.

The team lifted Larry on their shoulders and celebrated like they'd won the state championship. Cody understood their reason for savoring the moment. They weren't only on the verge of an upset, but they'd helped save the life of Larry's little sister.

Four minutes remained on the clock, and Herron made a run that took them from their twenty-yard line to the Lyle forty. Coach Schroeder was Cody's defensive coordinator. He called a timeout and Cody let him handle the moment. Schroeder had played linebacker in college but he'd never coached before. He'd learned much about motivating kids since joining Cody's staff. Whatever he told the guys, they returned to the line of scrimmage and proceeded to dismantle Herron's offensive attack. Three plays later Herron punted with little more than a minute left in the game.

The Lyle fans could smell a possible upset. They were on their feet, rattling the bleachers and sending up a shout of support that Cody figured could be heard to the city limits. All through the game Cody had kept his eye on DeMetri Smith. His star running back was capable of great things this year, but so far he had maybe sixty yards rushing in the entire game. He was tackled for a loss on his last carry, and he'd fumbled twice this half. Cody wasn't sure why, but DeMetri's confidence seemed a little off all night.

Cody gritted his teeth and made a decision. Only one player on the Lyle team had been openly praying for the team since the end of last season, one player who had believed this year's outcome would be different from last year's. They had time for maybe three or four plays, and running plays took the most time off the clock. Still, Cody sent the play into Arnie Hurley. Handoff to DeMetri Smith.

He put his hands on his knees, bent over, watching every detail of the play as it unfolded. But again as DeMetri took hold of the ball, he lost his grip and it dropped to the ground. He fell on it immediately so there was no turnover. But he could feel the frustration from the rest of the team along the sidelines. Even his coaches were looking at him like certainly he'd call a pass play next.

Cody did. And Arnie connected to Larry Sanders again, this time for twenty-six yards and a first down that stopped the clock. Arnie kept the ball for a three-yard gain and Cody used his last timeout. He hurried out to the huddle and he put his arm around the shoulders of his quarterback and running back. "You up to this, Smitty?" His eyes met DeMetri's. "You can do it . . . but are you up to it?"

Around the huddle the other guys slapped DeMetri on the shoulder pads and grunted their approval, their belief in him. Slowly DeMetri nodded. "Yes, sir . . . I'm sorry." He smacked his helmet a few times and shook his head. "I've been distracted and I'm sorry. I'm with you. I can do this."

Herron would look for a pass, of course. With just six seconds left in the game, this was Lyle's last chance, and they had seventy-two yards to cover. The outcome of the game depended on this play. Cody watched and suddenly it felt like the action was unfolding in slow motion. Arnie handed the ball to DeMetri but as he began to run he saw two Herron defenders coming at him. Even with Arnie leading the way, it looked like the play would go nowhere.

Then, in a move few kids had the athleticism to pull off, Arnie leveled both Herron players leaving a hole wide enough to drive a truck through. DeMetri didn't wait. He burst through the opening and on the other side found nothing but open grass. DeMetri's speed was breathtaking, and though no defender was close to catching him he ran for all he was worth.

The buzzer sounded as DeMetri crossed into the end zone and fell to one knee, his head bowed. Lyle won thirty-four to twenty-eight. The school's first win in two years. Herron's first loss to the Buckaroos ever. Cody glanced at the dark sky beyond the lights over the football field. *Thank You, God. All You . . . Your way.*

All around him the team was jumping and celebrating and pouring out onto the field to swarm around DeMetri. The fans responded the same way, breaking free from the bleachers and rushing onto the field to join the football players. "Let's go celebrate!" He motioned to the other coaches and the three of them hurried out onto the field to take part in the win. Already the town had started a chant. "We are . . . Lyle . . . we are . . . Lyle."

The celebration lasted another half hour on the field. DeMetri led the team and the townspeople in a prayer, thanking God for the ability to play beyond their best, and several of the players joined in. Larry Sanders held his little sister on his hip and the team filed past her, giving her high fives and understanding, the way all of them did, that wins and losses mattered little compared with doing their best. Most of the men worked their way over to Cody and shook his hand, congratulating him on the beginning of what looked to be the best season in years.

Coach Oliver found him too, his eyes full of peace and joy. "I couldn't be happier for you." He gazed at the guys still slapping each other on the backs, exchanging hugs, and posing for photos with their teammates. "They're a different group of guys with you." He nodded, again too emotional to say much. "I'm grateful God brought you to Lyle, Coleman. Very grateful."

"Me too." He shook the coach's hand. "I'd love to talk sometime . . . about your war experience . . . the counseling you're getting." He wondered if Coach Oliver could see the knowing in his eyes. "I'm a veteran too. You may not have known that."

The shock in Coach Oliver's eyes told Cody he was right. The man didn't know much about Cody, because he never stopped barking at everyone around him long enough to find out. But as the coach left, Cody had a feeling that would change in the months to come. Maybe one day he and Coach Oliver would even be friends.

Tara found him before she left and hugged him tight around his neck. "The impact you're making on these boys . . ." She waved her pointer finger in the air and shook her head a few quick times. "No one could've done it better. You're gonna win every game, Cody. Mark my words."

For a few seconds he and Tara's eyes held, and he had a sense that they were both thinking the same thing. If Art were still here, he'd be coaching right beside him, sharing in this win. "I'm going home . . . you take care of Chey for me, okay?"

"I will." Cody heard the double meaning in his voice, and he meant how it sounded. He would get her home that night, but he would take care of her beyond that too. He felt that way a little more every day.

Later, when most of the other players had cleared out of the locker room, Cody pulled DeMetri aside and put his hand on the kid's shoulder. "See what happens when people believe in you?" Cody smiled. "Great run, Smitty. Perfect."

"Thanks." DeMetri's grin proved he was still basking in the game-winning moment. His expression changed. "I'm sorry about the rest of the game, Coach. I don't know what got into me."

Cody didn't either. DeMetri seemed ready that afternoon on the way to the field. He had prayed about this season since the end of last year — faithfully hanging out in the end zone by himself after practice, asking God for a miracle this year, something special that could only come from the Lord. "God gave me everything I prayed for." DeMetri's tone was thoughtful. "Maybe it was all a little too much at first. How far we've come. Like I couldn't focus on the game."

He and DeMetri had much in common; they'd already established that a number of times over breakfasts and late-night talks. The fact that both their mothers were serving time in prison was just a starting point. "Or maybe . . ." Cody kept his voice soft so only DeMetri could hear him, "maybe you were thinking about your mama. How she couldn't be here tonight."

Nothing could've truly dimmed the happiness DeMetri felt that night, Cody had a feeling. But this came close. He blinked a few times and nodded. "It's not fair. She walked away from all this when she made the choice to do drugs."

"She did." There was no way around the

hard truth about their mothers. "But her addiction can only lose if she relies on God. She needs a lot of prayers, Smitty."

"I know." His smile was crooked and relieved, like he was grateful for a reason to be happy again. "That's the best part. If God does this when we pray about football . . . think what He's gonna do for my mom yet."

"That's right, buddy. Now you're talking." Cody patted him on the back again and left the locker room to find Cheyenne. It was like he'd expected all along. DeMetri hadn't been nervous or having an off night. He was simply thinking of all the other mothers in the stands, knowing that instead of watching him tonight, his mom was in prison. Cody could certainly relate.

They gathered their things, and the whole ride back to Indianapolis, Chey replayed the game from her notes, making sure she'd seen the details correctly and celebrating with them the beauty of their comeback. "It was the best game I've ever seen." She looked over at DeMetri and then at Cody. "Seriously. The best game ever."

"No offense, Miss Williams." DeMetri's tone was polite, but teasing. "But how many football games have you seen exactly?"

"A lot." She held her head higher. Art had

played football when they were in college, Cody knew that much. "I'll have you know I cheered for every football game my entire high school career."

"That's the thing about cheerleaders," a laugh sounded in DeMetri's tone. "They're always facing the fans. Which means . . . they have their backs to the game." He chuckled. "So thanks for saying it was the most exciting game you've seen . . . but maybe it was the only one you've ever really seen."

Cody raised one eyebrow in her direction. "Can't say I disagree."

"You two." She smacked her stat sheets at Cody and giggled. "Of course . . . you might be right."

The mood stayed light, the celebration still all around them even after Cody dropped DeMetri off at the apartment and promised to be back soon. Chey was back at her own place now, and she only lived a few blocks away. On the short drive there, Cody realized he had something to talk to Chey about, something to ask her. He'd waited long enough, and now he knew. He cared about her too much to walk away from her . . . so it was time to make their relationship official.

Cody was pretty sure he felt more nervous

as he walked up to her front porch than he'd felt at kickoff. Chey's street wasn't marked by any sort of light, and the stars overhead stretched like a canvas of light. She turned to him at the bottom of her stairs. "Tonight was amazing."

"It was." He searched her eyes, wondering if she felt it too. The connection that had grown stronger between them over the summer. "Hey, Chey . . . I was wondering . . . I mean, I really care about you a lot."

"I know." She looked at ease, relaxed . . . but her eyes told him she knew where this was headed. "I care about you too. Very much."

"Right, so . . ." He shifted, slipping his hands in the pockets of his khaki coaching pants. "What I'm trying to say is . . . do you have fun with me? When we're together?"

She let a light-sounding laugh sound on her lips. "Of course I have fun with you." She made a silly face. "You know that, Cody . . . We both have fun."

"I know." He uttered a single laugh, one that couldn't have possibly sounded more strained or nervous. "I mean, have you thought about whether . . . whether you're ready for something else?"

"Something else?" Her eyes danced, and again he was sure she knew what he was trying to get at. But she was enjoying watching him suffer. She bit her lip, clearly trying to keep from laughing. "What sort of something else?"

"Well . . ." Cody couldn't back down now. He took his hands from his pockets and without meaning to, he twisted the friendship ring. Then as soon as he realized what he was doing, he put his hands back in his pockets. He couldn't think about Bailey . . . not now. Definitely not now. He took a fast breath. "What I'm trying to say is . . . the way things are between us . . . maybe we should take things to the next level. I mean . . . if that's how you're feeling too, and —"

"Cody." She held out her hands and waited until he pulled his from his pockets. When their fingers were joined together, she lowered her chin, her eyes intent on his. "Are you trying to ask me to be your girl-friend?"

He sighed and hung his head, but the sound came out like a laugh. When he looked up, he could see that she was laughing too. "Yes . . . thanks for the interpretation." He straightened and tried to regain his composure. "Chey, would you be my girlfriend? I think it's about time . . ."

Even as he said the words, he realized they

didn't sound altogether romantic. Rather with all the time they'd spent together it was finally time to make their relationship official. He hoped she didn't take his words that way, but by the look in her eyes she seemed too happy to analyze exactly what he'd said. Cody searched her expression, looking for signs of doubts, signs that she maybe wondered whether Bailey was still an issue for him. But if Chey was worried at all, she didn't show it.

Instead she closed the gap between them and slipped her hands around his waist, her eyes still on his. "Yes, Cody." She smiled. "I'd love to be your girlfriend."

"Good." He felt relieved. "I've been thinking of a way to say that since our night at the coffee shop."

"You know what that means, right?" Her face was close to his, so close his senses filled with her perfume . . . the vanilla and cinnamon.

"What?" He brushed his face against hers, and he felt the moment become more intense, deeper.

"It means this is our opening night too. Just like Lyle." Her voice was playful, but it didn't change the smoky look in her eyes. "Kiss me, Cody . . . please."

A shallow breath caught in his throat, and

he tried to keep from looking surprised. This should've been his move, but he hadn't known if the time was right. Or he hadn't thought about it exactly. Either way, she didn't have to ask him twice. He leaned close and kissed her, kissed her in a way that he hoped told her just how much he cared, and that what he'd said back when she was in the hospital was all the more true now.

He wasn't going anywhere.

TWENTY-TWO

It was the last Bible study of the summer for Betty Keller and her friends, and Bailey wondered how she would've gotten through the weeks without this place of grounding and growing and learning. Most of all learning. Already the women had their Starbucks drinks and they were seated around Betty's living room.

One of the things Bailey loved about this group of friends was that they wasted no time getting to the heart of their struggles, the reasons that had brought them together for a study like this in the first place. Sara wore her red shoes — same as always — Marie had a new pair of cropped pants, and Barbara was tanned from a brief trip to Florida over the past week to see her daughter. But they spent only a minute or so on those details before they opened their Bibles and turned to Matthew chapter six.

"We always like to close our summer by

reading about forgiveness," Betty took the lead. "Forgiveness can be the one thing that truly holds us back in our Christian walk."

Bailey stared at the words in her Bible. If Betty hadn't said that she would've thought maybe the woman had chosen this section of Scripture for Bailey alone. For a moment she remembered what had happened a few days ago after her Bible study with the cast of *Hairspray.* A few more dancers had joined the group over the last five weeks, and Bailey thought they were making progress. Gerald and the others could see that Bailey wasn't out to attack them with Bible verses, and in fact they'd come to appreciate the time they shared together.

The problem was the rest of the cast, and long before this last meeting Bailey could sense the dissension between her and them. It came as no real surprise when Francesca showed up at the end of Bailey's Bible study a few days ago. She waited until it was over so they could talk, and she made herself clear. "You need to stop this . . . this Bible thing you're doing." Her tone wasn't angry, but it left no room for debate. "Whatever you're doing here . . . it's messing with the unity on my cast." She stopped and waved her hand toward the place where Bailey and Gerald and the others had been sitting. "At first I thought it would be fine . . . a little discussion time or whatever . . . something to honor Chrissy's memory." She stared straight at Bailey. "But not anymore. If you want to keep your spot with the *Hairspray* family, this is your last meeting."

"Yes, ma'am." Bailey didn't know what else to say. Ever since then she'd been angry with herself and angry with Francesca, frustrated at the other cast members who'd clearly gone to her and complained — even when they didn't know the first thing about what was discussed at the meeting.

That wasn't the only thing bothering Bailey. She'd updated her Facebook page over the weekend and there she had seen what she expected to see weeks ago. But that didn't make the realization any easier to take. Cody was in a relationship with Cheyenne. His Facebook status said so, and the photos from his team's first win showed one with Cody and Chey, their arms around each other, surrounded by celebrating football players.

The women were still catching up, talking amongst themselves about the struggles they'd faced that week. Bailey wanted to focus on what they were saying, but she couldn't stop thinking about Cody. It wasn't right that Cheyenne was sharing his football journey with him. She was the one with a lifetime of football knowledge. Her dad was the NFL coach, after all. If Cody had handled this right, Bailey would've been the one beside him in the picture, sharing with him his team's first win. She could've taken a weekend off for that, right?

Since then Bailey had caught herself checking his Facebook almost obsessively — every few hours. Every time she felt the unforgiveness in her heart, the way that the distance between them could have all been avoided if only Cody would've talked to her, if he would've believed her when she said she still cared, still wanted to talk to him.

"Bailey?" Barbara was looking at her. "Did you hear Betty?"

"I'm sorry." *Great,* she told herself. *The trouble with the cast . . . Cody's new relationship.* And now the women would think she didn't want to be here for their Bible study. She stared at her open Bible again and back at Betty. "Can you repeat it?"

"Definitely, honey." Betty's patience knew no boundaries as far as Bailey could tell. "We've already read the first part of Matthew six. It's your turn, if you'd read verses fourteen to fifteen."

"Yes, ma'am. Sorry." Bailey focused, silently asking God to speak to her heart as she read. "For if you forgive other people when they sin against you, your heavenly Father will also forgive you. But if you do not forgive others their sins, your Father will not forgive your sins."

The words hit Bailey like a sack of bricks, straight in her gut. Whatever she'd been holding against many of her castmates or Francesca Tilly — or even Cody — she absolutely had to let it go. She hung her head, her eyes running over the words one more time.

"This is always a hard part of the Bible for me," Sara sighed. "Like God wrote it just for me."

"I feel that way too." Barbara's voice was soft. "I especially like how that part . . . the part Bailey just read . . . comes after the plea in the prayer where we are to ask God to deliver us from temptation."

"Exactly." Irma nodded, thoughtful. "I always figured that was because our greatest temptation wouldn't be the big guns on the sin list — murder and theft and the rest. But something so simple we might overlook it. The temptation to hold a grudge."

"The call to forgive." Betty looked at Bailey. "What do you think, sweetie?"

A sad laugh sounded deep inside her. "I think Irma's right." She had learned not to hide things from these women. They had too much wisdom, too much to offer if she wanted to come out of this season in her life closer to God. "I've got a lot of forgiving to do."

"Tell us about your Bible study." Barbara crossed her legs and set her coffee down on the table beside her. "Is it still a struggle with the cast?"

Shame came over Bailey and she wished with all she had that she'd answered Francesca differently. She could've asked to move the Bible study to a local coffee shop, or to make it less about the cast and more of a talk open to anyone who wanted to come. But she had simply given up, and over the next ten minutes she explained the situation to the women.

"I'm sorry." Betty knew more than the others how much the Bible study meant to Bailey, and how she had wanted so badly to obey God by having the meeting in the first place. "You made a difference with your cast, even if you never get together with them again."

"But I'm mad at myself too. I gave up too easily."

Sara smiled. "Life can be hard on people who want to make a difference for God."

"It's true." Irma leaned forward. "I remember once when I was newly married seeing a bald eagle soaring overhead during a drive with my husband. For a while I watched it, soaring and dipping, riding the currents higher toward the heavens. But then out of nowhere came a couple of small-ish crows. Rather than do their own thing, the crows caught up to the eagle and began dive-bombing it, flying at its wings and talons, poking at it and irritating it."

Bailey let the picture play out in her mind. "I've seen that before. Out at Lake Monroe in Bloomington where I grew up. The eagle seemed unfazed by it . . . he kept flying in big arcs and circles, moving higher until the smaller birds left him alone."

"Exactly." Barbara's eyes told Bailey she, too, understood the analogy from God's creation. "And that's just what God wants us to do."

"The truth is, people pick on those who shine." Sara smiled at Bailey. "It's always been that way."

They looked at the Bible again, and they agreed that the most important thing they could do is forgive people who harmed them, and to fly — like the eagle — to higher ground until the problems of life, the hurtful people of life, were so far below they couldn't cause pain any longer.

"There is one thing to remember." Sara took a sip from her drink and looked around the room. "Sometimes we feel like the world is against us . . . and there are many days when we're the eagle. But other times we're the crow. And for that we need to make things right . . . change our actions and ask God to forgive us."

Bailey thought about that, and gradually a truth began to dawn on her. At least where Cody was concerned, he wasn't the only one who'd been quiet, who hadn't made an effort to stay in touch. She'd been mad at him since January, and because of that even when she might've otherwise worked to stay friends with him, she'd allowed the silence between them as much as he had. Sara was right . . . she needed to ask God for forgiveness over that and her ill feelings toward a number of her castmates . . . same as she needed to forgive.

By the time the Bible study was finished, and after the women had prayed — specifically asking God for protection and encouragement for Bailey — she was emotionally drained. She had already called the cast members in her Bible study and told them the meeting was cancelled for now. Gerald seemed most sorry about the situation. "I thought we could do all things through

Christ," he told her. He wasn't mocking her or the Bible verse they'd looked at a few weeks ago. But he sounded hurt. "I can't believe you'd give up so easy, Bailey."

That was earlier this morning, and now after the Bible study on forgiveness, Bailey missed home and her mom more than she had since she arrived in New York. Before she headed down the hall to her room, Betty came to her. "Honey, I think you need a good talk with your family back home." She soothed her hand along Bailey's arm. "Use that Skype thing you like to do. That'll help you feel better."

"Thanks, Betty." Bailey went to her room, grateful again for Betty Keller. She might as well have been family, and again Bailey thought she was a lot like Elizabeth Baxter. She flopped on her bed and for a few minutes she stared out the window at the buildings all around her. Times like this, New York City was suffocating. She wanted nothing more than to drive to LaGuardia Airport, hop on a plane, and be home in time for dinner.

But what would she learn from that?

She stood, went to her computer, and moved the mouse. As she did the screen came to life and she saw her Skype program light up. Betty was right — she could call her mom and ask her to chat on Skype for a while. Maybe her mom would know what she could do with her Bible study . . . how to stand strong for God without losing her job. She was about to call her mom and see if she had time to talk on Skype when a sound came from the lower panel of her computer.

"Brandon!" In her hurt over the fact that Cody had moved on, she had forgotten that Brandon was supposed to be back in Los Angeles over the weekend. For the past weeks he'd spent more time in a handful of exotic islands filming his next movie, but now — clearly — he must've been home. He couldn't Skype her if he didn't have internet — and he hadn't had it on location for sure.

A message popped up on her screen asking her if she'd like to have a Skype video chat with Brandon Paul, and Bailey clicked *yes*. Her heart felt lighter already. After a few more noises, the Skype window filled her computer screen and there he was — Brandon — smiling at her and looking so close he might as well have been sitting across from her. "Do you know how long I've waited for this moment?" He was always lighthearted, always more of a tease than a true romantic. But right now, even as Brandon's eyes sparkled, she was pretty sure he wasn't kidding. Not in any way.

"I've missed you!"

"Really?" He leaned closer to the screen. "So I should come see you, is that what you're saying?"

"I wish." She felt her spirits dip again. "You'll be busy for another four weeks, right? Isn't that what you said?"

"Not that long." His eyes held hers, and her sadness and guilt from earlier today faded compared to how he made her feel. "Besides, I have to see your show again. I'd see it every night if I could."

"Not tonight." She laughed, enjoying the feel of his eyes on hers. "We're dark today. I'm off until tomorrow."

"That's right." He leaned back and laced his fingers behind his head. "So that means our Skype date can last all day. Wouldn't that be great?"

She giggled. "If you want."

"I want." His eyes softened. "You have no idea how much I want that. How much I wish I was there with you." They locked eyes and stayed that way for a long while. Then as if he'd just remembered something he held up his phone and seemed to check the time. "Wow, it's almost one." He held up his finger. "Hold on. I'll be right back."

She waited, grateful that he was home, that they could talk through Skype this way. She had so much to tell him. But as she watched the empty screen facing what she assumed was his bedroom or his office at the studio, she sat up straighter, squinting at the details. The room where he'd been sitting didn't look like anything from his house or his studio or —

Suddenly someone put gentle hands on her shoulders, and she screamed. At the same time she whirled around and her hand flew to her mouth. "Brandon?" She stood, laughing even as tears flooded her eyes. "Are you serious? You're really here?" She jumped into his arms and they stayed that way a long time, holding onto each other.

"You should've seen Betty trying to think of a place to hide me during your Bible study." He laughed, his eyes tender toward Bailey's landlord. "And trying to explain Skype to her." He whistled low. "Wow . . . that was tough. But I needed you to get on Skype if I was going to make it happen like this."

"I love it . . . I mean," she looked at her computer screen and back at him. "It's like you transported yourself here or something." She hugged him again, and her voice lost some of its excitement. Instead there

408

was a depth in her tone that she had only recently started using around him. "You don't know how much I needed to see you today."

"God knew." He smiled at her, and then hugged her once more. Bailey couldn't believe it, couldn't convince herself she wasn't dreaming. Brandon was really here!

And because of that all was right with the world.

TWENTY-THREE

Brandon stayed at a hotel a few blocks away from the Kellers' apartment, and after a long day with Bailey he was finally ready for sleep. He had big plans tomorrow, but for now he couldn't stop thinking about the last ten hours. Right from the beginning when he surprised Bailey the day had been perfect. He'd brought an Old Navy baseball cap and dark sunglasses this time, and he wore beat up khaki shorts — too plain for anyone to think he was a celebrity.

They walked through Times Square holding hands, and shared dinner at a small pizza shop — all without being recognized even once. Brandon climbed into bed and thought about the last two months filming on the Tahitian Islands, spending every day making a movie with a handful of Hollywood's top talent. No matter how great the experience, he had missed Bailey with every breath.

His leading lady this time was Eva Gentry, a single, exotic-looking brunette in her mid-twenties. On the first day of the shoot she'd asked him to take a walk with her to the beach. Night had already fallen, and Brandon had his guard up from the moment they set out. Once they reached the shore, the actress started to take off her shirt. "Let's take a swim."

"Hey," Brandon grabbed her top and pulled it back into place. "You said you wanted to walk."

"It's the oldest line in the book." She had batted her dark eyes at him, moving closer. "Come on, Brandon . . . you and I know what's going to happen on this island. We're here for weeks. We're supposed to be in love."

Brandon explained that he was flattered. "But you need to know something." He kept his distance, his arms crossed, his voice filled with a new sort of passion. "See . . . I want to honor God. I haven't done that most of my life, but it's not an option now. God comes first."

Eva rolled her eyes. "Please . . ." She gave him a snobby look. "You've got to be kidding me, Brandon Paul. You and I made out at a party a year ago. And now you've got to honor God?"

"I've changed." He hated that maybe his response might hurt her, or make her feel like he was rejecting her. "I'm not the same person I was back then."

She took a step closer and grabbed a fist-ful of his T-shirt. "I bet I can prove you are."

"Eva." He had taken a firm hold of her hand and moved it off his shirt then. "I'm serious. He hoped she could see his heart, the fact that he truly *had* changed. "My life's so much happier . . . I'd love to tell you about it sometime."

"With our clothes on?" She sneered at him. Her laughter was an attempt to save face.

"Yes." Brandon was frustrated with him-self for how he had once lived. She wouldn't act this way if he hadn't been very available back before he chose a relationship with Christ. "With our clothes on."

She looked him up and down from his eyes to his feet and back — slow and measured, like she was sizing up his worth as a man. "Forget it, Brandon. You've lost it . . . I can see that now."

"It isn't only my faith," he called after her. It was a moment he would remember, because it underlined the fact that he wanted to go public about his feelings for Bailey.

Eva stopped and looked back at him, her expression mocking him. "What, Brandon? What else could make you tell me no?"

"I'm in love with someone else." He had crossed his arms, his toes deep in the sand. "Even if I wasn't a Christian, I wouldn't do anything to hurt her."

The memory of the conversation faded. Brandon rolled onto his side in the king-sized hotel bed and remembered the look on her face as she walked away, leaving him alone on the beach. Like whoever Brandon was in love with — compared to Eva — wasn't even worth asking about. Instead the look on her face told him the missed moment on the beach was his loss.

The amazing thing was he hadn't been tempted — even after their filming began in earnest. At first Brandon worried the encounter might damage their on-screen chemistry. But Eva was too much of a professional for that. If anything, she tried harder, so that when they shared a kissing scene she would trip a little or fumble her lines and the director would cut the action and ask for a retake.

"A dozen retakes," she whispered one day to him. They were standing in knee-deep warm blue water, and her words were shared between just the two of them.

"That's my goal today. A dozen retakes."

Brandon knew there would be challenges ahead — being a leading man in Hollywood, finding himself on location shoots with girls like Eva . . . He would always have to keep his guard up in this profession. But with his faith, he was ready for the challenge. Besides, no other girl mattered besides Bailey. If he had his way, tomorrow would help Bailey believe that — even if just a little more than the last time he was here.

He fell asleep thinking about their time in New York City, how Bailey had bought him a Statue of Liberty foam rubber visor and how he'd worn it over his baseball cap — enjoying the feel of her laughing beside him. He could hardly wait to see *Hairspray* tomorrow night. But only after the surprise he had for the daytime. He smiled to himself.

He could hardly wait.

The next morning Bailey was ready half an hour before Brandon arrived at the Kellers' apartment. During that time she had coffee with Betty and Bob. The couple shared more of their story, how Bob had met Betty when they were just twenty, and how she was dating someone else at the time.

"You stole me from him. In the middle of

our date." Betty grinned, and it was easy to see that she remembered the long ago night. "I don't think he ever forgave you."

Bob waved off the possibility. "It was your first date with the guy."

"Still." She smiled at Bailey. "It's true. He never forgave Bob."

Bailey laughed. These two were great, and gradually over the weeks she'd learned much about them. They would always feel like family, no matter how long she stayed in New York City or where God took her next.

"So," Betty's eyes twinkled. "Where's Brandon taking you today?"

"I'm not sure." She smoothed her pink T-shirt and white shorts. She had gone through three outfits looking for the perfect thing to wear today, and she was happy with her choice. It was the end of August, and she'd heard that the sweltering heat from last week was scheduled to let up a little. She smiled at Betty. "Life's always a surprise with Brandon."

"I see that." She smiled, but she looked slightly pensive. "He's full of life, that's for sure."

Bailey wasn't sure she wanted to ask . . . she had a feeling the Kellers weren't a hundred percent sold on Brandon. But she pressed on anyway. "What do you think of him?"

"We don't really know him. Just a few minutes yesterday when he got here." Bob grinned. His expression was far easier going than his wife's. "I let him in and told him hello . . . that's about it."

"I guess the better question," Betty leaned over the table, her coffee cup caught between her hands, "is what do you think about him, Bailey?"

She laughed. "That's easy . . . I mean, look at yesterday. I was so down I was ready to board the next flight home. Brandon shows up and changes everything."

"Yes." Her expression remained the same, the questions in her eyes not quite satisfied with Bailey's answer. "But is he someone you could love, Bailey?"

She thought about Cody, and his relationship with Cheyenne . . . the fact that he'd moved on and the reality that she'd most likely never talk to him again. "Yes . . ." She believed her answer to the center of her heart. "Yes, I could love him." She shrugged, her mood easy. "Maybe I already do."

They talked about the Bible study and the forgiveness God calls His people to do. "I feel a lot more able to forgive today . . . after spending the afternoon and evening with Brandon."

"Did you tell him what you were dealing with?" Betty would've made a good counselor. She raised one eyebrow, not prodding but pressing the matter just enough to make Bailey squirm.

"I tried a couple times." She remembered the chaos in Times Square, the crowds of people and their constant determination that no one would recognize either of them. "We'll talk about it today."

Bailey made a point to remember her statement, both then and later when she and Brandon climbed in the back of a black Suburban and the driver Brandon had hired pulled out into traffic. Not now, but sometime today she wanted to tell Brandon about her struggle with the cast and Francesca . . . and maybe even her thoughts about Cody.

He left some distance between them as he turned to face her. "You haven't guessed where we're going?"

"To the moon?" She turned and rested the side of her face on the seat. How thrilling to have a whole day with him. "With you anything's possible."

"Hmmm . . . the moon." He put his arm on the back of the seat and played with a strand of her hair. "That would be fun. But

417

not today."

She realized how little they'd talked about anything serious yesterday. "So tell me about your shoot . . . how's it going?"

"It's great." He hesitated. "Eva Gentry is interesting. She's made it a challenge."

Bailey wanted to ask. She knew a little of what it was like to date someone who was constantly filming love scenes with some actress. Her Christian Kids Theater drama instructor Katy Hart had dealt with that during the years she dated Dayne Matthews. Ultimately — before they got married — Dayne decided he wouldn't do love scenes, not unless they were with Katy. These days he spent his professional time directing and producing rather than acting.

The slightest wave of jealousy washed over her. Eva Gentry was gorgeous, and every week she was with a different guy on the covers of the tabloids. Bailey wasn't sure why, but she hadn't given the reality a lot of thought until now. Too busy trying to hold her life together — what with the sad loss of Chrissy and her Bible study and the eight shows a week. But now she pictured the setting — a sunny secluded island, a love story, and weeks and weeks with Eva Gentry.

A handful of questions came to mind, like whether Eva had hit on him or whether

Brandon had mentioned that he was sort of seeing someone. Brandon was watching her, and after a few seconds he put his hand on her cheek. "I know what you're thinking."

"You do?" Her heart skipped a beat and pounded faster than before. If she were going to let this sort of thing bother her, then she and Brandon didn't stand a chance. She tried to keep the mood light with a smile. "Fine . . . tell me."

"You want to know about Eva and me . . ." He didn't look bothered. If anything, there was more love in his eyes now than when they first got into the SUV. "From the first day she thought we'd be together — on and off camera. But I told her I'd changed and my faith was everything to me. I wasn't interested in cheap affairs."

Bailey would've liked to see Eva Gentry's reaction to that. "Did she laugh?"

"She did." He brushed his fingers against her skin, his touch light. "Betty tells me you've dealt with some of that too." He raised an eyebrow. "The Bible study?" He smiled. "We have a lot to talk about, don't we?"

"We do." She felt relieved. A part of her had wondered if Brandon would ever be as deep as Cody, as able to hear her heart and care about the important things inside her.

But here he was dismissing her fears with every word. He cared. Betty had talked to him, and he'd remembered to ask Bailey about it today. Not only that, but he was being an open book about his time with Eva. Her heart soared . . . wherever he was taking her they would have hours to catch up. She just hoped they'd have time alone so they wouldn't be distracted trying to disguise themselves or navigate the busy city streets.

They pulled into a parking lot just north of Chelsea Piers and Brandon nodded to a gorgeous yacht. "I rented it for the day. So we can talk."

She let her head fall back and she laughed out loud. Being with him was better than anything she could've dreamed. Every day more unbelievable than the last. They were escorted from the SUV to the boat and Bailey wasn't surprised to find a private staff ready to serve them. Again if they knew who Brandon was, they said nothing. But then that was part of their job — allowing celebrities the chance for privacy.

Brandon took her to the top deck, to a covered open-air patio. Two reclining beach chairs were there with a pitcher of iced tea and a table full of fresh fruit and other snacks. "Have I mentioned that I'm amazed?" Bailey looked at him as they took the chairs. "Is there any detail you don't think about?"

He gave a silly sort of modest shrug, and he slipped a pair of sunglasses on. "Come on, Bailey . . . you're worth all this and more."

The boat set sail fifteen minutes later, and they took off down the Hudson River. Bailey had always wanted to do this — ever since she'd moved to New York. There were public ship lines that conducted public tours around the Island of Manhattan. But always she'd been busy with the show, or unable to find someone to go with. Taking Brandon on a cruise like that had never been a possibility, because on a small three-decker public tour boat he was bound to get recognized.

But this was altogether perfect. Bailey sat down and settled back in her chair. She found her own sunglasses in her purse, put them on, and stared at the skyline. From this place on the top deck of the yacht, they could see the city and harbor perfectly.

"We're going to the Statue of Liberty first." His voice held the familiar sense of playfulness. "I figured since you got me my first Statue of Liberty hat, we should at least make a stop there."

"Definitely." The trip to the statue took about fifteen minutes, and in that time they simply let the breeze wash over them, grateful to be alone together. They stood and walked to the railing as they neared Liberty Island, and Bailey reached for his hand. "Thank you, Brandon. Really. I can't believe this."

He put his arm around her shoulders and pulled her close, both of them facing the water. "I love this . . . planning days like this for you." He leaned his head against hers. They stayed that way, watching as the yacht drew closer to the statue. Finally, they felt the captain cut the engine. A voice came over the intercom. "We'll take a few minutes here, like you requested."

Brandon smiled and he jogged back to his chair. A stuffed beach bag sat by his chair, something else he must have planned ahead of time. He reached inside, pulled out his Statue of Liberty hat, and slipped it on. Then he grabbed a second one from the bag and a small camera, as well. "The paparazzi wished they had this picture." He returned to her, handed her the second visor, and waited until she had it on. Then he put his arm around her, and — holding the camera out with his left hand — he took their picture. "Best happy snap ever. This'll be on Facebook by tonight." He winked at her. "Under my pseudonym of course."

He showed her the picture, and Bailey laughed hard at the way they looked, trying to be serious, their green foam visors waving in the wind. They tried to get a picture of the Statue of Liberty, but no angle actually did it justice. "It's one of those things you need to see in person to appreciate."

Bailey agreed, and after Brandon put their hats and the camera away he returned to her side. He put his arm around her once more and again they leaned on the railing, taking in the beauty of the river and the distant bridges. "So, Bailey . . . tell me about the Bible study."

It touched her deeply that he remembered to bring it up again. Now when they had time to talk. "It started with Chrissy's death."

"I'm sorry about that." He faced her, and held her arms, running his thumbs over her bare skin. "I wanted to be there for you."

"It's okay." She let her head fall against his for a few seconds. His presence would've only caused more tension. The memorial wasn't open to anyone outside the cast, anyway. She looked at him again. "It means a lot that you wish you were there."

"So . . . at the memorial you told everyone

you wanted to have a Bible study . . . is that right?"

Bailey nodded, and over the next half hour she went back to the beginning, how she'd ignored God's voice and let Chrissy down, and how she couldn't do that twice. She told him Francesca originally okayed the Bible study, thinking that anything in Chrissy's memory would be worthwhile. "But too many of the cast members thought we were sitting around judging them . . . and they complained." She felt awful about the admission ahead, but she had to tell him the truth. "Francesca asked me to stop the study, and I agreed. I called it off."

"Hmm . . ." Brandon waited, letting Bailey's words sit for a few seconds. He brushed a wisp of her hair back from her forehead. "Maybe it was just a season . . . a short time when God wanted the study, and now it's time to move on."

"Or maybe I'm supposed to try harder." She told him about Gerald and his questions about homosexuality, and how they had looked at Bible verses together, trying to grasp God's take on sin in general — all sin. And how people needed to never give up fighting against it.

"Wow . . ." Brandon looked impressed. "That couldn't have been easy."

"It wasn't."

He slipped his arms around her back and slowly drew her in, close to him. "I'm proud of you, Bailey. I'm not sure I'm that brave. And I have as many chances to share God's views on that topic as you do. Hollywood's full of people who feel the way your cast feels. Like I must hate gay people just because I love Jesus."

"Exactly."

One of the staff members appeared in the doorway and signaled to Brandon. "Lunch, sir?"

"Yes, that's great. Thank you." He led Bailey back to the table where a couple of chairs had been brought in for the occasion. The conversation lightened while they ate salmon and spinach and fresh baked bread. After lunch they explored the yacht, and finally wound up on the top deck at their spot alongside the railing.

"This day . . . it's been perfect." He grinned. "Well, not quite. After I get the chance to see you perform . . . then it'll be perfect."

She laughed, and the sound mixed with the breeze off the Hudson. "Don't get your hopes up. I'm still hanging on by a thread — at least that's how I feel."

They turned toward the water and allowed

a comfortable silence for a while. Finally Brandon turned, his face close to hers. "There is one thing I forgot to tell you. About Eva and the movie shoot."

Bailey's stomach tightened, and her next breath didn't come as easily. Was this it, the moment where he admitted some awful transgression, or some change of mind? She looked for answers in his eyes . . . waiting for him to explain.

Again he turned toward her. "Don't look so worried." This time he took hold of her hands.

"I'm not."

"Bailey . . ."

"Really." She laughed, but it sounded forced. "I mean . . . I'm interested in what you forgot to tell me." She emphasized the word forgot, but her light laughter kept the mood light. "But I'm not worried."

"You are." His teasing was meant to be playful, nothing more. "I like it . . . that you're worried."

"Oh, you do?" She laughed a little more easily this time. Whatever he wanted to tell her, it couldn't be too bad.

"Yes." He slid his fingers between hers and took a step closer. The rest of the world faded away. "I like that you care." He took his time, clearly enjoying this moment.

"So . . ."

"Well . . ." His smile let up and his eyes filled with a vulnerability she'd rarely seen before. He released her hands and put his arms around her waist. The boat swayed, and the two of them moved gently with it — like a dance that needed no music. "I told Eva I wasn't interested because I wanted to honor God." He brought one hand to her face. "But I also told her there was another reason."

Bailey felt dizzy, caught up in the moment, in the intimacy between them. "What . . ." She swallowed, her voice so soft even she could barely hear it. "What did you tell her?"

"I told her . . ." Brandon was so close he could've kissed her. "I was in love with someone else."

Bailey let that sink in for a long few seconds. Was he serious? "You told her that?" The sun on her shoulders . . . the view of the city and the sway of the boat . . . the feel of his arms around her . . . She had never felt this way in all her life.

"I said it . . ." He drew her closer, his voice a whisper against her cheek. "And I meant it."

Bailey wasn't sure what to say, how to respond. So she stayed in his arms, her head against his chest as the possibilities slow-danced in her heart. The boat docked and they found their way back to the Suburban. They shared an early dinner in a private steak house room in Manhattan and later that night she danced her heart out on the J. Markham Theater stage. After that they shared another carriage ride, this one through Central Park. Brandon made her laugh with a dozen stories from his recent weeks on set. When the time came, she hated telling Brandon goodbye. That night alone in her room she relived every moment with him and wished more than anything that he didn't have to go home so soon. Because even as she prayed for God to make sense of her swirling emotions, for the first time she was consumed by one very clear thought.

Maybe she was in love with him too.

TWENTY-FOUR

Ashley loved Friday night football at Clear Creek High because it gave her a diversion from the rest of the week. Every other day of the week, Landon was still restless, still not sure what his future held or if he'd find a career he loved as much as fighting fires. The pain of losing his ability to work was as great as if someone had died. And though Landon handled the heartache better than before the good news that he didn't have polymyositis, Ashley knew he was suffering.

Which was why the whole extended Baxter family looked forward to Friday nights. Her sister Kari's husband Ryan coached the team, and whenever they had a home game, as many of the family attended as possible. Pizza first at Ashley and Landon's house, then a caravan to the game. Tonight Ashley's sisters Brooke and Kari, and her brother Luke and their families had just arrived and were gathered in the family room ready to eat.

"Mommy, when do the pizza men get here?" Devin found her in the kitchen filling plastic water pitchers. He said the words pizza men with a special emphasis, like they were superheroes of some sort.

"Pizza man." She patted his head. "Just one pizza man, Dev."

"Oh." He looked slightly disappointed. "Okay, so when's he get here?"

"Any minute." She smiled at him. "You like pizza, don't you?"

"Sooo much, Mommy!" He ran off, yelling at the top of his lungs. "Mommy says any minute!"

The doorbell rang and Landon called out from the other room. "I'll get it."

Relief eased the cold and nervous edges of Ashley's heart. Landon sounded happy tonight, hopeful and confident . . . the way he had always sounded before he started coughing. She brought the water to the other room, and everyone gathered around the dining room table.

"That's a whole football field of pizza!" Devin held onto the back of one of the chairs and peered around it at the four large pizzas spread across the table. "I can't wait!"

Cole put his arm around his little brother's

shoulders. "Maybe we should pray first, buddy."

A serious look flashed on Devin's face and he nodded big. "Yes. Maybe we should."

Brooke's husband, Peter, prayed . . . thanking God for the food and the time together, and asking that the Lord be present in all they said and did that evening. When he finished, they situated the kids at the table, and the adults carried plates of pizza out to the family room.

The conversation was easy and upbeat. Brooke talked about the crisis pregnancy center she and Ashley helped run in downtown Bloomington. Under Brooke's direction, the center had started a Purity Pledge Program, where girls could come in and take a pledge to stay pure until they were married. In exchange for the pledge, they received a certificate, a booklet about the realities of premarital sex, and coupons from various local merchants. "Word's definitely gotten out around the high schools." Brooke looked comfortable next to Peter, his arm around her shoulders. "We're busier than ever."

They talked about Kari and Ryan, how it was to have him gone so much of the football season. "Jenny Flanigan jokes that she's a football widow every fall," Kari laughed lightheartedly. "I don't mind, I guess. I love being married to a coach. Every season is a new set of players and games and possibilities for greatness." She smiled at the others. "It keeps life exciting."

In the other room, the kids' voices blended together in a happy mix of laughter and teasing and pronouncements from Devin — who easily had the loudest voice of the group. Brooke noted that it was too bad Erin and Sam couldn't make it. Their girls had the flu, so they'd stayed back for a quiet night at home. "She loves these Friday nights . . . I hope the girls get better soon."

Kari's eyes lit up. "Speaking of football, Ryan tells me he heard from Cody Coleman. He's coaching at Lyle High near the Ohio border, remember? I think I told you all that a month ago."

They nodded, agreeing that they knew about Cody's position. Jenny Flanigan had talked to Ashley not long ago. She was interested in how his season was going. "How's he doing?"

"I guess incredibly well." Kari grinned. "His team is undefeated after three games."

"What?" Landon raised his brow. "That team hasn't won a game in two years."

"Exactly." Kari laughed. "God's doing something amazing out there in that small town. Ryan tells me everyone's got Cody slated as a hero. They could lose every game from here out and they would credit him with bringing life back to not only the football team — but the whole town."

"That's fantastic." Peter set his empty pizza plate on the arm of the sofa. "I always liked that young man. I wish we could've kept him here at Clear Creek."

A round of agreements came after that, and as the conversation lulled, Landon coughed a few times. Luke must've picked up on the fact. "What does your doctor say about your lungs . . . since the great news on the electromyography test?"

Ashley watched her husband closely. He didn't flinch, didn't let on that he was still suffering from the loss of his job. He clearly understood that Luke only asked because he cared. A casual smile played on Landon's lips and he gave a slow single nod. "It's good news . . . what they say now is I've got COPD."

"Chronic obstructive pulmonary disease." Brooke looked concerned. She was a pediatrician, but she was knowledgeable on all things medical. "Landon . . . that's still very serious."

"It is." The calm in his face remained. "I'll be working soon with an occupational therapist, learning ways to work around the disease, and how to keep my airways as open as possible."

"There's a lot they can do now . . . between medications and walking programs." Peter tried to sound hopeful. "What's the work situation?"

"A desk job for now." Again Landon didn't let on how much this subject hurt. He crossed one leg over his knee and sat back in his chair. "But I'm looking at a few other ideas." He smiled at Ashley. "We're praying about it. God has a plan . . . we know that."

Luke had been quiet since he brought the subject up, but now he leaned over his knees and laced his hands together, his eyes on Landon, his expression grave. "I've done a little research. More than eighty percent of the workers from Ground Zero are experiencing decreased lung function." He pursed his lips, as if he didn't want to share this information. Ashley understood. She and her brother had been best friends growing up. She knew Luke. The only reason he would talk about this was because he cared about Landon.

"I've read that about Ground Zero." Landon frowned and shook his head. "It's terrible. A couple guys have already been diagnosed with polymyositis . . . at least one has had a lung transplant."

"So . . ." Luke looked hesitant, like he wasn't sure he should bring up everything he knew at this moment. But he continued anyway. The Baxter family had always been close enough to talk about difficult things. Even this. "Are you aware there's a class action lawsuit filed against New York City over this subject?"

For the first time that night, Landon's expression darkened slightly. "I hadn't heard that."

"There is." Luke was a lawyer. He would know. "Hundreds of people have joined the suit or filed one of their own. To cover medical expenses and lost wages — that sort of thing."

Again Landon nodded slowly. For a long moment his eyes glazed over and Ashley wondered if he was thinking about his time at Ground Zero, the months he'd spent on the pile of debris removing one bucket full after another, searching for his fallen friend, Jalen. Whatever he was thinking, after a few seconds he blinked and turned his attention back to Luke. The half smile was back, and Landon's tone was kind and understanding. "Are you asking . . . if I'd like to sue the city of New York over what's happened to my lungs?"

An uncomfortable silence hung in the room for a few beats, and the attention turned to Luke. He hung his head briefly and then looked at Landon again. "I'm sorry . . . I wasn't sure how you'd feel about it. I just . . . you're entitled to settlement money, Landon. There's nothing wrong with joining the lawsuit at this point." His voice held no passion, no hint at whether he had an opinion one way or another about what Landon should do. "I just want you to know your options."

"Thank you." Landon looked ready to move on, to change the subject to anything but his lungs and his time at Ground Zero. "That might make sense for some people. But not for me." His smile held a finality, as if to say the subject would forever more be closed. "I went to Ground Zero by my own will. We couldn't see through the air, so obviously there were risks." He seemed to work hard to keep his tone even, so the conversation wouldn't put a damper on the entire evening. "I guess I'd have to say I took the risks willingly." He hesitated. "Whatever the risks, whatever the results . . . I'd do it all again." He shook his head. "So, no . . . I couldn't sue New York City."

Ashley was so proud she could've jumped

up and hugged him right there in front of her family. But she didn't want to drag the moment out. So instead she simply stood and smiled at the others. "More pizza?"

Landon raised his hand. "Pepperoni . . . if you don't mind." He handed his plate to Ashley and they shared a knowing look, a single glance that told her he had maybe found new purpose in the last few minutes. That if he could truly link his lung disease and lost career as a firefighter to his time at Ground Zero, then maybe he could live with the outcome a little easier.

She took orders from Peter and Brooke, and walked to the pizza table to get the pieces. The kids were still working on their dinners, excited about the football game. Little Janessa wore a child-size Clear Creek cheer sweater and Cole had brushed eye black beneath his eyes. The way the Clear Creek High School kids did before cheering on their team.

As she filled the empty plates, Ashley thought again about how much she loved Landon, how glad she was that he could gain something from a conversation like the one they'd just had. Like Landon said, he was searching for new career paths — possibly working with the sheriff's department, or as a teacher for other paramedics and firefighters. Nothing he was passionate about yet, but what he'd told Luke was true. He and Ashley were praying about what was next, trusting God that something would come through.

The bottom line was this: Landon didn't want sympathy. He didn't want to be a victim or blame someone for what had happened to him. Because Landon would've laid his life down to help out. It was why he could run into a burning house to save a stranger, and why he had gone to Ground Zero in the first place.

She gave Luke a quick smile as she left the room, to let him know he hadn't done anything wrong by bringing the topic up. He was only trying to help — they all understood that. But even though there were many people who would be right in suing New York City for the damage they'd received working at Ground Zero, she was glad Landon didn't want to be one of them. Like he said, he'd taken the risk on willingly.

Now they would all live with the outcome.

Cody grabbed his gear bag from the empty locker room and silently thanked God for the miracle he was bringing about for the town of Lyle. Tonight's forty-two to twenty-four win came against Arlington High — another local powerhouse that should've handily beaten the Buckaroos. But this year was different. God had heard the prayers of DeMetri Smith and Marcos Brown, and the rest of their teammates. He had heard Cody's prayers too.

There was no other explanation.

Not only were the kids winning. That helped, of course. But the town had come together too. People knew about Larry Sanders' little sister, and as a result, a fund had been set up at the bank. A local business owner put a thousand dollars in for every game Lyle won. When news got out about the man's generosity, two other businesses agreed to do the same thing. Already the family had access to more than ten-thousand dollars to continue the child's cancer treatment. Her face at every Friday night game was just one of the ways Cody could feel God working among them.

In addition, the local paper had done a feature story on Lyle's success at football camp, how they'd set a record by winning the first-place trophy every day of the week. When the reporter found out why they'd won, that they were raising money for a troubled team, only to find out that the troubled team was their own — he about went through the roof.

"This is the best story I've ever covered," he told Cody. The guy was in his fifties, a veteran who had spent his life covering the happenings of Lyle, Indiana. He had tears in his eyes as he took notes that day. "This will run on the front page. I guarantee it."

The story did indeed run on the front page of that Sunday's paper, and a week later it was picked up by the Indianapolis press. A week after that, a small story ran in *USA Today,* of all things. Now there was talk that *Sports Illustrated* might call, wanting to talk to Cody about his role as coach of the Buckaroos, and how small-town high school football could bring people together and even change lives.

One of the best parts was that every story included the team's chant, the words they said before every game and after every halftime, the words they shouted loud after every practice.

"Whose way?"

"His way!"

"Whose way?"

"His way!!"

Cody had received emails from other high school coaches. "Are we allowed to talk about doing things God's way at a public school?" one coach wrote to him last week.

"The idea scares me to death."

His answer was as honest as he could be. "Our constitution promises freedom *of* religion. Not freedom *from* religion. If you're worried about leading a chant like that, see if one of your players wants to do it. They're allowed freedom of speech."

It was crazy, really. Cody had only set out to build up the guys on his team, to make them close and give them an experience they'd remember long after high school. But in the process word was getting out around the state of Indiana . . . even around the nation. A coach who loved God and his players could literally change a town for good.

The story kept getting better, and Cody could hardly take credit for what was happening. Because of the feature story, people found out about Terry Allen, and his family's burned down house. Last weekend the team gathered at Terry's house and half the town showed up to help rebuild the home. People donated supplies and time, and now in the middle of September the house was almost finished. Long before winter, the Allens would have a place to live again — all because of what a group of football players had done at camp.

Last week a tray of fifty individually wrapped football cookies was delivered to the Lyle High athletic office — along with a check for the Sanders' family fund. Cody wasn't surprised to read the card and find a note from Jim Flanigan.

We're following your success, Cody, the wins on the field and off. We're so very proud of you. Please know that we continue to pray for you daily. With all our love, Jim, Jenny, and the Flanigan kids.

It was all so much more than Cody ever dreamed possible. He looked around the quiet locker room. He cherished this place in the postgame hours, the time after the fans had gone off to celebrate, and when only Cheyenne and DeMetri waited for him out in his pickup. The thought of Cheyenne made him smile. The two of them talked once in a while about where the future might lead, whether this might be a forever relationship. They'd kissed a few times, but only very briefly. Cody respected Chey, and they both wanted to honor God. Cody didn't have the roller-coaster feeling when he was with Cheyenne, but that didn't worry him. He was older now, more mature.

The way he'd felt with Bailey wasn't something he would feel again.

He zipped his bag, and for a minute he sat on the bench in front of the row of lockers. He breathed in deep, letting every wonderful thing about the season settle in his heart.

You're so good, God . . . beyond anything I could ever ask or imagine.

I am your Father . . . I go before you, always.

Cody basked in the reality of the truth, the certainty of the answer. He slid off the bench and dropped to his knees, humbled and grateful before a God who could turn even a smelly locker room into holy ground. "I am yours, God . . . lead me . . . teach me . . . help me to keep learning."

Cody stayed that way, on his knees before God, in the presence of the Holy Spirit. He rarely thought about his biological father. He had no connection to the guy whatsoever, and he doubted the man ever thought about Cody. There were times growing up when that fact had hurt more than a small boy could take, times when he would cry alone in his room wishing with all his heart for a dad. He had no father to play catch with or go fishing with . . . no man to cheer him on when he did well in grade school or for the local Pee Wee Football League.

His mom was always in and out of prison, in and out of her drug binges. When she wasn't around, Cody would stay with a neighbor or a friend from school. But none of the situations ever provided someone who felt like a father. Not until he came to live with the Flanigans. He smiled, his head bowed. "Thank You for Jim Flanigan, Lord." In some ways, the man would always fill that role — the father he never knew.

But in this private moment of serenity, as Cody pondered all the good God had done in his life, and in the last month . . . he was most grateful for the truth he'd just been reminded of. Even when he was at his loneliest as a little boy, and when he was fighting in Iraq or trying to deal with the heartache of losing Bailey, he was never without a dad.

God was his father.

Cody stood up, massaging his left knee, the one that still ached from the injury he'd suffered at war. He gathered his gear bag onto his shoulder and looked around the place. Stinky or not, he loved the smell of a locker room after a football game, loved the strong smell of rubber matting mixed with sweat and ripe football cleats. Being here, breathing it in, took him back to his days at Clear Creek High and the way Jim Flanigan had taken him in, treated him like a son.

How great are You, God . . . letting me be a part of something like this, something so much bigger than me. Please, Father . . . keep it coming. Let the miracle You're working here be so big the world will have to see You before they can understand this.

He smiled as he headed for the door, and at the same time he turned on his cell phone. It took only a few seconds for it to come to life, and as it did Cody saw he had a voicemail message waiting for him from a 212 area code. He paused, tapped his screen a few times, and held the phone to his ear.

"Cody, this is Hans Tesselaar, reporter with *Sports Illustrated.* I wondered if you might have a few minutes to call me back. We're watching your season and . . . well, if things continue the way they're going, we're thinking about doing a feature story on your team . . . maybe sometime at the end of November." The man rattled off a phone number. "I hope to hear from you."

Disbelief came over Cody. He'd heard this might happen, but he never really expected it. *Sports Illustrated?* He made a note to call Mr. Tesselaar back in the morning — assuming he would want to talk on a Saturday. He walked out of the locker room and headed toward his pickup. They were having a game night at Tara's house with Cheyenne and DeMetri. As Cody made his way across the field, he could only stand firm on one very great truth. He had the best Father in the world and something else too.

All of his life had led him to this.

TWENTY-FIVE

Six weeks had passed since Francesca ordered Bailey to stop having her Bible study, and now it was midway through October and Bailey still hadn't found a way to resume it. The advice from Betty Keller and her friends was strong — hold the study somewhere else. But Francesca must've suspected she might do that, because the woman pulled her aside a few weeks ago and said only this: "It would be a cast Bible time wherever you hold it. So don't think about having it somewhere else."

"What if it wasn't for the cast . . . but for anyone?" Bailey still felt nervous talking to her.

The director gave her a long look. "I can't stop you then. But given your public role in our cast, I don't advise you leading it."

Bailey could do what she wanted, of course. She could hold the Bible study at a local coffee shop, or in the lobby of the

Kellers' apartment building. But if Francesca found out, she could simply cancel her contract and send her home. She had the right to cut Bailey anytime, for any reason. That was how the contract read. Of course, Tim Reed and his girlfriend from the *Wicked* cast were involved in the church at Times Square, and they had their own Bible study. Bailey could join theirs, but she couldn't get her castmates to come along.

Gerald had already told her as much. "We meet with you or we don't meet. I can't sit in on a Bible study with a bunch of strangers. A few new people would be one thing. But I couldn't talk about my struggles with someone else leading."

Bailey understood, but she still hadn't found a solution. It was Monday night and the show was dark, so like most Mondays she and the Kellers went out for an early dinner. This time they ate at Sardi's on Forty-fourth Street. The place had long been frequented by celebrities, and the walls bore the caricatures of a number of them. It was the sort of place Bailey could never have come to with Brandon — because they wouldn't have made it out without attracting the attention of the local paparazzi and a sea of fans and tourists.

But she figured she and the Kellers could

eat there without much commotion. It surprised her then when, halfway through their meal, a woman walked up with a pad of paper. "I hate to interrupt you while you're eating . . . but could I have your autograph?"

Bailey wanted to look over her shoulder and see who the woman might be talking to. Even with her hit movie *Unlocked,* she rarely got recognized in the city. She looked like any other girl, as far as she was concerned. Any other dancer trying to make it on Broadway.

"We don't mind," Bob Keller was the first to speak up.

"Not at all." Bailey took the pad of paper and signed her name. "Did you like the movie?"

"I love it! I'll be the first to buy it when it comes out on DVD." She chatted on for another minute about how she'd spotted Bailey and how she'd told her husband, "That's Bailey Flanigan . . . I swear it is."

The woman hung around their table long enough that others in the restaurant caught on to what was happening, the fact that Brandon Paul's co-star from *Unlocked* was eating dinner among them. It was the first time anything like this had happened, and Bailey felt a little funny about the attention.

When they were back at the apartment, Betty asked her if she was alright. "You looked a little flustered."

"I'm okay . . ." She couldn't put her feelings into exact words. "I was happy to sign autographs and take pictures . . . I guess I kept thinking what if my life was always like that. The way it is for Brandon."

She was right to think about it, and as she made her way to her room around eight that night, she realized something for the first time. If she and Brandon became a couple, if she committed her heart to him, then that would become her life. She would move to LA so he could keep making movies, and their ability to hide from the paparazzi would eventually become impossible.

A sigh drifted from between her lips as she sat at her desk and opened her laptop. Brandon had been busy with meetings and reshoots this past week, finishing up his film with Eva Gentry. He hadn't texted as often as usual and Bailey missed him. She went to Yahoo.com, looking for any news on his new movie or what he might be up to next. It was crazy how she could find out more information from the Internet than she could in a conversation with him.

She was about to type Brandon's name in the search bar when something caught her eyes: An article featured in the top ten stories listed on the Yahoo home page. The headline read, "Small-Town Football Coach Changing Lives." A funny feeling ran through her, and without hesitating she clicked the words. Immediately the story appeared on her screen.

As it did, she gasped. A quarter of her screen was filled with a picture of Cody Coleman . . . and beneath it a shot of the Lyle High football field. She knew about Cody's success with Lyle. She kept up with his Facebook — even when she wasn't sure it was wise to do so. A few weeks ago her mom told her the media was all over what Cody was doing with the Buckaroos. She had sent Bailey a link to an online version of the feature story that had run in the Indianapolis paper.

But to see the story featured on Yahoo?

She read it, fighting back an onslaught of emotions. A part of her was hurt by the article, sad once again that in this amazing time in Cody's life, she wasn't there to share it. His Facebook page was still mostly about the Lyle football team. But there were occasional photos of Cody and Cheyenne, and references to her in the comments his players left on his wall.

But as Bailey read the Yahoo story, her

sadness was overshadowed by a pride in Cody she'd never really felt this strongly before. Sure, she looked up to him. He was the first guy to tell her not to settle for any reason, the first boy to assure her that what her parents had always said was true — she was one-in-a-million, and she should treat herself that way. And she'd been proud of him when he went to serve the country at war.

But this? The idea that he had taken a losing football program and not only breathed winning life into it, but that he'd rallied the guys to reach out to their teammates and their town? And the fact that he'd done all of this for God's glory . . . "His way" . . . as the article mentioned?

Bailey smiled at the image of Cody on her screen, and the impact he was making. "Way to go, Cody . . . I'm proud of you." She whispered the words in her empty room alone, and for a moment she thought about texting him, telling him she'd seen the story and she couldn't be happier for the way God was using him. But then . . . her mom had told her that they'd sent cookies and a donation. Anything she might say now would only confuse both of them. Someday they might be far enough away from yesterday to be friends again.

452

But not anytime soon.

Bailey clicked the search box and typed in Brandon's name. The first of seventy-three stories that came up made her smile too. "Brandon Paul Doesn't Mind Risking Popularity for Faith." A warmth spread through her, because a year ago she never could've seen this coming. It was one thing for an actor of Brandon's stature to give his life to the Lord. It was another thing to live his faith out — day by day in a city and industry that most often had no use for God.

The question had been posed to Brandon yesterday, apparently, as to whether he would tone down his talk about his faith if his Christianity started to cause a drop in his popularity. The article said that a smiling Brandon Paul had merely responded by saying, "I act because I love it . . . but I love God more. The Bible says our lives here are like a mist that appears for a little while and then is gone. I guess it doesn't matter so much how popular I am when you keep that in mind." Again, Bailey was thrilled. Brandon's statement might cost him his public popularity and something else — a lower paycheck. But he didn't care.

She was about to close the computer, play her guitar for a little while, or write in her journal and jot down the thoughts clamoring for position in her heart. But before she could close it an instant message popped up. Bailey smiled. It was from Andi Ellison, her college roommate from the last few years.

Hey, Bailey, how are you! It's been way too long!

Bailey typed her response. *Andi, it's so good to hear from you — lol. How are you? And how's the movie business?*

It's amazing! I might read for a speaking part next week. My dad thinks I have a good chance. It's a Christian film, different producers, but friends of my dad's.

A tenderness spread through Bailey's heart. Andi was another example of someone who had turned her life entirely over to Jesus. And in the process, God was blessing her, showing her that second chances existed for people who believed. She typed another reply. *That's great, Andi. I'm so happy for you. So you're loving LA?*

Absolutely. The sunshine and palm trees . . . the beach. What's not to love? And the traffic gives me time to pray, so yeah . . . I love it.

They talked another five minutes about New York City and *Hairspray* and Bailey's growing friendship with Brandon Paul. Andi thought the two of them were going to get married one day. *I always thought it would be you and Cody,* she wrote. *But now I've changed my mind. Brandon adores you . . . I can see it in your pictures.*

Bailey wanted to ask if Andi had plans to see her son, the one she gave up for adoption in January. The baby was thriving with his adoptive parents, Luke and Reagan Baxter. But there had been talk initially that every so often Andi might visit the baby, see how he was growing up. Still, the adoption seemed too recent to bring it up first.

As she and Andi were wrapping up, the Skype program popped up and a question appeared on her screen. Brandon Paul was inviting her to a video chat. Bailey uttered a quiet giggle. It was like he could read her mind, like he always knew exactly when to contact her. She said goodbye to Andi and agreed to Brandon's request. Like that, they were together, face-to-face, if only virtually.

"Bailey . . . ahhh, good." He was wearing a long sleeve gray buttoned-down shirt with a white T-shirt underneath. For a few seconds he put his hand on his throat and acted like he was only now able to catch his breath.

"What in the world are you doing?" She laughed, loving the way he could turn actor at any moment. "Don't tell me you're choking on an olive. One too many premiere parties."

This time he laughed hard and dropped his hand back to his side. "No . . . it's just that I can finally see you. Which means I can breathe better." He leaned close to the screen. "I need you like air, Bailey."

She felt his compliment to the depths of her soul. "I needed that right now."

"Then that makes us even." He leaned back and grinned. "So what's on your mind tonight, pretty girl?"

"You." She smiled. This probably wasn't the time to get into it, how she had been touched by Cody's efforts at Lyle and Brandon's strong faith in the world of moviemaking. Even Andi's ability to come back to God after living so very much against Him. Meanwhile, she couldn't figure out a way to stand up to her director long enough to get her Bible study going again. She leaned her elbows on the desk, her face closer to the screen. "I wish I could crawl through this thing and be with you. I could use a long talk on your balcony."

"Hmmm." He straightened, and his eyes lit up. "Hey, I have an idea. We can't be on my balcony . . . not tonight, anyway. But how about you take your laptop to the Empire State Building. I'll call ahead and talk to Joey, and you can meet up with him. He'll take you to the 103rd floor . . . and we can Skype from there."

"What?" Was he always going to be like this? One crazy idea after another? She had figured it would be a night of turning in early, but in light of his suggestion she felt newly invigorated. "Would that work?"

"Sure." He gave her a satisfied grin. "I already called and asked. Joey told me they have wi-fi throughout the building — even the top floor." He pulled a piece of paper from his pocket and unfolded it. Then he held it up for the camera. "See? This is the code. I'll text it to you, and we'll be all set."

"So . . . like what? Just take a cab there and tell them Brandon Paul sent me."

"Bailey, really?" He looked wounded, but she could see he was only teasing her. "I have a car waiting for you downstairs. It's just a matter of saying yes."

"You're not going to pop out from the other room, are you?" She was always on her guard with him now. He loved surprising her. Tonight's idea was just one more example.

"No." He laughed, almost like he wished he could. "But I'd love to Skype with you from the Empire State Building. Like, for an hour or so."

Bailey thought about it for a few more seconds. She had nothing else to do, no show until tomorrow night. Finally she shrugged. "Okay . . . but it might not work. I mean, you might not be able to see the view through the computer camera."

He held her eyes for a long time. "Oh, I'll be able to see the view, alright." His eyes couldn't hide the way he felt about her, how he was completely and utterly smitten in her presence. "I'll see it the same way I can see it now."

"You're crazy." She giggled, basking under his compliment. "Okay, then. I'll sign on again in fifteen minutes or so."

"I'll be waiting."

New York was still warm during the days, but the nights were cooling again. She slipped into a lightweight navy cardigan, grabbed her things, and explained to Bob and Betty that Brandon had arranged a ride for her. They laughed at his spontaneity and fifteen minutes later she was riding up the elevator to the 103rd floor. "That Brandon . . . he's got it bad for you." The man grinned at her. "I ain't never heard o' no one doing something like this."

"I know . . . skyping from the 103rd floor of the Empire State Building."

Joey smiled again. "Yeah . . . that."

458

She stepped off the elevator and, like before, Joey stayed for security reasons, anchored to his spot near the door. He motioned to the left. "You might want to walk that way. The best service is on the other side of the observation deck."

Bailey thanked him and began walking to the left, heading the direction Joey told her to go. She got a few yards out of view when she heard someone walking in the shadows, coming toward her. But before she could scream for Joey she saw his face.

"Hi." Brandon stepped out into the dimly lit deck area where Bailey had been walking. He gave an easy shrug, his eyes locked on hers. "I didn't feel like skyping, really. Not tonight."

A thrill ran through her, a thrill and the certainty that she was okay. She could let herself fall for the young man before her, because he adored her. She hadn't dared hope that tonight's adventure might culminate in something like this. But now that he was here she went to him and fell into his arms. "I needed this . . . I've missed you so much."

"I had to come." He still had his arms around her waist, and he eased closer to her. "If you knew what you do to me, Bailey . . ." He seemed like he might kiss

459

her and she was certain she wouldn't have stopped him.

But he seemed to find his composure, and he pulled back slightly. Enough so they weren't breathing the same air anymore. "I have something to tell you."

"So you came here in person?" She leaned her head back slightly and laughed, the way he always made her laugh. "Brandon, you do know that's not how the rest of the world tells someone something. By flying across the country like this."

"I'm not the rest of the world." His eyes still held the smokiness from a moment ago. "So . . . my agent gave me a handful of scripts last week, and asked me which one I wanted to do." He paused, clearly enjoying his ability to draw out the moment. "I told him, naturally, a love story with Bailey Flanigan. Nothing else, right?"

"Of course." She caught his hands in hers and felt the blush in her cheeks. A movie like that would be amazing . . . she could hardly imagine how much fun they'd have. "What did he say?"

Brandon looked disappointed, but not enough to change the mood. "No love story. Not for now." His eyes danced. "But maybe next time. So that's good news."

"Okay . . ." Confusion stretched out the

moment. "You came here to tell me that?"

"No . . . that's not why." He chuckled, giving up the game and finding a more serious tone. "Since I couldn't do our love story yet, I picked an action movie. We film on location for eight weeks . . . and guess where our location is?"

She thought for a moment. "Not Tahiti?"

"No, not Tahiti." He framed her face with his hands and searched her eyes, her expression. "We're filming right here, Bailey . . . in New York City."

"What?" She stepped back, her heart in her throat, her mind suddenly racing ahead, dizzy and overjoyed. "You'll be here for eight weeks?"

"Yes!" He hugged her again for a long time. "Maybe longer if I can stretch it out."

Bailey couldn't believe it, couldn't imagine how blessed she was. Other than Betty and Bob and their friends, she didn't have a person she could hang out with in the city. But now . . . now she would have Brandon. "You're really serious?" She took hold of his arms, looking deep into his eyes. "I can't believe it!"

"I'm moving here the first of December." He wrapped her in his arms again and held her that way for a long time. When they eased back, as they made their way closer to

461

the railing and the spectacular view of New York City, he put his arm around her shoulders. "I had to tell you in person."

There was no way Bailey could've been happier, not then or for the next hour as they talked about her struggles with the Bible study and his determination to pray for her. He had plans for the two of them tomorrow, and as he said goodnight to her at the steps of her apartment, he grinned. "I have a question for you . . . but not until tomorrow."

"Okay." The happy in Bailey reached all the way from her heart to her head and down to her toes. She grinned, willing the night to hurry up. "You can ask it then."

As she got ready for bed and slid under the covers that night, she thanked God for Brandon in her life, and for the adventures they shared every time they were together. And as she fell asleep she could think of just one thing.

The question Brandon Paul was going to ask her tomorrow.

TWENTY-SIX

Brandon had prepared for these few days in New York City since the last time he was here, a month ago. As the morning dawned, he walked to the window of his hotel room and smiled. God had given them a perfect day . . . the leaves as bright orange and red as they would ever be, the sky a perfect blue overhead.

His question later today after her show would come with a gift — something he'd had custom made just for her. It was a delicate white gold chain with a tiny yellow gold heart that hung at the center. Engraved across the front were the letters *B&B* and on the back was simply *Jer. 29:11.* Brandon remembered the verse because Bailey had talked about it back when they were filming *Unlocked.* God knew the plans He had for them, good plans to give them a hope and a future.

Now Brandon could only hope that the

future God had for them was one that would find them together. And that those same plans might begin in earnest tonight. He gathered the things he'd need. The necklace, already enclosed in a pretty box, and his baseball cap and sunglasses. He even considered a fake mustache today, but he changed his mind. Too itchy. Still, he would've worn any disguise that might give him privacy for this day with Bailey.

He met her at eight that morning and the two of them shared coffee with Betty and Bob. Then they rode in the same black SUV with the same driver, but this time Brandon took her to Central Park. On a Tuesday in October at this hour, Brandon was pretty sure he wouldn't need his entire disguise. He stuck with the baseball cap and brought the other things in a shoulder bag, which he wore across his body.

"The park?" Bailey's voice was filled with delight. It was one of the things he loved about her, the way she marveled at the mundane . . . her ability to find joy in the everyday pleasures of life. He could hardly wait to live in the same city as her — something the two of them had never done other than their time shooting *Unlocked*. And back then she was dating someone else.

"We've never been here together." Brandon took her hand and gave the driver quick instructions to stay close in case they needed to get away. Then he walked with her to the nearest path, the one that would take them by the pond and the zoo. Brandon hadn't spent much time in New York City, and he'd never taken this walk through Central Park. But he mapped it out a week ago, so he was very familiar with the trail.

Everything about being with her was wonderful. Brandon loved the way her fingers felt in his, and the feel of her arm as it brushed against his.

She seemed to know he was thinking about her, because she turned and smiled at him. "It's a perfect day."

"It is now." He wanted so badly to kiss her, to call her his girlfriend and never have to wonder another day whether she felt about him the way he felt about her. No wonder he was nervous. He would have her answer soon enough.

They stopped at the pond and found a park bench. For a few minutes they were quiet, enjoying the feel of the sun on their faces, the feeling that somehow here in the middle of the city they had found a country setting, green grass and the vast pond stretched out before them. After a while Bailey leaned on his shoulder and sighed.

"I'm still thinking about my Bible study." She lifted her eyes to his. "I have to find a way to start it up again."

Brandon didn't think the problem seemed very complicated. "Come on, Bailey, you can figure this out."

"Meaning what?" She wasn't irritated, but her eyes proved she was flustered. "Francesca told me to quit holding it." She put her hand over her chest. "But in here I can feel God telling me not to give up."

"So don't." Brandon smiled gently at her. This was a serious matter for her, he understood. "Tell the dancers who were meeting with you that you're starting up again. Hold it at the Starbucks near the theater. Make it once a week in the morning, and they'll come." He was careful not to sound flippant. "What can Francesca do about that?"

"If she finds out?" Bailey straightened and turned so she could see him better. "Fire me. I'll be home by the next afternoon."

"Okay . . . so she fires you." Brandon soothed his hand over hers. "Then you move to LA and get back into making movies."

Bailey seemed to think that over. "But what sort of example am I if I go against what she asked?"

"The kind that's all through the Bible."

He chuckled quietly. "Bailey, come on. I might be new at it, but I'm pretty sure people like Paul and Timothy went against a lot of people in authority to spread the gospel of Jesus." He hesitated, hoping she could hear him with her heart. "It's not like you'd be breaking a law. Americans are still allowed to hold public Bible studies, last I checked."

He was right — about everything. Peace smoothed out the concerned lines on her forehead. "You make it sound simple."

"The cast already thinks you're weird, right?" He slid a little closer and ran his hand along the back of her head, her hair. He felt his grin lighten the moment. "And I have to say, sometimes I agree."

Her laugh told him she was going to be okay. "I'm definitely weird. No question about that." She breathed in and seemed to find new life, new hope in the moment. "And if I lose my job, I lose it. But at least I'll be following what God wants from me."

"Exactly." He stood and helped her to her feet. "But if you do lose your job, I have to say I'll need an assistant through the end of February." His smile was sheepish. "Don't you think?"

"You're funny."

"Betty and Bob would be down with the

idea . . . I'm sure."

She laughed again. "Okay . . . I'll have the Bible study. If Francesca fires me, I'll be your assistant."

"See? That wasn't so hard."

"Yeah." She rolled her eyes and laughed again. "You haven't worked with Francesca Tilly."

They set out down another pathway, benches on either side. It was a part of the park that had made its way into countless movies. They slowed, and Bailey turned to him. "I love that you were bold in that article . . . I guess I just think of the whole industry as pretty Godless. Everyone except producers like Keith Ellison and Dayne." She put her arm around his waist and gave him a side hug. "And you, of course."

"Maybe it's changing." Brandon put his arm around her. More people walked through the park now, so he kept his sunglasses in place, the bill of his hat pulled down. "A guy at my agency wants to make it an industry thing, reading Scripture." He stopped and gave her a pointed smile. "He wants me to memorize a Bible verse every week. Life is a mist . . . that was the first one."

"I love it."

"People act like they'll live forever, like

the whole world will always revolve around them." Brandon had thought about this long and hard after his friend showed him the Bible verse. "The truth is, there won't be autograph lines in heaven. We have to be so careful how we spend our days . . . since most of our lives will be spent in eternity."

Adoration filled Bailey's eyes, and Brandon drank it in. They stopped again and stepped off the path. An enormous maple tree anchored the walkway and together they leaned on it. "Do you know how many movies have been filmed on this path?" She gazed down the walkway and then up at him. "Maybe we can film our movie here someday."

"I'd like that." Again he wanted to kiss her. He touched her face, let his fingers move lightly down her arm. He had to wait. This wasn't the time. "You know what's next?" Anything to put a little distance between them, as far as Brandon was concerned. He truly cherished her, and he understood her desire to wait until she got married. It was what he wanted for himself now too. But still, the closeness of her was almost more than he could take.

They started walking again. "I'm still thinking that trip to the moon is possible." She laughed a little and looked at him.

"With you, right, Brandon?"

"Well," he raised one eyebrow. "I am intrigued by the idea."

This time they both laughed and a little further down the path he pointed to the entrance to the zoo. "That's next. The zoo." He chuckled. "I mean, I have to see this. A zoo in the middle of New York City? We couldn't spend a day here without at least stopping in."

"The zoo is perfect!" Her voice was like music in his heart, and he savored it as such.

Bailey held his hand as they walked into the zoo, and again he was careful to keep his eyes down, his face shaded. At least until after they were inside. Once they were past the front gates, they walked toward the mongoose exhibit. "Mongoose pups were born a few days ago." He'd done his research. "We can't miss that."

She looked at him, like she truly marveled that he would know about the pups. "You amaze me, Brandon . . . I love this."

They walked a little quicker, holding hands even when Bailey broke into a skip. Brandon kept up with her, loving how the moment made him feel like a kid, like they were back in high school. How different his life would've been had he and Bailey known each other when they were younger. But then maybe that didn't matter as much as what he was praying for now.

That they might know each other when they were old.

Bailey could hardly wait to see the mongoose pups, but more than that she couldn't stop thinking about whatever question he wanted to ask her, and when that might happen. The day had been nothing but magical since the moment he'd shown up at her apartment, and even now she only wished she could slow the hours. Their time together was never enough.

On the walk to the mongoose exhibit, she remembered something she hadn't told him. "Hey . . . I have a surprise for you too."

"You do?" His fingers felt wonderful between hers, and she hoped no one would notice him. So far the day had been theirs alone.

"I called in . . . I haven't used hardly any vacation days. The standby dancers were available, so I'm off tonight."

"Really?" He stopped and turned to her. They were just off the main pathway, so they weren't in anyone's way. "Bailey, that's great!" He made a silly face. "Of course, that means I'll have to fly home tomorrow, and you'll have to put up with me for another day." He started walking again, his eyes still on hers. "Because I'm not leaving New York City without watching my favorite performer."

Comments like that reminded her why she enjoyed her time with Brandon so much. He made her a priority, and he loved watching her perform. She put her arms around his waist and hugged him. Then she took hold of his hand again and ran a little ahead. "Come on . . . the mongoose pups are waiting."

They were the only ones at the exhibit when they reached it. "Ahhh," Bailey stooped low, bringing herself to eye level with the pups. "They're so cute."

"They are." Brandon chuckled. "They sort of have a nervous look."

"Nervous and cute."

"Kind of like you used to be around me at first." He elbowed her softly in the ribs.

"Hey . . ." She returned the gesture, and for a moment they had a teasing sort of tickling battle. "You have the most recognized face in the nation." She laughed as he poked at her other side, and she did the same to him. "That would make anyone nervous."

"Alright you . . . Nervous Nelly. Let's go check on the sea lions."

Bailey could practically hear the romantic music in the background as they made their way around the zoo. They were almost back to the front gates again when they came head on with a high school class — or maybe two classes. At that exact moment, Brandon had his head upturned, laughing at something she said. Bailey could see what was going to happen seconds before it actually did. And by then it was too late.

"Brandon Paul?" A big girl at the front of the group stopped and screamed his name. Then she pointed at him. "Yes. It's him! Brandon Paul!"

If there had been more people at the zoo he might've been able to escape in the crowd. But they were the only two people heading out of the zoo at that moment, and with the girl's announcement, the fifty teenagers let loose in their direction. Brandon cared a lot for the people who liked his work. He would sign an autograph at dinner or take a picture just about anytime.

But in this moment, Bailey was glad he responded the way he did. He pulled the cap of his hat firmly down on his forehead, grabbed her hand, and the two of them took off. They darted past the group of high school kids and out the gate. "To the car," he shouted.

But the students didn't give up that easily.

They took off down the same path they'd walked in on. But a number of the teens stayed close behind.

"That's Bailey Flanigan!" one of the guys shouted. "Hey! Bailey, wait up."

She almost wondered if it would be easier to stop and deal with the kids, sign autographs, and take pictures. But then Brandon was far more experienced at this, and the crowds he could draw in a very short time would make her night at Sardi's look like a quiet affair. They held hands, staying fifteen yards ahead of the kids, but the commotion they caused was drawing other people into the chase.

"We're a parade," she smiled at him, yelling so he could hear her above the shouts from behind.

"Always." He picked up their pace, and as he ran he pulled his cell phone from his pocket and called their driver. "Same place, five minutes," he told him.

Whether one of the kids called the news or flashed the information on Twitter, they would never know, but by the time they passed the pond, more than a hundred people ran after them, and a host of paparazzi jumped out from a cropping of bushes and began snapping pictures.

"Keep running." Brandon didn't seem upset, just determined.

Bailey was glad she was in shape. They'd already run for a few minutes.

"Don't worry about the pictures. There's no way around them."

She had been with Brandon at premieres where she wondered if she'd ever seen so many flashes or heard so many cameras clicking. But a red carpet event was supposed to be like that. Here . . . with a couple dozen cameramen snapping rapid-fire shots as they ran toward them, Bailey could only imagine the pictures they were getting.

The paparazzi continued to shoot as they ran up and passed them, and then they joined the throng of people still chasing them. They reached the drop-off spot and there was the driver, the back door already open. He saluted Brandon as they ran up, and like a scene from a movie Brandon and Bailey jumped into the car and the driver slammed the door shut.

"Wow . . ." Brandon was breathing hard, but still able to laugh. "I didn't see that coming."

"I did." Bailey doubled over, laughing and trying to catch her breath at the same time. "There was nothing I could do. Not enough time."

"There never is." He leaned back against the seat, his arms sprawled out at either side like he was exhausted. He turned his head and grinned at her. "Okay . . . so we got through that, right?"

"We did." She turned sideways and laughed again. "It's crazy . . . like what are people thinking? They'll catch us and then what . . . tackle us to the ground? Force you out for a cup of coffee?" She exhaled, her heartbeat almost back to normal.

"You're not freaked out?"

"No." She was a little, but she didn't want to say so. They'd survived it, right? "It was a onetime thing. Compared to all the hours we've had in the city, I guess it isn't so bad."

Brandon winced. "Except one thing . . . now they know we're a couple." He was quick to correct himself. "What I mean is . . . we starred in a movie together, and now we're holding hands in Central Park months after the movie hits theaters." He nodded, his expression resigned. "They'll think we're a couple for sure."

"Which means . . ." Bailey thought she understood where he was headed with this. "We'll have less of a chance hiding next time we check out the mongoose pups?"

"Exactly."

Bailey wasn't sure what to say. She appreciated that Brandon had a plan, that he'd arranged for the driver to be nearby in case something like this happened. She could live with this if she had to, right? If that's where God was leading them? They fell quiet then, and Brandon reached for her hand. Once their fingers were together, Bailey's questions fell away. She could tolerate any amount of paparazzi or wild fans if it meant being with him.

She had never been more sure.

TWENTY-SEVEN

Paparazzi followed them to Bailey's apartment, but Brandon caught the eye of the doorman, and whisked Bailey inside before the photographers could take more than a few pictures. They took the stairs to the second floor and the elevator the rest of the way, and Bailey tried to imagine the pictures in the tabloids over the coming week. "I'm sure they'll have a field day with the one of us running into my apartment."

"Probably." He looked intently at her, the way he might if she were sick or if she'd had an accident of some kind. "But you're okay? You're not going to hold it against me, right?"

"Brandon . . ." They were in the elevator, and she put her hand on his shoulder. Her heart melted at the thought that the concern in his eyes was over whether she would hold the paparazzi incident against him. "It's not your fault. You've done everything you can to avoid that."

"Okay." He seemed to breathe a little easier. They got off at the eleventh floor and went into the apartment. The Kellers were gone for the afternoon — headed to Jersey to see Betty's sister. They might not be home until nine or ten, according to Betty. She knew that Brandon might come back with her, and though she and Bob had a house rule that their tenants couldn't have visitors in their bedrooms, they'd assured Bailey that Brandon was welcome to hang out in the living room with her. Bailey checked the clock on the microwave. It was a little after three in the afternoon, and they hadn't eaten since breakfast.

"Let's see what's in the fridge." She checked and found very little she could make into a meal. She gave Brandon one of the yogurts she kept at the back of the top shelf, and she took one too. But that wouldn't work for dinner. And now that the paparazzi knew where she was staying, they'd be waiting downstairs.

"We can order in." Brandon took a seat at the dining room table. "How about I beat you at Scrabble and then we get Chinese food?"

Bailey felt the night become magical once again. "Perfect." Suddenly the idea sounded better than any place they might go out in the city tonight.

They played Scrabble for an hour, and Bailey lost both games. Then they called for sweet and sour chicken, broccoli beef, and an assortment of other vegetable and noodle dishes. The time alone was wonderful, and Bailey loved that they didn't have to worry about paparazzi here. It was dark outside by then, and the lights from the city twinkled from both walls of glass windows that bordered the living room. Bailey took a spot on the sofa, and Brandon sat beside her. But she noticed he left room between them — something she appreciated, even if she would've liked him to sit closer. They were alone, after all, and Brandon knew the same as she did that the Kellers wouldn't be home until much later. The distance told her he didn't want to put either of them in a situation they couldn't escape from.

Bailey flicked on the TV and they found a special on Broadway shows. This one was titled, *Wicked — Making of a Broadway Musical.* Halfway through, the camera caught a ten-second shot of the ensemble dancers practicing. "Hey . . . that's Tim!"

"Tim?" Brandon glanced at her, his expression mildly confused. "Do I know him?"

"No." She giggled. "I used to date him."

"Oh." Brandon leveled his gaze at the screen. "So you're saying I should know him."

"No, silly." She angled her head, loving how he could make her laugh. "He's dating someone else. We were never really more than friends, anyway."

"I see." Brandon nodded, absently. "I like him better now."

The special ended just as the Chinese food arrived. Bailey paid — mostly so the delivery guy wouldn't catch a glimpse of Brandon. She wondered if the paparazzi would follow the man up, hiding behind the bags of Chinese food. But the doorman downstairs wouldn't have allowed that.

When the man was gone, Bailey handed the food to Brandon and followed him to the table. He sat at the head of the table and she took the spot beside him, so they shared a corner.

But before he sat down, Brandon held up his finger. "Hold on." He hurried into the kitchen and rummaged through a couple drawers before he found what he was looking for. "Here." He returned to the table and held up a book of matches. Then he lit the candle at the center of the Kellers' table, and before he sat down he dimmed the lights. "Most romantic Chinese restaurant

481

in all of New York."

Bailey tried to focus on her dinner — which was truly delicious. But she kept wondering about the *question* . . . and whether this was when he'd finally ask it, or if maybe he'd been teasing or possibly forgotten altogether. She didn't bring it up, and the dinner hour breezed by — the two of them laughing and talking about his funniest movie moments and her brothers' greatest sports victories.

When the meal was over, Brandon cleared their plates and the two of them washed the few dishes and put away the leftovers. Enough for the Kellers and Bailey to eat for a week. Finally, with the kitchen clean and the beautiful night beckoning them, Bailey turned to him. "I wish we could take a walk . . . go somewhere outside. The night's beautiful." It was one thing the Kellers' apartment didn't have: a balcony.

"Is there roof access?" A sense of adventure brightened Brandon's expression.

"Ummm," Bailey tried to remember if the Kellers had ever said anything about the roof. "You know . . . I'm not sure."

"Well," he took her hand and led her to the front door. "Let's find out."

Bailey often wondered what life would be like with Brandon if their friendship led to something more serious, more long-term. Marriage, even. Would their lives always be a series of adventures and surprises, the adrenaline rush of escaping paparazzi and searching for hidden places to share their time? Bailey smiled to herself as they hurried into the hall. She wouldn't mind, that's for sure. Bailey loved everything about their time together recently — even the chase through Central Park today was fun. He brought a sense of magic to any situation, never knowing where he might show up or what new memories they might make together.

A lifetime of this would be practically perfect, right?

Bailey didn't stop long enough to answer her own question. She and Brandon tiptoed to the other end of the hallway. "Shhh," he whispered back at her, his eyes alive with the thrill ahead. He snuck a glance over one shoulder and then the other, pretending that someone might jump out at them at any moment. Bailey had to work to keep her laughter at an appropriately quiet level.

The door at the end of the hall led to a stairwell, and Brandon raised his brow at her. "See? We might be onto something."

Bailey had no idea how many floors made up the apartment building, but she hoped it wasn't more than twenty. She could climb stairs all day long, but between laughing and trying to catch her breath, she wasn't sure how many flights she could take. At first Brandon kept up the light steps and whispers, like he was playing a part in an espionage movie.

But after six floors he began dragging his feet, exaggerating every breath in. "I need . . . to get . . . to the gym more."

Again she was overcome by a bout of laughter, this time strong enough that she grabbed the railing and stopped, bent over. She laughed so hard tears came to her eyes, and when she finally regained her composure enough to move on, she gave him a playful slap on the shoulder. "Quit it . . . I can't breathe when I laugh that hard."

"Risks of hanging out with me, I guess." He shrugged, again moving lightly up the stairs, the out-of-shape act finished for now.

As it turned out there were eighteen floors in the Kellers' apartment building. Only then did Brandon stop and turn abruptly to her. "Of course . . . we could've taken the elevator to the eighteenth floor and then looked for roof access."

Again they both started laughing, holding each other up from the silliness of their walk up the stairs. It was one of those times when a person looking in on them might not understand, a time when every moment seemed funnier than the last thing. Bailey thought about all the hours she'd spent with the *Hairspray* cast, and how little she'd laughed. A night like this, laughing until she couldn't see for her tears . . . was more wonderful than anything else they might've done for her tonight.

One last flight of stairs went up after the last floor, and as they rounded the corner they saw a door printed with the words *Roof Access.*

"Ahaa!" Brandon stopped and thrust his hand in the air. "The explorers are victorious!"

"Exhausted . . ." Bailey trudged up the last few steps. "But definitely victorious."

The minute they walked onto the roof, Bailey drew a quick, quiet breath and stopped, shocked at what she was seeing. A garden filled up most of the roof, and through it pathways and benches that gave it a feel of Central Park. There were lights along the winding walkway, and pretty bushes marking every ten feet or so along the railing that ran along the perimeter of the roof. Suddenly Bailey remembered a conversation with Bob a month ago when he'd said something about hanging out with

Betty on the roof. Bailey hadn't given the idea another thought. Where she grew up, people didn't hang out on rooftops of buildings.

"Wow . . ." Brandon stopped and slid his hands in his pockets. The goofiness from earlier was gone, and clearly now he could do nothing but stand frozen in place, in awe over the beauty here. He looked back at Bailey and grinned. "Who would've known?"

"Bob said something about the roof once, but . . . yeah, I had no idea." It was one more example of how she shared new vistas with Brandon, how they experienced things Bailey had never imagined. She smiled. "Ummm . . . definitely a good idea. Coming up here."

"Even with the stairs." He still had laughter in his voice as he reached for her hand again and they walked along the path to the other side of the roof. "Let's check out the view."

The air was cooler now that night had fallen, and Bailey realized she should've brought a sweater from the apartment. She ran her free hand along her arms and stayed close at Brandon's side.

"Cold?" He slowed and put his arm around her shoulders.

"A little." She felt a different sort of chill at the touch of his hand against her bare arm. And his body beside her kept her warm against the cool of the night.

They reached the far side and found a pretty patio that ran alongside the railing. Flower bowls dotted the edges and benches anchored either side. "It's beautiful." Bailey took the lead and they walked slowly to the railing. She looked back at him. "Our own personal Empire State Building."

"Mmmm." His teasing eyes danced again. "With you, who needs another eighty floors?"

She giggled quietly. "Exactly."

For a little while they stayed that way, side by side, leaning on the high railing, soaking in the lights of the city and the view of Times Square. But then he faced her, sliding his arms around her waist and looking to the places in her heart that were beginning to feel like they belonged only to him. "I had another great day."

"Me too." The mood between them was suddenly more intimate, deeper than before. Bailey felt her heart beat hard. She laughed a little. "I don't think I've had this much fun ever."

"See?" His smile warmed her soul. "That's why you're supposed to be with me."

"Hmmm . . . is that right?" She lowered her chin, her eyes on his.

"It is." He ran his fingers lightly through her hair. The depth in his eyes turned more serious, a sort of mesmerizing look that left no doubt about his feelings. "I have something for you." He slipped his hand into his pocket and pulled out a tiny vintage-looking brown leather box. He held it out to her. "Here."

The box alone was the most beautiful thing . . . like something a person might only find in an antique store. She ran her thumb over it and then lifted her eyes to him. "Can I open it?"

"Of course." His smile told her how much he enjoyed this. "I've been waiting for this all day."

Happiness filled her, consumed her. She had no idea what to expect, but as she opened the box she caught her breath again. "Brandon, it's beautiful."

The white gold necklace had a heart charm and on it — in the faintest engraving — were their initials. *B&B*. He reached in and turned the heart around. "It's engraved on the back too."

She peered at it in the moonlight and what she saw brought tears to her eyes, tears because for all the ways she'd missed opportunities and struggled in her season here on Broadway, somehow God still loved her enough to give her a moment like this . . . a guy like Brandon Paul. She looked at him. "My verse. You remembered?"

"I remember everything about you, Bailey." He took the necklace out and set the box on the nearby bench. Then he carefully slipped it onto her neck, his fingers cool against her skin. After he'd fastened the clasp, he faced her once more and she wondered if his heart was pounding like hers. "Can I ask you something?"

This was it . . . the question. She put her arms around his neck, curious . . . barely able to breathe. "Yes . . . please, Brandon." She couldn't take her eyes from him, didn't dare move or blink.

"You're beautiful . . . you have no idea how much." He looked mesmerized, lost in her eyes.

"I feel beautiful . . . with you, Brandon."

"Bailey . . ." The rare vulnerability was back in his eyes, the brash confident, carefree guy the rest of the world knew gone in this moment between them. "Will you be my girlfriend?" He didn't wait for her to answer, but rather put his hands on her shoulders, his expression intense and filled with a love that surprised her. "I know it won't be easy . . . but I'll try my best to make it normal. As normal as we can be."

"Normal?" She laughed, and the sound held the slightest cry in it. "Brandon, you could never be normal." She hugged him and when she pulled back she felt the depth in her own eyes. "Which is why I have to tell you . . . yes. Yes, I'll be your girlfriend."

"Really?" His question came loud and with a fresh burst of life.

"Really!" She laughed again. "I wanted you to ask."

He picked her up and swung her in a full circle, and when he set her back down again he leaned against the railing and shouted. "Hey, New York! I'm in love with Bailey Flanigan!"

"You're crazy." She beamed at him — glowing from the inside out. The necklace. The question. And now this . . . Brandon wanted the whole world to know how he felt. That he was in love with her.

She still felt breathless, her heart still pounding as he returned to her and took her gently in his arms again. They hugged for a long time, until Bailey was glad when he eased back a little. If they were going to do this . . . be in a serious relationship . . . they would have to take every step carefully . . . make every decision slowly.

He kept his arms around her waist, and now he looked into her eyes. "Girlfriend?"

"Yes . . ." She laughed, but not enough to pull her from the bond between them.

"I have an idea."

"You're good at that." At this point she was willing to go with just about any idea he had. She put her arms loosely around his neck and tilted her head, curious . . . waiting.

"So . . . you know our love story?"

"The one we *are* going to film someday . . ." She loved the feeling of being in his arms.

"Yes . . . that one." He looked like he was struggling to concentrate, as caught up in the closeness between them as she was. "Anyway . . . I think maybe we should practice . . . you know, just in case they call us in for a cold read or something."

"Right . . ." She had a feeling she knew where he was headed with this, and she was glad. "Cold reads can be tricky."

"Exactly." He moved closer, brushing his cheek against hers, capturing her, mesmerizing her. He looked straight at her and suddenly there were no words needed. He brought his hands slowly to her face and he kissed her . . . tenderly and with great restraint, in a way that showed her how much he wanted her, but even more how much he cared.

The kiss didn't last long, and Brandon didn't try to kiss her a second time — even though Bailey sort of hoped he would. Instead he stepped back, trembling. "I promise you, Bailey . . . I'll respect you. We'll do this God's way."

She wasn't sure what to say, or how to respond. This was what her parents had prayed for her since she was born — that the guys in her life might cherish her. And now Brandon was promising just that. She hugged him again. "That means so much."

Bailey held tight to the way it felt to be kissed by Brandon Paul on the rooftop of her apartment building amidst the prettiest secret garden in all of New York. After they'd said goodbye, and after he left the building to what was no doubt a flurry of photographs and shouts from paparazzi, she knew one thing with absolute certainty.

She was totally and completely in love with Brandon Paul.

TWENTY-EIGHT

The miracle continued to play out, and Cody could do nothing but stand by and humbly credit God for every great thing happening to the Lyle High football team. The changes happening to the small town. After the Arlington win, the Buckaroos played road games against Lawrence Central, Warren Central, and Cathedral and pulled out wins at each.

Tonight they were back at home against John Marshall High — their last Friday night game of the season. A win tonight and Lyle would go from a winless two years to an undefeated run heading into play-offs. Cody was alone in the locker room again, this time at his desk in the office, going over plays. But he couldn't keep himself from thinking back over the last three months.

His flashbacks to his time in Iraq had all but faded from his waking hours. Only in a dead sleep did he occasionally have nightmares of that time. His counseling hours had dwindled because he simply didn't need them. On top of that he'd kept up on the visits with his mother, usually every Sunday afternoon. Cody hadn't brought Cheyenne along yet. Not when his mom still asked about Bailey at least every other visit. She still wanted to blame herself, believing that Cody and Bailey would be together if it weren't for her. Privately, Cody agreed with her, but her situation wasn't the only problem. Bailey didn't need him . . . he understood that now. At any rate, things had turned out this way, and now there was no going back and rewriting the past.

"I want you to meet Chey one day," he told her last time they were together. "But you can't bring up Bailey."

"I know." His mother nodded, obviously frustrated with herself. "I'm trying, Cody . . . but that girl's in my heart." She reached for his hands and gave them an understanding squeeze. "I know somewhere . . . deep inside of you . . . she's in your heart too."

Comments like that meant that bringing Cheyenne was still a long way off. But the rest of their visit had gone better than most, more uplifting and encouraging. Cody brought a makeshift scrapbook with some of the articles that had been written about him and the team. His mother had only limited computer access, so the scrapbook gave her a window to his football season and all that was happening.

Before he left, her eyes teared up. "Cody . . . I'm so proud of you." She pulled the scrapbook close and gave a bewildered look, as if there were no words that might sum up how she was feeling. "Look at you, son . . . you're famous. Everyone knows about you."

Not everyone, he reminded her. But he told her then about the *Sports Illustrated* article, and the possibility that they would do a feature story on him after this week's game. Again she was stunned, happier than he'd seen her since she'd been locked up. "The impact you're making . . . I can't believe it, Cody . . . even with a mess-up of a mother like me."

Cody spent their last ten minutes together convincing her that she wasn't a mess-up, but just a person whose addictions were stronger than her. And like always he encouraged her to keep up with her accountability group. "I love you, Mom." He stood and hugged her shoulders, letting her lean on him. "Read your Bible and believe what it says. You're free. Now you need to start living that way."

The memory of their visit faded and Cody stared at the playbook on his desk. But once again the images and words blurred together and all he could see was Bailey Flanigan's Facebook page, the way it looked last night. He and DeMetri had talked long about the game and then the kid had turned in for bed. And like he hadn't often done in the last few weeks, Cody found his way to Facebook.

She was in a relationship, of course. Same as him. Facebook photos didn't lie, and now in addition to the photos they'd taken of themselves, the one Bailey had in her album marked "Fun in the City" . . . there were pictures taken by fans, where Bailey and Brandon were tagged as a couple. Of course, he didn't need to go to Facebook to see how close the two had become. He could see that at the local Safeway. The two of them had been photographed at the zoo in Central Park, and again heading into her apartment building.

As much as it still hurt to see her with Brandon, he wished he could make a public statement in response to some of the comments people had made about those pictures. People wondering why a good Christian girl would take Brandon into her apartment. Cody released a sad chuckle. Anyone who would question Bailey's faith and innocence didn't know her. It was that simple.

Anyway, at least she was happy . . . as much as it was hard to think about. Still Cody was glad to see the smile on her face, glad she was making an impact in New York City. And she was . . . Cody had no doubts. Bailey wouldn't have settled for anything less than making an impact on the people around her. So the fact that she was smiling had to mean her life was going well.

Cody sighed and tried once more to focus on the playbook. Cheyenne had looked over it with him last night, and they both laughed at the way she tried to interpret the *X*'s and *O*'s. "Okay," she finally admitted, "I give up. It looks like a tic-tac-toe game."

Sweet girl, Cody told himself. *Wonderful girl.* Cody gathered his thoughts and ordered them safely to the back of his mind. If he was going to help his team take care of business tonight against John Marshall, he needed to focus. And with an hour before the team arrived, there wasn't a minute to lose.

The time passed quickly, and in a rush of activity the team arrived and dressed down in their uniforms, taping ankles and adjusting shoulder pads, their voices a chorus of anxious nervous energy and absolute determination that tonight the league title would be theirs to take.

Cody gathered them twenty minutes before kickoff. "You've risen to the challenge . . . you've done what we set out to do that first day at spring practice. You've played Lyle football His way . . . God's way." Cody didn't want the season to end. He'd loved these guys, their struggles and foibles and miracles and mishaps. The few who had been drinking had sworn off partying, and Arnie Hurley's girlfriend found out she wasn't pregnant, and the two of them broke up when she wouldn't adapt to the cleaner life Arnie wanted. Yes, Cody's players had listened and believed him. And along the way they had allowed Cody to lead them in faith through the most unlikely football season of all.

Not an eye in the room wasn't full of intensity and passion as they came together, their fists raised in the center of their huddle this one last time before the regular season came to an end. "One more time, men . . . you're going to go out there and take care of business one more time." He raised his voice. "Whose way?"

"His way!"

"Whose way?"

"His way!" The sound grew and filled the locker room.

"Whose way?"

"His way!" The guys shouted and bellowed their approval, their belief in the common purpose between them.

"Okay, men . . . league title on three." He hesitated, feeling the echo of their battle cry deep in his heart and soul. "One . . . two . . . three . . ."

"League title!"

With that Cody and his assistant coaches jogged out to the field behind a stampede of Lyle football players. As he reached the edge of the field, Cody almost stopped midstep. If he'd thought the place was packed before, it was half empty compared to the people who had flocked to the field tonight. Before he could go another yard, a man jogged up to him and motioned for him to stop.

"Coach . . . I'm Hans Tesselaar . . . reporter with *Sports Illustrated.*" He grinned. "I had to see this one for myself."

"Great," he shook the man's hand. Of all the writers at *SI,* Hans wrote the best stories. He had a way of mixing real life with lore and leaving a person deeply moved by the power of competition and the bond of teamwork. "You can follow me over to the bench. Hang out on the sidelines. Then we can talk afterwards, if that's okay."

"Perfect." Hans was younger than Cody expected . . . in his midforties maybe with a kind smile. Cody had a feeling the guy would be blown away by tonight's game. Not just his team's performance, but the presentation that would happen at halftime. Yes, this was the perfect game for the reporter to attend. Now it was a matter of getting down to business and winning it. Cody hurried the rest of the way to his team's bench, organized his clipboard, and reviewed his plays once more. Then — with the roar of the crowd behind them — John Marshall kicked off.

Cody called in a play for DeMetri, a fake pass that if done right could open the game with a touchdown. He crouched low over his knees, his eyes on the team. "Come on, Smitty . . . you do this . . . you got this . . ."

The snap was good, Arnie reeled back like he was going to throw to one of his wideout receivers, but in a blur of motion DeMetri took the ball and sprinted for daylight. Cody and the rest of the team ran along the sidelines, cheering him on. As the Buckaroos took a seven-zero lead, Cody exchanged a quick grin with the *Sports Illustrated* reporter. Already he could see the man was swept up in the small-town support and the miracle unfolding beneath the Friday night lights.

John Marshall hadn't had a losing season in ten years, so it was no surprise when they responded with a touchdown, marching eighty yards and knocking seven minutes off the clock to tie the score. Lyle was up by just three points heading into halftime, but before the team ran for the locker room, they lined up on the field and watched as Larry Sanders met up with his little sister near the jam-packed stands. He hoisted her onto his sturdy shoulders and brought her out to the fifty-yard line.

The athletic director handed him a mic, but before he could say a single word, the applause began. Slowly at first and then louder, with an intensity that brought the entire town to their feet, cheering and hollering and clapping for Larry and his sister and the love of a football team that would give everything they had to save the life of one sick little girl.

In the end, there wasn't much Larry could say, not much he needed to say. He thanked the businesses and families, the backbone of Lyle . . . and then he turned to the sidelines and thanked his teammates. Finally he hugged his sister tight, holding onto her for a long time before the two of them left the field together, the girl on his shoulders once again.

Cody caught a glimpse of Chey and Tara in the stands, the two of them hugging the way so many of the fans were. The clapping continued and Cody looked back at the reporter again. He was wiping his eyes, and the sight made Cody know for certain one thing: Hans Tesselaar got the story. Got it with his heart — where the message mattered most.

The reporter joined them in the locker room for Cody's halftime talk, and though he didn't ask questions, he scribbled furiously. As Cody drew his men into a huddle once more, and as they chanted the words that had become familiar, Cody mouthed a message to the man. "You might want to get this."

Hans nodded and pulled out a small video camera. Cody led the guys one more time through the cry that by now came from deep within their souls. When it was over, the team ran out onto the field and proceeded to tear apart the John Marshall defense. Hurley threw touchdown passes of seven and thirty-eight yards to Larry Sanders, and after he caught the last one he ran by the stands and pointed to his little sister.

Again the crowd erupted into a standing ovation, one that lasted through much of the fourth quarter. At the final whistle the Buckaroos had soundly taken hold of the league title with a forty-five to fourteen thrashing of John Marshall. Like most of their home games, the fans poured onto the field, filling every open spot and clamoring around the football players for a chance to congratulate them, pat them on the back, or wish them the best for their upcoming run through play-offs. But before they could do that, DeMetri yelled for the team to follow him.

Every day after practice last spring, De-Metri had taken the jog to the end zone and prayed by himself, prayed for the coaches and the players and his role on the Lyle team. But here, beneath the lights of their last league game, the entire team took the jog with him. In the end zone they all dropped to one knee, close together so that it was impossible to tell who had their arms around whose shoulders. Cody and the other coaches ran over to join them, and for the next several minutes the guys took turns thanking God . . . for the season, for the unlikely wins, and for bringing Cody to them. But most of all for the miracle He was giving Larry's little sister.

"Really, God," DeMetri finished the prayer, "the miracle was for all of us. We were all sick in one way or another."

Cody thought about DeMetri's low point — when his mother had been put in prison and the kid had been sleeping in the wrestling room at school. He blinked back tears, listening.

"We set out to play football your way, and we did that," DeMetri continued. "Now we ask that You do one more thing for us . . . help us never forget this season. In Jesus' name, amen."

Hans found Cody and shook his head, his eyes wide. "I didn't know this still existed. I feel like I'm on a movie set."

Cody grinned and looked around him, at the celebrating and rejoicing, and even at Cheyenne still grinning ear to ear up in the stands. "Yes . . . I've felt that way all season long."

They made a plan to talk more the next day. Hans even hoped to fly Cody to New York for a weekend to meet the rest of the Sports Illustrated staff. Again Cody could hardly take it in. He agreed, and they parted ways. Cody finished talking with parents and well-wishers from the town, and finally an hour later he and Cheyenne drove back to Indianapolis. DeMetri was staying the night at Joel Butler's house — where most of the team was meeting to watch *Remember the Titans* and get pumped up for the play-offs.

Cody was glad the team wanted to spend time together. Better than going their separate ways when they had so much to celebrate — and certainly better than partying the win away like so many football players around the country would do after a game like tonight's.

The ride home was quiet, and Cheyenne admitted to having a headache. "I'm sorry, Cody. I'm so happy for you . . . really. Maybe I need more sleep."

"Don't be sorry." He smiled, hiding his concern. "I want you to feel good, Chey." He held her hand and let her sleep the rest of the way home. When they reached her apartment he walked her to the front door and kissed her goodnight. "Get some rest."

"I will. Thanks, Cody." Her smile tugged at his heart. "You were amazing out there. Your guys . . . the town . . . Larry's sister. All of it."

"You forgot one thing." He backed up a step, not wanting to keep her when she didn't feel good. He gave her a final smile. "You were there, Chey. I felt your support every minute."

She grinned, clearly grateful for the compliment, and then she waved once more and went inside. When the door closed behind her, Cody climbed in his truck and drove home to his apartment. Once he was inside he stepped out on his small patio, sat in his folding lawn chair, and stared at the stars. Cheyenne was amazing. He was blessed to call her his girlfriend. She deserved a guy who would cherish her and treasure her and maybe he was that guy. In time he would have to think about taking their relationship to the next level. That was the right thing to do.

Cody breathed deep and leaned over his knees. He had so much to be thankful for. His football team . . . the town of Lyle . . . the love from Cheyenne . . . his mother's progress . . . and his faith. So much.

Cody absently twisted the friendship ring he still wore on his finger. He still loved what it stood for, the Bible verse it contained. There was no reason to take it off, really. Besides, never mind about the past. God had blessed him completely and fully — beyond his expectations. He had learned much these last months . . . lessons that would last a lifetime, he was sure.

What more could he possibly ask for?

■ ■ ■ ■

Bailey dug her ladle into a vat of gravy and poured a scoop over a mound of mashed potatoes. Then she passed the plate to the bearded guy on her right. It was his job to add several turkey pieces, and then at the end of the line of volunteers a homeless person would be given an early Thanksgiving dinner.

It was the Monday night before the holiday, a perfect time for Bailey and her castmates from the new Bible study to serve at the mission in downtown Manhattan. The crowd of hungry people filled the room, more so than Bailey expected. The work would last another few hours at least, and Bailey was grateful. This sort of faith in action could truly change the lives of her castmates.

And they were open to change now. They met Monday mornings at Starbucks across from the J. Markham Theater. Francesca had expressed her disapproval a few times, but she had also admitted that since it wasn't an official *Hairspray* Bible study, there wasn't much she could do. Somehow, Bailey still had her job.

She ladled another scoop of gravy over

another mound of mashed potatoes. Gerald worked on her left, making pleasant conversation with the people who passed through their line. Gerald had the kindest heart of anyone on the cast. He understood better now God's calling for him. He hadn't given his life to Jesus yet, but that would come. Bailey had no doubt.

"You're moving a little slow, lady," the bearded guy on her right elbowed her lightly in the ribs. "Pick it up."

She looked at him, at the familiar teasing eyes she had come to love over the last few months. "Hey," she leaned close, her voice a whisper. "Don't hassle me, Brandon. I'll pull off that beard and they'll chase you out of here."

He chuckled, pressing the fake beard firmly into place. Even the cast hadn't figured out who he was with this disguise. Of course, Brandon had arrived separate from her and just as the meal was being served — all intentionally. Bailey had merely introduced him as Jorge, a friend in the business.

They went back to work, serving tirelessly for the next few hours. After that, she and Brandon found a quiet table and shared dinner with the street people gathered around them. Moments like this she was sure she'd made the right choice, and she was grateful beyond words for Brandon. He was moving here in a week, and that combined with the fact that they were going to have Christmas together with her family made Bailey thrilled about all the future held. She had learned so much in New York City, and she had much to be thankful for. Her Bible study . . . the fact that she still worked a dream job on Broadway . . . her family's health and love . . . and Brandon Paul. Bailey smiled at him and memorized the way she felt right now.

Because she could hardly ask God for more than this.

READER LETTER

Dear Reader Friends,

Now that you've journeyed with me through the first two books of the Bailey Flanigan Series, I'm sure you're thoroughly confused. That's okay . . . I feel that way a little too. As we learn from God, we're bound to feel a little confused. I think God must like when we can't see the happy ending ahead. It makes us rely that much more fully on Him.

As I mentioned before, the character of Bailey Flanigan was inspired by my daughter, Kelsey. In real life there is no Cody Coleman, no Brandon Paul. But the way she lives for God, and her passion for His word and His truth are a mainstay in her real-life story — the way they are with her fictional character: Bailey.

In addition, Kelsey is the oldest of six — the others all boys, three of whom were adopted from Haiti. When I write about

Jenny and Jim Flanigan, I am — for the most part — writing about my family. Kelsey and I have the relationship that Bailey and Jenny share — an open communication that has allowed her to trust me with any conversation, any decision, any heartbreak. I have had the privilege of raising this one-in-a-million girl, and the very great responsibility of seeking God's wisdom in helping shape her into the young woman she is today. Along the way I love hearing about your one-in-a-million daughters, and the way God is working in their lives too.

And so, along the years — through the Firstborn Series, Sunrise Series, and especially during the four books in the Above the Line Series, we watched Bailey grow up. We watched as she developed a love for Cody Coleman and musical theater and a longing for the dreams God had placed in her heart. When Cody pulled away from her and Brandon Paul stepped in, I knew Bailey needed her own series.

Of course, that story wouldn't be complete without a season of learning.

The story of Bailey has many twists and turns ahead. The books to come will be *Longing* . . . and finally *Loving*. I think you'll be amazed at where God takes this fictitious girl. Here's a funny, fictional fact: The books in the Bailey Flanigan series will release over the next eighteen months. But during that same time, we'll follow Bailey through three years of life.

Ahh, the marvels of storytelling.

Anyway, thanks for joining me on Bailey Flanigan's journey . . . and yes, the journey of one more ride with the Baxter Family. Some of you may have ideas about where Landon's story is headed, but I think you might be surprised. I guess I have to always remember what Jenny Flanigan told Ashley . . . when we're too weak to walk on our own, God will carry us.

As always, I look forward to your feedback. Take a minute and find me on Facebook. I'm there every day — hanging out with you in my virtual living room, praying for you, and answering as many questions as possible. I have Latte Time, where I'll take a half hour or so, pour all of you a virtual latte, and take questions. We have a blast together, so if you're not on my Facebook Fan Page, please join today. The group of friends there grows in number every day, and each of you is very special to me.

You can also visit my website at *www.KarenKingsbury.com.* There you can find my contact information and my guestbook. Remember, if you post something on Facebook or my website, it might help another reader. So please stop by. In addition, I love to hear how God is using these books in your life. He gets all credit and He always will. He puts a story in my heart, but He has your heart in mind. Only He could do that.

Also on Facebook or my website you can check out my upcoming events and get to know other readers. You can hear about movies being made on my books and you can become part of Team KK — a community that agrees there is life-changing power in something as simple as a story. Please post prayer requests on my website or read those already posted and pray for those in need. If you'd like, you may send in a photo of your loved one serving our country, or let us know of a fallen soldier we can honor on our Fallen Heroes page.

When you're finished with this book, pass it on to someone else. By doing so, you will automatically enter my "Shared a Book" contest. Email me at *contest@KarenKings bury.com* and tell me the first name of the person you shared with, and you might win a summer day with me and my family. In addition, everyone signed up for my monthly website newsletter is automatically entered into an ongoing once-a-month drawing for a free, signed copy of my latest novel.

There are links on my website that will help you with matters that are important to you — faith and family, adoption, and ways to reach out to others. Of course, on my site you can also find out a little more about me, my faith and my family, and the wonderful world of Life-Changing Fiction™. You can also follow me on Twitter. I give away books all the time, and I'd love to see you there!

Finally, if you gave your life to God during the reading of this book, or if you found your way back to a faith you'd let grow cold, send me a letter at *office@KarenKingsbury .com* and write, "New Life" in the subject line. I encourage you to connect with a Bible-believing church in your area, and start reading the Bible every day. But if you can't afford one and don't already have one, write "Bible" in the subject line. Tell me how God used this book to change your life, and then include your address in your email. My wonderful publisher Zondervan has supplied me with free paperback copies of the New Testament, so that if you are financially unable to find a Bible any other way, I can send you one. I'll pay for shipping.

One last thing. I've started a program where I will donate a book to any high school or middle school librarian who makes a request. Check out my website for details.

I can't wait to hear your feedback on *Learning!* Oh, and look for Bailey Flanigan's Book No. 3: *Longing* . . . in stores this fall. Until then my friends, keep your eyes on the cross and remember this:

When you see just one set of footprints, God is most definitely carrying you.

In His light and love,
Karen Kingsbury
www.KarenKingsbury.com

DISCUSSION QUESTIONS

1. What does the word *learning* stir in your heart? Explain.

2. Have you or someone you loved learned a major lesson lately? Tell about that.

3. What did you learn about growing in your faith by reading this book?

4. Explain how Bailey felt she was a failure after Chrissy's death. Explain how you do or don't relate to this personally. Share an example.

5. Have you ever felt like you failed God? Talk about that time.

6. What does God want us to learn when we feel we've failed Him?

7. The Bible tells us in Lamentations that

God's mercies are new every morning. How can that truth change the way we view our failures?

8. What lessons did Cody learn in this book? Describe the characteristics that make Cody so willing to help.

9. Do you know anyone like Cody Coleman? Talk about how they love to be needed, and what that has looked like in their lives.

10. What lesson from your childhood made the most impact on you? Why?

11. There is a cost to pursuing dreams. Lessons must always be learned along the way. What dreams did you have when you were growing up or what dreams do you still have, and how did God teach you lessons about those dreams?

12. The story of the Lyle High football team coming together to earn prize money for a sick girl with cancer was one that touched Cody deeply. Talk about what this part of the story meant to you.

13. Have you ever seen people come to-

gether to help someone in your church or family or community? Tell about that time.

14. Brandon Paul learned that our lives are but a mist that appears for a little while. What does that mean to you?

15. Did you learn anything from the character of Brandon? Do you think there are real-life celebrities like him? Why or why not?

ABOUT THE AUTHOR

New York Times bestselling author **Karen Kingsbury** is America' favorite inspirational novelist, with over fifteen million books in print. Her Life-Changing Fiction™ has produced multiple bestsellers, including *Leaving, Take One, Between Sundays, Even Now, One Tuesday Morning, Beyond Tuesday Morning,* and *Ever After,* which was named the 2007 Christian Book of the Year. An award-winning author and newly published songwriter, Karen has several movies optioned for production, and her novel *Like Dandelion Dust* was made into a major motion picture and is now available on DVD. Karen is also a nationally known speaker with several women's groups. She lives in Washington with her husband, Don, and their six children, three of whom were adopted from Haiti. You can find out more about Karen, her books, and her appearance schedule at www.KarenKingsbury .com.

DATE DUE